A Lasting Promise

Mary Wood was born in Maidstone, Kent, and brought up in Claybrooke, Leicestershire. Born one of fifteen children to a middle-class mother and an East End barrow boy, Mary's family were poor but rich in love. This encouraged her to develop a natural empathy with the less fortunate and a fascination with social history. In 1989 Mary was inspired to pen her first novel and she is now a full-time novelist.

Mary welcomes interaction with readers and invites you to subscribe to her website where you can contact her, receive regular newsletters and follow links to meet her on Facebook and Twitter: www.authormarywood.com

BY MARY WOOD

The Breckton series

To Catch a Dream
An Unbreakable Bond
Tomorrow Brings Sorrow
Time Passes Time

The Generation War saga

All I Have to Give
In Their Mother's Footsteps

The Girls Who Went to War series

The Forgotten Daughter
The Abandoned Daughter
The Wronged Daughter
The Brave Daughters

The Jam Factory series

The Jam Factory Girls
Secrets of the Jam Factory Girls
The Jam Factory Girls Fight Back

The Orphanage Girls series

The Orphanage Girls
The Orphanage Girls Reunited
The Orphanage Girls Come Home

The Guernsey Girls series

The Guernsey Girls
The Guernsey Girls Go to War
The Guernsey Girls Find Peace

Stand-alone novels

Proud of You
Brighter Days Ahead
The Street Orphans
A Lasting Promise

A Lasting Promise

Mary Wood

PAN BOOKS

First published 2025 by Pan Books
an imprint of Pan Macmillan
The Smithson, 6 Briset Street, London EC1M 5NR
EU representative: Macmillan Publishers Ireland Ltd, 1st Floor,
The Liffey Trust Centre, 117–126 Sheriff Street Upper,
Dublin 1 D01 YC43
Associated companies throughout the world

ISBN 978-1-0350-3678-3

Copyright © Gaskin Hinckley Ltd 2025

The right of Mary Wood to be identified as the
author of this work has been asserted in accordance
with the Copyright, Designs and Patents Act 1988.

All rights reserved. No part of this publication may be reproduced,
stored in a retrieval system, or transmitted, in any form, or by any means
(including, without limitation, electronic, mechanical,
photocopying, recording or otherwise)
without the prior written permission of the publisher.

Pan Macmillan does not have any control over, or any responsibility for,
any author or third-party websites (including, without limitations, URLs,
emails and QR codes) referred to in or on this book.

1 3 5 7 9 8 6 4 2

A CIP catalogue record for this book is available from the British Library.

Typeset by Palimpsest Book Production Ltd, Falkirk, Stirlingshire
Printed and bound by CPI Group (UK) Ltd, Croydon, CR0 4YY

MIX
Paper | Supporting
responsible forestry
FSC® C116313

This book is sold subject to the condition that it shall not, by way of
trade or otherwise, be lent, hired out, or otherwise circulated without
the publisher's prior consent in any form of binding or cover other than
that in which it is published and without a similar condition including this
condition being imposed on the subsequent purchaser. The publisher does not
authorize the use or reproduction of any part of this book in any manner
for the purpose of training artificial intelligence technologies or systems.
The publisher expressly reserves this book from the Text and Data Mining
exception in accordance with Article 4(3) of the European Union Digital
Single Market Directive 2019/790.

Visit **www.panmacmillan.com** to read more about all our books
and to buy them.

To the memory of two lovely friends and members of my family who I lost during the writing of this book: Ann Geraldine Knowles, known to all who loved her as Geraldine, mother-in-law to my son James; and Margaret Gradwell, mother-in-law to my daughter Rachel. Brought to me by my children, you both enriched my life. Thank you – I miss you both.

Chapter One

Angelica

The Past Collides with the Present

1963

Pain seared every part of forty-four-year-old Angelica's body. Thin and frail, she lay still, clinging on to the last thread of life she had left.

She couldn't let go and die.

She had to stop this cancer taking her until her soul was ready to rest peacefully.

How can that happen when I have sinned? How can I hope to gain forgiveness and salvation?

'Mama . . . Mama, it's all right, I'm by your side.'

The tearful voice of her daughter, Mia, penetrated the pain and brought comfort, but didn't allay Angelica's fears. If anything, Mia's very existence deepened the gulf she felt between gaining peace and forever living in the agony of hell.

'The doctor will be here soon, Mama.'

Angelica opened her eyes. The usual bright light of the sun shining through the window was dimmed by the presence of a red bus standing at the bus stop outside their home in

Globe Road, Stepney, East London. The hustle and bustle of life didn't stop because she was about to die.

Her hazy mind reminded her of what a journey it had been, going from her beloved France in 1943 to living here in London, where she had lived for the past twenty years. A journey that was the cause of her angst today.

As she closed her weary eyes, another voice came to her – a distant voice from long ago.

'*Sœur Angelica, nous voulons sortir, s'il vous plaît. Laissez-nous sortir.*'

Marcia begged her to let her and the other Jewish children come out of the hot, stuffy cellar. But Sister Angelica, as she had been then, could not allow it.

The Nazis were at the gate of the convent. If they discovered the children she loved and cared for, it would mean their certain death.

Angelica floated back in time to when it all began – she was a young woman of twenty-three again. Her clothes weren't of the modern day. Instead, she was wearing the timeless flowing gown of a nun.

1942

Sitting on her favourite bench in the convent grounds, under the large oak tree that shaded her from the hot August sun, Sister Angelica found no peace. Her huge hazel eyes were saddened and her mind troubled as she looked at the children playing during their break from lessons.

Run as a boarding school, the Maria-Madeleine Convent, near Limoges in the south-west of France, housed over fifty children aged between six and sixteen. Children from all walks of life. Mostly from rich families, though some were the children of fighting soldiers, and some were orphans. Children whose lives were safe and closeted here in the convent, in a world untouched by war and hunger, though occasionally by loss.

A letter from the Archbishop of Toulouse, Jules-Géraud Saliège, had been read out in mass that morning and had troubled Angelica. He'd written it to his own diocese of Toulouse, but a copy had found its way to them and was very relevant to what was happening around Limoges:

In our diocese, disturbing scenes have occurred, the bishop had written. *Children, women, men, fathers and mothers are being treated like lowly herds. Members of a single family are separated from each other and carted away to unknown destinations. The Jews are men, the Jewesses are women. They are part of the human race. They are our brothers, like so many others. A Christian cannot forget this.*

To Angelica, the words were a rallying call not to sit back and do nothing, but to help in some way.

She couldn't help the adults, she had no means of hiding them, but their children . . . Somehow she must help the Jewish children!

The bell of the gate tolling interrupted her thoughts as she looked around for Sister Frederica, the nun on duty. But when there was no sign of her, Angelica rose and went to see who the visitor was.

The hem of her habit brushed the pebbles of the path as she walked, calling out, 'I'm coming.'

Quickening her pace as another chime rang out, Angelica stumbled on a stone. Her sandals didn't give much protection from the pain of this and unwittingly she let out a curse. 'Damn and blast!'

The sound of male laughter from the other side of the door made her blush. She hadn't meant for her slip of the tongue to be heard!

The gate creaked open.

'So, you're human in this convent after all! And here was me shaking in me shoes, as for sure I thought I was going to be turned away, or you wouldn't be for understanding me. But that curse was in English!'

Angelica smiled. 'Yes, I speak English, and for a curse it is the better language to use as the children don't understand. God always understands motive, so I'm sure He won't condemn me.'

The visitor chuckled. His twinkling, liquid-blue eyes would have given his heritage away even if his accent hadn't.

'I am used to the Irish way of speaking too,' Angelica told him. 'I trained in Ireland. What can we do for you, and how is it you are so far from your country?'

'I was captured at Dunkirk, but the little people were with me, and I escaped. I made me way down here and found the Maquis Resistance workers. They have cared for me since, and I am honoured to do their work with them.'

'And what part of that work brings you to our door today, Mr . . . ?'

'Shane. Shane Flannagan . . . We need your help. Will you be asking me in?'

'I would have to speak with the Reverend Mother before I could let a gentleman in. Can you tell me what it is you want?'

'The Maquis have come across many Jewish children hiding in the forest. We have been taking food to some of them, but more need to be found and given help, and all need a safe shelter.'

'It is as if the Lord himself has sent you. I have been

pondering on the question of the safety of these children . . . So, some are in the forest, you say?'

To Shane's nod, Angelica straightened her back and in a determined voice that would brook no argument, said, 'Well, I have my free time at this very moment. I will come with you and see them.'

'Won't you be needing permission?'

'Some things are best done without asking. But if I can see the plight of the children, then I can put a case for them. I'll be with you in just a moment. I must tell Sister Frederica – the sister on duty today – that I am leaving to go for a walk. Please wait for me.'

'But, Sister, it can be very dangerous. I was for thinking that if you can take them in, I'd be waiting until it is dark and then be bringing those I know of to you.'

'That way I won't be able to see where they are for future trips to find others, or what help is needed. No. I will come, Shane. I am not afraid of the Germans, or Pétain's men. They are unlikely to question a nun.'

Turning and closing the gate before he could protest further, Angelica sucked in her breath. She had the chance to do something, and she wasn't going to have that taken away from her by asking permission that might be refused. She almost skipped into the large hall where she knew she would find Sister Frederica at a small desk – probably snoozing and not paying attention to her duties.

This was exactly what Sister Frederica was doing.

Always playful, Angelica slowed her pace and crept over to her. 'Boo!'

'Oh, may all the saints have mercy! You frightened the life out of me!' A girlish giggle followed this and Angelica laughed out loud. 'Ha! I caught you napping on the job.'

Frederica playfully hit out at her. 'You bad girl! What do you want?'

Still giggling, Angelica informed her that she was going out for a walk and asked if Sister Frederica would sit outside and watch the children.

'You're a one, Sister. But hurry back as the convent is not the same when you are missing.'

'Ah, come here.'

Sister Frederica, a small, chubby woman, came into Angelica's hug. She patted her back. 'I'll be about an hour. Then we'll sit together, and I can tell you of any adventures I have had.'

Unsure whether she would tell of the children or not, Angelica left that decision until she saw how things were and what she could do to help.

Shane looked apprehensive when she opened the gate and joined him. 'Have you no ordinary clothes, Sister?'

'No, none.'

'I have come under the guise of a farmer delivering vegetables to market. You will draw attention if you are in me cab dressed in your habit.'

'Right, help me up onto the back of the truck and put that tarpaulin over me. I'll be fine.'

Though looking astonished at the request, Shane did as she asked.

'It is that the sacks here at the back of the truck contain the veg. Those at the front are full of straw to be giving the appearance of a full load. Make your way to them, and I'll be for throwing the tarpaulin over you.'

They hadn't gone far before Angelica regretted her impulsiveness. The swaying of the truck threw her from side to side, but she knew it wouldn't take long to reach the edge of the forest and from there they would have to walk.

Suddenly the truck halted. An angry French voice demanded to see Shane's papers. Sweat beads trickled down Angelica's face as she heard, 'What is it you are carrying and where are you going?'

As if born in rural France, Shane told of his cargo and direction in a word-perfect country accent.

Angelica held her breath. The jolt of them coming to a halt had sent her body towards the cab and she was now wedged between it and a sack of straw, but she dared not move.

'Vegetables, you say . . . Raphael, prod those sacks!'

Angelica's breath caught in her lungs; her heart fluttered with fear. But then, knowing she must do something, she inched herself further into the gap until she was on the floor of the truck. As she did, a vicious blow missed the sack and hit her foot. She bit down on her lip willing herself not to cry out. At last, she heard, 'On your way!' and felt the truck move forward.

Trapped as she was against the cab, Angelica's body moved with every bump and twist in the road, scraping the skin from her thighs.

Tears ran down her face. But she quickly wiped them away when the truck came to a halt once more.

'Sister! Sister, are you for being all right?'

'Help me, Shane. I'm trapped.'

The truck shook as Shane climbed aboard, then two strong arms lifted her. 'Be Jesus, how did you get yourself down there? But then, if you hadn't, you would have been discovered. Are you hurt?'

'My leg . . . it's bruised but I can manage once I'm on my feet. Are we in the forest?'

'That we are. You're safe now. But we must hurry.'

Stepping down from the truck, Angelica winced with the pain in her ankle, but then as she looked around her, it was as if she'd been transported to a wonderland.

The branches of trees formed a canopy as they met above her, letting through rays from the sun and throwing shadows over her that made a lace pattern on her black habit.

In front of her was an archway over a path, ready to welcome her tread. The air was full of twittering birds disturbed by their presence, and the sweet aroma of pine floated on the breeze.

But then, she thought, this may look like a little piece of heaven but it was probably hell to the lost and hungry children taking shelter here.

They hadn't gone far when they heard a sound as if someone had started running.

Once more in his country-sounding French, Shane called out, 'Don't be afraid, it's me . . . Shane. I've brought someone with me to help you.'

Angelica looked into the frightened eyes of four children, now huddled together as they came out onto the path. Her heart went out to them. She opened her arms. 'Come.'

Four shivering bodies almost knocked her over. But she stood firm and held them to her. 'Are there any more of you?'

'Yes, many. They are deep in the forest. We came foraging for food.'

Dark, red-rimmed eyes looked up at Angelica.

'What are your names, little ones?'

'I'm Noah.' This was said by the tallest of the children. 'And this is Ruth, my sister.'

The little girl, no older than six or seven, didn't speak, but just stared out of frightened eyes.

A girl of around twelve spoke next. 'My name is Rona.'

'Hello, Noah, Ruth and Rona. Now, what is your name, little one?' Angelica looked into the almost defiant eyes of the fourth child, also a girl of around twelve years old. When she spoke, her words held a challenge. 'My name is Madeleine . . . Are you going to help us?'

'I am going to do my best. How long have you all been here?'

'Many weeks.'

Angelica could see they all had a harrowing story to tell, but decided not to press them. She would let them tell her when they were ready.

Madeleine, it seemed, was ready now.

'I was the last one to come into this forest. The Germans came along our street. They were taking our neighbours. Mama went out to ask what was happening. One told her that they had to go with them. Mama ran inside and told me and my sister, Marcia, to run . . . I lost Marcia . . . I don't know if she fell. I just kept running. We come from Toulouse.'

The bishop's letter came into Sister Angelica's mind, confirming to her that her mission was to help these children.

Madeleine was now saying, 'Mr Rodkin, our baker, saw me and picked me up. He brought me over the border into free France . . . I – I hid on a train, then jumped off when the trained slowed and ran into this forest.'

'We found her,' Noah added.

'Well, you are safe now. You're coming back to the convent with me.'

With this snap decision Angelica trembled with nerves.

Would the Reverend Mother accept the children? And if so, would she take in more of them?

But then, how many more? These children spoke as if there were hordes hiding in the forest . . . Could they feed them all? Yes, their produce was plentiful, and their cupboards were stacked with jams and preserves, and flour that had been milled from the wheat they'd grown in their field. They also had plenty of vegetables growing in their garden, but already they had many mouths to feed, besides helping the poor who begged at the gate.

But then, what else could she do? These children needed protection, love and food. Somehow, she and her fellow sisters must provide it.

A hand came into hers. She looked down into the huge, tear-filled eyes of Madeleine. 'You will find Marcia, won't you?'

Angelica couldn't speak. She just held the head of soft dark hair to her and tried to soothe the little girl's pain.

1963

'Mama, Mama.'

There it was again – the voice that brought her back to this world where all she knew was pain and anguish.

Mia, her beloved daughter's voice.

'Please don't fret, Mama. Lie still and rest.'

'But I must find Marcia . . . I – I left her, Mia.'

'Who's Marcia, Mama? Is she someone you knew during the part of your life you never talk about? Your life with Papa and before?'

'Yes. She came to me. I loved her . . . She came to us, like so many children . . .'

'How, Mama? And who is us? Do you mean you and Papa? . . . Oh, Mama, why have you not told me about your past and my papa?'

'I – I could not . . . I made vows . . . I – I must find Marcia . . . I must. I need her forgiveness.'

'I will find Marcia, Mama, I promise. But where shall I look?'

'The Maria-Madeleine Convent, Limousin.'

'A convent!'

Angelica closed her weary eyes. She wanted to tell Mia all she was reliving but she hadn't the strength and was afraid of her judgement. But in going back down the path she'd chosen and looking at the life she'd given up, she hoped to find some peace.

Chapter Two

Marcia

Acceptance Leads to Freedom

1942

Marcia crouched in the long grass next to the river. Her breath came in short pants as fear clutched at her heart. Were her mama and Renée, her lovely little sister, safe? And what had happened to Madeleine?

When their neighbour had warned them that the Germans were coming and were knocking on everyone's doors seeking out Jews, and that they had a list too and were asking for Jews by name, Mama had told Marcia and Madeleine to run. To make their way into the forest, imploring Marcia to care for her sister.

But Madeleine could run like the wind and had gone ahead of her. She dared not call out for fear of being heard, and then Madeleine had disappeared. Would she make it to their aunt who lived in the free zone of France?

Marcia trembled. Her thick black hair fell over her face, where beads of her sweat dampened the tresses and stuck them to her cheeks. And yet, she was cold – cold and hungry. She'd been lying in the damp thicket for weeks, eating only berries and drinking from the river. Always she hoped Madeleine would come back to her. And always she was thinking of her Mama and little Renée. But in the dead of night, tales that had circulated for months of the fate of those Jews who'd been captured had frozen her body with fear.

A tear plopped onto her cheek. With it, she made up her mind to return to her home and to try to find out what had happened to everyone.

When darkness fell, stiff-limbed Marcia rose from her hiding place and made her way back. She needed to check if perhaps Madeleine had returned. And she needed to find food.

What met her wasn't home as she knew it, but a hollow emptiness.

Her voice calling out for her Mama, Renée and Madeleine echoed around the kitchen, until realization dawned: they had gone . . . Would she ever see them again?

The sound of the wooden chair scraping along the stone floor as she pulled it out from under the table enhanced the loneliness and the fear that vied in Marcia for prominence.

Her bottom bruised as she flopped down onto its hard surface, her head bent forward with the weight of her despair.

The door opening and the gentle voice of their neighbour, Madame Conté, asking who was there lifted Marcia. Maybe she had news?

Looking up into Madame's lovely face, whose tiny features always looked smiley and were enhanced by her deep blue eyes, Marcia asked, 'Did they escape, Madame Conté?'

Arms were opened to her. Marcia jumped up and ran towards the comfort offered, but she knew by the soft strokes of her hair and the whispered, 'All will be all right, *ma petite*,' that all wasn't all right.

'Where is it that you have been, *ma chérie*?'

Shivering and near to tears, Marcia told of how she had not travelled far, of how she had lost Madeleine, and how she'd been torn between returning and going on.

'I will make you safe. I will take you to my sister tomorrow. She lives on a farm on the outskirts of Montressor village. She will take care of you and find you work on her farm. If you are busy, you will not have so much time to think or to dwell on the bad things that are happening.'

'Madame Conté, why are these bad things happening? What have we Jews done that makes the Nazis want to get rid of us? . . . Is it true . . . are they murdering us?'

'*Ma chérie* . . . you must not talk of such things . . . *Non* . . . I – I mean . . . Oh, *ma petite*, we do not know the truth, but you will be safe, I promise you, and we must hope that Madeleine is too. Come, you can sleep on my sofa tonight, then we will go in the morning. I have prepared coq au vin. Monsieur Conté says that no one can make better!'

Madame Conté puffed out her chest with pride.

The thought of the chicken dish made Marcia's tummy rumble. She went gladly to the cosy welcome of Madame Conté's kitchen, with its shutters still open letting in the light of the low September sun.

How could the sun still shine when nothing seemed real any more? It hadn't been since her papa had left. Where was he? Why did he go?

These thoughts crowded Marcia.

Papa had left to go on business weeks ago. But what business? He had a jeweller's shop in Tours, but he never travelled further than that or for any other reason than to open his shop and his workshop.

But one night, he didn't return at his usual time. Mama had been fretful, but she'd told them that Papa had sent her a note saying he had to go away and would be away for a long time, but that they weren't to worry as he'd left money in an account for them and would write when he could.

But no letters, or messages had come from him . . . Realization made Marcia gasp and pull away from Madame Conté.

'What is it, *ma chérie*?'

'Papa . . .'

The way in which Madame Conté quickly took hold of her once more and her head shook from side to side confirmed for Marcia the awful thought she'd had. 'The Nazis have taken Papa!'

'There, there, everything will be all right.'

Marcia came out of the hug. 'But it won't! It can't be! Mama . . . Renée . . . Papa . . . The Nazis, they've taken them all!'

Madame Conté didn't deny it but stood as tall as her tiny frame would let her and put on a stern voice. 'Well, they're not going to take you! *Ma sœur et moi*, we will not let them!'

Suddenly, though heartbroken, Marcia did feel safe. Madame Conté had said that she and her sister would not let the Germans take her and she believed her.

'You, Marcia, you will live for your family. You will make them proud. You will grow beautiful and have children that you know your mama and papa would love and will always watch over. You will do this for your family and for all Jews everywhere.'

This made Marcia want to stand tall too. She felt a trickle of the courage she'd always been known to have find its way into her heart. She would be strong. Nothing would stop her. She would live for her family.

Life on the farm with Madame Slater proved to be almost ideal, if only Marcia's nights weren't haunted by the images conjured up by the rumours. Rumours of gas chambers that the Jews were forced into and never came out of; of mass shootings and long graves into which the bodies fell, after being piled high on top of each other and then bulldozed into the ground.

Sometimes she wanted to join them and lamented that she wasn't there, holding Mama's, Papa's and Renée's hands as they faced death together.

Always her pillow was wet with tears.

During her sixth week on the farm, Marcia did as she had done countless times and searched through the letters that had plopped through the door, hoping one of them would be from her aunt telling her that Madeleine was safe and with her. But this time, as before, there was nothing.

As she finished searching through the letters, a knock on the door made her jump.

Opening it, Marcia found a young woman standing there, dressed in a light grey wraparound coat. She was tall and wore a navy small-brimmed hat perched on one side of her head. Her dark hair curled under in a smooth roll. Her pale blue eyes didn't show any expression as she asked, 'Marcia Karmi?'

'*Oui?*'

'May I come in? I have come from your aunt.'

Feeling wary of this stranger, Marcia called out to Madame Slater. 'We have a visitor, Madame!'

As Madame Slater arrived, the young woman was taking something from her handbag. 'I have come from Marcia's aunt, Madame. I have been asked to take her over the demarcation line to the safety of her aunt's home. My name is Mademoiselle Layla Henchman. I work with a group that are trying to save the Jews. Here, I have a picture of Marcia's aunt, to show that I am genuine.'

Marcia's heart flipped over when she cast her eyes over the photo, for there were her mama and her aunt. Two loving sisters, smiling out at her.

Memories flooded her of their giggles whenever the families met. Mama and Aunt Felicia had such a wicked sense of humour, often one that only they understood.

Tears stung Marcia's eyes. How had her aunt taken the news of Mama and Renée having been captured by the Nazis?

'Do you want to go, Marcia?'

Marcia looked at Madame Slater and nodded. As she did her tears plopped onto her cheeks.

Madame Slater reached for her and held her close. A buxom woman, there was always a lovely feel to Madame's cuddles. One that soothed and reassured.

'Oh, I do. I am sorry, Madame, to leave you, but I would like to be with my family.'

'I understand. You go and pack your things while I give our guest some refreshment.'

Layla spoke then. 'We must hurry, Marcia, you cannot pack your things. We must not look as though we are going on a journey to stay somewhere different as that would raise suspicion, but rather we must appear to be on a shopping trip. See, I have nothing with me, and I have travelled from over the border. The trick is to wear two pairs of knickers, so that you can discard the pair next to your skin and feel fresh. But other clothes will have to last you. We will journey by road. I have my car outside the gates of the farm. I have papers for you . . . but I must make changes to your appearance in case we are stopped, as one look at you will give away your heritage.'

With this, Layla took a pair of tweezers from her handbag.

'I will be grateful for a drink, Madame, and while you are preparing it, I will make Marcia's eyebrows much thinner and apply make-up to her, to make her look older. We must pass off as two friends going on a fun day. I will also dress your hair in a modern style, Marcia.'

When all this was accomplished amid many instructions from Layla as to how to conduct herself, Marcia could not believe that the young woman looking back at her from the mirror was truly her.

Her hair was parted in the middle and swept off her face into a fold at the back, with tiny tendrils left on her forehead. Her eyebrows were shaped like the film stars', thin and bowed, and her skin appeared much paler than its usual olive colour while her lips looked fuller due to the dark red lipstick. She now resembled a fashionable lady of French, but not Jewish origin. In some small way, Marcia felt like a traitor to her people, but she so wanted to live. To do all Madame Conté had said she should do. And she knew that this disguise would help her to do all of that.

When she was handed her papers, she was told that her name was Maria Dubois and that she was nineteen years old. That she lived in Tours and was spending the day exploring and shopping in Bourges.

'The Germans like to think of us living our lives as normal under their rule but are very suspicious of us too. Try not to look as though you have something to hide, rather flirt a little as is the French way, and giggle in a girlie way. We will practise as we drive . . . And Marcia, do not worry. Where I am taking you to, you will be safe.'

'You mean, we aren't going to my aunt's?'

'No, that is not safe for you . . . Yes, I know, your aunt lives in Vichy, which is still under French rule, but its leader, Pétain, is not to be trusted. We fear that one day he may give in to the Germans' demands of rounding up the Jews.'

'Will I be able to let Madame Slater know how I am?'

'She will know.'

It was strange to Marcia how accepting she felt of these arrangements. It was as if she'd entered a new phase where the most important thing was to protect her life – she wanted to live. She didn't want to die.

Chapter Three

Angelica

Returning from the Forest

1942

Sister Angelica breathed a sigh of relief as Shane pulled his wagon up to the gates of the convent.

They hadn't been stopped and challenged and were now safely back with the children. Sister Frederica opened the gate before the chime of the bell had ceased.

'Angelica! Oh, my dear sister, where have you been? You're late and we were all afraid for you . . . But . . . what have you here?'

'We must hurry, Sister Frederica. This is Shane, he is a Resistance worker. Together we have found these children and brought them to safety. We must get them inside quickly; they are in danger!'

Not waiting for a reply, Sister Angelica called out, 'Come along, children! Jump down, hurry!'

Four small bodies scurried past Sister Angelica and the surprised Sister Frederica.

'I'll be on me way then, Sisters. Thanks for looking after the kids, it is a good deed you have done.'

'But, Shane, when can you come again? We must bring more in.'

'I am not sure that I am able to, Sister Angelica. I can only do what the leader of my group is telling me I can. Everything must be planned so that nothing leads the gendarmes or the Germans to the Resistance workers. It is sorry that I am.'

With this, he was gone.

'Sister, have you gone mad? Who are these children?'

'I can only tell you that they need our help, Sister Frederica. God has sent them to us. He is calling me to do his work – to save these children . . . I must speak with the Reverend Mother. Will you take the children and feed them? I will be with you shortly, as after they are fed, they will need bathing and to be allocated beds. We will need to get more beds from the cellars.'

'You mean, they are staying? But we are full!'

'We have the left wing. It hasn't been used for years but is always kept aired. We can get many beds in there . . . Please believe me. These children's lives are in danger, we must hide them and care for them. God is calling upon us to do that.'

Sister Frederica shook her head but didn't object further. 'Come with me, little ones. There is some soup that only needs heating and plenty of bread that was baked today. I will feed you and then we will see.'

Putting her hand up to shield her words, Sister Frederica said for Angelica's ears only, 'Good luck with the Reverend Mother. I hope you're not trying to rehome these children in the morning, but I fear you will be.'

This parting shot filled Sister Angelica with trepidation as she turned and ran up the stone steps to the Reverend Mother's office.

And the feeling deepened when she knocked on the door and a cross-sounding voice called, 'Enter!'

She swallowed hard as she prayed, *Holy Mary, mother of God, be with me and help me to achieve the safety of these Jewish children.*

'Sister Angelica! And what have you to say for yourself? You have been missing for a long time and we were all frightened for your safety. And you didn't make evening prayers, which were mostly said for you. Where have you been?'

Sister Angelica held her head high and in a strong voice that didn't show any fear, or signs of begging, she recounted all she'd been doing and the decisions she'd taken. To her, being late back and missing prayers paled into insignificance in the face of the plight of the Jewish children.

The Reverend Mother's face showed astonishment and then, to Sister Angelica's relief, softened. Her ready smile beamed. 'So, you have answered the call of the Archbishop? And of course, God, for He guides the Archbishop in all his teachings. I am very proud of you, Sister Angelica. We will of course help the children.'

'Oh, Reverend Mother, thank you. There are many of them. I have only found four and brought them back with me, but I wish to make further trips and to find them all . . . I – I took the liberty of asking Sister Frederica to open the left wing.'

'That is an excellent suggestion. Well done. I will get all our sisters to lend a hand. The dormitory in that wing will take no time to get ready. What else is needed?'

'Clothes, medical help, comfort and . . . Oh, Reverend Mother, above all, secrecy. It is best that only you and I know where the children have truly come from and their heritage. Maybe just tell the others that they are orphans, which isn't a lie. That way, no one can unwittingly betray them. I have instructed them to tell the other children that they have come from a Paris orphanage that is overflowing.'

'You mean, we cannot tell our sisters?'

'I cannot ask you to lie to them. But perhaps you can find a way of not telling the truth? You see . . . Well, I believe we will be putting them under a great deal of strain if they knew. Maybe just tell them that though you had been informed of the children coming, some have come a lot sooner and you sent me to pick them up? Perhaps I can take uniforms with me when I go to collect more of them? That way the children will be safe when we are travelling.'

'My goodness, you have thought this through . . . But yes, I agree. And we have many uniforms in the basement donated by past pupils. But we will need help, Sister Angelica. You and I cannot launder, mend and press the uniforms in readiness. The sisters will be curious.'

'But our story covers that. I am collecting them from a train bringing them from Paris. They have nothing. And you wanted them to fit in when they arrive, so that they will be accepted by the other children.'

'*Mais oui*, that is a good suggestion, and we're not lying, we're doing God's work.'

'Oh, Reverend Mother. Thank you. I will be sure to instruct the children. They are used to saying and doing things to save their own and other's lives. Poor mites, they have lived in fear and have lost their families and need help.'

'Mama, Mama! Oh, Mama, you were so peaceful, now you're upset again. Are you in pain?'

'Mia?'

Angelica fought through the fog in her brain. She tried to grasp on to her daughter, but then, how did Mia get here?

'They're safe, Mia. We're going to care for them.'

'Who's safe? You haven't told me anything, Mama. Nothing of whatever it is you're playing out in your head . . . But rest now. It's time for your pain relief and that will help you. I will get it for you and then you will sleep.'

Everything was so vividly real to Angelica that she didn't question how it was that she could talk to Mia, and then be back as she was – the young nun trying to master the monster of a car she drove to and from the forest on her missions to find as many Jewish children as she could and to save them.

Suddenly it was two weeks after her first trip with Shane and here she was with another six Jewish children!

This meant the count would be twenty altogether. Twenty beautiful little souls who might have died of hunger or been caught and murdered by the Germans. But instead they had been given a happy home with good food and were carrying on with learning and playing and doing what they should be doing but within the safety of the convent walls.

Not a good driver, Sister Angelica rounded a bend and sent a farmer jumping out of her way and running for his life. She had no time to stop and apologize, she had to concentrate on swerving around the cattle and trying to slow the enormous car she had no control of.

The children screaming in her ears panicked her further. Then fear gripped her as ahead she saw a checkpoint, and she swerved to miss a stupid cow that had changed its mind over which direction it wanted to go.

Finding the brake at last, the car came to a halt.

'Children, do not say a word. If any of the soldiers speak

to you, just nod or shake your head. They will have no reason to suspect you are anything but pupils of mine.'

None of the children acknowledged she'd spoken. She could feel their anguish – she shared the same feeling, for one day it could happen that the soldiers did not believe her and they could take the children from her.

A gendarme came sauntering over.

'Sister, you need more lessons in how to drive, you will end up killing someone.'

'I'm sorry. None of the other sisters will take to the wheel and the children need to be taken for appointments. I am improving and will master it.'

'No doubt, but in the meantime, you should not be practising with children on board. Who do you have with you today? I don't seem to recognize any of them, as I didn't on the last two times I stopped you.'

Sister Angelica froze for a second, but then took a deep breath. 'That's because we have so many, and once they have been to the doctor's they don't need to go again, but others may.'

Another officer came up to them.

'So, where have you got these children from? I saw you going past earlier, and you had no passengers.'

'These are a new intake. We are taking more and more children whose fathers have been killed in this awful war. Every day we are approached by convents in occupied France who cannot cope with all the children they take in.'

The first gendarme sighed. 'Well, you do a good job, Sister, but please find someone who can teach you to drive properly. Good day.'

Sister Angelica nodded as she grated the gearstick in a desperate attempt to get away quickly. At last, the car moved off, did one or two kangaroo jumps, then glided ahead as if it was being driven by a professional.

It was getting dark as they approached the convent gates. In the shadows of the tall trees outside the wall, there was a movement. Sister Angelica's reaction was to tell the children once more not to talk if they were questioned again.

But as she pulled the car up outside the gates, two figures appeared – two young women.

Winding the window down, she looked into the darkest eyes she'd ever seen, and a face she thought for a moment she recognized. Glancing towards the older-looking woman, she asked, 'Can I help you?'

'We hope so, Sister. It is known to the Maquis that you take in Jewish children.'

'Who are you?'

'I am a Resistance worker with the Maquis, and I have brought a girl to you. Her name is Marcia. Please take care of her. She has escaped the Germans, but lost all of her family.'

'Where is Marcia from?'

'Toulouse.'

Sister Angelica glanced at the frightened-looking girl. 'Have you a sister named Madeleine?'

'Yes, yes, I do! Do you know where she is?'

'We have a Madeleine here who came from Toulouse and who lost contact with her sister Marcia. Praise the Lord, it is you.'

'So, you will take her, Sister?'

'I will, and any others you know of. Bring them to us but be careful. Never come this early again.'

Once inside the gates, many sisters came to help with settling the new children in and making them feel at home, taking them off to feed and wash them and introduce them to the other children.

All had been instructed of the stories they should tell even to the other nuns, and how they should never show signs of being Jewish, except when the dormitory was meant to be still for the night, then they could pray together, swap stories and find comfort from being with others who had the same tales to tell and the same beliefs.

'I will see to Marcia,' Sister Angelica told the other sisters. 'Please have Madeleine come to see me.'

Tears pricked Sister Angelica's eyes as she watched the two girls hug, cry, ask questions and then weep with distress and grief.

After a while she took them both into her arms. 'You will be all right, girls. You're here now. Your mama, papa and little Renée may be safe somewhere. Hang on to that and pray for them every day.'

Within days, Marcia had proven that she was far too grown-up to be classed as one of the children and had taken on the role of teaching the smaller ones about their faith and helping the older ones with anything they needed of her. To Sister Angelica, she was a rock, helping to settle those who were finding it difficult to understand all that had happened to them and their families, and instructing in the kind of foods the children could and couldn't eat and what each day meant to them.

Marcia encouraged one of the older boys to take prayers on a Friday night and instructed that until Saturday night the children must observe prayers and fasting.

To Sister Angelica, it was all fascinating, but secretive too, as all had to be carried out without raising the suspicions of the other sisters. And so it was mostly done in the dormitory after the children had retired so that it was only them who knew they were observing the Sabbath the next day.

Everything ran smoothly – the runs to collect more children and the settling of them – until there were now fifty Jewish children in residence.

To Sister Angelica, her mission was complete. They hadn't heard for a good while of any new children, the raids of houses were lessening, and the walls of the convent contained a happy routine for the children and the nuns.

Worryingly, though, Pétain was allowing more and more German intrusion into their lives. Every time Sister Angelica went into the town, which was often as she was the only driver and she had to fetch the supplies they needed, she always encountered a German soldier or two, leaving her feeling afraid and threatened.

That threat increased one day when the bell rang in a way that demanded attention. Sister Angelica sensed danger, and this was confirmed as Sister Frederica hurried across the garden to open it and a distraught Marcia grabbed her arm.

'Sister, it is the Germans!'

'What . . . ? Why . . . ? Oh, my dear God in heaven, have mercy on us . . . Hurry, Marcia, we must get all the Jewish children into the cellar. It is undetectable so you will be safe . . . Make a game of it, so as not to frighten the children.'

As Marcia scurried away, Sister Angelica ran over to where a group of her fellow sisters were huddled together staring at the uniformed men who were now demanding to be let in.

'Sisters, I cannot tell you why, but please do not mention the children I have been bringing in. It's a matter of life and death that you don't.'

To her surprise, the eldest of them, Sister Benedict, replied,

'We understand and have from the beginning. We will protect the Jewish children.' She turned then to the others, 'Right, come on, let's occupy the rest of the children and keep them from being asked any questions . . . Hurry now. We'll gather them all into the playground and begin exercises with them.'

Sister Angelica felt a sense of relief that all knew and would work alongside her to protect the children as she turned and walked as if nothing was untoward to the room at the back of the convent to access the cellar. She needed to reassure herself that the children were all down there and were okay.

All was quiet. But before she rolled the carpet over the entrance, she lifted the heavy wooden door.

'Sister, please let us out. It's hot and stuffy and hard to breathe.'

'I dare not, Marcia. The German soldiers haven't gone away. They must not have a chance to question any of you. The young ones may give you all away.'

'But it is unbearable.'

'Marcia, you are to rise above that and soothe the younger children. Look at Madeleine, she is shivering with fear because you are showing weakness. She, and all the children, look to you to reassure them.'

A tear ran down Marcia's face. Her young shoulders bore so much, but all that was at stake depended on her and the older boys being able to keep calm.

'God is with you, my dear. Now, I must close the hatch and put the rug in place.'

Feeling like a jailer, Sister Angelica made everything seem normal as she replaced the huge, faded, musty-smelling rug and stamped out any rucks.

Her own face was wet with tears as she prayed that the children would be safe.

Brushing her tears away, she ran through the maze of whitewashed stone-walled corridors, her feet squeaking on the red-tiled floor, polished till it shone, as everything was in the convent, from wooden carved banisters to heavy mahogany furniture. As the Reverend Mother would say, 'Cleanliness is next to Godliness.'

Taking a moment to catch her breath, this last thought made Sister Angelica reflect on how hard the sisters worked, keeping this huge building with its chapel, assembly rooms, classrooms and dormitories, not to mention its many washrooms, clean and sparkling. And on top of that they kept the gardens looking neat and tidy and the kitchen garden well stocked with fruit and vegetables, besides teaching and looking after the children. It made her feel tired to think about it all.

She was tired, she realized. Tired to her bones . . . and unfulfilled.

Shocked at this last thought, she crossed herself and asked for forgiveness. And yet, did she really want forgiveness? Could she help being herself? Help having feelings of not being where she should be, that she'd somehow drifted into becoming a nun – or had she been steered into becoming one?

After the train crash that had killed her parents, and having no other relatives but an elderly grandmother, who died shortly after from the shock, she'd been taken in by the sisters of this very convent.

Staying her progress and leaning against one of the walls that seemed to suffocate her at times, Sister Angelica closed her eyes against the rush of emotions attacking her.

She could see her laughing mama calling out, 'Stop, Albert, put her down!' as her handsome papa swung her round above his head.

Clenching her fists, Angelica swallowed hard as the pain of the much-visited scene stabbed her heart.

These walls had become her sanctuary ever since, the sisters her saviours. She'd done everything to please them. And when it was suggested that she was sent to a convent in Dublin for a retreat of prayer and learning to help her to make her mind up about joining them, she'd been broken-hearted at leaving.

But had it really been her choice? As now it all seemed to have been part of a plan to guide her along this path.

They must have known she would do anything to please them. That she loved them and wanted to be like them. Surely it would have been better to have sent her out into the world to have different experiences, and then if she was still of the same mind, to help her to become a nun?

At first it had seemed to be her destiny, her calling, but doubts began to creep in when she started caring for the children schooled here, or the orphaned or abandoned children they took in. Suddenly, longings awakened inside her – she wanted children of her own and to know the love of a man.

She gasped against the impact of the pain this gave her – against her own betrayal of God.

Once more tears ran down her face. *Why am I visited by these doubts? And why now, when there is danger to us all?*

Feeling remorse, she made her way to the chapel. There, she slid into a pew and closed her eyes once more as she bent her head in prayer.

But no matter how hard she begged of God to help her, she didn't feel at one with herself. Somehow, in her mission of finding and looking after the children, she had lost herself and with that had allowed the part of her that didn't feel right in the life she led to come to the fore. But there was more to life, wasn't there? Couldn't she serve God in other ways . . . by being a mother? Remorse clothed her in guilt . . . *Forgive me, Father, forgive me.*

The door bursting open made her jump. With her sleeve she wiped her tears and turned around to face the Reverend Mother.

'Oh, I have found you . . . Sister Angelica, why are you so upset? Were you afraid?'

The wooden bench creaked as the Reverend Mother sat down and slid along to be by her side. 'What is it, my dear? Did you lose faith that God would help us in our mission? Because He has. The Germans have left, though it is obvious that something has raised their suspicions.' Sister Angelica felt the warmth of the Reverend Mother's hand as she took hold of hers and squeezed it. 'I appealed to the Christian side of them – if you can call the facade that they put up of being Christians a true faith. Anyway, it worked, and they left, so you have no need to be afraid any more.'

Removing her hand, the Reverend Mother put her arm around Angelica. 'But it isn't that, is it, dear Sister Angelica? It isn't fear that has you in this state . . . You know, we all have our inner battles. You will win yours, believe me.'

At this moment, Angelica didn't think she would. The truth had been shown to her: the vocation she'd believed was hers had been stripped away, leaving her with longings she didn't know how to deal with. She'd let her demons have a voice, and now knew they would never quieten again.

Chapter Four

Mia

An Instant Attraction

1963

At the gasp from her mother, Mia shot from the chair she was sitting in to a standing position. 'Mama . . . Mama?!'

Mia's heart banged heavily in her chest, but as she looked down on her mama, she could see that the sound hadn't marked her end as had been Mia's first thought.

Taking hold of her mama's hand, she gazed at her anguished face. 'Are you in pain, Mama?'

'No. Only . . . only the pain of all my wrongdoing.'

'Mama, dear, tell me about it. It may help you.'

There was no response to this. Mia sighed. 'Mama, the doctor will be here soon. Try to rest. I don't want to give you any pain relief just in case he wants to prescribe different medication.'

Her mama's hand going slack in hers told Mia that she was resting once more. 'I'll be back soon, Mama. I must be downstairs to hear the doctor knocking, and to let him in.'

With no response to this, Mia went down the stairs of the two up, two down terraced house she and her mama had called home for as long as she could remember. As she did, she puzzled over it all. Every word Mama uttered – even though there weren't many – told of a dramatic happening that had something to do with someone called Marcia. And that it happened in France.

She knew, of course, that her mama was French, and that she had come to England with Papa during 1943, but that was all she knew. She'd never known her papa and had asked many times about her mama's past – what she did during the war, who her family were. But all she'd been told was that her mama had been orphaned as a young girl, nothing more. If only her mama would tell her now, maybe she would find some peace. But the cancer had rendered her weak and hardly able to function, let alone talk much. *Oh, Mama, how am I to bear losing you? And yet, how I long for you to rest and not suffer this torture of your mind any longer.*

Sighing, Mia glanced in the mirror at the bottom of the stairs. The image that looked back at her had the same features as her mama – large hazel eyes, long lashes, dark brown hair that had a natural wave to it, and the same slight figure, which some called dainty.

But as a young woman, Mama had lived in a different world to the one Mia knew. Her world hadn't had the freedom of today. War had raged, persecutions were happening, death and fear. What part did Mama play in it all?

A knock on the door took these thoughts away and had Mia begging that this would be the doctor calling on his promised visit.

On opening the door, a young man greeted her and introduced himself as Doctor Granger. Tall, slim and with blond hair flopping over his forehead, it was his blue laughing eyes that seemed to make him appear as far from her idea of a doctor as it was possible to be.

'Oh, hello. I did hear that there was a new doctor joining the local surgery. Come in.'

As he stepped over the threshold, he grinned. 'But no one told you he would be fresh out of medical school and still very much wet behind the ears?'

Mia laughed. 'Well, no, they didn't tell me that bit.'

His chuckle at this had a lovely sound.

'Well, here I am, for my sins . . . I've come to see your mother, who I believe isn't in a good way?'

'No. I'll take you to her, she's bedridden.'

When they entered her mama's bedroom Mia's heart lurched as Mama lay in a ball, her face red and hollow-cheeked, with sweat beads standing out on her skin.

'Mama, the doctor is here.'

'*Non, je ne veux plus de médicaments.*'

'Your mother is French?'

'Yes, but I know little about when she lived in France . . . Only, she seems very troubled about her former life there. I – I feel she must have done something very wrong . . . I mean, well, she cannot get inner peace and keeps begging for forgiveness.'

'Oh dear, that is distressing. Can you get her to talk about it?'

'Only snippets. She's very concerned that someone called Marcia forgives her. I have promised to find Marcia and tell her that Mama asks for her forgiveness, but I cannot do that until . . .'

'No, I understand . . . Look, nursing your mother is a huge strain on you. We could arrange—'

'No! I – I'm okay, I just want you to help Mama to rest and for her to know I am by her side. I couldn't abandon her to others to care for her.'

'Mama? Is that her preferred way for you to address her?'

'Yes, or Maman. Her native language is the only bit of her French heritage she has hung on to . . . until now. As now it seems the life she lived there is troubling her. You see, somehow, during the war, she met my father – a British pilot – and came back to England with him . . . I never knew him, or what happened to him. Mama would never speak of that time.'

'It would help her if we could get her to.'

'I have tried, and I desperately want to know myself, but if I press her, she becomes more agitated.'

A hand came onto Mia's shoulder. A strange sensation came over her. She cast her eyes down as the doctor's gentle words soothed her. 'You have to look after yourself too, Mia.'

Lifting her eyes, she held his gaze. As she did it seemed that something passed between them. Mia wanted to lean into him, have him hold her. Was it wishful thinking, or did she see a return of her feelings in his gaze?

Her loneliness engulfed her when he removed his hand and looked away, and she told herself that it was just having him there that had made her feel comforted and the sensation of his touch had been nothing more than that.

Didn't she feel the same sense of everything being all right when Angie came home? That feeling that there was someone there for her after the stress of hours of lovingly tending to Mama?

Brought up together, she and Angie were like sisters. A little older than herself, Angie worked in journalism, as Mia had before she'd given up work.

She smiled to herself as she remembered the fun they'd had working together and how Angie had been known in the office as 'the Mad Redhead' due to her head of glorious red curls, and her always getting herself into scrapes.

But now there was very little fun to be had as life seemed full of sadness, anxiety, and long night hours of sitting with Mama.

Angie felt that sadness too, as Mama had brought her up as her own after Angie's mum had died.

She and Angie knew so little about their mothers' lives other than that they'd met during the war.

Mama saying, '*Puis-je être pardonnée?*' brought Mia's attention back to her.

Doctor Granger was leaning over her. 'I don't understand what she's saying, Mia.'

'She is asking again if she can be forgiven.'

Doctor Granger stood up straight and looked over at Mia. 'Has she ever gone to church?'

'No. She's always prayed every night and morning with me and my adopted sister, but there has never been a formal structure to her beliefs. Though she did tell me once that we were Catholics. It was when I had to fill in some forms for a position I applied for.'

'I see . . . Look, maybe you should try asking a local priest to come and chat to her? It might help. I can only give medical assistance. I can give her morphine to rest her body from pain and help her to relax, but I cannot ease her troubled mind.'

'Thank you, Doctor. It would be good to know she is out of pain . . . Does she . . . I mean—'

Doctor Granger interrupted. 'I do know what you're asking, but let's talk about that downstairs.'

Mia nodded. She didn't want to talk about losing her mama at all, but if she was to help her to find some release from her anguish, she needed to know how much time she had and if it was enough for her to try to find and contact the convent and see if that led to finding Marcia.

Once downstairs, Doctor Granger spoke in gentle tones. 'I know you want to have some idea of how much longer you have your mama for, but it's a question that is impossible for a doctor to answer. A patient's own need for life is a strong factor. There are those who fight to stay alive, no matter how much pain they are in and even though they know they cannot ultimately survive. And those who give in and go peacefully. I see your mama as a fighter. Is there nothing you can do to help her gain peace?'

'I wish there was. Though she has mentioned a convent in France. But how I go about finding an address for it, I don't know.'

'Maybe it would be best for you to go and see a priest. Not only could he perhaps help your mama to find appeasement for her conscience, but it's possible they have a directory within the church of all churches and convents. After all, they're all controlled from Rome.'

'Thank you, Doctor Granger, I will.'

'It's Steve, by the way. My name's Steven, but I'm called Steve by all my family and friends. I'd like to think of you as a friend.'

Shocked, Mia couldn't answer him for a moment, but then she felt a smile tugging at her sad face. 'I'd like that too. It's a lonely world when you're indoors most of the time.'

'Does your adopted sister live here?'

'Yes, she's out at work. But I don't look on Angie as an adopted sister as we're as close as any real sisters, and good friends too. I sometimes live for the moment I hear the latch lifted.'

'She sounds just the kind of friend you need. I have only been in London a few months – I'm from a village in the Midlands – and I have found it isn't easy to make friends here. I have my partner, Doctor Jones, and his wife and family, but that's about it . . . Maybe I could . . . No . . . I'm sorry, I won't ask that.'

'What was it? You can't leave it there!'

'Well, I'm a good cook as well as a good doctor.' He grinned in a way that said he was mocking himself. 'So . . . I – I just wondered if maybe I could come round one evening and cook dinner for the three of us? . . . I shouldn't have asked, only I'm lonely and you're in this predicament, and Angie is too, really, as I'm sure she doesn't get much relief from work and helping at home?'

For a moment he looked sheepish and embarrassed, but then his sideways grin made her laugh. 'I'm being very forward, but I feel at home with you. And it's the first time I've felt like that since arriving here.'

'Not at all. Me and Angie would love that. As long as you like Elvis and Cliff, as we'll have their music on all evening!'

'I love them both.' With this he curled his lips in the way that Elvis always had, and Cliff had imitated of late, and then he burst into song, singing the first line of Cliff Richard's hit 'The Young Ones'.

When Mia stopped laughing, she was surprised further by Steve saying, 'Mind, I like Frank Ifield too. Especially "I Remember You". I love it when he yodels. I have all his records; I can bring some with me, they might make you a fan too.'

Mia couldn't believe this was happening. It was like someone had switched on a light in her life and given her hope. In Steve she knew she had a friend, and deep in her heart she hoped for much more.

'I already like Frank Ifield, but not as much as Cliff or Elvis, so you won't have a difficult job in converting me. And I love the cinema and theatre, though haven't been able to go to either for a long time. At least with music you can enjoy it in your own home.'

'They're my loves too, especially musicals.' He looked around. 'Oh, you don't have a TV?'

'No. It broke down – the tube went, and we haven't bothered since. Though Angie wants one. She's always going on about *Coronation Street* and how those at work watch it.'

'I don't blame her. It sort of draws you in seeing how other people live their lives, especially those up in the north of England. It's a world apart from London life . . .'

He sighed, making Mia think that living in the Midlands, he'd been a lot closer to that kind of easy-going life.

'Well, I'll have to go, I have a list of patients to call on. I'll call again tomorrow unless you need me before. If you do, just call the surgery number. I'm on duty all night tonight so will be kipping down in the back office and manning the phone. Bye for now, Mia.'

Mia felt bereft as Steve stepped out onto the pavement immediately outside her front door and walked towards his car. When he got to it, he turned and waved to her, giving her a lovely smile.

The gesture sent Mia's heart racing. She closed the door and leaned on it. *How did that happen? This morning, I never knew Steve existed, and now I fancy myself in love with him! It's madness!*

But even so, she skipped across the living room, plumping

the cushions on the huge beige sofa as she came up to it, and then plonked down on it and put her head back.

Looking up at the ceiling, she giggled like a schoolgirl, grabbed the cushion she'd just shaken and hugged it to her. Something good had come out of her agony of facing the loss of her beloved Mama – she'd met Steve, and she knew he was going to be a big part of her life.

The sound of her mama calling out brought Mia out of the lovely world she'd entered and had her running upstairs.

Mama was asleep but not resting, as Steve had insinuated. Her head writhed from side to side and from what Mia could catch and translate, she was saying, 'Yes, there are more, but they are out on a nature walk.' Then in a cross voice, she said, 'André, go and line up with the rest of the children!'

Then her voice softened as she said, 'I'm sorry, but you should never give any information to the Nazis or the gendarmerie, André. If questioned, just shrug your shoulders, or say you don't know.' It seemed a strange thing to say and deepened the mystery surrounding Mama's past.

But Mia knew she could do nothing to help her mama unless she talked and explained all that had happened. Especially who Marcia was and what wrong she'd done to her.

Thinking of Marcia, she vowed that she would keep her promise and find her, no matter what.

Chapter Five

Marcia

A Cold, Dark, Damp Place

1963

Marcia swallowed hard. No matter how much she tried to forget, she couldn't.

Lifting her head from the task of sewing a gown for her fourth child's imminent appearance, she closed her eyes.

As she did, she could feel the heat and the clawing darkness suffocating her, and she became that child again, loved by Sister Angelica, and cared for by all the nuns, but with a sick feeling of fear in the pit of her stomach.

1943

Willing herself not to show the other children how frightened she was, she told herself that Sister Angelica would come soon. Once the Germans had left, she would come and let them out.

With this knowledge, Marcia listened for the slightest noise that would indicate she was on her way. But she could hear nothing but cries of anguish from the other Jewish children crowded into the cellar with her.

Fingers curled around hers. Not the soft, smaller ones of Madeleine, but the large calloused ones of Joseph, made rough by all the gardening he did for the sisters.

'We will be all right, Marcia. This is nothing to what we have heard our families have been through.'

Joseph gave a sound like a sob. Marcia clutched his hand tighter. 'You're right. For them, we must be brave, we must survive.'

'The Germans must have suspicions about the sisters' activities, as why do they visit often and question Sister Angelica when she drives any of us out in the car?'

'I know, it is frightening, but Sister Angelica is doing all she can for us. Listen now as I want to hear the gate close as then we know they have gone.'

Joseph lowered his voice. 'We should do something to prepare this cellar. It needs more ventilation. I could dig down to it as it reaches out into the garden where part of the building that stands over it collapsed years ago. I could install a grid.'

Marcia wondered if such a thing could be achieved, and if so, with ventilation, they could have lanterns down here. Then her mind went further – maybe toys, and crayon books could be stored, as with light these would occupy the children.

She told Joseph her thoughts and he agreed, adding, 'And we need a toilet – a soakaway toilet and washbasin. Many of the children soil themselves due to fear, and we can't help them.'

'I will speak to Sister Angelica about it if you really think it can be done.'

'I – I need to keep you safe, Marcia, and so I would not

be reckless with how I positioned the grid . . . I – I have something to tell you. You see, I'm older than I look, Marcia. I dared not tell my real age as the sisters might not have rescued me, but I am seventeen, almost eighteen.'

Marcia caught her breath in surprise.

'And that's old enough to know that I am in love with you, Marcia. I love you. You are what keeps my world going.'

'Joseph! I – I don't know what to say.'

'Say how you feel about me.'

'I am only fourteen, but in my heart, I know I am old enough to love you, Joseph, and I do.'

'Oh, Marcia. We must survive this horror. We must survive to one day marry and bring into the world happy children who know no fear.'

His arm came around her and they fell silent. The feelings Marcia had as she leaned against Joseph's small but strong body filled her with joy and hope. They would have a future, her and Joseph, they would.

'Listen! I heard the gate close. They must have left. We're safe!'

Joseph's kiss on her cheek was wet with his tears. They mingled with her own. But she wiped them away and showed no trace of them in her voice as she shouted, 'Children, it's all right. The Nazis have gone. Sister Angelica will soon let us out . . . Madeleine, did you hear that?'

'She's asleep, Marcia. Nothing phases Madeleine,' Joseph told her.

Marcia smiled. Her little sister was the bravest soul she knew.

The creaking of the hatch above them gave them the sight of Sister Angelica's beautiful, tiny face. Her lovely hazel eyes told them all was well as she smiled down at them. '*Mes chéris*, you're safe. And that's despite one of our younger pupils having been questioned by a Nazi officer about where all the other children were.'

This struck a terrifying chord in Marcia. '*Non, mais non!* This cannot be. What if he or she gave us away and they come back?'

'Don't worry. They came to me and I was able to give a good reason why so many children were missing. I told them you were out on a nature walk, though I had to be sharp with the little boy to stop him protesting that as a lie! We must school the children on what to say if the Germans question them . . . But oh, Marcia, just listen to the distress of the other children! They should not have to go through this!'

'Joseph and I have been talking, Sister Angelica. We need to make things better.'

'Oh, Marcia, somehow we must, but you do well to keep them quiet.'

'I . . . we do our best, as Joseph helps me, and Elsie. She's good with the little ones. But many have been hidden in cupboards for long periods of time, or in cellars too, and have a deep fear of such places.'

'Oh, my dear, I am sorry. But I must keep you all safe. Come along and get some fresh air. You can all have extra playtime. I'll get the sisters to bring jugs of water out for you . . . And children, all of you, listen to me: whatever I do, I do it to keep you safe. Trust me. That's all I ask.'

'But there is more that can be done, Sister. Joseph and I have plans.'

'Plans? But how? What are you thinking? . . . Look, tell me after, my dear . . . Come along, children, line up and let us make our way in an orderly fashion to the playground.'

Shocked at how cold this order sounded, Marcia looked towards Joseph.

'It's all right, Marcia. Sister Angelica is probably thinking that it is best to bring back the normal teacher–pupil relationship to help the children to see that all can carry on as before. But you can see that these visits are a massive scare to her. She is trembling.'

Marcia understood. She never wanted to think badly of Sister Angelica. She loved her with all her heart.

'I'm trembling too, Joseph. What will happen if the Germans come back again, and we can't get to safety in time?'

Joseph said, 'I have another idea to put to Sister Angelica about that. I and the other older boys could take shifts looking out from that huge oak. We could keep the road under surveillance and see when a convoy comes along in the distance. Then we warn the sisters, and we could hide much more quickly.'

Then Elsie, a girl of the same age as herself, took hold of her other hand.

Marcia squeezed it. 'We're all right now, Elsie.' Elsie smiled, but still clung on to Marcia's hand. 'Joseph is really clever and he's going to make the cellar more comfortable for us all.'

Joseph beamed.

It didn't seem long before all was back to normal, and Marcia found herself gazing out of the window of the nursery where she was helping with the under-four-year-olds. She could just see the top of Joseph's black cap and knew he was working away, pruning the fruit trees.

She just wanted to run to him and to put her arms around him and squeeze him.

His small size didn't worry her, though she hoped she would not grow any taller so as not to tower over him. This made her giggle just as the door of the nursery opened.

'Ah, there you are, *ma chérie*. Is everything all right? The older children are all back behind their desks and working diligently on their maths. Are the little ones settled?'

'Yes, Sister Angelica.'

'Ah, that's good. I never get over the resilience children show.'

Paulette, the youngest Jewish child, turned and ran to Sister Angelica, who lifted her and cuddled her to her. With this, the others followed suit, and all were given hugs and kisses. Marcia looked on with a feeling of warmth filling her body.

'Your turn, my dear Marcia.'

In Sister Angelica's arms, Marcia felt loved and safe. And she remembered, too, the cuddles of her mama and papa. A tear plopped onto her cheek. Sister Angelica held her tighter for a moment, before holding her at arm's length. 'Right, I need to know these plans you and Joseph have, *ma chérie*.'

After listening to all Marcia had to say, Sister Angelica clapped her hands together. 'I remember that hatch! And yes, everything is possible. Especially the idea of the boys keeping watch. Boys love climbing trees and it will be an adventure for them. I can see them now arguing over whose turn it is.'

'And I was thinking that perhaps each child could make up a pack of things to do – crayons and colouring book, books they would like to read, that sort of thing – and have them stored down in the cellar. Then it will be like an adventure for them as they open their packs.'

'Excellent . . . Marcia, you have renewed my faith in this project of rescuing and being able to look after you all. And you're my inspiration to continue.'

Sister Angelica held her shoulders once more and looked intently into her eyes before again cuddling her to her.

Marcia was filled with a deep and unbreakable love for this nun, who had risked everything for her and her fellow Jewish children, and she wanted to stay with her for ever.

It was a few days later when she and Sister Angelica were working together in the sickroom tending to the elderly Sister Maria, who'd been bitten by a widow spider, that news came that a visitor was at the gate for Sister Angelica.

Marcia's heart felt heavy with worry. She instinctively knew that the caller was the bearer of bad news concerning herself. Her body tensed and she bit on her bottom lip to try to stop it from trembling. Her eyes fixed on the door.

The gnarled hand of Sister Maria gently took hers. 'Don't worry, Marcia. Sister Angelica has many visitors. She is a very courageous young lady. She takes her vows seriously and does much of God's work for him, inside and outside of the convent. Everything will be all right . . . God willing.'

Marcia managed a smile and patted Sister Maria's hand but though she tried to look as though she was calm, she trembled inside.

Her fear was realized when Sister Angelica returned. 'Come with me, *ma chérie*. Let us go and sit in the garden for a while . . . Sister Maria, Sister Frederica is on her way to look after you.'

Marcia didn't ask why. She didn't want to know. She didn't even want to go to the garden, so stood her ground.

'Marcia, Madeleine is going to need you.'

With this, Marcia followed, knowing that her worst fears were going to be realized. When they reached the bottom of the stairs Madeleine stood there with Sister Frederica, who handed her over to Sister Angelica without saying a word, then glided towards the stairs.

Taking Madeleine's hand, Sister Angelica said, 'Let's sit on my bench.'

Everyone knew the bench under the old oak tree and near to the gate as Sister Angelica's bench. Marcia loved it and liked to sit there when Sister Angelica went out of the convent as doing so made her feel close to her.

'*Mes chéries*, I have a heavy heart. Shane has brought some very sad news.'

'Is it our aunt?'

'Yes, Marcia . . . I'm so sorry, but . . . Oh, *mes chéries*, the Germans have taken her.'

Marcia gasped. Her head shook from side to side. '*Non, non.*'

The sound of Madeleine's sobs brought the full force of her grief rushing at her. She clutched her heart to ward off the pain, then rose and ran to the only person she wanted to be with at that moment.

'Joseph! Joseph!'

And then he was there, in front of her, his arms open. He knew.

As he held her, he kissed her neck, patted her back, whispered words of comfort. But they were words that held desolation as he too would feel the hopelessness of the situation they and their people were in.

An anguished cry of, 'Marcia!' and then 'Marcy!', the latter telling her this was Madeleine, helped her to control her sadness and be strong. She had to be there for her sister. Turning, she took the full force of her sister running straight into her arms. Hugging her, she told her, 'Don't worry, *ma chère soeur*, all will be well. Mama and Papa will come for us once the war is over and we will be with them and little Renée once more . . . I promise. We'll be a family again and you and I will picnic in the forest, just like we used to.'

'No! Not the forest. I never want to go to a forest again . . . But what of Aunty?'

'She will come and visit, and you and I will go and stay with her.'

'So, why are you crying? . . . I want Mama, Marcy . . . I want Mama . . .'

Tears rained down Marcia's face as she clung to her sister. Together they felt their hearts were breaking. For despite her brave words, Marcia knew they would never see any of their loved ones again.

Joseph's arms came around them. He didn't speak – he didn't have to. Marcia could feel his love and that was all she needed from him.

But a worry niggled away at her, and one she couldn't answer. 'Joseph, look after Madeleine for me. Give her some weeding to do. You love gardening, don't you, Madeleine?'

'I do, Marcy. I used to help Mama with the weeding.'

'Well, one day you will again. The British will win this war and free all of our people and then we'll be back in our cottage. There'll be so many weeds unless Madame Conté has managed to keep them at bay for us.'

Madeleine gave a giggle, a lovely sound. 'Ha, Madame is beautiful, but she doesn't like getting her hands dirty!'

They all laughed. Joseph's was a concerned sound and a caring one, but her own was false as her heart was breaking. Only Madeleine's was natural, reassuring Marcia that everything was all right in her sister's world.

Marcia found Sister Angelica still sat on her favourite bench, but with her eyes closed as if she was praying.

'Sister, can I sit with you?'

Opening her eyes, she looked up. 'Yes, of course, I'll hotch up.'

'I wanted to ask, what will happen to us . . . me and Madeleine, when the war is over?'

Sister Angelica put her arm around her. The gesture gave immediate comfort and reassurance.

'I will always take care of you both. You've nothing to fear.'

Marcia's eyes filled with tears. 'You're all we have left in the world now, Sister. We both love you as if you were our mama.'

Sister Angelica pulled her closer and stroked her hair.

'But, Sister, how can you care for us? Would we be allowed to stay here?'

'God really does work in strange ways, *ma chérie*. He called me to Him long ago, and yet now He is showing me a different path to walk. He has sent you to me and He will show us the way. I will always make sure you keep your heritage and your faith. I will protect you and that part of you.'

Sister Angelica leaned her head on Marcia's and told her, 'We'll find a way, little one. I will always be by your side. I will never abandon you.'

* * *

Coming out of the past, Marcia slumped back in her chair. *But you did! You abandoned not only us, but all the children, and your faith!*

And yet, she understood. She was a woman herself now, with needs and longings that were fulfilled. Sister Angelica was too, and she'd followed her heart.

Something must have stopped her from being able to come back. But then, if she had, she wouldn't have found them as the Germans came soon after she left and . . . No! She refused to think about that time . . . *Oh, Madeleine . . . Madeleine, I miss you . . .*

Chapter Six

Angelica

For the Love of Her Life

Angelica lay peacefully on her back, her mind at rest and her physical pain easier to bear. In her dreams she'd been visiting some of the better times of yesteryear and mulling over how for over a year after her promise to Marcia, they'd lived an almost serene existence without incident. And how they'd settled into a routine that meant they coped well with the much larger numbers of children.

Many of the older Jewish children, which included Marcia, had moved on from being pupils with care needs to being self-sufficient and holding down jobs within the convent walls. Some were cooks, others were gardeners or cleaners – all greatly easing the daily toil of the work the sisters had to do.

Angelica filled with warmth as she thought of how Marcia, at age sixteen, had become a beautiful young woman and been firmly woven into her heart. Of how she helped in the sick bay looking after any of the children who suffered ailments, and sometimes the sisters if they fell ill too. And how it was obvious that her feelings for Joseph were very deep, as his were for her.

But, Angelica thought, despite the peace within the walls, war had still raged outside of the convent.

With this thought, the life she'd known became alive once more. She no longer reminisced in fear. Nor did she feel the anguish of her past.

Instead, she felt the gentle breeze of the early summer on her cheeks as she sat on her favourite bench, not knowing then that life would take a drastic turn that would change her future for ever.

And that change seemed to begin with an excited voice:

'It's coming to an end! I just know it is, Sister.'

Angelica smiled as she felt the bench bounce a little when Sister Frederica plonked her body down beside her. 'I feel so hopeful now that the Americans have at last joined the effort to crush Hitler. It's as if our old life really will come back. Praise be to God!'

Angelica didn't answer but knew the same euphoria had settled her own fears.

'You don't seem so troubled lately, Sister, and it is good to see.'

This surprised Angelica. Had everyone noticed her inner turmoil?

But yes, it was true. She had found a kind of peace. Had made herself accept that she must settle once more into the life she had. And had come to a compromise that had helped as she'd made herself see that she was a mother figure to so many, and in that she was fulfilled.

All that changed the moment she opened the gate to a caller on the morning of 16 June 1943.

Shane stood there, telling her that he had a British casualty they needed her to take in and to care for until they could arrange for him to be lifted out.

'It is that we don't have the right conditions, the resources or the time to take care of Captain Jamieson – Philip Jamieson. He's a British agent, so he is. A very brave man. But he's been injured badly, shot in the leg. It's been operated on by a local surgeon who is a sympathizer of our cause and the bullet has been removed, but that's all we've been able to do for him. The wound isn't healing well and he's for being in a bad way.'

Without hesitation, Angelica told him, 'Bring him in, Shane, we will care for him.'

But the compassion held within her for all who needed help wasn't what came to the fore when she gazed down into Philip's pain-filled eyes as he was brought through into the courtyard on a make-do stretcher. For this man, she knew, had come to capture her heart – to give her the answers she'd long forgotten she needed.

In the depths of his deep blue eyes, Angelica knew her soul lay. God had given her the answer to the long-suppressed question. He'd sent her a man to love.

Shaking this insane idea away from her, Angelica set about organizing for the necessary arrangements for Philip's care to be put into place.

She had the stretcher bearers take him straight to the sick bay, and saw to it that he was laid on the only bed that had a curtain and was usually kept for the purpose of giving privacy when any procedure was needed that would mean baring the flesh.

'You will be all right now, Captain. Do not be afraid. Here in the convent walls you will find sanctuary.'

'And . . . and you . . . What . . . name?'

'I am Sister Angelica. Now, don't try to talk. We will clean you up and dress your wounds and take care of you.'

'Angelica . . .'

The sound of her name on his lips stopped Angelica in her tracks. She stared at him.

When he reached out his hand and took hers it was as if her earlier thought had come to fruition, as the simple gesture seemed to claim her as his.

Shaking herself, she told herself not to be silly, that she was a nun committed to do God's work for the whole of her life.

But chastising herself didn't help. Something had happened between her and Philip in the simple gesture of a touch – and not of her bidding. But whatever it was, she knew it would change her life for ever.

With Philip bathed and his wounds dressed, a troubled Angelica made her way to the chapel and fell on her knees in the aisle. 'Lord, what do you want of me? Why do you send me these torturous temptations? Help me . . . Feelings in my heart and body are pulling me away from the work I promised I would do – from the vows I took. Are you testing me?'

With this last she lay flat with her hands spread out. 'I implore you to take this longing from me and give me peace.'

There was no peace to be found for Angelica. Each day that she tended to Philip, he took more and more of her heart. She loved him. Not with the kind of love she was committed to give to all mankind, but with a love that consumed her and gave her thoughts she shouldn't have.

A love that gave her no peace as her body began to need more than ever to know the love of a man – not just any man, but Philip.

Her heart pounded whenever she knew she was going to be near to him. Nothing she had to do for him repulsed her. But rather tending to his needs enhanced her love for him.

And she knew Philip loved her too. She saw it in his eyes and felt it in the times she touched him as she steadied him or washed him – in everything about him. As now, as she gently bathed his back, then massaged his skin with oils to keep his circulation going and prevent sores, and he reached out and caught hold of her hand.

'Angelica . . .'

Angelica gasped at the sound of her name. Always he'd called her 'Sister'.

'I – I have feelings for you.'

Her throat tightened and her heart raced.

'I've fallen in love with you . . . Oh, Angelica, forgive me, I shouldn't have spoken of it . . . You're a nun . . . I'm sorry.'

'No, don't be . . . I – I feel the same.'

Philip's eyes opened wide. 'You do? You love me . . . truly love me, not just as you're commanded to love all mankind?'

Biting her lip as the pain of her sin burned her heart, Angelica knew there was no turning back. She'd crossed the line. 'No, not like that. I'm *in* love with you, Philip, and have been since the moment I set eyes on you.'

His smile filled out the pain lines in his face and for a split second made him look well and strong. His hand took hers, sending shivers through her. All sin was forgotten as she clung on to it.

'What do we do now, Angelica? Can our love be allowed?'

Doubt made her cast her eyes downwards. How could it? Would she be released from her vows, or would she just have to turn her back on them? . . . And could she?

'I love you, Angelica. I love you with all that I am. I can never leave you now.'

Suddenly, she knew the meaning of the saying 'Wherever you make your bed, I make mine.' For she knew she would follow Philip to the ends of the earth.

Lifting her hand, she took off her veil and let her long dark hair fall around her face and into the nape of her neck. It was an act that symbolized her freedom, of her shaking off her old life and accepting whatever life lay ahead.

Philip's eyes lit with a light she'd never seen – a light that had been dulled by pain and a light that held his love.

'You're beautiful.'

His words brought the woman that she truly was to the fore. The feelings racing through her body were the true her. She would no longer be suppressed.

Lowering her head, she let her lips touch Philip's, and then it happened. Sister Angelica, the obedient servant of God, became Angelica, the woman.

The kiss was gentle but held the promise of tomorrow – of all her tomorrows – as, with the touching of her lips to his, her world burst into glorious flames of love and desire. It was done – she no longer belonged to God, but to Philip.

It was three weeks later before Shane called again. He had news that there was an arrangement in place for Philip to be airlifted out in four days' time. He was to be taken back to the UK.

Angelica's heart sank.

Although making progress, Philip still had an infection in his leg that they couldn't stem. But it was their deepening love and all they'd shared – kisses, touches, and the plans they'd made for the future, a future that saw the end of the war, of her renouncing her vows, of them marrying and having a family – that had tied them to one another and made this news unbearable.

How could she live without him? And yet, yes, at times, she'd been so conflicted and in agony over the sins she was committing that she'd begged of God to take away the feelings she had for him. That had never happened. For their love was a deep love neither of them could deny.

Nor did she when Philip was told the news, and he took her hand and looked up into her eyes. 'Angelica, I cannot leave you. I love you.'

The words zinged through her and seemed to wipe away the feeling of being a sinner as her body swayed towards him and she bent over him, giving him her lips.

When they parted, Philip's words set up a turmoil inside her as he begged, 'Come with me . . . please. I will take care of you. I need you. I have no one . . . well, a distant cousin . . . My family . . . they were all killed in the Blitz on London. Our home was destroyed . . . I cannot cope without you . . . I love you with all my heart.'

Angelica's stomach lurched. Could she give up everything? Could she abandon the only life she'd ever known and become a different person? The answer came to her, leaving her in no doubt that she could. What she couldn't do was let Philip go out of her life.

She nodded. 'I will go and speak with the Reverend Mother.'

As she walked towards the Reverend Mother's office, Angelica wanted to rip off her veil once more and strip herself of her vows. She wanted to be married to Philip. With this feeling came a determination that would brook no argument. Her life no longer belonged to God. He had given her the love of a man. He was showing her that it was a different path she must choose to take.

* * *

'Oh, Mary, Mother of God! What are you thinking? No, Sister Angelica, please don't do this. It is the devil tempting you. It happens to us all, though the sin calling us is different in each case.'

'Is it a sin to fall in love, Reverend Mother?'

'Well . . . no . . . but you are already married. You are married to God.'

'Yes, and God sent me my real reason for living. He Himself wants to divorce me and send me to happiness . . . Please, Reverend Mother, I must go with or without your blessing.'

'Then you have my blessing. No one has done more to serve God in Heaven than you have. Maybe He is now satisfied that your life's work here is done, and you have a different path to choose . . .'

'Those were my thoughts too. Oh, thank you, Reverend Mother. Thank you.'

'Be happy, my dear child, but remember, we are always here to welcome you with open arms.'

Angelica went gladly into the hug offered and felt the motherly love that she knew the Reverend Mother harboured towards her and all the nuns.

It was as she left and walked the hollow, echoing corridors back to Philip that Marcia came into Angelica's mind. Would she be able to take her and Madeleine with her?

Please God, let it be so, and then I can keep my promise to care for them for ever.

But when she put this to Philip, although he was overjoyed that she would be released to go with him, he told her, 'It won't be possible to take the girls. There won't be room on the aeroplane as they will only send a small craft and I will be on a stretcher . . . But we will come back for them . . .

I – I promise. Once this war is won and is completely over, we will come for them.'

With this he pulled her to him and kissed her. A kiss that burned into her as she gave her heart and soul to him. Her life was his now.

His fingers ran though her hair. 'You're the most beautiful woman I have ever set eyes on, Angelica. Will you do me the honour of being my wife?'

Happiness surged through Angelica as her true destiny shone brightly for her to see clearly. 'I will, my darling Philip, I will.'

They held hands then and it was to Angelica as if her soul and Philip's joined at that moment.

A movement of the curtain made her turn. Marcia stood there, her face holding an astounded expression. 'Sister Angelica . . .'

'Just Angelica, Marcia . . . I – I have something to tell you. I'm not a nun any longer. I am to be Philip's wife. I'm going to England with him. But I have not forgotten my promise to you. I will come for you when the war is over. Until then, be happy for me. I will always be a mother to you, I will not leave you and Madeleine behind.'

Angelica gestured that she wanted to hug Marcia. There was a hesitation but then she dashed forward, and her arms came around Angelica's waist.

Stroking her hair, Angelica told her, 'I have always said that God moves in mysterious ways, haven't I? Well, for a long time I have felt that He only needed me for a short while to do His work – to save His children. I have done that. You are all safe now. And so, God is freeing me to find the happiness and the fulfilment I seek.'

'Promise you will be back . . . promise.'

'I promise. You have lost so much in your life; you won't lose my love.'

Saying goodbye to the Reverend Mother, the sisters, especially Sister Frederica, and to the children tore Angelica apart but she smiled bravely and the courage she needed was helped by catching a reflection of herself in the glass door that led to the chapel.

She was just a woman – one who hadn't yet got used to wearing ordinary clothes but felt a freedom in doing so.

A shopping trip to buy them with the very generous allowance made to her by the Reverend Mother had been exciting and yet daunting. Funny, too, as the shop assistant was faced with her in full habit, wanting clothes a nun would never normally be seen in.

For Angelica, it had been her first taste of the outside world as someone who was going to join it, and she no longer felt different and at odds with it.

In the end when the young girl helping her relaxed and began to treat her like any other customer, it had become fun, and they'd had a giggle together.

She'd chosen a grey costume with a slight flare to the skirt and a fitted jacket. To team with it she bought a short-sleeved white blouse. The transformation astounded her.

Next, she'd picked a black skirt that would alternate with the grey one of the costume to give her a change of clothing. This she wore for the journey.

As the sisters gathered around her, she didn't feel too dissimilar to them in her black, white and grey, but they told her how lovely she looked, and how pleased they were for her. They told her how they loved her and would miss her and that she should write often and tell them about her new life.

'We want every detail,' Sister Frederica said, and then she doubled up in a fit of giggles. 'Well, not all!'

They all laughed at this, and Angelica detected a look of envy in several pairs of eyes. Suddenly the life in the convent that she'd loved showed its true colours to her. The restrictions, the small world they were contained in and, apart from the priest, the lack of any male company. How had she ever felt it was the life for her?

And yet, there was a lot she would miss – the peace, and the feeling of being safe. The outside world seemed full of noise and hustle and bustle and, yes, it was frightening. But she was ready to embrace it and would do so with her beloved Philip by her side.

As the sisters went about their duties, Angelica took a moment to sit on her bench and look up at the sunlight cascading through the branches of the old oak tree.

Once all was quiet, she allowed her thoughts to go to what her new life might be like. Was she up to it? How did normal people live day to day? She supposed she would keep house – cook and clean . . . But what about at night? What would it feel like to be in bed with Philip? To have him touch her and . . .

Her body filled with a warm feeling. Her cheeks flushed and her mouth dried. Anticipation tickled muscles she'd only recently become aware of, making her clench her thighs. She couldn't imagine what it would be like and yet, just the thought of it gave her sensations and longings.

Blushing, even though there was no one who could possibly know her thoughts, Angelica rose and went towards the convent. She needed to make sure Philip was ready for the journey and just to be with him.

Being by his side, holding his hand, intensified the feelings she'd had when sitting on the bench as he gazed into her eyes.

'I love you, Angelica.'

'I love you, Philip.'

His hand tugged at her, compelling her towards him. Slipping off her shoes, she climbed onto the bed and lay next to him.

'You're so beautiful, you look lovely. If only I were stronger. I want so much to make you mine.'

'I want that too, my darling, but it will be so. You are getting stronger every day.'

He was quiet for a moment. When he spoke, his words made her realize just how much he'd been through and had to face.

'I so want to go home, Angelica, and yet here, none of it seems real. It will all be so when I see the destruction that took my parents, grandparents and sister away from me. I – I don't know if I can face it.'

'I will be by your side, my dear. Together we will find a way, but where will we live if your home is very badly damaged?'

'We will live in an apartment my family . . . I own. But I would like to renovate the family home. The apartment is in London. The family pile, as Father called it, is in the countryside in the county of Surrey. It was a stray bomb that took it. The family were all gathered for my sister's birthday – her last day.'

'Oh, my dear, I can feel your pain. Have you never been back since?'

'No. I was here in France. The family solicitor managed to get information to the War Office, and they relayed it to me. It has been agony living with the knowledge, but I had my duty to do.'

'Oh, Philip. You weren't even able to bury your family?'

'No, but I know they are all buried in the grounds of the estate. We have our own little chapel and family cemetery. You and I will be married in the chapel; the local priest will perform the ceremony. We can stay at the inn nearby.'

Angelica thought it strange for a family to have its own chapel and graveyard. Only the very rich had such things in France. She'd no idea of Philip's status but was beginning to realize that he wasn't an ordinary run-of-the-mill young man.

'What did you do before the war, Philip?'

'I was studying law at Oxford University. When war broke out, I and several of my fellow students joined up to become pilots, but then I was singled out as having the qualities needed to become a special agent. No one knows this, it is so hush-hush. Where they think I've gone, I have no idea!'

His grimace told her of his anguish and of his physical pain. Was he well enough to take the flight? They hadn't been able to stem the infection in the wound in his leg and now it seemed that it raged through his body as she could feel the heat of his temperature and the clammy dampness of his skin. He closed his eyes.

'I – I need a minute, Angelica . . . I'll be all right . . . It's just bad for a short time and then it eases.'

She knew it didn't. Not always. She knew, too, that the biggest fear they all had was that the infection would become gangrenous . . . Oh, God, if that happened, he might lose his leg. Would he cope with such a devastating thing happening?

More than anything, he needed to see a doctor, but they didn't know one they could trust. She and the sisters had done their best for him, but they hadn't got a source for the medication he needed. All they'd been able to do was to give him the morphine Shane brought for him and to keep his wounds clean and dressed.

Getting off the bed, she went in search of more morphine which they kept in their refrigerator in the kitchen. She'd hoped to keep it for the flight as Shane had said he didn't think he could get any more . . . Maybe she would just give him half a dose and hope that would help.

As she crossed the courtyard she met Father Damion.

'Ah, our errant sister. Tell me, are you at peace with what you are doing, or is this terrible sin you're committing searing at your soul?'

Taken aback, Angelica stammered, 'I – I'm not sinning, Father. God is releasing me.'

'Vows are for ever! Don't you think that we all have moments when we want to abandon them? But it is then that we turn to God and away from the sins of the flesh, not run to partake of them . . . You will live to rue the day you discarded yours, Sister Angelica. Your sin will come to haunt you and to lay you low.'

Fear trembled through Angelica. Her body physically shuddered with the force of it as her stomach muscles clenched and doubt set up in her mind. Was she doing the right thing? Was it a terrible sin she was committing? Could God forgive her, or would she one day do as Father Damion predicted and regret the day that she left the convent and her life here? But then, God would be with her, wouldn't He? He had led her down this path.

Lifting her head, she looked Father Damion in the eyes.

'I have God's blessing and that of the Reverend Mother, Father. That is all I need.'

'I will pray for you, my child, and for the salvation of your soul.'

The force of feeling this evoked catapulted Angelica out of her life back then as she gasped with the force of the fear clutching her. 'Is he still praying . . . Will . . . will my soul be saved, my sin forgiven?'

'Oh, Mama . . . Oh, Mama, what is it that happened to you? Who? Who was praying for you?'

Angelica looked into the pleading eyes of her adored Mia. Should she tell her? But then, how could she? How could she admit to being a fraud – a woman who made vows and broke them?

'I – I can't tell you . . . Oh, Mia, I'm sorry, but I can't. I want you to know me as you know me. To remember . . . my . . . my love for you.'

Mia's desperate sigh cut through Angelica. She knew that in one way she wasn't being fair, but how could she destroy the picture Mia had of her? The life they'd had together? *Knowing the truth of her birth would shatter Mia's perception of everything I have let her believe . . . I can't do it, I can't . . . Oh, Philip, Philip, be with me.*

Mia's hand tightened around hers. Her other hand gently rubbed her mama's back. The action soothed Angelica.

She closed her eyes and for the moment found peace.

Chapter Seven

Mia

Sisterly Love Helps

Mia gently closed the bedroom door and then sighed as she went downstairs. She was glad that Mama was asleep, but she was now at odds with herself.

As a journalist – well, a trainee one – she knew she could find out more about her father, and just doing that might lead to her knowing more about her mother. But something stopped her. It was the feeling that she would be prying into things her mama held as secret and didn't want her to know. But then, did her mama have a right to keep it all from her? Wasn't her own heritage hers to know?

The front door opening and Angie putting her head around it lifted Mia's spirits. They hugged, then Angie asked, 'How's things with Aunty Angelica, love?'

Another sigh escaped Mia. 'Oh, Angie, her pain increases, but so does her anguish.'

'Sit down and I'll put the kettle on. A cuppa always sorts a lot of problems.' As she walked towards the kitchen, Angie looked back. 'Hey, it's a pity we didn't take to that smoking lark. We could go outside and have a fag. Everyone at work is still causing billows of smoke when they light up. The office gets that full of it sometimes that I've asked to sit near to the open window.'

'I can smell it on your clothes and hair, love.'

'Ugh, really? Do I stink?' With this Angie giggled. But then she became serious. 'They should ban it indoors. It's not fair on us who don't smoke. I can taste it all the time . . . disgusting.'

'We'll start a campaign – let non-smokers breathe fresh air!'

'Hey, that's not a bad idea, especially in light of the rumblings lately about how damaging smoking is to the health of your lungs and to those around smokers who breathe in their smoke!'

'Oh, don't. There's enough gloomy news without thinking that we're all doomed – even though at times it feels like we are with the threat of nuclear war hanging over us.'

'I know. I still feel trembles of fear when I think back to last year and Kennedy standing off against Khrushchev. I really thought our lives would end before they'd properly begun.'

'Ooh, I love John Kennedy. Jackie's a lucky girl . . . Though there are rumours . . .'

'What? What rumours? . . . About John Kennedy, you mean?'

'Yes. We get a lot of snippets from the American press boys. They talk of an affair John Kennedy had with a very well-known lady.'

'Really! Oooh, tell me more.'

'Ha, you're a typical journalist. I don't know any more, it's all been hushed up. We can't have the flavour of the month tarnished now, can we? And Jacqueline looks happy, so there's probably no truth in it anyway.'

'What a story if there was, though . . . You know, I so miss everything about my job . . . I mean, I wouldn't want to do anything different than to nurse Mama at the moment . . . Oh, God, what am I saying, of course I would. I would want her well again and everything to be as it was.'

'It's so sad, it breaks my heart. She's always been like a mum to me. Though she never let me call her that, or Mama. She always said that I had a lovely mum in heaven, and no one could replace her.'

'Oh, Angie, you've been through this, when you lost your mum.'

'Yes. But I was so young I didn't really know much about it, and now I only have hazy memories of her, which is sad . . . Look, let me pop that kettle on. We'll hear it when it boils – the blinking thing's got the loudest whistle I know!'

When Angie sat opposite her on Mama's favourite chair – a high-backed winged, beige velvet chair covered in tiny pink roses – Mia told her about Mama's latest ramblings.

'She never says anything that will help me to understand who she was. Why? How could she have committed some awful wrongdoing that haunts her now but must remain a secret from me?'

She'd curled her feet under her as she sat on the sofa that matched the centre of the roses on her mama's chair.

'Look, Mia, why don't you look into who your father was – his story, I mean? After all, as a pilot being brought back from France injured there's bound to be stuff about him in the library or the British Museum. There is about everyone who served and especially those injured or killed.'

The kettle suddenly demanding attention with its high whistle and rattling lid made them both jump.

'While you make the tea, Angie, I'll go and see if Mama's all right and, if she is, we'll enjoy our cuppa. We could sit on the step, it's a lovely day.'

'That would be lovely. I've been cooped up all day.'

Mama was sleeping soundly, which settled Mia's heart and mind. She tiptoed out of the bedroom and down the stairs. As she did, the thought stayed with her that Angie was right, and of course she knew of these sources of information. Maybe now it was time to start researching her father.

Once they were settled Angie said, 'I love our neighbourhood, you know. We will stay here after . . . ?'

'Of course we will. Though you'll have to take turns in scrubbing the step then. I'm not doing it every day, I feel like an old housewife out there with the lot of them – scared in case I'm a bit late doing it!'

They both giggled at this, but then became sombre again as they sipped their steaming tea.

'What will it be like when Mama's gone? Part of me wants her to go, to be out of pain and out of this anguish, but the other part of me doesn't think I can bear life without her.'

Angie's head came onto Mia's shoulder.

They sat like this for a while. Then Angie said, 'Life used to be so different. I can see us now skipping up and down this road, two little carefree kids. We were lucky to have the childhood we had. The friends we had here, and still have. The games we played. The love we had . . . and not just from your mama, but from every woman in the street who treated us like we were theirs.'

Mia didn't speak, just let herself see the scene of yesteryear and find happiness in it until a memory came to her and she asked Angie, 'Do you remember how Maisie's Dad used to give all the kids piggyback rides?'

'Oh, I do, and we were so jealous of her having a dad, we wanted to share him.'

'Well, it's not surprising. Neither of us knew our real dads. And it made us feel normal for a time to have someone who was like a dad to us.'

'He was lovely, wasn't he?'

'He was. I still miss Maisie since they moved to the Midlands.'

'I do too, and her dad. But that's life. Folk come in and out of it. Anyway, what's troubling you, Mia? . . . I mean, other than Aunty Angelica? There's been something different about you since you told me about that new doctor.'

'It's just that I've been mulling over something he said. He suggested I get a priest to visit and to see if he can help to calm Mama.'

'Mmm, not a bad idea. She's always prayed with us . . . You know, Mia, it is a mystery where she came from. Maybe I can look into it – use my journalistic powers and investigate. I could start by trying to find out who your father was. We have his name, Philip Jamieson, and your birth date, February the eighteenth. And we know he died before that.'

Angie began to do some calculations on her fingers. 'We also know that you were three weeks early, so that means that your mother and father must have been together in June of 1943. If we're assuming they met in France, then the only way that could be is if your father's plane was shot down . . . But that's strange as I don't think we had aircraft flying over France in forty-three . . . But it is the only answer if your father was a pilot . . . How else would they have met, and he bring her to England?'

'Oh, I don't know. Nothing fits. I know Mama came from

France, and that I was born in England. That my father, as you say, was Philip Jamieson, but that's it. But I am certain that Mama has done something bad. And I want to put it right for her . . . But how? She won't tell me anything! All I pick up is from when she's talking in her sleep.'

'It means a lot to you to know, doesn't it? Well, I'll try to find out what I can for you. I can't promise, but I can try.'

Two days later, when Angie came in from work, she shouted, 'I have news!'

'Oh, Angie. Really?'

'Yes, but . . . well, I don't know if it is of any help as it contradicts what you already know. But there is no record of any pilot being brought back to England having been shot down over France during the time we think it must have happened . . . But an amazing coincidence came about. Henry's been helping me.'

'Henry? How is he? I always loved him and his quirky ways. He brought life into the office.'

'He still does. Good old posh Henry. He never forgets how we both helped him to fit in with the crowd when he first arrived at the office.'

'Well, he did have a tough time of it, what with his battle with his titled family who disapproved of him wanting to be a journalist.'

'They did, but since he's been assigned to helping our royal correspondent, they are quite pleased as he gets to mingle in circles he's used to being in. Very useful too, as he gets inside information . . . Anyway, he was interested in your story and wanted to help. And guess what? He only came into work today with the revelations that his dad and yours were at Oxford together, studying law!'

'Oh, Angie, someone who knew my father! I've never known that. I've always envied how everyone in the street knew yours and could tell you about him – give you little memories you wouldn't have otherwise. I have nothing.'

'No. That's very unfair of Aunty Angelica. But we both know she has something to hide about her past. We've always known, so talking about your dad would have made her feel she might slip up.'

'Oh, Angie, it must be something wicked!'

Angie took her in her arms. 'Look, let's not jump the gun, eh, Mia? Let's see what we can find out. I have loads already to tell you, but I'm hungry and whatever's cooking smells delicious.'

'Shepherd's pie. It's nearly ready.'

'Right, while you dish it up, I'll nip upstairs and see Aunty, then we'll eat and I'll tell you what I know so far.'

'Okay, but try not to wake her, love, she's had another bad day.'

When they sat down at the table that stood under the window in the kitchen, Mia said, 'Tell me all that you know now, Angie, I can't wait any longer!'

'Well, Henry's father remembers your father leaving the air force under a veil of secrecy and disappearing, but now knows what he ended up doing.'

As Mia listened to how her father landed up in France as a special agent, she was filled with awe and pride.

'So, he was a hero! But why haven't we heard anything about men who did such work?'

'Henry said his father doesn't know. He assumes it is still a national secret and one which involved both men and women.'

Mia couldn't take this in. Not only that there were special agents during the war, but why her mama hadn't ever told her. But then her thoughts darkened. Did her father do something bad too?

'Hey, I thought this news would put to rest part of your speculation, but by the look on your face, it's opened up new doubts and misgivings.'

Not wanting to cast a shadow on her father's memory, Mia quickly said, 'No . . . It's just the not knowing. I mean, why should such heroism be kept a secret?'

'Some things just are. But I'm sure it will all come out one day. At least you have the answer to one mystery – how he was in France and why . . . Though it does open up many more questions for you.'

Mia nodded. All sorts of scenarios were going through her mind. Somehow, this Marcia girl seemed to have the key to it all. With this, Mia vowed to herself that she would keep the promise she made to find Marcia. She had a good starting point with Mama telling her the convent she should go to to begin her search.

'Look, Mia, there are records. You could find out all you need to know in the future, but until you're free . . . I mean . . . Oh, it's all so sad . . .'

Angie stood and came around the table and took Mia into her arms. As they hugged, Mia told her, 'I'll shelve it all for now, I promise. I didn't mean to make such a thing of it . . . But, oh, Angie, what would I do without you?'

Angie held her a little tighter. 'You'll never know as you'll never be without me.'

This warmed Mia's heart. Angie would be there for her when the worst happened. Just knowing she would have somebody helped.

As they came out of the hug, Mia said, 'I've decided to do what our new doctor suggested and ask for a priest to come and see Mama.'

'Oh, that was sudden. But I agree, it's a good idea. The Church of Our Lady of Assumption is only just up the road and, as you know, I pass it going to and from work. I can call in and ask if one of the priests could call if you like?'

'I would like that, ta, Angie. Tell them that Mama is a lapsed Catholic but is very troubled and needs help to die in peace . . . Oh, Angie . . . I – I can't face that day.'

Once more Angie was holding her. She didn't tell her not to cry, but gently rubbed her back.

Something let go inside of Mia and she found she couldn't control her sobs.

Angie cried with her. When at last they calmed, Angie made her giggle by saying, 'The tea lady's here, love, all will be fine.'

'Oh, Angie! I'll make the tea, it's my turn.'

Angie plonked herself back down. 'That's not a bad idea. I want to finish my pie, it's delicious. Anyway, I'm always running around after you!'

Mia burst out laughing at this complete twisting of the truth. She felt better for it. And for the tears. Although they'd left her bunged up and sure that her eyes were bulging, they'd released what had felt like a painful pressure in her chest. She took a deep breath as she turned the gleaming brass tap and water gushed into the shallow pot sink.

Putting the kettle spout under the flow in readiness for making tea, Mia thought about how her mama still preferred coffee. And not the chicory that most folk drank, but real ground coffee. *Oh, Mama, how different your life must have been to mine. What were you like at nineteen years of age?*

Having never been to France, Mia couldn't imagine. Though she did know a little about Mama's country – snippets she'd pieced together from what her mama had told her and from geography lessons at school. She'd learned about how the French grew grapes in neat rows, and she had seen pictures of farmers wearing their berets and the sun shining on shuttered houses.

'The kettle, Mia!'

With this from Angie, the sound of the shrill whistle penetrated Mia's thoughts and brought her out of the world she knew nothing about, but often dreamed of.

Father Benedict had a lovely smile when Mia opened the door to him a couple of days later. Angie had told her that he would be coming and what his name was. She'd said he was a nice man and, from what she knew, well loved too.

'Mia?'

'Yes. Come in, Father.'

'How is your mother today? . . . I was very sorry to hear of her being so sick, and of her being troubled in her mind. I hope I can help.'

'Thank you. Would you like—'

'A cup of tea? No thank you. Priests are full of tea, you know. We drink it out of politeness usually, but I feel that I don't need to stand on ceremony with you, Mia. Am I right?'

Mia grinned and felt herself relax. She nodded her head. 'You are. I won't force-feed tea to you, I promise.'

'Ah, someone who can be natural around me. We're off on a good footing, Mia.'

Mia liked him and felt at ease when she'd been dreading his visit. A man of no striking qualities, average height, fair hair, and not even good-looking, it was his ready smile and sense of humour that endeared him to her.

'Your sister – well, she explained that you look on each other as that – told me that you know little of your mother's life, that she won't share anything with you. You do know that if she shares anything with me by way of a confession that I cannot divulge it to you, don't you, Mia?'

'Yes. I understand. I just want her to find peace of mind. And I'm trying to make myself accept that I might not know about Mama's life, or my own history until after she . . .' Still Mia could not utter the word that would mean saying goodbye to her adored mama. 'Well, anyway, I'll take you up to Mama, Father.'

Mama opened her eyes when they entered her bedroom door. As she looked from Mia to the priest, it was as if God Himself had walked in. Her face lit up. 'You . . . have come . . . to help me? *Merci, merci, Monsieur.*'

'*Oui, bonjour, Madame. Je viens apporter la paix.*'

'Oh, Father, you speak French! That alone will bring Mama peace. Thank you . . . I'll leave you now . . . I'll just be downstairs, Mama, dear.'

Back in the living room once more, Mia let herself out of the front door and sat down on the step hugging her knees. She cast her eyes heavenward. *Please, please let this work. Please God. Forgive her.*

But then, for some unexplained reason, Mia's mind turned to thinking of Steve. Her thoughts turned to longings and then a deep sigh as she told herself that a man such as him would never look at a girl like her. She couldn't understand why she wasn't able to get him out of her mind, until she admitted to herself that he hadn't just got into her head, but into her heart.

Chapter Eight

Angelica

Revisiting Love Lost

'Angelica, *je suis Père Benoît* – known as Benedict here. May I continue in English?'

'*Mais oui.*'

Angelica wanted to say more than yes, as his French was so like that of Father Damion and brought back the terrifying curse he'd uttered:

You will live to rue the day you discarded your vows, Sister Angelica. Your sin will come to haunt you and to lay you low. How right he'd been, for over the years, she had been laid low on many occasions. Though never lower than now. This agony – not just of her wretched body, but of her soul – was akin to how she'd felt soon after she and Philip arrived in England.

And yet what had happened in the first few weeks had been a high point in her life too.

'*Non . . . Non . . .*'

'What is it? Speak to me, Angelica.'

She tried to tell him. His lovely smile encouraged and inspired her, but then his face faded and became Philip's –

beautiful Philip. And the silence of the bedroom filled with the roar of the plane as it left her and Philip on the tarmac.

People were running towards them. She didn't want them to come as she knew they would take Philip away from her, but she knew too that he desperately needed to be in hospital.

'You must be cold, darling. You should have brought a thicker coat. I don't know how long it will be before you are taken to my flat.'

'I didn't know it could get this cold. But now you're home, Philip, and my heart will warm me knowing you will now have a chance to get well.'

'And my arms will warm you too, darling, once I am fit.'

And now he was. The long two months that she'd visited him, sitting with him for hours, had passed, and he was back with her in his flat that now felt like home, although at first it had seemed damp, cold and unwelcoming.

But since then, she'd thrown her heart into getting it clean and ready, made possible by Philip instructing his solicitor to make the funds available to her that she asked for.

'Come here, my darling. We haven't had a proper cuddle while I was in hospital . . . I'm so happy they've allowed me out, though I had to tell them that you were a nurse and would be able to care for my leg in between the doctor's visits.'

Just one of so many lies they'd had to tell, the biggest being that she was Philip's wife.

'Necessary for convention, darling,' Philip told her, before going on to say that she would be as soon as he was well enough. 'But first we have to register you as living in the area, and that has to be for three weeks.'

'But I have been here for that time now. Please, Philip, couldn't we get one of those special licences I have heard of?'

'This set-up doesn't sit well with you, does it, my dear?'

His hand waved around the lovely but small apartment, with its one bedroom. 'Look, I'll sleep on the sofa till we're wed. How will that be?'

Philip sat down on the small couch. What its original colour had been, she didn't know, but now it had a fitted linen cover in a pale blue. Beside it was a matching chair with the same-coloured cover. She'd washed both and now they were fresh-looking and complemented the mahogany table in the corner, the small occasional one between the sofa and the chair, and a china cabinet in the corner of the room, all of which she'd polished until they gleamed and now sat on a huge clean rug that she'd beaten for hours.

A long window, with curtains of the same blue as the chair and sofa covers, gave plenty of light, often glittering with the reflection of the River Thames that flowed by at the end of the small garden and through Windsor, where this house was situated.

Philip's apartment was on the ground floor, so access to the garden and river was just through French doors leading from the living room.

The upstairs apartments were let out to people who, Philip said, only came for a few weeks each year in the summertime.

It was beautiful, outside and in. Angelica had come to love it in the short time she'd lived here.

'The sofa isn't big enough for you . . . I – I think you should have the bed.'

'Come and sit beside me and then we can decide. Only, I have something for you.'

As she sat, Philip put his hand in his pocket. 'I want you

to have this, my darling, as a symbol of our love and something to mark us becoming engaged to be married.'

A gold chain holding a blue stone caught the light as Philip took it from a small pearl box.

'It was my mother's. She gave it to me to carry everywhere with me while I was away.' His face creased as he fought the tears, but one seeped out of the corner of his eye. He dropped his head.

'Oh, Philip, Philip, I will treasure it for ever. Tell me about your mama.'

As he turned and clasped the necklace in place, he kissed her neck. The sensation was as if someone had run a feather down her back, giving her delicious tingles.

Philip's voice was husky as he pulled her to him, setting her senses on fire.

'Let me hold you first, my darling. I feel stronger than I have since we met and need to feel you in my arms.'

She went willingly to him and accepted his kisses. She allowed the caressing of her – she wanted it – and when he stood and pulled her up, she followed him into the bedroom, noticing that he hardly limped, the first sign that he was truly on the mend.

Once there, she let – no needed – Philip to take her clothes off, to gaze on her, to touch her and to kiss her in the most intimate places. She heard her own voice crying out her exquisite pleasure. She explored Philip's body and came to know it in a different way to how she'd known it before – as that of a sick man. Now, it felt strong, and her touch made his cries join hers.

And then it happened – her ultimate sin. And yet, the most beautiful moment in her life.

She became one with Philip. She winced at the discomfort,

but then was soothed by his gentle words and persuaded to relax.

'It will be all right, my darling. I'll go slowly, till you're ready.'

Soon she whispered, 'I'm ready,' as her body cried out for more, and though not bidden, her back arched in a gesture of acceptance.

She was no longer in control as she cried out, 'My love, my life,' as an almost unbearable but beautiful ecstasy pulsated exquisite feelings through her body.

A cry like no other he'd uttered came from Philip as he made her truly his.

Rolling off her, he smiled a sweaty smile, which then suddenly twisted into agony as he clutched his heart. Beads of sweat from their lovemaking became huge droplets.

'Philip! Philip, my love, what is it? Darling, are you in pain?'

He didn't answer. His eyes bore into her. They held a plea for help, a desperation that said, 'Save me, Save, me . . .'

But before she could turn to get up onto her knees, a terrible rattle came from Philip's throat, and he flopped back onto the pillow.

'Philip! Philip! No . . . no . . . no!'

Her scream pierced her own ears.

A strange voice penetrated her agony. 'Angelica, Angelica, it's all right. I'm here. Father Benedict, remember? I've come to help you if I can. You can talk to me . . . You drifted off to sleep, my dear. A troubled sleep. Tell me, unburden yourself . . . God's mercy is waiting for you.'

The sensation of coming from the past to the present disorientated her when the past had been so real.

'No one can help me . . . I've lost so much, even my soul.'

'No one can lose their soul while they are still alive, dear lady, as there is still time to redeem it. Talk to God, tell Him your sin, and ask for forgiveness. You will receive it.'

She wanted to tell this lovely priest that her sins were too mortal – she'd given up the same vows he lived by, had a child out of wedlock, and abandoned two helpless children when she'd given them her word.

But her mind took her swirling back and she left him to pray over her as she gazed down in horror at her beloved Philip's still body.

Somehow, soon after, Angelica found herself in the street, dressed and screaming at the top of her voice. People gathered around her, took her back to the apartment, fetched help and held her as Philip's body was taken away and a police officer went through his papers trying to find an address for his cousin.

When at last they'd all gone, Angelica fell to the floor, lay prostrate as she had in the chapel back at the convent, and sobbed until she fell asleep. Never had she felt so alone. What would she do? Where would she go? *Oh, Philip, Philip, my love, why did you leave me?*

Her bones ached when she woke. Stretching out her limbs gave her the knowledge that she was in bed, but she couldn't remember how she got there. Her hand reached over, but there was no one there. Memories flooded her. Grief overwhelmed her.

Rolling over, she tried to bring Philip back to her by sniffing the pillow he'd laid his beloved head on. Then she buried her head in it and wept – for Philip, for her own plight, and yes, from shame at what had passed between them. And yet, she knew that the beauty of that moment would stay with her – even if it was forever tarnished by her loss.

Somehow, she functioned enough to bathe and dress, and to brush her hair and roll it back before pinning it neatly into place.

Wandering into the kitchen, she gazed out of the window at the beautiful peaceful view, of rippling water, running to eternity past the lovely homes on its banks and overhanging willows that seemed to be weeping tears for her.

It was when she placed her hands on the windowsill to give her strength and asked why they had been punished in this terrible way that she began to question her beliefs, and ranted and raved at the vile revenge she was suffering. She sobbed as loneliness engulfed her – for not only had she lost her beloved Philip, but she had lost her love of God too.

Weeks had gone by – Angelica didn't know how many – when suddenly the sound of a key turning in the lock and the front door opening filled her with fear.

She'd been told that the solicitors were trying to trace Philip's cousin, but that he was away serving in the air force.

Taking a deep breath and straightening her back, Angelica turned from her position of gazing out of the window and was confronted by a man in uniform who had the look of Philip.

'So, you're the French hussy my cousin was besotted with?'

Shocked by his tone, all Angelica could think to say was, 'What is a hussy?'

'A woman like you. One that would move in with a man

before wedlock. Well, now you will pay for your action. You killed my beloved cousin. He needed rest and loving care, not the demands of the flesh.'

Incensed, Angelica pulled herself up straight. 'It wasn't like that . . .'

'The police told me that you were sobbing about how you had just made love and he died! The only person who allows a man to do that out of wedlock is a hussy.' He put his hand in his pocket. 'Well, I don't know how much your pleasuring of a very sick man cost, but here, I have a few coppers. Take it and leave. I never want to see you again! My wonderful cousin wasn't well enough for such antics. You must have cajoled him into them, and they caused his death!'

Aghast, Angelica told him, 'We loved each other, we were going to marry . . .'

He strode over to the door and opened it. 'Just get out! Gather your things and go!'

Fear gripped Angelica. 'But I have nowhere to go . . . Please, just let me stay until I can contact my Reverend Mother.'

'What? Your . . . Reverend Mother! Just who the hell are you? . . . Good God! You're not a nun, are you? I had been told Philip had been kept safe in a convent until they could get him home. Safe! Ha!'

'I – I cared for him . . . We fell in love. He brought me back to England. We were to marry. Please don't throw me out, please help me.'

Her fear of being on the streets put a desperation into her voice.

His grimace showed his disgust as he stared at her. When he spoke, he said, 'You're not my responsibility. I suggest you seek out a priest and get the help of the Church . . . Go back to where you came from. I'm a respectable man, I cannot be involved in your sordid affair with my cousin. I've never heard of anything more disgusting than a nun sleeping with a man! It goes against everything I believe in. I want you to leave, and to leave now!'

Angelica trembled as the implication of her situation hit her. *Oh, Philip, Philip, why did you leave me? My love, my life . . .*

A tear dripped from her eye, followed by others as she felt herself crumbling.

'Don't even think that turning on the waterworks will help you as it won't! There are churches around here, you just need to ask. It's up to them to take care of you or send you back to where you came from. I just want you to leave and to leave now!'

Angelica could see there would be no arguing with this man. Nor did she have a leg to stand on. All that had been Philip's now belonged to him. She was trespassing. He had a right to demand that she left.

On a cry of anguish, she ran into the bedroom. She could not look at the bed that had been the scene of her greatest moment and her worst, but she gathered her things into a small case she'd found in the bottom of a wardrobe, picked up her purse containing what was left of the money that Philip's solicitor had given her and, mustering all the dignity she could, she left.

Lost in a world of cars, buses and horse-driven vehicles, Angelica stood staring around her. A car pulled up and a cockney voice asked, 'Taxi, luv? I'm on me way back to the East End and looking for a fare.'

Over the time she'd nursed Philip, he'd told her many tales of London, and of how he owned tenement buildings in the East End. He spoke fondly of it, saying the folk there always had a cheery word for you. In an instant she made her mind up that she'd find more help there than in this area where no one looked at you, let alone showed a friendly gesture.

'How much would it cost to take me to a Catholic church in the East End, sir?'

'Blimey, you ain't from England with that accent. And yer don't 'ave to call folk by formal names. Mister'll do. But why the East End, eh, luv?'

'It's . . . I – I've been abandoned . . . I – I heard they're kindly people there.'

'Well, you hop in. I'll take yer to a good priest who'll help yer. I don't need any fare as I'm going back that way anyhow.'

This kindness broke Angelica. The tears that had dried earlier now flooded her face as she got into the car.

'Hey, things ain't that bad, luv. Yer'll be all right. Father Kevin is known for his kindness. He takes in all waifs and strays, and there's a lot of them, I can tell yer. Especially after what the Jerries 'ave done to our lovely East End.'

As they drove through London, Angelica became aware of just what war meant. Her heart went out to these brave people they'd heard so much about, and yet they hadn't really imagined what devastation they'd been going through. There were buildings with their hearts ripped out, burned-out vehicles, piles of rubble and worn-out women pushing prams piled high with what looked to Angelica like all their worldly goods.

And as they got deeper into what the driver told her in a proud voice was the East End, the destruction took away her pain for herself and replaced it with sorrow for those who lived here, as their poverty was visible in shattered windows covered in cardboard, and their houses being no more than hovels built in rows with hardly an arm-stretch between them. Some were reduced to a pile of bricks. Rubbish littered the paths, and the gulleys ran with brown liquid that contributed to the putrid air. Angelica wanted to help them in any way she could. *Maybe that's why God has steered me here . . . But then, will He ever forgive me enough to place any trust in me again? I have lain with a man out of wedlock . . . Oh, Philip, my Philip, how am I to live without you? Why did we do what we did? You were so weak . . . your poor heart couldn't take it . . . I – I killed you!*

'Now, now, young miss. Tears never 'elped anyone. Look around yer. There's been a million tears shed, but at the end of the day, folk 'ave got on with life. That's what you've gotta do. Pick yerself up and dust yerself down. There'll be folk who'll help yer . . . I wished I could meself, but I'm a man on me own since me ma died . . . I never married, yer see. But I'm happy in me own way. You can be too. Yer just need a leg-up and a bit of kindness.'

What a leg-up was, Angelica had no idea, though she thought it must mean something like a helping hand. She needed more than that. But would she find it?

'Here we are. You go in and ask for Father Kevin, luv, yer'll be fine. He'll help yer.'

'*Merci* . . . You're so kind.'

'French, is it? I wondered where that accent was from. Well, luv, you lot copped it good and proper. We did our best, but the Jerries beat us in the end. We ain't done yet, though. We'll get 'em out of yer country, yer'll see, luv.'

'Your soldiers did a wonderful job, we'll always be grateful to them, and we are sorry you lost so many . . . Thank you again for your kindness . . . Let me pay you your fare, I have a little money.'

Angelica wasn't sure how much as she hadn't got used to pounds, shillings and pence. It hadn't seemed like real money after the franc.

'You keep what yer 'ave. I'm glad to help. But I have to get on me way, luv, I've still time to pick up a few fares.'

Without thinking Angelica said, 'God bless you.' But then she wondered if she had any right to call on God to bless anyone.

Looking up at the huge church in front of her, which stood on a corner and seemed to majestically defy the destruction around it, Angelica felt it gave the air of being a place of sanctuary . . . Would it be so for her?

The door creaked as she opened it. And then shame washed over her as she looked up at a statue of Our Lady holding her toddler son. Feeling her knees give way, Angelica grabbed hold of a pew. It was then that the sound of sobbing brought her up as she looked towards the bent figure of a young woman crouched over a pew, her weeping now echoing around the empty building.

Compassion steered Angelica towards her. Her own troubles forgotten, she slipped into the pew beside the young woman and put her arm around her.

Anguished, tear-filled eyes looked up at her. Angelica smiled through her own tears. The young woman, who looked no older than Angelica's twenty-three years, leaned into her. The gesture broke the strength Angelica had tried to muster, and together they cried out their pain without knowing what was hurting the other, and without knowledge of who each other was.

When they calmed, Angelica asked, 'Will you be all right?'

'I'll never be right again, luv . . . I – I lost me man . . . me Bert . . . me best friend . . . He were fighting in Italy . . . He caught a bullet . . . I just don't know 'ow I'm to carry on . . . I 'ave me belly up, yer see . . . He came on leave . . . Oh, me pain when I think I'll never see him again . . . I can't even bury him . . . he's out there somewhere . . . Oh, Bert . . . Bert.'

Angelica held her to her again.

When she pulled back, the young woman asked, ''Ave you lost someone, luv?'

Angelica could only nod.

'Here, let me hold you for a while. We're in the same boat by the sounds of things.'

There was comfort in being held as there had been in holding someone in the same distress.

'Me name's Irene. What's yours, luv?'

'Angelica.'

'Well, that's about right, as you are an angel. It was like you'd been sent to me when yer put yer arms around me. I was so lost . . . Me and Bert have been together all our lives. We were orphans in the same home. We always looked out for one another, and then as we got older, we fell in love and married . . . Then the war came and . . . now, he's gone.'

'Oh, Irene. I am so sorry.'

'What's your story, luv? You're foreign, ain't yer? Have yer got someone who can help yer?'

Angelica felt that she was with a friend and could tell all. Once she started, she couldn't stop. Everything came out, her past, her meeting Philip, his death, and being thrown out.

Irene didn't interrupt her or show disgust. She just patted her back.

'And now I have nowhere to go. I'm hoping the priest will help me. I've been told he's a kind man.'

'He is, but you've found your help in me. I told yer, you've been sent to me. Well, we need each other. If you'll accept it, yer can come and live with me in me house. It ain't much. Just two rooms upstairs and two down, but we'll jog along just fine. It's not far from here.'

'Really? You would help me like this?'

'If for nothing else but to hear that lovely accent every day, luv . . . Yes, I would gladly help yer . . . Well, we will help each other. Me army allowance has been stopped and I'll be due a war widow's pension, but it'll take a while to come through. I have a job, but it don't bring in much, so I'm struggling to pay me rent. But with us both working we could manage . . . Yer'd be very welcome. Yer'd be company too.'

'Oh, Irene, I will gladly accept, thank you. I do have a little money, but I will get a job. Only I don't have papers. I don't know how long I can stay for.'

'We'll sort that out. I know folk. Most who were brought up in an orphanage have to make their own way in life. Some go down the route of activities that ain't quite legal, but they do such a good job, they get away with it. We'll get yer some papers, don't you worry, girl.'

As Irene looked up and smiled, it seemed that everything was possible.

Even with her tear-swollen eyes, Irene was beautiful. Her red hair fell around her face in a natural curly mass. Her blue-green eyes were full of compassion and, yes, love.

Angelica felt a return of that love as a feeling for Irene surged through her. Somehow, it made her feel safe. She had found a friend.

* * *

Irene's little house stood third from the bottom of a row of similar houses, all joined together. Two at the other end of the row were just a shell, with blackened beams hanging at angles, making it look as though they would fall at any moment.

'The bombing did that. Took two families in the one night. It was the worst night of the Blitz for us. But it's over now and we're getting back to normal – well, not proper normal, we still have to beat them bleeders, but the Yanks will help us do that. And everything's short on the shelves in the shops and yer have to fight for what yer need. And then there's a lot of folk who are homeless – some sleeping in school halls, others in churches. There're soup kitchens everywhere . . .'

'What is this, "soup kitchen"?'

'It's run by the Women's Voluntary Service, and some are run by the Sally Army. They set up a stall and give out meals, and soup and bread. A godsend they are. I've used them meself lately. Mind, when I had me money coming in, I used to donate what I could – a bag of spuds, or a meat pie that I'd made.'

'And now your kindness is being repaid in food being available for you.'

'Yes. I ain't looked at it like that, but that makes me feel better.'

Angelica observed that though the streets looked clean, the houses reflected the hardship and poverty that made these soup kitchens necessary. Most had ragged curtains, and washing hung across the street that didn't look as though it had been washed, suggesting to her that maybe soap was hard to come by as well as food.

Angelica had seen many atrocities but the plight of ordinary people who didn't ask for war always tore at her heart. Marcia came to her mind and her sister, Madeleine. How glad she was that they and all the children she'd gathered from the woods were safe, happy and cared for.

Inside, a cosy little room greeted them. A brown sofa and matching armchair faced the fireplace, with embroidered antimacassars giving them a cheerful look. A small dining table and two chairs stood under the window and just past them there was a door that Angelica guessed led to the kitchen. The floor was tiled with two big, multi-coloured rag rugs covering it.

'It's lovely, Irene. I love it.'

'Ta, luv. I've done me best with it. We got the furniture from the second-hand shop – some nice pieces, I reckon. And I made the rugs, the antimacassars and the curtains. We were taught skills in sewing and knitting at the orphanage and the boys learned to work with wood.'

'They're so good. You're very talented.'

'Ta.' Irene beamed before resuming her tour of her lovely home. 'Right . . . through here is me kitchen. I whitewashed the walls a couple of weeks ago, so it looks better than it did. I'll put the kettle on, and we can have a drop of tea. I've a couple of scoops of tea leaves left, so I'll make it fresh. Though I do dry me leaves out and use them again. Yer get used to it . . . Oh, and I ain't got any sugar, but I've got some milk and saccharine.'

'I'll have it without. I'm not really used to tea. We drink more coffee, and wine.'

'Ha, I heard about the French and their wine. Well, we ain't got any of that, and nor 'ave the shops, but I've got some chicory coffee if yer want that instead of tea?'

'Thanks, I will . . . You're being so kind to me, Irene, I will pay you back, I promise.'

'Don't be daft, you don't know how much you've 'elped

me. You've made me look forward to the future now, as there's been times when I was thinking of ending it all.'

'Oh no! Oh, Irene, I'm so sorry.'

'It's hard knowing yer man's gone, ain't it?'

'It is. I – I didn't have Philip for long. I – I didn't even see him laid to rest. His solicitor was waiting for the wishes of his cousin.'

'That adds to the hurt, don't it? As I said, I ain't never going to see me Bert's body, nor can I lay him to rest nearby. But as for not knowing your Philip for long, it doesn't matter, yer loved him, and that's where the pain is. It's like you've been cut in half.'

They were quiet for a moment.

'Look, while the kettle's boiling, I'll show yer upstairs. I've two bedrooms. The lav's outside and there's a tin bath hanging on the wall out there for bath night.'

Angelica guessed that lav was short for lavatory, but the tin bath was a novelty, and why it was hanging outside instead of in a bathroom she didn't know!

Upstairs, one room was furnished with a double bed and a huge walnut wardrobe, which Angelica couldn't imagine getting up the stairs, or through any of the tiny windows. Its gleam caught the sunlight, making the grain of the wood look beautiful.

'Me pride and joy, that wardrobe, luv. Me Bert unscrewed it bit by bit and rebuilt it up here for me, just because I loved it. Mind, I ain't got much in it – me Sunday best frock, and me undies on the shelves, and Bert's Sunday best suit, and that's it.'

'It's so lovely . . . I can sew too, so we'll make ourselves some clothes. I've only got a couple of outfits in my bag. The Reverend Mother kitted me out before I left France.'

'That'd be lovely. I ain't never done any dressmaking, but I'd like to learn. There's a market in town, and a stall that sells material. Once we get some money coming in, we'll go and have a mooch. Yer know, you being a nun is the one bit of yer story that I can't get me head around, luv.'

Not sure what a 'mooch' was, Angelica ignored it and said, 'You won't tell anyone – not a soul? Only . . . well, I'm ashamed. Not of being a nun, but of leaving and doing all I've done.'

'No one'll hear it from my lips, girl, but try not to be ashamed. Yer ain't done nothing wrong. Yer fell in love, that's all.'

Relieved, Angelica followed Irene through to the second bedroom.

'I've only got a bed in here. And it ain't up to much. It were left by the previous tenants. But I've some clean sheets. Though I ain't got any blankets, only a couple of old grey coats we picked up in a jumble sale. They're lovely and thick and warm, we put them over us in the winter. And yer can have my pillow. I'll have Bert's. I always sleep on it anyway as it brings him to me and still smells of his Brylcreem. He used to plaster his hair down with Brylcreem and part it in the middle . . .'

Irene's body shook.

Angelica took her hand. And, trying to keep the mood light, said, 'It's lovely, thank you. I will be very happy and cosy in here.'

The kettle whistling loudly was a welcome distraction.

'Ah, I'm dying for a cup of Rosie Lee. Come on, let's get our drinks and we can sort your bed out in a bit.'

One sip of the dark brown chicory coffee made Angelica grimace, but she hid her distaste from Irene.

'D'yer want anything to eat, luv?'

'No thank you. I – I'm not eating much. I feel queasy most of the time . . . And, well, I am not able to drink this . . . I'm sorry.'

Irene's brow knitted together as she looked intently at Angelica. 'When did yer say yer laid with your Philip?'

'A few weeks ago.'

'And 'ave yer seen yer monthly since?'

Angelica had to think what her monthly was, but then gasped . . . '*Non, mais je n'ai pas!* No! it cannot be!'

'It can, love. If yer man finished the act, it can. I reckon you've got your belly up.'

'Belly up?'

'Pregnant . . . You're having a nipper . . . a child! I know the signs. I knew them the moment they happened to me too – many a girl in the orphanage got caught, poor things. There was a lot that went on as shouldn't 'ave done in that place, but me Bert always protected me from it. He was a fighter was Bert.'

Most of this went over Angelica's head as she tried to absorb the shock of the possibility of what Irene had said. '*Non! Non, ce n'est pas possible!*'

'I don't know what yer saying, luv, but I understand "*non*" . . . Sorry, but yes, you could well be having a baby.'

Angelica sank back into the sofa.

'Look, luv, we're in the same boat. We'll get through it together.'

'But how? . . . A baby . . . and no papa!'

Mia's voice penetrated Angelica's anguish and catapulted her back to the present, leaving her confused and lost in time.

'Mama, it's all right. I'm not a baby any more . . . Oh,

Mama, Mama, you were left alone to have me, but you got through it . . . Tell me, what happened to my papa?'

How can this be? I have only just found out!

'Don't cry, Mama. It's all right. Everything's all right.'

Gentle arms held her. Mia's arms.

Her heart rested. It had been all right. Irene had made it so . . . Though times were often difficult, they managed to have fun too. Irene always made her laugh.

'Oh, Mama, that was a lovely sound. You giggled.'

Chapter Nine

Marcia

Safe No More

The sun scorched the little lawn that Marcia had tried to cultivate outside her house in Limousin. She'd always loved gardening. Joseph had taught her so much during the times she'd been able to stand and chat with him as he'd worked.

Sighing, she listened to her three boys playing out in the street. Joseph, her eldest, was now six, Amos was five and Hans was two.

Despite the heat, they weren't fractious, but happily kicked a ball about with other children from the neighbourhood.

The heat was getting to her, though. Number four was only weeks from being born and her body felt heavy and cumbersome.

Sitting down on the bench in the shade of the tree – a place she loved as it made her think of Sister Angelica's bench – memories began to flood her.

Now she'd let the past in once, Marcia found it was helping her to remember and that she shouldn't always try to shut it out. But though she'd thought a lot about it lately, she hadn't let herself go to the very worst bits.

They niggled at her, though. Wanted her to remember.

Wanted her to record them to let the world know. She would. She would write them all down. But not today. Today, she would just remember another bench.

Closing her eyes, she could see herself running towards it on that fateful day.

1944

Marcia ran across the yard to where Joseph was sitting on Sister Angelica's bench. 'Joseph, Joseph!'

Now almost as tall as her, Joseph, who'd grown at least three inches in the past two years and now looked more like a man, stood up. His smile showed even white teeth and his love for her. But that smile changed to horror when a loud banging of the gate signalled danger.

They looked up into the tree and saw that Isaac, their lookout for today, was fast asleep!

'Run, Marcia, get everyone down into the cellar! Hurry!'

But before she could move, the hack-hack of automatic gunfire rang out and the gate shattered, freezing her to the spot.

In an instant German soldiers marched in, their shouts terrifying and confusing.

Marcia looked around her. 'Madeleine! Madeleine!'

Children ran in all directions, their screams and cries silenced by another bout of gunfire. Their bodies were like statues as they stared wide-eyed at the German soldiers.

Sister Frederica came running from her little office, followed by the Reverend Mother. In French, the tall, evil-looking German in charge said, 'We have reason to believe you are harbouring Jewish children here.'

Sister Frederica pulled herself up to her full height, though still she looked tiny. 'We harbour no one. We take care of children!'

A single shot and she lay on the ground. Blood seeped from her head and made a pool of red that told of her life having gone.

Sobs and cries broke out once more.

'Silence!'

'Now, by your habit, I would say you are the leader of this operation, Madame.'

He marched towards the Reverend Mother, his back turned towards Marcia and Joseph. Joseph motioned to Marcia to follow him, but she couldn't move. Fear for Madeleine had her rooted to the spot.

Her head swivelled from one direction to the other, trying desperately to find her sister, but she was nowhere to be seen.

'I am the Reverend Mother, yes.'

Marcia could hear the fear in the tremble of the Reverend Mother's voice, but she kept her dignity and looked the German officer squarely in the face.

'So, you are responsible for the illegal harbouring of Jews?'

'As my dear sister said, before you slaughtered her, our mission is to look after all children, regardless of creed, colour or race.'

'They are not children! They are scum and should be wiped from the face of the earth!'

The Reverend Mother crossed herself. 'May the Lord have mercy on you.'

The officer raised his gun. Suddenly Madeleine appeared and threw herself at him, kicking and punching him.

Marcia took in a deep and painful breath that burned her

throat and made a noise that showed her agony as the gun was lowered. A crack resounded and Madeleine's body slumped to the ground.

A tangible silence enveloped them all. Shocked faces stared at the horror. Marcia couldn't move, couldn't breathe.

Her body crumbled and blackness took her into its depth, releasing her from the searing pain that had sliced her heart in two.

Rough hands grabbing her and pulling her along brought her to. She opened her eyes to see a German uniform, and then his young, fresh face flooded with tears.

Pandemonium reigned around her, and children's screams pierced her ears as soldiers grabbed them by their hair and roughly threw them onto the back of wagons waiting outside the gate. Marcia looked from the bloodied mess that was her darling Madeleine to the Reverend Mother who stood staring in shock.

'Please, please do as you're told, miss. I'll help you all I can. Walk with dignity towards the trucks. Show the children how to save themselves from further pain.'

Marcia looked into the face of her would-be rescuer and saw his pain. 'Why? . . . Why?'

'I – I do not know . . . I can do nothing.'

Straightening, Marcia shouted, 'Children, line up in an orderly fashion. No, only the Jewish children. Pierre, you are not Jewish. You stay and pray for us.'

Her words seemed to mobilize the Reverend Mother. She came over to Marcia. 'Marcia! Oh, *ma chérie*! I'm sorry, so sorry.'

'Mother, you have done all you could. Help the children now, help them to go with dignity.'

Where this calmness came from, Marcia didn't know. She

only knew that now Madeleine had gone and Joseph too, as he was nowhere to be seen. Nothing mattered any more. She was an empty shell. A nothing. Her life mattered to no one, not to these vile Germans and least of all to herself. All that mattered was that she helped the children to suffer as little stress as possible and she could do that by her acceptance and by guiding them.

When she sat on the back of the truck with little bodies pressed against her, and feeling Elsie's arm around her, Marcia looked back, hoping to see that Joseph was all right, but she guessed he'd climbed the wall when everything was chaotic, and she hoped with all her heart that he got away. That would be her mission till the day of her death, to be accepting and to pray for her lovely Joseph to make it. Someone had to. Someone had to survive to tell those children of the future what had happened.

As the trucks drove away at speed, throwing the little bruised bodies about like rag dolls, Marcia allowed her tears to fall. *Soon, my mama, papa, Renée and Madeleine, I will be with you. We'll meet in the promised land and dance and sing and be happy for eternity.*

With this it was as if her spirit seemed to die and she sat, allowing her body to sway violently, just staring ahead of her, not letting her mind open to the horrors that awaited her, but accepting her fate.

They hadn't been driving long when they stopped, and they were all transferred to buses. At least now they could sit, though they were crowded in like animals.

Marcia had several children clambering over her. She tried to cuddle them all and to quieten their fears.

No windows would open, and the air became unbearable. Several children slipped into a deep faint, but Marcia could do nothing to help them. Once more, though she muttered soothing words and gave cuddles, she was dead inside. She couldn't allow herself to be otherwise, or she would break.

The journey was eternal. Night had come and given way to daylight once more. Now, children slept through sheer exhaustion.

Marcia had been in and out of a fitful sleep. But now she was wide awake as the bus she was travelling in came to a halt.

Fully conscious of everything around her, she wriggled her nose against the smell of urine and faeces that hit her senses.

Once more they were bombarded by angry voices shouting at them, and roughly pushed and shoved forward.

'You stink! You're disgusting! Jewish bastards!'

Marcia knew she must smell as more than one child had urinated on her. Her damp skirt clung to her.

The young German must have travelled in the truck that had followed them as now he was by her side. 'I will see that you and the children get a shower. It won't be a pleasant one, it will be cold and there is no soap, but at least you will feel better.'

'What about clothes?'

'You will be given uniforms . . . I'm sorry, so sorry.'

Marcia managed a smile, but as she did, spittle landed on her cheek. 'Hun lover!'

A woman had snarled the words at her.

'No! It isn't what you think, he has been kind to us.'

'Ha! Of course he has. He's priming you for later, and you're playing into his hands.'

'I'm sorry, I didn't know.'

'Well, be careful. A young girl like you ain't safe around these love-starved Germans.'

Fear of a different kind visited Marcia then. She'd heard of the rape of her people and other atrocities, but what did it matter? They were all going to die. And for her, that would be her salvation. She didn't want to live. Not now Madeleine had gone to join her parents and Renée.

For the first time, the full impact that Madeleine had truly gone hit her. Tears engulfed her, her knees gave way. The hard gravel gave her pain, but she welcomed that. It took the edge off the agony of her heart, but only for a moment. Then it was as if all the sorrow she'd ever suffered flowed from her as she sobbed loud, wretched tears.

A thud in her ribs had her gasping in her cries and falling forwards under the impact of the blow.

'Just kill me! Kill me now!' She knew she was screaming the words but couldn't stop herself.

'You've killed my whole family already, you filthy murdering bastards! My . . . my sisters, my mama and papa, all dead at your bloodied hands! You'll all rot in hell!'

Another blow and Marcia knew a blessed peace. No sound, no agony wrenching at her, just a swimming blackness that let her float around in its depths.

But then she was shocked out of it. She gasped as her body shivered after being drenched in icy cold water. Opening her eyes, she saw a gun pointing at her. Suddenly, she didn't want to die. She wanted to live for her family, just as Madame Conté had said she should.

'Get up!'

Struggling through the stinging, throbbing ache of her side, Marcia mustered all the strength she could to obey the order.

The kindly young soldier stood just back from her aggressor. Once more, his eyes were full of tears. His head shook from side to side as if he was willing her to be compliant.

Why did he care so much? She'd never met him before. Was he not truly a Nazi, but forced to pretend he was?

With this thought, some compassion for the German people entered her. Were there millions of them who hated the regime and what was happening to her people? Did they live in fear that their views would lead to reprisals and so they kept quiet and obedient?

Was that young soldier one of them?

Somehow, these thoughts helped her. She would try to live for them too. Defy the regime that kept them oppressed. She wouldn't hate the Germans as a nation any longer, but pray for them, but she would hate the Nazis till the day she died.

'Move! Get back in line, now!'

Another blow to her shoulder increased the excruciating pain wracking her body, but she turned and stepped into the gap made for her in the line of children and adults and walked with as much dignity as she could muster.

They were in a yard, having passed through gates in a wired fence. The building surrounding her was of a horseshoe shape. Someone had said they were in Drancy, near to Paris, and that it was a transit camp, meaning that they would all be shipped out from here and taken to concentration camps. Marcia knew that no one came out of such places.

She turned her gaze upwards and surveyed the grimy-looking building that was five storeys high and looked like a tenement block found in any inner city – even to the odd bits of washing hanging on the balconies. Almost normal homes.

A girl standing in the doorway of one of the blocks, and who looked the same age as herself, smiled at Marcia.

Her smile didn't reach her eyes. Her hair, clipped back from her face, looked dirty and greasy. Her eyes were sunken into the dark circles surrounding them. But for all that, Marcia could tell that she was a pretty girl.

When she entered the building, the reality was different. The rooms contained rows of bunk beds, smelled of sweaty bodies, and were dark and dingy. Some of the stairs were separated from others by barbed wire.

Marcia couldn't fathom the reason for this.

Allocated a bunk bed with a filthy, thin mattress, Marcia sat down on it. Never had she been so dejected in all her life. She bent her head. She wanted to shout out for Sister Angelica to come and save her but knew that couldn't happen.

Hunger and the need to pee took over these thoughts. Her stomach rumbled. She looked around her. None of the children who came with her were anywhere to be seen.

A sound had her turning towards the door. Uncertain, she waited. When it opened it was the girl from the doorway downstairs.

'Hello, I'm Janina.'

'Marcia. How long have you been here?'

'Twenty months.'

'Really? We could be kept here that long? . . . But the war may be over then!' Hope warmed Marcia's heart.

'We're special. That may not happen to you. My mama found out that those here for a long time were the wives of POWs and they were held as POWs themselves. Some special convention or other. Anyway, Mama lied and said that her husband was a POW, and got away with it, so here we are, living out the war.'

'What's it like here?'

'It's actually a little better now than when the gendarmes guarded us. We were starving then, but since the Germans took over, we get a lot more food. But it's boring. There's nothing to do . . . and very sad too, to see people come and then watch them go, knowing that they . . . Anyway. I'm glad to meet you, I just wish it wasn't here. Where are you from?'

Marcia told her briefly, not giving a lot of details. It was too painful to recall how a few days ago she was so happy and relaxed.

'I saw what happened to you in the yard.'

'I – I wasn't being a coward . . . I . . . my sister . . .'

Telling Janina about Madeleine hurt, and yet helped. She'd had no one to talk to about it, to release some of her agony by recalling it all.

'I'm sorry. I know what it's like to lose someone . . . My father and brother were taken earlier than me and Mama. We don't know where, or if we'll ever see them again.'

Impulsively, Marcia put her hand out and took Janina's. Janina hitched up closer to her. It felt good and comforted Marcia to have this contact.

She had so many questions. 'Why is there barbed wire dividing the stairs, Janina?'

'It's part of the sadness. You will see a list posted every day in the stairwell. If your name is on it, you will go down the stairs on the other side of the barbed wire and await transport. All those you saw coming down were going on the buses that brought you all here. They'll be taken to the station and transported in cattle trucks to camps in Poland . . . We all know what happens there, but we never speak of it.'

Marcia's eyes opened wide; her mouth dropped open. Realization had dawned on her. She could be on that list any time soon.

'No! Oh, God. I – I don't want to die.'

Janina's arm came around her. Marcia knew she had no words of reassurance to offer. No one had. Nothing could save her.

'You might be here for a little while. Some are here for weeks. We could be friends. And we could pray that God saves you, Marcia.'

'Has . . . has anyone ever escaped from here?'

Janina shook her head.

The nice German came to Marcia's mind. 'Are there some good Germans? . . . I mean, do any of them show acts of kindness? Only, one has to me, but a woman in the yard said that he was doing that to get me ready . . . I just don't know what to think.'

'Ready for sex, you mean?'

Marcia nodded. She had no idea what sex entailed, but knew it was how babies were made.

'They don't get you ready for that. They just drag you out of sight and do it. But it's best not to struggle . . . Then there are those women who curry extra favours by prostituting themselves.'

Again, Marcia's eyes opened wide. 'Has it happened to you, Janina?'

Janina nodded. A tear plopped onto her cheek.

'Oh, God, no. I'm sorry, so sorry . . . Did – did you have a baby?'

Janina shook her head. 'The Germans don't want babies by us. They pull out when their stuff comes.'

'Stuff? And pull out from where?'

'Don't you know about sex, Marcia? But then, living with nuns, you wouldn't, I suppose.'

'I know that I get a feeling in my privates when Joseph kisses me, or holds me, and that it makes you have babies.'

'I'll tell you . . .'

As Marcia listened, she just couldn't imagine such a thing happening, and yet a big part of her wanted it to with her Joseph, except . . . 'Does it hurt?'

'Not after the first time . . . but I hate it. Mama does too, though she said it's not like that when you love someone, and they love you.'

Janina blushed, but then said, 'I'd like to tell you what Mama told me, as it helped me. Would that be all right?'

Marcia nodded, not sure what she was agreeing to.

'Well, Mama embarrassed me really, as she spoke frankly to me, but she said she didn't want me to look on the act of making love as horrifying but beautiful.'

Marcia felt confused but didn't interrupt.

'Anyway, she sat me down and told me that when you're in love, the feelings you get when you go with your man are beautiful and consume you. That you long for it to happen and it makes you very happy. That it's the pinnacle of your love. So now, I just look on what the Germans do as dirty. I just let it happen and then forget about it. Well, I try to. Mama said it is their sin, not mine.'

Marcia couldn't speak for a moment. She was imagining doing this thing with Joseph and, yes, nice feelings were tickling her and making her want to. But would she ever get the chance? Would she ever see Joseph again?

Somehow, she didn't feel the despair of not doing so as always there was a flame of hope in her heart. But fear was nestled there too, as she feared a German ever doing the sex thing to her.

'Are you all right, Marcia? I know it's all a shock. The best thing to do is to try to keep out of sight as much as you can.'

Marcia nodded. Then once more she had the urge to hug Janina. It didn't feel as though they'd just met but had known each other for ever. The hug was returned, and Marcia knew she'd found a friend.

Chapter Ten

Angelica

Fortunes Can Change

Angelica stirred.

'Are you awake, Mama? You've been giggling in your sleep. Was it a good dream?'

'It . . . was Irene . . . I . . . we giggled often . . . *Oh, Irene, I love and miss you.*

As she thought this, pain gnawed at Angelica's stomach. *When will this cancer take me? Why must I suffer so?*

And yet, she wanted – needed – to suffer, for hadn't she made others do so?

Her mind swirled, took away the pain of today and left the pain of the past – a milder pain, from hunger gnawing at her as she and Irene walked towards the soup kitchen. They hadn't eaten since their visit the day before.

With her baby almost due and her grief weighing her down, Irene hadn't been able to go to work for the past two weeks.

Angelica did all she could to help, but her money had all gone now. As had most of her strength. But she had the best friendship she'd ever had. She and Irene were so close that when either of them allowed their tears to flow, the other joined in. Their hugs were a comfort, though. And they hugged often.

When they reached the van, the sight of the long queue increased Angelica's desperation for food.

But that feeling dampened as a nasty voice called out, 'So, we have that stranger in our midst again. I don't like strangers these days with us being at war. Who is she really, Irene?'

'Mind yer own bleedin' business, Maggie. I told yer, Angelica is me cousin.'

'Ha! How come yer have a French cousin then?'

'Look, Maggie, leave it, eh?'

Shaking inside at this confrontation, Angelica moved closer to Irene.

'No, I ain't leaving it. We ain't took in by your lies, Irene. You told us you were an orphan, now all of a sudden you have a cousin!'

'All right. Angelica is a refugee. She managed to get out of France and was homeless. I've taken her in.'

'Why didn't yer say so, you daft bleeder? Well, you're very welcome, Angelica. We were just afraid as to who yer really were. No one can be too careful these days, you know.'

'Thank you. You're all very kind.'

Another voice called out, 'Is she up the duff? Her belly's well rounded.'

Angelica's hands went to her stomach as if to protect the little one she knew for certain nestled inside her. Philip's child – the only thing she had left of him. 'I lost my . . . my husband . . . He was killed, just weeks ago.'

Maggie stepped forward. 'So, you're both in the same boat then, eh? Well, if I can do anything to help, just ask. I've a few of me Elsie's baby clothes in a drawer upstairs if either of you have a girl.'

'And I've some nappies. I always boiled me nappies, so they're fresh-looking.'

'Ta, Maggie, and you, Peggy. You may be nosy cows, but yer hearts are good.'

Both women burst out laughing and the moment lifted.

Angelica's shoulders dropped with relief and she found herself laughing too, and with that, she felt they had accepted her as one of them.

'You've not long to go, Irene, luv. Give us a shout when the pains start.'

'I will, ta, Maggie.'

As Maggie and Peggy reached the counter, Irene said, 'Maggie delivers most of the kids around here. Unless there's complications, then she calls in that lot from Our Lady of Assumption Convent. A couple of the nuns are trained nurses and look after the community . . . It's strange really, them not having much to do with stuff like that.'

'Oh, but we do . . . I – I mean, nuns do. Their work is to help all who need it. And there are many skills among them. I was a teacher-cum-nurse. Mostly I nursed the sick. I've never delivered a baby, though, and don't know anything about the process.'

'Except how they get inside yer . . . You know about that, luv.'

Angelica blushed. It wasn't a comfortable blush as she felt the impact of her sin.

'Look, luv, stop thinking of yourself as a wrongdoer. Yes, it's classed as wrong, but why? The coming together of two people who love each other is natural and no bit of paper saying you're wed changes that. Getting wed is only a few words said over you and you saying a few. The real binding of yer is in the feeling you have for one another. There ain't many go up the aisle a virgin, me included.'

'But . . .'

'No buts. God made the act of making love pleasurable, and something everyone wants, so He must take the blame on His shoulders for us all getting up to antics before He says we can.'

Angelica burst out laughing. 'Like a child taking a cake before his mama gives him permission?'

'Exactly that! We're all God's children. So, what's He going to do about it, eh? He can't smack our bums like a mother would, so He names it a sin and makes us all suffer guilt.'

'But like a mama, he'll accept us saying we're sorry.'

'He will. So, do that and get on with the practical side of what your so-called sin has landed you in, girl . . . Oh, good, it's our turn. Me belly feels like me throat's been cut!'

What Irene meant by this last, Angelica had no idea, and she thought it wise not to pursue it.

With a bowl of hot soup and a chunk of bread handed to them, they sat on the mound of grass behind the truck.

'Irene, we cannot go on like this. I should leave. The Red Cross will help me.'

'No, don't do that. I couldn't carry on without you now . . . Look, I'm feeling all right again, though I've lost me old job through being absent. But the biscuit factory is still taking folk on. I'll go there tomorrow.'

'No. That's not possible for you. You're not well enough . . . Look, I'm hardly showing, and I have an idea. I could alter one of your frocks into a loose-fitting garment that would hide my condition, then I could get a job, just until your widow's pension comes in.'

'I know you're willing and would do that, luv, but we need to get yer some identity papers first, and we ain't got the money for that.'

It all seemed so hopeless that Angelica felt near to tears.

'We'll be all right, luv, I promise yer. Now enjoy your soup, it's bleedin' delicious.'

Angelica couldn't agree with this last statement. She found English food very bland and longed to be able to make proper food with taste. But from what she'd seen as she'd passed by the greengrocer, she would struggle to find the ingredients she needed to cook the French way. No garlic bulbs and no herbs. And then there was the lack of wine too.

To her, the soup with floating vegetables was passable, and hot, and the bread was stodgy and nothing like the fresh, crusty bread that she was used to, but it stayed in your tummy and kept your hunger at bay for hours.

But when would they eat again? And what was their constant hunger doing to their unborn children?

Her hand went to her neck and her concealed necklace tucked into her frock. 'Irene, is there somewhere that I could go and borrow money on the strength of the value of my necklace?'

'A pawn shop, you mean? Yes, there's plenty of them robbing bastards about . . . Oh, excuse me French . . . I mean . . .'

Irene's giggle set them both off. 'It – it's a saying . . . I didn't mean . . .'

'It's all right. We have sayings too. We call you English "*les rosbifs*"! It means roast beef, and stems from your way of cooking beef!'

By Irene's expression she didn't understand this, but then she giggled. 'So, I'm a roast beef, and you're a frog!'

Angelica knew this expression from when she'd been in Ireland, '*Mais oui*. And so called because we eat the great delicacy of frogs' legs!'

'Ugh, how could you? And why "may we"? May we what?'

Angelica burst out laughing. 'It means "but yes". I shall have to give you French lessons, Irene.' Suddenly the idea appealed. 'We should do that. It would be fun.'

'I'd love to. I ain't ever been taught a foreign language. Only kids as go to posh schools are taught such things. It's reading, writing and arithmetic and that's yer lot when you're a poor kid.'

'I was an orphan, but I was lucky, the sisters who cared for me believed in preparing us for the world. Girls as well as boys. So, I was well educated. But here, you have something that is called a class system and it categorizes you as to what you can and can't have. There's no such thing in France . . . Anyway, we should take my necklace to one of those robin bastilles and then we can buy some food.'

Once more Irene was laughing. Angelica didn't know at what until she corrected her English. Then Angelica saw the funny side and joined in.

When they calmed, Irene said, 'We can get some spuds and veg and some bones to make stock with. That'll make us a few soups, and if I can get hold of a bit of flour, I can make some bread. I've got yeast and fat, but we should spend most of what we make on getting you your papers, luv.'

'I've been thinking about that, and Philip told me that when we got to England, he would apply for papers for me. Why can't I do that?'

''Cause yer not married to a British citizen, as was the

intention when you came, and yer didn't really come as a refugee. The authorities might just send yer back.'

'This is possible? But maybe that would be the best thing for me. The sisters would look after me and I could find work once my baby is born.'

'Oh, Angelica, I couldn't bear to lose you too. And besides, you've been through hell to make a new life, why go back to your old one?'

Angelica knew this was true. She bit her top lip. She didn't want to go back to the convent, but though she knew she was loved and needed here, and even accepted by the community now, she couldn't see a path her life could take in this country, or how she would look after her child. Conflict raged inside her.

'Angelica, please don't go.'

Irene's plea made her mind up to stay. 'You're right. Let us get to the pawn man and then get the papers I need.'

'Ta, luv, and I won't let you lose your necklace, even if I have to stand on the corner of the street!'

Angelica was shocked at this as she knew that a woman standing on the corner of the street was selling herself to men.

'No! I can never let you do that!'

Irene stood. 'Ha! Can yer see me getting a customer?' With this she walked with a swagger, bending backwards to thrust out her huge belly. They doubled over and Angelica thought her sides would burst; they were so painful with her uncontrollable laughing.

When they calmed, Angelica stood up too. 'Irene, I'm willing to take my chances of losing my necklace, and if I do, it will not mean you becoming a prostitute, so let's go there now.'

'But it's all you have of Philip!'

'Philip would look on it as taking care of me in the only way he can, and we will get it back.' A little doubt crept in as Angelica said this. 'We will . . . won't we?'

'Even if we have to rob a bank, luv.'

Once more, Angelica laughed out loud.

'Here, what you two got to laugh about then?'

'Our bellies are full, Maggie, and that's excuse enough, luv.'

'It's a wonder yer don't pee yourself with you being pregnant!'

'Ah, *mais oui*, we do!'

'What? Are yer off your head? You're not making sense, girl?'

'Oh, she is, Maggie. It's French. It means, "but yes".'

'You've both gone daft if yer ask me. But you keep laughing, girls, it's better than crying.'

Angelica watched Maggie walk away, thinking how her appearance so belied her forthright ways. A small woman in her fifties, she had one tooth in the front, and a fag hanging from the corner of her mouth. This made her squint and gave her a sinister look which helped her to maintain an air of fear around her, despite her lack of height.

Not that Irene feared her, but then Irene had been brought up the hard way and feared nothing and no one and this helped to give Angelica confidence too.

The pawn shop was a scruffy-looking place with everything you could imagine stacked high behind its dirty window.

'Right, luv, this is it. You'd better take your necklace off ready.'

Angelica stopped dead. She suddenly felt that she didn't

want to step inside the horrible shop, filled with people's treasured possessions that they'd been unable to retrieve.

'Angelica . . . Look, yer don't have to do this. Let's go to the post office first and see if they know anything about me war widow's pension. They might have a payment book for me . . . Come on, it's only just around the corner.'

Glad to be heading away from the pawn shop and still have her necklace, Angelica prayed as she walked along.

I know I don't have a right to ask, but please make it possible for me to keep all I have of Philip.

The clanging of the bell as they opened the post office door went through Angelica, but then the words of the postmistress answered her prayers.

'Hello, Irene, luv. I've something for yer . . . There. Your money's come through.'

Irene burst into tears. Angelica moved to her side and held her.

'It's payment for me man's life . . . But I want me man, not this bleedin' blood money!'

Angelica's face was wet with tears as Irene clung on to her.

Lifting the counter and coming over to them, the post mistress put her arms around them both.

'Ah, Irene, I feel for yer, but it's happened now and you've to think of your little one. He or she is part of Bert, and will bring him back to yer, luv. Come on, let's cash your payment slip in and you two can go on a shopping trip, eh?'

Irene nodded. 'Ta, Rita, luv. You're right.'

'And you will be when yer see what you're due. You've chits in that book that date back from when you were widowed six weeks ago! And at thirty-two shillings a week, that's nine pounds, six shillings! You're rich, luv!'

Irene let out a sound which was hard to distinguish between a giggle and a sob. Angelica squeezed her, torn between wanting to cheer with relief but wanting to be careful of Irene's feelings too. But she needn't have worried as Irene looked into her eyes and said, 'We're going to be all right, luv,' and gave her a beautiful smile. 'You've no need to pawn your necklace now.'

Before Angelica could answer, the post mistress said, 'I wouldn't cash all the chits at once, luv. Just take as many as yer need to get sorted. There's a lot of folk out there waiting to take what yer have from yer, and they hang around this shop knowing folk are coming out with their dues.'

'I'll just take three of them for now, Rita, ta. That'll be enough to catch up me rent and get us some food in.'

There was an excitement about Irene that lifted Angelica as they linked arms and went out of the post office.

'Where to, luv? The butcher's or the veg shop?'

Before the clanging bell had time to die down, Angelica was pulled roughly by the arm and slammed against the wall. Shocked, she looked into the grimy face of a young woman with evil-looking eyes. Her arm was raised above her head and her fist was clenched. She hissed, 'I'm having that!'

As a stinging punch landed on Angelica's ear, she felt a tug on her necklace.

'*Non, non, s'il vous plaît, ne le prenez pas!*'

The woman stopped tugging. 'What the bleeding hell's the matter with yer? Yer talking gibberish . . . Hey, gerroff!' Irene had waded in with her handbag, but the woman swung her arm in a violent movement. Irene crashed to the ground.

'Bleedin' mad, the pair of yer.' With this, she turned and ran.

Angelica let go of her necklace and sank to the floor next to Irene.

'Irene, Irene . . .'

'Mama, Mama, why are you clawing at your neck? Oh, Mama, have you had one of your dreams again? It's all right. You're safe.'

'I thought it was gone . . . Oh, no, Irene . . . Help her.'

'Hush, Mama. It was just a dream. Everything's all right.'

Opening her eyes disorientated Angelica. She looked around her. 'The . . . priest?'

'He will call tomorrow. You seemed so peaceful for a while I thought the priest had really helped you, Mama.'

Angelica managed a smile and nodded her head.

Beautiful Mia deserved something from her . . . If only her past would let her rest.

Oh, God, help me, please . . . Please stop my two worlds colliding . . . I'm sorry. So sorry . . .

Chapter Eleven

Mia

An Evening to Remember

Mia sat on the last step of the stairs. The door to the living room was ajar, giving a little light to the otherwise gloomy staircase. She looked over to the front door, and suddenly felt trapped. She had an urge to run through it and never stop running.

Her head dropped into her hands. She so wanted to weep her heart out but dared not let go, or she'd cry for ever.

Mama had had one of her worst days, repeatedly referring to her necklace and how it was the only thing she had of Philip. But why was it so?

At times it felt as if she had already lost her mama. That her mama lived out her 'other' life without them. At these times she and Angie didn't exist. Mia didn't want that. She wanted her mama for as long as she could have her. Or at least to be a part of what she was going through, and to be told everything about her own history.

A knock on the front door, and then it opening, made Mia jump.

Steve put his head around the door. Mia's heart skipped a beat as it did every time he called. Each time, her love for him had deepened, until now when he filled her thoughts day and night.

'Hello! . . . Oh, Mia, I didn't expect to see you there, I thought you'd be upstairs and so I let myself in . . . What's wrong? Is it your mother?'

Shaken, Mia clutched herself as a defence against the force of the conflicting emotions that hit her – the utter joy of seeing Steve, and the sadness that enveloped her. The feeling rendered her unable to move or to speak.

'Mia?'

Coming fully into the room and dropping the shopping bag he'd been clutching, Steve was in front of her in a few strides, his hands outstretched. When she took them, he lifted her. She swayed into him, wanting his comfort, needing his strength.

'Mia . . . Oh, Mia, I – I . . .'

He pulled away from her. As he did, the charged atmosphere changed.

'I'll just go up and see your mother . . . Only, well, I haven't come as a doctor. I – I was remembering when I said I would cook for you one night . . . Only, over the weeks, I felt we had become friends enough for me to do just that.'

Wrestling with feelings that were overwhelming her, Mia managed to smile up at him. She kept her voice steady as she asked, 'Is that night tonight?'

Steve visibly relaxed. 'It is. I have my bag of goodies, and my Frank Ifield record!'

His grin made her giggle. But oh, she wanted so much more and for a moment she had thought Steve did too. She was wrong. He just wanted to be friends . . . *Can I do that, feeling like I do, and now having been in his arms and experiencing the surge of sensations that zinged through me at his touch?*

'Are you all right, Mia?'

She nodded, keeping her forced smile on her face as she fought the urge to say, *No, I'm not. I want you to hold me again and to never let me go!*

'Right. I'll just make sure your mother is okay, and then, hey presto! I'll turn into a chef.'

They both laughed and the tension eased a little. Though for Mia, her life had changed. Did Steve feel the same way? But then, if he did, why didn't he show it?

He was downstairs before she'd had time to move from standing staring out of the window. She'd been looking for answers that weren't out there, or anywhere it seemed, other than in her heart for Steve, and in her mama's mind for past events.

'All's as fine as it can be. Your mother is resting, though I wish I could say peacefully. Wasn't the priest able to help her?'

Steve's words brought Mia back to reality. Could anyone help her mama? It seemed that only the mysterious Marcia could.

'The priest helped a little, and Mama was asking for him when she last woke.' Mia's lips pressed close together as she shook her head, and then released her breath on a sigh. 'If only she'd talk to me.'

Steve was by her side in an instant, his eyes holding concern. His hand came onto her shoulder. 'I know it's hard, Mia, but perhaps it would help if you allowed your mother her memories and didn't feel so much angst about her sharing them.'

'How? How do I do that? Do I ignore the fact that I know nothing about my mother's past?'

Suddenly, it all seemed hopeless. Mia shrugged her shoulders in a resigned way and let out another sigh. Then, to lighten the mood, she smiled. 'Anyway, I'm hungry. What delight are you going to cook for us?'

His hand left her shoulder, making her feel bereft of its comfort, but then he shocked her as he strode towards the door and picked up his shopping.

'I'm going to make my speciality . . . baked beans on toast!'

Mia burst out laughing.

'What?'

'I thought . . . Oh, that will be lovely, thanks.'

'Ha! Got you there! No beans, I promise. Though I do love them, and they are my go-to quick fix for my hunger. But tonight, Mia Jamieson, I'm making spaghetti Bolognese!'

This last he said with a flourish and a mock Italian accent.

Mia laughed at him. 'Ooh, I've only had it out of a tin before!'

'That's spaghetti in tomato sauce, nothing like the Italian dish at all! And I have the authentic recipe from Mario, the chef at the Italian restaurant in Chelsea. I'll take you there one of these days. It's wonderful!'

Mia could only dream of such things now, though when she went to work, she used to love to try all the different foods of the world and she and Angie had visited some of the many restaurants that were springing up around Carnaby Street . . . Oh, how she'd loved the excitement of walking down that famous street during her lunch break, gazing at the fashions by designers such as Mary Quant.

'I haven't been in an Italian restaurant, but I love Chinese food . . . And Indian. Well . . . I'm not quite so sure about some of the really spicy dishes but I love the creamy korma.'

Remembering the different life she used to lead, Mia had a sudden attack of loneliness. Of missing her many friends in the office and how they would meet sociably and go to a club or to have a meal together. The giggles and the camaraderie. The silly chatter, and . . . well, just being herself.

She wondered if Angie missed it, as she faithfully came straight home every evening forgoing any invites that would keep her out later, just to be with her and to help her all she could.

With this thought, Mia decided she would insist that Angie went out on a Friday night with her friends. This cheered her as she didn't want to spoil Angie's life. There was nothing she could do about her own . . . Though did she want to? As change could only come when Mama passed, and she dreaded that happening. And yet she knew it would, and very soon. With this thought, Mia felt her heart would break.

'Hey! No doldrums.'

Steve's cheerful voice brought Mia out of her sadness as he continued, 'Steer me in the direction of the kitchen and supply me with a chopping board and a large pan and I'm at your service . . . Oh, I hope you have a mincer? The stewing beef I've bought needs to be minced with the onions.'

'Yes, we have everything, even a garlic crusher. Mama is French, remember? We've always had the most delicious food in this house, so you have a lot to live up to!'

'Well, to find anything to do with garlic is unusual for one, so I brought my own crusher, thinking you may not have one.'

'If you'd have come a few months ago before Mama became ill, your nose would have told you, as this house always smelled of garlic. But Angie and I have just been eating plain old English food for speed, though we can both cook the French dishes that Mama used to.'

'Mmm, I love French food, so it'll be your treat next time.'

The mention of the 'next time' thrilled Mia. It seemed to mark a new era for her – one that contained all the promise of becoming closer to Steve, as surely she would on social visits . . . And just maybe . . .

It was while Steve chopped, minced and sprinkled, and they talked, that he told her, 'I've been finding out about you, Mia . . . Well, how old you are, anyway, as it's hard to tell these days. Anyway, I know that you're only nineteen. I've looked at your medical notes – not that there's anything of interest to a doctor in your envelope: your baby jabs, and that's about all. Oh, and you had mumps when you were six and your polio vaccination at age eleven!'

'That's a fat lot. Why did you want to know my age?' She knew she was prodding for some little spark of him saying he was interested in her other than just as a patient.

'Oh, just interested . . . But . . . well, I'm almost ten years older than you, and I was worried you might find me old and boring . . . as a friend, I mean.'

'No, of course not! What does it matter? You've brought a little spark into my life . . . I feel I have someone other than my poor sick mama and Angie. But you know, you've almost summed up my history there. I've no knowledge of my past, other than what's in my own memory, so I've little to tell you about myself. I did well at school, and that was down to Angie doing so as I've always followed her lead. She went to college, so I did. She went into journalism, so I did, though I loved it from the first.'

'Hmm . . . that suggests a nosy nature then.'

Mia laughed. 'Yes, I like to know everyone's business, not that there's much to know in this street. Everyone lives their lives in a textbook way – rising, working, annual two weeks' holiday, and that's that. No scandal, no intrigue, absolutely nothing to report!'

'So, what did you report on? Anything exciting?'

'Oh, I'm just a junior . . . was, I mean. I had to leave to take care of Mama, but they've kept my job open for me. I loved it and was sent on a variety of assignments. Usually assisting a more senior reporter . . . I'd say my most memorable assignment was being allowed to attend the premiere of *Lawrence of Arabia* and meeting Peter O'Toole.' She closed her eyes, reliving the moment. 'Oh, but to be so close to Queen Elizabeth, who looked beautiful in her long, ivory frock, was a dream. Mostly, though, I worked on fillers and was allowed to write those up myself.'

'Fillers?'

'Oh, that's those snippets of news you see in a small block on the pages of every newspaper. Things that are very important to the people involved, but not world-changing news.'

'Ah, I see. It all sounds so exciting, even if they were lesser news pieces you investigated and wrote about. People still read your work.'

'Yes. And that's the bit I love the most . . . I . . . well, I've not been completely idle on the writing front . . . I've . . . It's silly really, but I want to write a book.'

'Really? That's amazing. Have you done anything towards it?'

'I have an outline, that's all. A murder mystery . . . But I thought you'd laugh at me.'

'No, why would I? I think it's something very special . . . like y— I mean, I think you're very brave to have a go.'

Was he going to say, *Like you*?

But then there seemed no trace of that as he asked, 'Will it be like Agatha Christie's novels?'

'Not exactly, though I do enjoy her books. I'm thinking two girls who come across a body and get involved in being amateur detectives. It has a comedy slant as the old and wise detective gets very annoyed with them and they have to keep dodging him, convinced that they have more and better clues than he does!'

Talking about her project made her forget the thought she'd had, and she was able to put a humorous tone into her voice as she said, 'Your turn. What secret desire do you harbour?'

'Well, mine stems from . . . well, I'm from a family of two children, brought up in Leicestershire, where my mum and dad still live . . . Well, there used to be two of us.' He bowed his head and stirred the delicious-smelling dish with vigour.

'Used to be? Have you lost your sibling?' As she asked this in a gentle tone, Mia put her hand on his back. He turned to her. Tears filled his eyes. 'Yes, my sister. Andrea was older than me and cared for me. I loved her dearly. I – I wanted so much to save her, but Mum told me I couldn't. There is no cure for leukaemia. But then, she took me in her arms and told me, "But one day, in honour of Andrea, you could save other people. If you work hard at school, you could become a doctor, like your grandfather. You could do that for Andrea, she would love that."'

'And I'm sure she does, Steve . . . One day, I'd love to hear all about Andrea, but I can see now isn't the time.'

'No. But I need to find that time. I have a heavy part in my heart that I've never released. I've always thought of it driving me forward to achieve something for Andrea.'

'And you have. You are a doctor!'

'Yes . . . but, well . . .' He turned back to stirring the contents of the pan. 'I followed that path as it was what my mother wanted, and she motivated me by making me think I was doing it for Andrea. But what I really want to do is research. I want to help to find cures, not just make people comfortable until they die. I want to make them better.'

'Then you should do that, follow your dream. Just imagine if there was a cure, you wouldn't only be saving patients' lives, but the lives of their family. People like me who are going through agony watching their loved ones slowly and painfully die of cancer – leukaemia is a form of cancer, isn't it?'

'It is, it's a cancer of the blood. A lot is known already about it and there are treatments – some successful. But we need to know more, and research is reaching an exciting peak with chemotherapy making a great deal of difference and more patients surviving longer.'

He turned to her then and she so wanted to take him in her arms as still she could detect a wretchedness about him.

'You're right. I must follow my own dream, not my mother's. I'll talk to Doctor Jones, I'm sure he would help me to take the right steps into the research field.'

'Couldn't you do both? You really are a wonderful doctor – approachable, believable. I – I mean, you have an air of faith that you can make things right. Mama has had a lot more peaceful moments since you've been visiting her.'

'Thank you. That's very kind. But the answer is that I don't know. I'll look into it. You see, I do love administering to people and helping them, but I just have this deep need in me to make all cancers curable. Whether it can ever be done, I don't know, but I must try.'

Angie coming home at that moment stopped them going deeper into how such an ambition could be achieved.

'Hi, sis. Mmm, what's that delicious smell?'

'In the kitchen, Angie. And we have a visitor!'

Angie came through the kitchen door grinning widely. 'The much talked about Steve, I presume?'

Mia's cheeks burned. She could have killed Angie at that moment. But Steve grinned. 'Pleased to meet you, Angie. I wondered why my ears often burned. And thank you, Mia. You've just been praising me for my skills with your mother, and nice to know you shared that with Angie too.'

'Did she ever! . . . Ow!'

'Sorry . . . I – I could feel cramp coming in my foot . . . I kicked out to relieve it.'

There was an embarrassed silence, during which she and Angie looked daggers at each other. But Steve smoothed things over. 'Hey, I didn't come here to be with warring young women! I want nothing to take centre stage over my exceptional cooking!'

Angie, always the one to get over any spat the quickest, laughed. 'It had better be good! You've to go some to beat Aunty Angelica's offerings.'

Her arm came around Mia. 'Sorry, love, I didn't mean to embarrass you. Just having a bit of fun at your expense.'

Still seething, Mia made a huge effort. 'Come on then, let's leave the master to his work and set the table together.'

'Not until I've had a pee. Or I'll make puddles that you'll need a boat to cross!'

They all laughed at this, and Mia relaxed once more.

They worked in a companiable silence while Angie was gone – Steve set about cooking the spaghetti and Mia got the knives and forks out of the drawer in the kitchen table, feeling grateful as she did that Angie's teasing hadn't made Steve uncomfortable.

When Angie came in, she hugged Mia.

'It's all right, love,' Mia whispered to her. 'But you did make me look a fool. Though I'll forgive you if you promise to be good for the rest of the evening.'

'*Moi*? Good! Ha, you may have seen him first, but he's so dishy, how can a girl be good?!'

Mia giggled, but then held her breath as Angie went towards Steve and looked over his shoulder. Her breath released in a sigh when all Angie said was, 'I see it's spaghetti Bolognese on the menu then?'

Steve answered her in the same flamboyant manner he'd told Mia what his dish was.

Angie grinned. 'It had better be good. That's what we had for my friend Patsy's birthday lunch last week, and it was delicious, though not easy to eat. It turned into a comedy as we all tried to master twisting the long strands around our forks. We ended up with the meaty tomato sauce plastered around our lips.'

Their laughter warmed Mia's heart. She'd so wanted Angie to like Steve too, and it seemed they were already friends. She'd have hated Angie not to have liked him. She wouldn't have been able to stand hearing any critical remarks about him.

'That's a sound I love – laughter. And I hope you two do plenty of it. It will help your mother to hear it . . . But I also like music and expected it to be blaring out when I came after what you told me, Mia.'

'I'll soon fix that – Cliff, Elvis or the Beatles?' Angie asked as she went to leave the kitchen.

'There's another choice, Angie. Steve's brought Frank Ifield's LP with him. Let's put that on.'

'Oooh, I love his "I Remember You". His yodelling is brilliant.'

The whole atmosphere changed as Frank's voice filled the

house. Steve sang along, making them howl when he tried to yodel, and it came out like the strangled cry of an injured animal.

Suddenly, he grabbed Mia and began to dance around the kitchen, jigging her around as if she was a rag doll.

'Stop it! Stop it! You're crazy!'

At that moment, the sauce threatened to boil over, rescuing Mia as Steve leapt to save it.

The meal was wonderful, and hilarious as they had competitions to see who was fastest to suck in the longest pieces of spaghetti. But all too soon it was over, and they were saying their goodbyes to Steve.

As the door closed on him, Angie said, 'You've got it bad, love. Come on, I'll make us a cuppa, eh? We can take it outside into the backyard and sit on the wall. I love it when we do that.'

The air had a slight chill to it, so they snuggled up close.

'He feels the same way for you, you know. He couldn't take his eyes off you and hung on to your every word.'

'Oh, Angie, I wish. But earlier, he pointed out the age difference between us, and it really seemed to matter to him.'

'Give it time. Men take longer to admit their feelings. Look at Freddie with me. He knows I love him to bits, and I know he loves me, but he won't commit.'

Mia looked up at the stars defying the smog to twinkle through like a million diamonds. *Please make Steve love me*.

Sipping her tea, she hoped with all her heart that her prayer would be answered.

Chapter Twelve

Marcia

A Good German

Marcia looked at the clock. There was another hour before Joseph and Amos would be in from school.

She went to the window. Little Hans was quite happy digging away at a small patch of the front garden with his tiny spade. He looked up and grinned, his blue eyes twinkling, taking her back to the first time she'd realized that Shane's did that.

Always on his visits to the convent, Shane had never been allowed inside the gates, but she'd met him a couple of times when she'd been out in the car with Sister Angelica.

How brave the Resistance was, and how she admired them, and yet it had been one of them who had taken Sister Angelica from her.

For the millionth time she wondered if Philip had made Sister Angelica happy. Had they had a family together? But mostly, why didn't they come back for her when the war ended?

Her mind began to think over her journey back to the convent.

Turning away from the window and reaching for her

writing pad and pencil, Marcia sat down on the brown sofa that always seemed to envelop her in softness and comfort.

She loved her little home, loved the light coming through the tiny windows and rarely shuttered them as was the normal thing to do. The dimness terrified her, and had done since those first days in the war when they'd been put into the dark cellar.

But there'd been other times too.

As she put her pen to paper, Marcia drifted back in time. A voice came to her, calling her name.

'Marcia, Marcia!'

The urgency of the sound of Janina's call dried Marcia's throat.

She shot up from where she'd been lying on her bunk thinking about Madeleine, shedding tears and lamenting the hopelessness of her situation, even trying to imagine what it would be like the moment she herself died.

From what she'd heard, if she died in a concentration camp, she would know her death was imminent as she'd be herded with hundreds of others into a gas chamber.

This had brought sobs that shook her body. She didn't want to die.

Janina burst into the room. 'Oh, Marcia, I – I . . . Oh, God! Your name is on the list!'

Marcia's heart dropped like a concrete block. Shocked, she could only stare at Janina. She saw her face awash with tears.

'Oh, Marcia!'

Then she was in Janina's arms being held, and clinging on in the hope that somehow Janina could save her, yet knowing that she couldn't.

'Oh, Marcia, I'll never forget you . . . This doesn't always mean . . . Well, a lot are known to stay in the camps they're taken to, especially if they are useful. You're young, I'm sure they will see you as a strong girl who can work. I've heard they use us for labour, on the land, or for building extra blocks. Not everyone is put to death . . . And listen, the war is coming to an end.'

Marcia could hardly speak as she asked, 'How do you know that?'

'There's been a new intake. They aren't Jews, but some Resistance workers who've been captured. One, a man with a country accent, told us that the Allies are making huge gains.'

A little hope seeped into Marcia. If she was put to work, she'd work hard and keep her head down. Maybe, just maybe, she would make it to the end of the war when the British and Americans would surely find them?

'Do I have to go now to the other side of the stairs?'

'Yes. I thought you'd already gone. Didn't you check the list?'

'I never check it.'

'Oh, Marcia. When I asked and no one had seen you, I thought you were already over there, and then Mrs Reuben told me that she thought you were up here . . . Please, hurry, Marcia . . . I have witnessed those who tried to hide being shot!'

Marcia jumped off the bed at this. She knew the rules. Knew that the first job every morning was to check if you were to be deported, but she just hadn't thought it would happen this soon.

'Come on, I know a way around the back. If we bang on the window, someone will let you through. There's always a lot of the folk who are going mulling around in the basement area. What they're doing I've no idea, but if we can attract their attention, you'll be safe.'

Safe? How can I ever be safe?

With Janina pulling her along, Marcia ran down the stairs. As they reached the ground floor, her heart stopped to see a German soldier standing in the doorway. He turned abruptly. A small amount of hope filtered into Marcia when she saw it was the kind one.

'Ah, Marcia. I saw your name. Please don't be afraid. I'm not going to hurt you.'

His French had a coarse sound to it, but his words soothed her a little.

'I've been looking for you and when I didn't find you where you should be, I guessed you were still in this block. What I want you to do is to go with me. It will look as though I have rounded you up and am taking you to where you should be. That way, you won't be harmed.'

Marcia nodded, though a little fear trickled through her. Could she trust him? Could she trust any German? Didn't they all hate the Jews?

'Come.'

As she went to go, Janina caught hold of her. 'One day, we'll meet again, Marcia. I will find you. I will pray you survive, my lovely friend.'

Tears ran down Janina's face. But Marcia couldn't cry. It was as if she'd closed down her emotions.

Janina went to cuddle her, but the soldier said, 'No! Marcia must come! Try not to worry.'

Following him out and then stepping in front of him as he indicated she should, Marcia walked with her head held high.

When they reached the corner of the building, she looked back and waved. Janina blew her kisses.

It was when she turned the corner that the German soldier surprised her.

'My name is Hans. I hate the Nazi regime. I do all I can for the Jewish people.'

Marcia stopped and looked back at him. He smiled. 'All will be well. You're scheduled to go out on a train this afternoon . . . I . . . Look, I feel I can trust you and I want to help you not to be afraid.'

Hans sidestepped until he was against the wall. Stealthily, he peered around the corner.

'We are safe for a moment . . . Look, I have always helped the Resistance. Those captured have been for a reason.' Continuing to keep watch, he said, 'They put themselves in a position to be. You see, they have a job to do . . . A very dangerous job. But they are the inside men on a mission that will see the train ambushed. I made sure your name was on the list so you would be on that train.'

'Oh, Hans, does this mean I will escape?'

'That is the plan. But . . . Oh, God! There's a few of my comrades heading this way. Forgive me for what I must do!'

With this, Hans turned her and grabbed her. 'Struggle. I want it to look like I'm forcing myself on you.'

Pressing her against the wall, he ripped at her top.

Marcia protested loudly, 'No! Leave me alone!'

In French the soldier said, 'Ha! Hans is at last finding he has a cock!' then still in French, 'Wait! Is that the girl we're looking for?'

'It is, I have fancied her since she came . . . Give me a couple of minutes. I'll deliver her after.'

One of them put his hand on his crotch. 'I might take her after you, comrade. She looks like a good lay.'

Marcia was left in no doubt what might happen to her. But when Hans said, 'I'll call you. Now, leave a man to do what he has to do, Fitz,' the men laughed as they moved away.

'Keep resisting. Make some noise.'

As he lifted one of her legs, Hans made movements that bumped into her. Marcia cried out.

'I'm sorry, we must look like I am taking you. But listen, one of the Resistance men knows you. His name is Shane. He asked for you and as many of the children who came from the convent as possible to be among the passengers. But I could only arrange for you – I added your name secretly. Don't tell anyone, just be ready to run as soon as you're let out . . . Oh, Marcia. I – I've had feelings for you since I first saw you. I will pray for your safety and hope that one day we will meet again.'

Marcia was shocked at this revelation. She wanted to tell him that she was spoken for, that one day her Joseph would find her. But suddenly, he was yanked away from her.

'What is this? You haven't moved for a while, what are you doing?'

The colour drained from Hans's face. He pushed her. 'Go, bitch! You're not worth the struggle!'

Marcia didn't want to go, she feared for Hans, but she knew she must. Turning, she ran towards the door that led to the other side of the divided stairs and took them two at a time. Then she pushed her way through what seemed like hundreds of others who'd congregated on the landing, making it to the window and gasping in the fresh air.

It was then that she saw trucks leaving the compound. On one of them she caught sight of Elsie.

Despair overtook her, but this turned to shock as she continued to stare and saw Hans being marched across the courtyard at gunpoint. Her heart, already heavy, seemed to split with sorrow.

Suddenly, Hans turned and made a dash for the gate. The shots that riddled his body brought the camp to a deathly silence.

Marcia slid down the wall and crumpled into a broken heap on the floor.

Strong hands lifted her. 'Don't despair, it was one of their own. Good riddance! And we always have hope. We're still alive. Do all you're told to do and pray that Adonai means for you to live.'

Marcia wanted to scream that the Good Lord hadn't done much for her to date. That he'd taken all she loved from her. But instead she prayed to Him to take no more, only to help her.

As they were all crowded onto the station, Marcia spotted Shane standing apart from them and with others – one of these, she was shocked to see, was Layla, the lovely young woman who'd taken her from the farm to the convent.

She wanted to wave but knew she must not.

A train pulled in – no carriages, just cattle cars. Marcia imagined it would pull out again, but then the German soldiers guarding them opened the cars and began to hoard her people into them.

When it came to her turn, Marcia thought they would surely take her to another car as already the one they had been loading was packed solid. But no, she was roughly shoved forward.

A pain sliced her back when she hesitated. She'd been hit

with the butt of a gun. Turning, she saw a face full of vile hatred and a raised gun about to smash down on her.

Leaping out of the way, she hurriedly went up the step and into the car.

As the doors rattled closed, it seemed to Marcia that she would suffocate with the heat and the proximity of the other people. A baby cried, and her heart went out to its mother. She tried to turn to see if she could help, but it was impossible, they were so tightly packed in. Her legs felt like jelly, but she knew she couldn't sit down, there was no room to.

Someone at the back began to wail – a sound so desperate that it cut into Marcia. Others joined in. Those near to a side began thumping on it, calling out that there were too many cramped together, that they couldn't breathe.

A banging on the side quietened them for a moment.

'You're all going to the gas chamber anyway, so who cares!'

Sobs and cries of, 'I don't want to die,' put a sick fear into Marcia. A trickle of water came from her that she had no control over, and she knew that the same had happened to others as the air became pungent with the smell of urine and puddles appeared at her feet.

Suddenly the train moved with a jerk that sent them all swaying one way. Desperate cries of, 'I can't breathe!' were gasped out.

When the train steadied to an even chugging, one man shouted, 'This woman and her child are dead . . . crushed! God help us.'

Marcia wondered if it was the crying baby as there was no longer any sound coming from it.

She let the tears flow, and yet felt no emotion. It was as if the horror was too much for her and she was already dead.

* * *

Marcia didn't know how long they'd been travelling when there was a change in the rhythm of the train. It seemed to be slowing.

Her heart filled with hope, but at the same time, she became aware of what had happened around her. Everyone was quiet. Some she could see were still standing, but no longer lived. The smell that now penetrated her senses made her heave. Something heavy leaned against her. Turning, she looked into the dead face of an old lady.

Unable to cry or to move anything other than her arm, she stroked the lady's soft, grey hair. 'Rest in peace. Your horror is over.'

Suddenly, there was a jolt that sent everyone to one side again. Though she shouldn't think it, Marcia couldn't help feeling grateful that it was to the other side to where she was. But her heart went out to those gasping that they couldn't breathe.

The train came to a halt and the strong among them were able to right themselves.

Gunfire held them all rigid when they did. And then the door to their carriage was being opened, and the surge towards her pushed her out.

Arms held her. 'Marcia, come, quickly, don't look back! Run!'

'Oh, Layla!'

'Run! Run! Go towards those trees, we will find you.'

Not stopping to see who else got out, but hearing footsteps matching her own, Marcia gathered all the strength she could and ran into the wood as gunfire sounded around her.

Distracted by the chaos, not watching where she was going, she stumbled and fell heavily to the ground.

With the wind taken out of her, Marcia couldn't move. She lay her head on her arms and sobbed the last bit of her strength out of her.

How long she'd lain there, Marcia didn't know. She only knew when a voice came to her saying, 'Well, it is that you're all right, me darlin',' that Shane had found her. The English that Sister Angelica had taught her gave her understanding, but the feeling of being safe at the sound of his voice would have anyway.

She clung to him.

'Everything's for being all right now, I promise. We will be for keeping you safe. The war is nearly over.'

With this, he lifted her and carried her through the woods.

When they arrived at a camp that resembled a small village – although the homes were tents, not built of bricks – Shane said, 'Sure it is that I have a surprise for you.'

He lowered her to the ground. As he did, Marcia hugged her knees to comfort herself as a feeling of being bereft washed over her. She wanted to stay close to him. His body offered warmth; his strength gave her strength.

'Come and be sitting next to the fire.'

When she sat, he held her hands. 'Joseph is safe!'

'What? Oh, Shane, that's such good news . . . Where?'

He lifted her chin and it was then that she saw the twinkle in his eyes as they shone in the light of the fire. 'Now, don't you be worrying about details. Just accept, eh?'

She nodded, knowing for the first time in a long time a feeling of being at peace with herself. But oh, how she longed to see Joseph, to have him hold her, to hear his voice, to mess around with him, and to just love him and have him love her.

'I am seeing that that news has cheered you, me little darlin' . . . Well, go along with you to Layla. She will help you to get showered and give you some clean clothes.'

'Did many get out of the train?'

'Yes, a lot did. They will make their way here in the next few days, no doubt. Then they will be helped to get to safe houses, but you will stay here with us. Now that I have you, I'm not for letting you go. Sister Angelica would be having me guts for garters if she ever came back and found that I had.'

Marcia found that she could laugh with him. And again, his eyes twinkled.

'She will come back, she promised me.'

'Aye. It was a strange set-up. Something I've not been coming across before – a nun leaving her vows behind for a man. I am hoping that Philip makes it and can be taking care of her. She's one of life's angels is Sister Angelica.'

After a hot drink of black coffee, Layla came to take her to shower. As soon as they were out of sight of the men, she put her arms around Marcia and hugged her to her. 'I've been so worried, *ma chérie*. Out of my mind.'

Marcia hugged her in return. 'That's twice you've saved me, Layla.'

'And I always will. I'll always be here for you, my poor Marcia.'

Marcia felt her hair being stroked as she asked, 'Do you know if the Reverend Mother is all right? . . . They . . . they shot Sister Frederica, and . . . and . . .'

Marcia could go no further. Her body shook with sobs.

'Cry it out, *ma chérie*. You have so much inside you. We heard what happened to dear little Madeleine. I'm so sorry. So very sorry.'

When at last Marcia calmed, she said, 'I wouldn't have been able to keep her safe, Layla. And I'm glad she didn't land in that camp or know what it was like to be transported to her death. She died so quickly; she wouldn't have known anything about it. I would want that for her.'

'Yes, that is the best way to think of it. She is with your God.'

This surprised Marcia. 'But my God is the same one as yours, Layla. It is the role of Jesus that we question. We believe the Messiah is yet to come.'

'Well then, Madeleine is with our God.'

Marcia knew Layla was pacifying her and loved her for it.

'Well, inside that tent, Marcia, you will find all you need. The shower will be very cold, but it is invigorating. I'll leave you to it as you have grown into a young woman. And one who is already in love. Joseph is a very nice young man. I'm glad for you that he is safe.'

Wanting to ask where he was, but not wanting to break faith with Shane's instruction not to ask, all she said was, 'One day, we'll be together and that will be a good day.'

As she went into the tent and welcomed the feel of the cold water, Marcia thought that until that day came, she would hold Joseph where he'd always been, and where he belonged, deep in her heart.

Tears were flowing down Marcia's cheeks as she put her pencil down and came back to the present. For the most part, she had come to terms with all that had happened – it was twenty years or more ago now – but there were many things that her heart would never let go of. It was these she wanted in her memoir more than anything.

Chapter Thirteen

Angelica

Life is Looking Hopeful

Angelica's pain eased as the morphine she'd been given took effect. The music drifting up to her was different to usual and it soothed her as she caught the words, '*I remember . . .*'

Yes, I remember. Oh, my beautiful necklace . . .

Suddenly Irene was there, shouting, 'It's started, Angelica! . . . Ooh, it hurts!' Angelica sat up in bed. Irene was standing just inside her bedroom.

'You mean the baby? It is coming?'

'Yes.' Irene clung on to the door. 'Help me . . .'

Jumping out of bed, the thoughts that had been going through her head left Angelica as she hurried to Irene's side. 'Let's get you back to bed, Irene. I'll help you . . . Oh, but this is so exciting!'

'It bleedin' ain't! I told yer, it hurts!'

Angelica was taken aback. Irene had never spoken to her like that before.

'I'm sorry . . . Oh, Angelica, help me . . . I want Bert . . . BERT, WHY DID YOU LEAVE ME?'

This scream, full of anguish, cut through Angelica.

'*Ma chérie, non, non*, you must stay calm. Bert is with you as you bring his child into the world.'

'Oh, Angelica, I want him here!'

'I know. I am feeling the same way. But you're about to have your and Bert's child, and you are bringing a part of him back to life. Please stay calm. Getting worked up can only harm you and may harm the baby.'

At this, Irene took several deep breaths and smiled. 'I love that – a part of Bert will live again, won't it, Angelica?'

'It will, my dear Irene. It will.'

'Right. I'm going to get on with it as I can't wait to see him again . . . My baby will look like him, won't it?'

Angelica closed her eyes and prayed that it would. The photo of him on the mantel shelf showed a cheeky grin, dark black hair and a handsome face. Irene had told her that he'd had blue eyes.

Irene lay back. 'I sort of want the pains to come, but I don't. I know they mean that I'm opening up to let the baby out, but I don't like anything hurting me.'

'Well, you cannot have it both ways, my dear Irene. But I'll be by your side. I know a massage that I gave to any of my sisters when they were in pain that works, so I'll try that and see if it helps.'

At first it did seem to help as Irene took long, slow, deep breaths, but as morning dawned Irene made Angelica jump as she screamed, 'Go and get Maggie to come and get the bleedin' thing out!'

Angelica ran down the stairs and out into the street. Dodging under sheets hanging on lines across the road, she banged on Maggie's door.

When Maggie opened it, she didn't give Angelica a chance to say what she wanted, but pushed her sleeves up, spat out her fag onto the pavement and said, 'Right, girl, I'm with yer. How far gone is she? And have yer got the kettle on?'

Angelica hadn't thought to make Irene a cup of tea. Then she giggled at the thought of her probably throwing it all over her, she was in such a bad mood.

This had surprised Angelica as she'd thought it would be a joyous event. It also scared her as she hadn't expected it to hurt so much. She wondered how she would cope when her time came.

'I thought she had longer than this. A few weeks at least!'

'Well, she did have a shock, and seemed unwell after that. We were attacked and I was almost robbed of my necklace.'

'Ah, that would be it. Are yer all right? Is the necklace valuable then?'

'I'm a bit bruised, and yes, the necklace is very valuable to me . . . It came . . . it was from my husband.'

'Well, if you're not hurt bad, that's all that matters.'

For the next half an hour the air was blue with swearing as Maggie and Irene seemed to be in competition with each other in the cursing stakes. But at last, the baby slipped out and let them all know that it could compete with any of them.

'It's a girl, Irene, love. And you did good. There! The cord's cut and tied . . . Now, Angelica, that water, has it cooled enough? We need to clean the baby up.'

The next ten minutes passed in a haze as Maggie washed the baby, gave out orders for nappies, pins, a vest and a shawl, and Irene cried gently for her Bert and begged for her baby.

'I've to clean you up first, Irene, you're a right mess.'

While this was done, Angelica held the baby. She looked

like an angel with her cherub face, tiny tufts of red hair and blue eyes.

At last, Maggie allowed Irene to hold her.

At that moment, Irene's face shone with love and pride. 'She does look like my Bert, even though she has my hair . . . You do . . . You look just like your daddy . . . He would love you so much.'

Her sob was curtailed by Maggie saying, 'Well, she needs a name, yer know.'

'Oh, I have that already, and now I see her, it's perfect for her and honours me best friend. Angelica.'

A surge of love hit Angelica at this very great honour. She knew she was smiling, and yet her eyes were misty with tears.

'Well, we won't know who you want when yer call for Angelica! But it is a lovely name and Angelica has brought a lot of love to your life, we've all seen that.'

'I can shorten it to Angie . . . Yes, that's a lovely name too.'

'Good. Well, let's get Angie suckling on your breast, and then I'll leave yer to it.'

With this done and Irene at first wincing, and then loving the feeling, she said, 'Ta, Maggie. You're a diamond. I've put an envelope on the side for yer.'

'Don't be daft! You'll need any money you've got, luv.'

'No. I'm all right, I promise yer. Me pension came through with back pay. I want yer to have something.'

Maggie picked up the envelope and looked inside. 'Ten bob! Oh, Irene, luv . . .'

An astonishing thing happened then. Maggie – staunch Maggie – burst into tears.

Angelica went to her side and hugged the little woman to her.

'I – I was facing eviction . . . I ain't paid me rent for a few weeks. This'll save me, Irene, luv. Ta.'

It was then that Angelica realized the true spirit of these East End women. Maggie had been going to refuse payment, even though she was desperate, because she thought that Irene needed it more.

Holding her close and not feeling any resistance, Angelica told her, 'Never go without. We're always here for you. With Irene's pension and me going to get a job, we'll have more than we'll need.'

'A job? What sort of job, girl?'

'Well, I speak English and my own French language and someone may need an interpreter.'

'Well, I think that'll be a well-paid job. I wish yer well in it.'

'We just have to wait for her papers to come through. I've a friend—'

'*Non*, I'm not doing things that way, Irene. I've been thinking. I will go to the authorities and put my case. I think I will be accepted as—'

'Course yer will, yer were married to an Englishman. You get applying, luv. Anyway, I'd better get going. I'm going to Aggie's to see what I can get to eat. I can have at least three bob of this and give the rent man seven. He'll be happy with that.'

Angelica breathed a sigh of relief. She'd nearly given her true circumstances away.

But no one seemed to notice as Irene said, 'Maggie, we've a full cupboard. Help yourself from that, luv. Only don't take all me sugar, or all me flour – they were black market. I only managed to get them late last night.'

'You're a good girl, Irene. Anyway, I'll do that. I'll raid

your cupboard on me way out, luv. Ta. Now you enjoy your nipper.'

When she'd gone, Irene said, 'Well, who'd have thought Maggie had a soft side, eh?'

'She's really a lovely person. The Reverend Mother always said there's good in everybody, you just have to bring it out.'

With this, Angelica had a pang of homesickness. She sat on the end of the bed. 'I miss them all, you know. But most of all I miss Marcia and her little sister, Madeleine.'

'You've mentioned them before. One day, yer must tell me all about them. I love hearing about your life at the convent.'

Angelica held Irene's hand. 'I will, but, oh, little Angie is so beautiful. I will make her a christening gown . . . You can buy the material.'

'I'll do better than that. I'll buy you a second-hand sewing machine.'

'Oh, that would be wonderful! I love to sew and to make things.'

As she looked at Irene, she was treated to the loveliest of smiles and it warmed her heart. Raising her eyes, she thanked God for bringing such a beautiful friend to her.

'Mama, it's so lovely to see you smile. What's making you so happy?'

'Angie, she is born. She's beautiful.'

A voice that Angelica knew well came to her then, but who was it?

'Is Irene all right, Angelica?'

Then Mia was reprimanding someone, but Angelica didn't know why.

'Angie! I've never questioned Mama about whether any

of what she talks about actually happened. I don't want to confuse her more.'

Am I confused? Why is everything so vivid to me? But Irene is all right, and I must tell the anxious person . . .

'Yes. Irene is fine. Maggie has made sure of that. Look, Irene is rosy-cheeked and smiling, holding her little Angie to her breast.'

There was the sound of a sob. 'I always think of my mum as smiling, even though I sometimes have difficulty in remembering her face.'

Then they were gone, the two girls who had visited her. They didn't come downstairs with her as she went to get a cup of tea for Irene. It was now Irene's voice calling after her. 'Remember, make sure the kettle boils, and warm the pot. Then, three scoops of tea leaves – I've plenty now, even though I hope Maggie took some . . . Anyway, once the hot water is on the leaves, let it stand for at least three minutes.'

'Yes, Madame. I'm sure the tea will be to your liking.'

Irene burst out laughing.

Angelica giggled to herself. *These rosbifs love their tea . . . Urgh! How they can drink it, I'll never know.*

A few days later, Angelica stood inside the Labour Exchange. Her nerves made her feel sick. She didn't want to be sent home. Of course she would like to see everyone, but from the news, the Germans were taking more and more charge of Vichy, and Pétain was following Hitler's lead like a puppy dog. She prayed that the Allied forces would soon win through.

Someone calling her name took these thoughts away.

As she walked forward, sweat beads ran down her back.

'I want to apply for a work permit, please.'

Then the questions began: where was she from, what were the circumstances of her being here. And so on and so on, until at last, the clerk told her, 'It will be a few weeks before you hear. Next!'

'Oh, but . . . I need to know. I need to get a job!'

'As soon as we verify who you are and why you are here, we will contact you. But if you're suffering hardship, there's the Red Cross and the Salvation Army.'

'No, my friend is looking after me, but how will you verify me?'

'Well, we'll start with Mr Jamieson's family and then contact the convent you came from. It will all take time.'

Feeling defeated as she knew that Philip's cousin would take great pleasure in denouncing her, Angelica thought again about the illegal route she could take. But then she decided that the best thing to do was to go to see Philip's cousin and beg him to help her.

Seeing the apartment again tore at Angelica's heart. She'd arrived with Philip, dreaming of her future and with such hope of a new life in her heart . . . *Oh, Philip, Philip, my love!*

Standing a moment looking at the bell, nerves took her. Could she face the abuse she was sure she would get? But then, what choice did she have?

Ringing the bell took a lot of courage for her to do and once done, set her heart racing.

But the reception she dreaded didn't happen.

The door opened and the hateful cousin appeared, taking the wind out of her sails by saying, 'You! What are you doing here? I mean, well, I'm so glad you have called. We tried to find you.'

It took a moment for Angelica to answer. 'I – I came because I need your help . . .'

'Of course, of course. What is it you need?'

'I need you to verify who I am so that I can get a work permit . . . I just need to know that you will back up my story as it is the truth.'

'We will do anything, anything . . . We . . . I have a lot to make up for. Won't you come in?'

Shocked by this change of heart, Angelica was unsure of whether she should. He'd called her a hussy – a prostitute! Did he still think that of her?

'I'm not alone, so don't be afraid. I have my wife with me. Please, just give me a chance to make things up to you.'

'That's very kind of you . . . Mr . . . ?'

'I'm George Jamieson, I'm the son of a cousin of Philip's father. What that makes me to Philip, I'm not sure . . . We only really knew of one another . . . I made a lot of assumptions when it all happened . . . Please, come in and meet my wife.'

This was a turn of events that Angelica couldn't ever have imagined happening, but she was relieved. What had changed his mind, she couldn't think. Maybe it was her saying she had been helped by kind people? Or saying she wanted to work? She just couldn't fathom. Whichever it was, she hadn't been given the impression on first meeting George that he and Philip only knew of each other. He'd spoken as if Philip was a beloved cousin.

She was lost for words, but as she stepped over the threshold, she did manage to say, 'Thank you . . . I didn't expect this, but I appreciate it.'

Angelica followed him, still feeling a little apprehensive, but glad now of this chance to hopefully gain a little understanding.

When he opened the familiar door to the lounge, he said, 'We have a visitor, Philomena. This is, well, the . . . Philip's fiancée.'

'Oh, my dear, I'm so glad you have called at last. What my husband did to you was despicable!'

As she spoke, she came over and guided Angelica to a chair.

Everything in the room was different to what it had been, which made it easier for Angelica, but what was going on, she couldn't think.

George looked very sheepish and wasn't a bit defensive of himself.

Once she was sitting, Philomena said, 'We found papers that Philip had written while in hospital. They were in a bag that hadn't been opened. He must have brought it home with him and . . . well, he wasn't home long, I gather.'

Angelica looked towards the door that led to a hall. Just along the hall was the bedroom, where everything had happened. Her mind went back over the heartbreaking scenes of what had occurred in the short time after Philip came home. And no, they hadn't unpacked anything he'd brought back with him after his hospital stay, when she'd taken many things in for him, including his writing box – a wooden box with a carved lid, which contained all he needed for writing and opened into a small desk. She remembered that Philip had told her the design had been inspired by one that George Jefferson, the third president of the United States, had had made for him.

'Anyway,' Philomena was saying, 'there was his writing box inside and what he'd written told us that George had made a big mistake. Only we didn't know where to start to find you.'

'What had Philip written?'

'The whole story of what he'd done in France – his special operations work with the Resistance, and how he'd found you. How you'd fallen in love, and what it cost you to follow him. His plans to marry you. And, well, not only what war effort he'd been involved in, but what he'd discovered you had done. You are a remarkable woman, Angelica.'

'I only did what was asked of me by the Resistance. Anyone would have. It's wicked what is happening to the Jews in Europe.'

'We agree. So much so that we've sent money to the convent to help with looking after the children.'

'Really? Oh, *merci, merci*.'

Philomena looked up at George. 'It's the least we can do in the circumstances. We're truly sorry that George got the wrong impression and about the way he reacted to you.'

'I understand. Things didn't look good . . . What we – I – did wasn't right. We should have waited. It . . . Well, it just happened out of our deep love for one another. No one could have dreamed of the consequences in their worst nightmare. And now I find myself in a predicament.'

George spoke then. 'Angelica needs a permit to work. She came to ask us to verify why she is here. I can only say that I'm sorry. Very sorry for what you've been through.'

'It hasn't all been bad.' Angelica told them then how she'd met Irene and had come to love her as a friend, and Irene's circumstances.

'We've been through some very tough times, but things are getting better now. And if I can get a job, we could live very comfortably together and help each other to bring up our children.'

Philomena looked shocked. 'Children? You're pregnant!'

Angelica nodded.

'I'm so sorry. It shouldn't have happened – any of it. Philip should have taken care of you . . . I mean, well, anyway, he has in another way.'

'He did take care of me . . . We loved each other. We sinned, I know, but we were to be married just as soon as all the legal requirements were in place.'

'There are things you don't know, my dear. It has come out through the post-mortem report that Philip's heart condition was known, and he'd been warned he should take things easy.'

'Oh, no! He never told me!'

'I know. You see, when he wrote about his life and yours, he also wrote what his intentions were. It was a kind of will, but not one that would stand up in court. He should have had his solicitor come to see him and put things in place. But the main thing is that we know he wanted you to be looked after properly, and we intend to do that for him.'

Angelica burst into tears. Philip knew he didn't have long. He'd tried to put things in place for her . . . He'd made her his, and yet he never told her she would be left alone . . . *Oh, Philip, Philip, my love. You should have given me a choice.* And yet, would she have chosen to do anything differently? And Philip couldn't have known he'd be taken so quickly. He'd have hoped they could be married, and that she would be given proper protection before he had to tell her the worst news.

Philomena was by her side, holding her, but Angelica felt no sincerity in the gesture.

George stood where he'd been throughout it all. His words held compassion but, yet again, Angelica detected something wasn't ringing true.

'I'm truly sorry, my dear. We will make it up to you and put things right. I promise.'

How can anyone put things right? She didn't have Philip and would never have him.

When she'd calmed, Philomena said, 'Let's have tea while we discuss what we would like to do.'

'May I have coffee, please?'

'Oh, of course. I was forgetting. Your English is very good.'

Over coffee and biscuits – both very welcome to Angelica – they discussed her future.

By the time she left, Angelica could have skipped along the pavement. It had been agreed that she should look for a house that she wanted, and it would be bought in her name. That she was to get an allowance and that funds were there for her future.

There had been one stipulation. A stipulation that had shown Angelica that the George she'd first met was the true George. And that Philomena wasn't at all a sweet person. They made her agree that once all this was in place, she'd never contact them again.

The atmosphere had changed to a business situation. She had once more become a stranger – a fallen woman.

But none of that mattered to her. All that did was that she and Irene, and their children, would be secure. That's all she needed out of life . . . Well, except the impossible – to have Philip back by her side.

Chapter Fourteen

Mia

On a Mission

Mia always looked forward to Saturday. Angie was home and stayed with Mama, while Mia had a couple of hours to go around the shops or have her hair done – whatever took her fancy.

This morning, she was going to the local Catholic church to seek out some information. She needed to know how to find the address of the Maria-Madeleine Convent in Limousin.

The creak of the church door seemed to split the silence within and the smell of burning candles and polish hit her as she stepped inside. A figure knelt at the altar.

Feeling she was in an alien world, Mia crept up the aisle, but no matter how hard she tried to be quiet, her footsteps echoed around the walls.

The kneeling man turned and watched her progress.

'How can I help?'

She recognized Father Benedict, who'd called at her house. His voice was kind and gentle and put her at her ease.

'I don't know if you can, Father, but I thought I'd try you first. You came to visit my mother recently.'

'Ah, yes, Angelica. How is she?'

'No different, though I think your visit helped her.'

'I was unable to do very much, I'm afraid. Would you like me to call again?'

'Yes, please, Father, whenever you can. But that's not why I'm here. You see . . .' Mia told of Marcia and how she thought finding her would help her mama.

'Mmm, yes, she spoke of Marcia to me. Now, as it happens, I do have a friend who may be able to help – another priest. He's French but studied with me here in England. He has his parish in Lyon. I'm sure he will be able to look in a directory and find the convent you speak of . . . But are you sure that you're not opening a can of worms? I mean, the young lady may not want to be found, or your mother may not want you to have information that she may have. There are a lot of possible scenarios, you know.'

'Yes, I understand that, but I have to try to do something to bring peace to Mama.'

'Very well. I may get into trouble for making an international call, but I'll do it anyway. Come through.'

Mia's heart filled with hope as she followed him through to a room hung with vestments.

'Just through this next door and we will be in the hall of my home. Would you like a cup of tea? My housekeeper, Lilly, will make you one and you can enjoy it while you wait. She'll show you into the little sitting room we keep for visitors.'

'Thank you, yes, I would. I haven't had time for one since breakfast.'

'Good, follow me.'

Lilly, a pretty lady with dark hair spiked with grey, brown eyes and a trim figure, seemed to Mia to be in her late fifties. She was friendly and welcoming, making Mia feel at home as she chatted about the usual things – the weather being so lovely this summer, and how everywhere looked beautiful with flowers blooming.

It was when they sat drinking their tea out of delicate china cups that the conversation took a different turn.

'It's nice to have you visit, Mia. I heard about your mother being so poorly. Not much happens around these parts that passes us by. And Father Benedict was very glad to be called in to see her. It's very sad, and if there's anything I can do, you must let me know.'

'Thank you, that's very kind.'

'I'm not just saying that. I am often an extension of Father Benedict's work. You see, I used to be a nurse, and so can help the sick. I'm free in the evenings, so if ever you need a break, I'd be willing to sit with your mother for you.'

A little unsure how to treat this offer from a stranger without hurting her feelings, Mia said, 'I do have my . . . well, she's a sort of sister.' She explained the relationship between her and Angie.

'Well then, how nice if you two could go out together occasionally. I'm sure you were used to doing that . . . Look, I could come around and visit first and sit with your mother while you're there so that she gets used to me and you build confidence in me.'

Mia couldn't believe the kindness of this lady who she'd never met before. 'I'd like that, though Mama doesn't hold a conversation with anyone, Lilly.'

'Then I will just sit there, tell her about myself, and become a friend to her.'

The idea began to appeal to Mia. Mama needed a friend. Someone who would talk about different things and maybe she would then talk about herself. 'Thank you, I think I'd like to give it a try. And I'd be downstairs for the first couple of visits just in case Mama gets distressed.'

'Has she had many friends in the past?'

'Oh, yes, so many loved her, and are so sorry about her illness. I'm always being asked how she is by our neighbours and those whose lives she made a difference to.'

'Has she ever been back to France?'

'No, but . . .' Suddenly, Mia wanted to confide in Lilly. She knew Father Benedict would only have told her so much.

'I so wish she had. She's troubled by something that happened there when she was young. She won't talk to me about it. I don't know if she has to Father Benedict, but he told me when he visited that he couldn't reveal anything she told him as a priest.'

'Oh dear, poor Angelica. Father did say she was very distressed, but not what about. I'll help all I can, but I can't force anything, just be a friend to her . . . Would it have been possible for her to go back to France? I mean, financially, and with her commitments? . . . I'm just trying to get a little background, not to pry, but to help me understand.'

'Well, it wouldn't have been easy. It's not money, though I don't know how much it would have cost to go to France or to get to a particular area of France.' Mia sighed. 'To be honest, I don't know anything about her. She never spoke of her past. She always told me she was an orphan, but nothing about my father, except that he was a British pilot and he brought her to England.'

'You say it wasn't money? So she does have an income?'

'Yes, but I don't know where from. I only know that I'm authorized to collect the money we need from the bank each month and that Mama owns the house we live in, which tells me she must have had – or come from – money. You see, I know nothing of my own background either.'

She was finding it strangely cathartic to speak openly to someone who wasn't involved in any way. 'But commitments, yes, she had those. Me and Angie, and Angie's mum – they were devoted friends. I do know, from people who have lived in the street as long as us, that Mama dedicated herself to caring for Aunty Irene and was devastated when she died. But then, Irene had been a saviour to her.'

'It sounds like a wonderful friendship. And the commitments you have mentioned would have made it difficult for Angelica to leave you all, and the cost of taking you all would be prohibitive too.'

The sound of footsteps brought the conversation to an end. 'Ah, Father's coming now. Let's hope he has news for you.'

The door opened. 'I heard that, and I do!'

Mia jumped up, her hopes soaring high.

'My friend is able to get the contact details for the convent. He will ring back later with them as he has a lot of appointments today. As soon as I have an address, I'll bring it round to you.'

'Oh, Father, how can I thank you?'

'Well, it would warm my heart to see you at mass. It's on my conscience that I have lapsed Catholics in my parish, but I've never been a pushy or condemning priest. Ha! I often get it in the ear from my bishop for not being so!'

His little giggle made Mia laugh. 'I will try. I do believe and I do pray. Mama always taught us about our religion, but would never take us, or encourage us to go to mass.'

'Well, I think that is all tied up with the guilt she carries inside her. I will keep trying to help her.'

'I'm going to do that too, Father. I'm going to befriend Angelica and help with her care.'

'Lilly, you're a marvel. A real marvel. If women could be priests, you would be the best priest ever.'

Lilly blushed with pleasure and Mia knew she'd met a good and genuine woman and one who might help to change her life.

Not wanting to stay out any longer, Mia hurried home to write the letter she now knew would at least reach the convent one day.

'Hey, you're back early!'

'Oh, Angie, I've such good news . . .'

Mia shared all that had happened with Angie.

'But that's amazing – both bits. Oh, we may have a chance to go out together again! That will be wonderful. And the contact! I did try to get this myself, you know. I asked if I could get in touch with our French correspondent but wasn't given permission. He's freelance, you see, and would have charged as if on a consignment.'

'Oh? You never said.'

'I didn't want to raise your hopes. But I'd do anything to bring peace to Aunty Angelica . . . You know, sometimes I want her to go. She's in so much pain, both mentally and physically.'

They hugged as their despair hit them afresh.

Then Mia said, 'Steve once said something about how a person can cling on to life by using their will, especially if they have something unfinished. I'm hoping by finding Marcia Mama can let go.'

Angie nodded. 'Yes, you have to do this, Mia.'

Mia hung her head. Though she'd accepted she needed to help Mama go to her rest, it wasn't going to be easy.

'How has she been today?'

'The same, really. A lot of mumbling about a George, who she hated, but nothing making any sense.'

'I'll go up for a few minutes and then I'm going to write a long letter to Marcia, telling her of Mama's state of mind and asking for her help. It may never reach her, but we can hope and pray it will.'

The letter was harder to write than Mia had thought. Not knowing the connection Marcia had to her mama was a big stumbling block. She didn't know if she was a friend of the same age, or a child, when Mama lived in France, but she leaned more towards her being a child from the mutterings she'd heard. What she did know was that Marcia was somehow the key to most of what troubled Mama.

Dear Marcia,

You don't know me, but you do know my mama, Angelica Jamieson. Her surname is her married name, which I am not sure whether you will know or not.

So sorry to be vague, but Mama is ill and is distressed about something to do with you . . .

After that, Mia hit a block. She bit the end of her biro and tried to compose the little she knew into something that made sense, even though it didn't do so to herself.

Angie was no help as she knew even less than Mia.

'Look, why don't we talk to Aunty Angelica? We listen and beg her to tell us things, but maybe if we asked direct questions?'

'Oh, I don't know. What if we cause her more stress?'

'Well, I'm just going up to try to get her to drink some water, I'll see how she is and . . .'

'I'll come with you, but what will you ask?'

'How did Aunty Angelica cope with the two of us and in

a foreign land and with no husband to help her? I was only three, and you were a few months younger when Mum died. It must have been like having twins.'

'Yes. And now she's come to this. And yet, I don't remember her being troubled in her mind. As we grew up . . . Oh, Angie, I can't bear it.'

Angie rose and opened her arms. Mia went gladly into the hug offered, wanting comfort, wanting this not to have happened to her mama. But it had, and she was powerless to do anything about it.

'We'll carry on supporting each other, Mia. We'll get through this and help Aunty Angelica as much as we can.'

When they entered the bedroom, Mia looked down on the beloved face that no longer resembled the mama she'd known, and prayed that soon she would be at peace. She could do that now as she was no longer in conflict over that happening. She'd found the courage to face it as only then would Mama be able to rest – the past would no longer matter . . . And yet, Mama's anguish was hers too, as the past did matter to her. She so longed to know who her mama had been and what had happened to her and, yes, what her grave sin was.

She knew this wasn't a healthy wish, but to be forever wondering would be torture.

Angie spoke first. 'Aunty Angelica, I want you to know how much I love you and how grateful I am to you for the life you have given me. It must have been so sad for you and Mum that your husbands weren't there when we were born.'

Mama cringed, then her voice, full of anguish, spoke words that froze Mia. '*Mais je n'avai pas de mari. J'ai péché!*'

Mia covered her mouth with her hands. *My God! Mama was never married!*

Angie, whose French was excellent too, grabbed her by the shoulders and pulled her to her. 'Oh, Mia. Mia . . .'

A sob from her mama took Mia to her side. Climbing onto the bed, she took her into her arms. 'It doesn't matter, Mama, no one will ever know. You loved me, and struggled to bring me up, but you did it. And for Angie too. Please don't look on anything you did as bad.'

'Philip loved me . . . I loved . . . he died . . . Oh, God! Philip . . . Philip . . .'

'Aunty Angelica, that's the loveliest and saddest thing for you to have gone through. And for Mia, to know she was born of such a beautiful love. Don't be ashamed. Be proud. We are, aren't we, Mia?'

'We are, Mama. I am so proud of you. To be left in that predicament and yet to carry on and care for your child is wonderful. Many poor girls that happens to have to give their children up.'

'It was . . . Irene . . . She helped me . . .'

Mia looked up at Angie. Her eyes had filled with tears.

'Your mum was a wonderful person, Angie. How Mama found herself alone and pregnant, and in a foreign country, we don't know, but we do know that Aunty Irene took care of her, and that's such a good thing to do.'

'We can find out more about your mum. We know so much about your father now. Let me do it, Mia. You need to know. Let me research further. Your father must have family . . .'

Again, Mama cringed. 'No. I'm to have nothing to do with them . . . I will tell . . . I'm so tired . . .'

Mia went back to her mama and held her gently. Her own tears ran freely down her cheeks. 'Rest, Mama . . . Rest, knowing you haven't done anything wrong.'

'Marcia . . .'

'I will find Marcia and explain all to her. You can sleep, Mama. You no longer have to fight.'

Mama lay her head on Mia's shoulder and relaxed.

After a moment, Angie said, as she wiped her tears with her handkerchief, 'That's the most peaceful I've seen her for a long time. Let's leave her to sleep. I'll pop down and make a cuppa, eh?'

Mia looked out of the window and saw the sun was going down. 'I'm hungry, Angie, hungry and tired, and yet somehow relieved that at last I know. And I feel that you will find out more for me.'

As she turned and saw her mama looking so peaceful now, Mia felt a surge of love for her and bent and kissed her cheek. 'Be back shortly, Mama.'

Once downstairs, sipping her tea and greedily munching on a cheese sandwich, Angie asked, 'Are you all right now, Mia?'

'I am. I feel strangely calm and accepting, and yet so sad for Mama. I can only think that she and my dad were planning to get married when my dad died before they could.'

'I think that too, and it's so sad. And that she then met my mum, and my mum helped her, even though she was bereaved herself.'

'Maybe they helped each other.'

'Yes, I mean, we've always been led to believe from the little we've been told that my mum took yours in, and yet your mum owns this house . . . Oh, it's all such a mystery . . . But we have the key to unlock most of it and I'm so glad you're going to let me.'

Mia smiled. 'It's a wonder you haven't done it already. Nothing stops you being a journalist usually!'

'I was afraid of knowing and not being able to tell you as you weren't ready. But now we know that we both have the same need, I'll do it. Anyway, get on with that letter as that's another part of the puzzle.'

By the time the letter was composed, Father Benedict was knocking on the door.

His smile told her he had good news.

For Mia, as the priest went up to her mother, putting the letter into the addressed envelope and sealing it was a pivotal moment.

Maybe many doors would be unlocked at last.

After dinner Mia suddenly yawned and collapsed heavily onto the sofa.

'You look exhausted, Mia. Look, I'll sit with Aunty Angelica tonight. You can grab an early night . . . I know you like to work on your book while you sit with your mama, but you need rest . . . How's your book coming along, anyway? You haven't spoken of it for ages.'

'I always think people will laugh about it. I mean, it's a sort of an "above your station" thing to want to do.'

'You're a very talented writer, Mia. I loved what you'd written up to where you'd last got to and I want more. But for now, get yourself into a hot bath and then get into bed and dream of Steve making love to you.'

'Angie!'

'Ha, don't look so shocked. I dream about that happening with Freddie all the time . . . It nearly did the other night.'

Mia grinned. You couldn't help it with Angie, she had a different way of looking at life. None of what they'd been taught was wrong seemed wrong to Angie. She was a free spirit.

'You're incorrigible, and very naughty!'

Angie giggled before becoming serious. 'I mean it. You get off to bed and I'll stay by Aunty Angelica's side.'

The dreams Angie had said she should have began in the bath as she lay soaking. They took Mia to a different world. A world where Steve loved her, and she lay beside him every night, and they awoke feelings in her that didn't give her peace, only longings. But when she got into bed, she closed her eyes and slept a dreamless sleep. Today had been full of revelations that had given her mama some peace and had gone a long way to her at last knowing more about herself. All she had to do was to hold hope in her heart.

Chapter Fifteen

Angelica

Finding a Settled Feeling

'I've a lot to tell you.'

'What is it, Mama? I'm ready to hear anything.'

This surprised Angelica. Why was Mia answering her? She'd been talking to Irene. They were sitting on the bench just by the mound behind the soup kitchen, only this time they'd brought bags full of homemade bread to donate as they'd promised they would.

Confusion threatened to unsettle her, as she said Irene's name but Mia came through again.

'It's all right, Mama. You go to your yesterdays. But be happy there. Try not to get upset.'

She went to thank Mia, but Irene was saying, 'Go on, tell me. Only don't say you're thinking of leaving when your kid gets here. Yer know that upsets me.'

'No, Irene, it's nothing like that.'

When she told Irene about her visit to Philip's cousin a few weeks ago and how she could look for a house for them that no one could put them out of, Irene reacted by bursting into tears.

'Oh, *ma chérie*! What is it? I thought you'd be overjoyed.

We need never worry again, what with your pension and my allowance, we'll be self-sufficient, and with a house on top that we don't have to rent, we can have a good life and give that to our children too.'

'It's a shock and, well, mostly relief. I didn't know how to tell you, but I had a letter from me landlord's solicitor. He's selling up the three houses that he owns in the street – ours and two at the bottom . . . Not the one that's been bombed, but across the road. I thought we could be made homeless if someone bought ours who wanted to live in it, or the new landlord charged extortionate rent.'

'Oh, Irene. Never hide anything from me. How long have you known?'

'A couple of weeks.'

'And you'd not long had your little Angie. Something like this can affect her too. She's so close to you, she may pick up on your anxiety.'

'Well, you didn't.'

'No. Sorry, Irene. I've been preoccupied. But, well, that letter I received yesterday confirmed something for me and gave me details of what Philip's cousin was offering me, and where it would be paid and how much I could spend on a property.'

'Oh, Angelica, it's all so much to take in. And you didn't say anything either!'

'Ha! That's true. And for the same reason really. I worried that it wouldn't happen as I had nothing in writing, but now I have. My allowance is going to be a very generous sixteen pounds a month!'

'What? We're going to be rich! With my two pounds six shillings a week, we'll have . . . Oh, I can't add it up!'

'Well, it's no good asking me, I haven't a clue. Let's do

it on our fingers. We can do it at four weeks. Four times two . . .'

They were laughing by the time they came to the answer as not only was it an enormous sum, but their antics at getting there had given them the giggles.

'Twenty-five pounds four shillings!'

'Oh, God! And no rent!'

'If you say it enough times, you'll believe it, Irene. Yes. No rent.'

'Couldn't we buy my house? Only . . . well, I love it and it's a place I've memories of.'

'We'll see how much it is, but yes, I would love that. And with our money we can do it up – paint it and get new furniture. At least for my bedroom. Because I'm going to need loads of wardrobes to put all my new clothes in!'

They laughed again, unable to believe it was all true.

'Let's nip over to Kelly's cafe and have a cup of Rosie Lee, eh? I think we can afford that, don't you? I can park the pram outside and keep me eye on Angie through the window.'

'Yes, but first, do you know who the solicitor is who is selling your house?'

'Do I? I've enough bleedin' threatening letters from him to paste one of our walls! And he's only just around the corner. He's a rotter, though, so watch how you deal with him. It's Mr Roderick of Wesham and Wesham Solicitors.'

'I'll go there now. You get your tea and order me a glass of water. I won't be long.'

Mr Roderick looked her up and down when he finally consented to see her. 'Look, missus . . . whatever your name is, I really don't see why you're asking about house prices.

You look as though you haven't got the price of a bag of potatoes.'

'Well, sir, you are wrong. I – I've recently come into my inheritance from my . . . husband, a Mr Philip Jamieson, and the waiting has been a time of poverty for me as his cousin contested the will.'

Angelica mentally crossed herself for the white lie.

'Philip Jamieson? Well, that's different, but there are far nicer houses for sale for you to consider, madam.'

'No. I want that one, please.'

He raised his eyebrows, but didn't object further. 'Let me see.'

He opened a portfolio. 'The asking price for that house is five hundred and fifty pounds.'

'I'd like to offer four hundred, as it does need a lot of repairs. Kindly put my offer to the owner.'

'I don't have to. I have his bottom figure, and he'll accept that. Do you want a survey on the place?'

'No. I'll take it whatever is wrong with it. I can give you a deposit now.'

Angelica got the brand-new chequebook out of her handbag. It had come in the post with the letter containing details of her settlement.

'Will one hundred pounds secure it until all the paperwork is done and I can sign the deeds?'

'It certainly will, madam.'

Angelica's hand shook as she wrote the cheque. Never before had she been in a position to hand over so much money. What that was in francs she couldn't work out, but she knew it was an enormous sum and that it would probably keep the convent going for years.

It had been good to hear George and Philomena say they

had donated a sum of money to the convent. She would do that too. She needed a solicitor of her own now, but it wouldn't be this one. She would find a good one and ask him to help her to send money to the Reverend Mother.

With this she thought of when she would be able to go back and collect Marcia and Madeleine. Of how good it would feel to bring them here. But not yet. With war still raging, and France still occupied, it would be too dangerous for them. Better they stayed in the safety of the convent.

As she walked back to the cafe with her precious receipt for her part payment of their home, she pondered on how she'd come here without her identity papers and worried if that would hinder her buying and owning a house. *Why didn't anyone advise me to bring my identity card with me?*

But then, it had all been such a rush – getting her clothes and the plane coming that night, and no clearance needed at borders as it was a military plane. But maybe no one had thought it important, thinking that as soon as she was Philip's wife, she would be given British papers. Now, she was stuck. But maybe a good solicitor could sort it out for her.

On her way back to the cafe, Angelica passed a group of men, all injured. One had only one leg, another missed an arm, two were leaning on crutches, and the last one had a scarred face as if it had been burned. She smiled at them but wished with all her heart she had more than a little change in her pocket. They were thankful for that, with one of them saying, 'Ta, missus. Are yer sure you don't need it, luv?'

'I'm sure. God bless you.' Putting her head down and hurrying on, Angelica's heart was heavy. How could she, a sinner, call on God to bless anyone?

With this thought, her mood dropped. Did any amount

of money make up for what she'd done? It couldn't clear her conscience for her, nor cleanse her blackened soul.

'Hey, what's that face for? . . . You didn't get the house!'

'*Non, non*, all of that is secure . . .'

'But that's wonderful! Pick up your glass of water, luv, let's have a toast, eh? Me tea's still hot. Kelly only just brought it, he'd been busy.'

Angelica guessed that Irene was thinking she'd gone into the doldrums because of the money coming indirectly from Philip, so made her mind up to allow Irene her own thoughts and not to dampen things with telling her what really troubled her.

But it was never easy to remain downcast when with Irene.

'I've been thinking of things we could do – we could extend the back and make a bigger kitchen. Marion down the road did that as she owns her own home. It's lovely. She can get a table and chairs in there and she only has to go through a door to her bathroom – no outside lav. She even installed one of them flush lavs and doesn't have the stinking honey wagon call to empty her pan.'

'That sounds wonderful. And maybe we could have a bath fitted and a sink and have a proper bathroom. There'd be room if we knocked through to the coal house.'

'Yes, but we'd have to see where we could store the coal. Some of the bigger houses have it tipped down the cellar, but we ain't got one of them.'

'We'll get around it, but oh, wouldn't it be wonderful to have a bathroom and not have to drag the tin bath inside?'

'Ha! I think we're getting a bit ahead of ourselves! Not only are there shortages of materials and manpower because of the bloody war, but we ain't got running hot water, and here we are talking of having a bath installed!'

They both giggled.

Some things did seem insurmountable, but were they when she had enough money to cover them? Even with the fees the solicitor would put on top of the sale price of the house, she'd have nearly two hundred pounds left – you could do a lot with that!

Their giggles turned to belly laughs when Irene put down her cup and said, 'Well, that should fill me jugs for little Angie, and she'll be crying for it soon, I know!'

The other customers looked over towards them as if they were naughty children. This made Angelica laugh even more.

The blanket covering little Angie suddenly lifted and her cry could be heard through the glass of the window.

'What did I say? Right on cue! Have you got that change you had to pay for the tea, luv, as I've nothing on me?'

Angelica coloured as her eyes opened wide and she stared at Irene.

'Yer have got it, ain't yer?'

All she could do was to shake her head.

'But . . .'

'I gave it to some wounded soldiers down the road. I didn't think!'

'Oh, Angelica, yer heart's good, but what the bleedin' hell are we going to do now?'

'I'll pay by cheque.'

Irene's face twisted in disbelief. 'I wouldn't think Kelly's ever seen a cheque, let alone know what to do with one. His bank is a rusty old tin under the counter!'

Feeling desperate but wanting to soothe Irene, Angelica said, 'Don't worry. You go to Angie and I'll sort this out.'

How she was going to do that, Angelica didn't know, but honesty was the best policy.

Kelly looked at her with raised eyebrows. 'Yer can't pay?'

The murmur of conversations died. The silence seemed to accuse Angelica. She felt like a criminal.

'I do have money . . . but not on me. I thought Irene did and so I gave what I had to the wounded . . . It's just a mistake, I will bring the money in to you.'

'Well, that was a kind act. And I've heard that you and Irene donate regularly to the soup kitchen. Some folk won't give the drippings of their nose!'

Kerry looked around. One or two of his customers looked away shamefaced; another couple folded their arms and nodded, looking around at the guilty ones with an expression of disdain.

One woman stood up. 'I'll pay for Irene's tea. She's a good girl and wouldn't have done this on purpose. But not even you, as mean as they come, can charge for a glass of water, Kelly!'

'Oh? So, I ain't got to supply the glass then, nor use me soapy water to wash it up? And me labour in doing that ain't worth the half-penny I charge then, is it, Florrie?'

Florrie clucked her teeth. 'Extortionate. But here yer go, yer mean bleeder!'

'Thank you so much. I'll tell Irene what you did, and we'll give it back to you.'

'No need. What you two did for Maggie more than enough covers it. Maggie's me mate, and she struggled. I gave her what I could, but you two have kept the wolves from her door. She's a good sort and'll be there for you when you have your nipper, luv.'

As they walked away from the counter, Angelica thought for the thousandth time how generous in love and spirit these Eastenders – as she'd learned they were called – were.

When they stepped outside, Florrie went to the pram. 'Ah, who's a lovely little girl then?'

'Ta, Florrie. I saw through the window what you did. I'll do the same for you one day, luv.'

As she said this Irene jerked and seemed to be about to fall. Angelica went to catch her, but as usual, she made a joke of it. 'Me bleedin' leg gave way, and I ain't had a drop either!'

'You daft sod, yer made me jump then. I thought you'd gone!'

'Sorry, Florrie, I don't know what happened. I just stood here and then wallop!'

Angelica was by her side the moment she'd almost fallen. 'Are you feeling all right, Irene? Oh dear, you gave us a fright!'

'I'm fine. Honest. It was just me leg gave way. Probably because I've been standing here a few minutes, and I was anxious about the bill and Angie needing her feed.'

When they reached home, Irene acted as if the incident hadn't happened. She cheerfully fed Angie and did all that was needed to make her baby comfortable.

'I think you should have a lie-down now, Irene. I'll look after Angie for you.'

'I do feel tired, ta, Angelica . . . You're a real pal, yer know. The best mate a girl could have. I want you to know that I love you like the sister I've never had. And . . . well, if anything happens to me, I know you'll take care of little Angie for me.'

She closed the stair door behind her then and Angelica listened to her going upstairs. Her tread seemed slow.

For the first time since she'd left the convent, Angelica slid off the sofa onto her knees and prayed fervently, over and over, that Irene was all right. That these were all symptoms following childbirth. But no matter how hard she prayed, a little voice inside her wouldn't still.

Rising and feeling drained, instinct told her there was something dreadfully wrong with Irene's health and yet there was nothing she could put her finger on – just a series of odd things happening.

Going to the window and gazing out as if looking for inspiration, Angelica came up with a plan. She would write everything down as it occurred, then she'd take Irene to see a specialist to find the cause and to seek a cure for her. She didn't care if it cost her the rest of her money, she couldn't bear anything happening to her beloved Irene.

How could she face life without her?

Please, God, don't let me have to.

Chapter Sixteen

Marcia

Love and Loss

Marcia had schooled herself not to let her thoughts take her into the past for a few weeks now. Dwelling on all that had happened didn't help.

To this end, she hadn't picked up her notebook, which in the beginning she'd only meant to use to help her to cope mentally, but which had now turned into something of great importance to her. Doing so would force her to go over more chapters of that time.

She straightened herself from folding the clean, dry washing, fresh from the line, and felt compelled to place her hand on her side. The niggly ache was still there but hadn't developed into labour as she thought it might.

Massaging the spot, she thought she could feel a little foot. She smiled and gently pushed on it. Her stomach lurched. 'Ah, so you will be a thorn in Mama's side, eh?'

She laughed to herself as the pain eased, and then leaned a moment with her hands on the table and looked around her little kitchen with its stone floor, pot sink in the corner, wood-burning stove that served as a cooker too, and the bright yellow walls that brought the sunshine inside.

A door led from this to the living room, a much brighter room, which she loved – that was, except for the green curtains. But they were there for Shane, her beloved husband who wanted something to show his Irish heritage to the world.

She had to admit, though, that they went well with the beige sofa and chair. She'd tied in the green on her beige cushions with something that had warmed Shane's heart – she'd embroidered each one with a picture of a shamrock in a silk thread of the same green. Smiling at Shane's almost child-like reaction to them, Marcia sat and did what she'd tried not to do – she allowed the past in . . .

1944

'Is it that you're feeling refreshed now, Marcia?' Shane asked her as she came out of the shower.

'*En Français!*'

'*Pardon!*'

He winked and made her laugh as he put on his best French accent and then repeated his question.

This made her giggle. Shane was so lovely, she thought, but then she realized he was staring at her.

Her hand went self-consciously to the strands of her wet hair.

Shane turned away. 'I have coffee percolating. Come and have a mug.'

Marcia watched him walk towards the fire that burned in an old metal drum with holes punched around the sides. 'Yes, please. But not there, I'm too hot.'

'I'll bring it over for Madame.'

She giggled again.

As they sat together on the stump of a tree, Shane asked her if she wanted to talk about what had happened. She shook her head.

In French, he told her, 'Well, I can tell you that the Reverend Mother is doing fine. She collapsed after the Germans took you all away and couldn't help her sisters, who were all heartbroken and very shocked at what took place. But they are gradually getting some normality back. And they are all pleased that you got away. Quite a few others did, and they're all hidden in safe houses for now.'

'Were many recaptured?'

'We're not sure but we think so. We set up ambushes to try to help any children who had been recaptured, but nobody came their way, and there are men searching the woods now for any that did escape. But all we can do is to give any we find tents, pans, utensils, water and traps to catch rabbits. Most have the skills to start a fire to cook on and once the water is gone, they will be left with a container to refill from the stream. We haven't enough food to share with them.'

He looked down to the ground. Marcia saw his shoulders droop as if the weight of all he knew was too much to bear.

'The reason is that the war is set to heat up. That's not common knowledge so you tell no one, but a big push will be made soon to liberate France. We will need all the resources we have, and that includes food, to keep the men strong. The children will survive – we have to believe so.'

Shane sniffed and a little droplet of water trickled down his face. Marcia put her hand on his back. 'You're a good man, Shane. Sister Angelica always said that of you. You have done your best . . . Maybe, if I went to the children and cared for them . . .'

'No! I – I mean, well, we need you here. Your baking skills will help us . . . But most of all, your nursing skills. Sister Angelica was always praising your way of finding how to heal. She said that at times you were like a doctor.'

For a moment, Marcia thought Shane was putting the needs of the men and women Resistance workers before those of the children, but then he said, 'By keeping us fed and well and able to do the job in hand, you'll be making a massive effort towards France winning through. We have many ailments visit us that lay us low – itching, bad feet, fevers – and they spread rapidly.'

'The fever will come from your lavatory facilities. There are so many flies around the latrine and they carry disease. You need to clean that up and have a system of burying any excrement deep into the ground.'

Shane's eyes opened wide, and his chin receded as he looked at her. 'You see! How did you know that?'

'I have learned many things from Sister Angelica's books and mostly from her. When I went to relieve myself I noticed that there was a problem. I couldn't go near for the stench, so went into the bushes, but they are well used too and smell bad. They too have flies circling them and almost as many as the latrine.'

'Well, I've learned something today! I just thought flies were pesky and brushed them off. You really are so much older than your years, Marcia, and Sister Angelica taught you well.'

'Oh, I miss her, Shane.'

'Be happy for her. She is safe in London with Philip and will be well cared for. There have been no raids on the city for a while now, and Philip isn't a poor man. She will have all she needs in life . . . Though I still can't get over her doing what she did. It's unheard of. And, well, it doesn't seem right. But then, who are we to judge? Love is a powerful thing. But the important thing is, what should we do to improve the camp and rid ourselves of the causes of our ill health?'

'Well, order that the latrine is dug in and buried, and a new one is built, and give instructions for a new system of burying everyone's waste. And tell the men to wash their hands after using it.'

'Yes, Madame.'

He dropped his French and went into English then. 'I am for being your servant. And always it will be that way.'

'*En Français!*'

Shane saluted. 'I just said I am your servant . . . The last bit I hope to say to you again one day. When you are older.'

She didn't understand all of this, but something stopped her from pressing him to tell her. She wished her English was better. Joseph had spoken it perfectly and had tried to help her with their English lessons. Maybe Shane could help her too.

It was the next day as the Resistance workers were preparing to ambush another train that a messenger arrived. Joseph had been caught. The safe house he was hiding in had been raided.

'It is that we have a traitor!'

The man broke down and cried as he continued. 'The owner of the house was shot, his wife raped . . . and . . . and . . . the girls . . . all raped . . . before being shot!'

He sat down on his haunches. It seemed the burden of what he'd discovered was too much.

Marcia's body trembled. Spittle ran from her open mouth.

She stared at the man with such intensity that her eyes dried and stung as the shock of what she'd heard vibrated through her.

The man was openly weeping now. 'The children are not safe. If the Germans know of one safe house, they will know of more.'

The horror of it crumpled Marcia. She landed on the ground in a deep faint.

Shane was bending over her when she came round. Trickles of cold water ran from a sponge he held on her face.

'Try not to worry. Joseph is strong so will be useful to the Germans. We know they put the strong young men to work on their farms surrounding the camps or set them to build more blocks. I promise you, the war is coming to an end. We must pray that it is in time to save him.'

In a weak voice, Marcia managed to say, 'And the girls . . . those poor girls.'

'They are at peace now. More and more, the Germans – and more so the gendarmes – are using swift methods of instant murder as they cannot cope with the numbers they detain. They just haven't the resources.'

Marcia gasped. 'They're dead? All the children from the convent?'

'We don't know. But we must prepare ourselves that many won't survive. But have faith that Joseph will. And always pray for the others that they will too.'

His touch on her hair and the look in his beautiful shining blue eyes told Marcia that he loved her and made her feel safe in that love, giving her the knowledge that he would protect her. *But, oh, Joseph, my Joseph . . .*

* * *

As she stared into space, almost twenty years later, Marcia remembered her first love – Joseph. She cherished his memory as it was later found that he was on the list of those murdered at Auschwitz. He would always remain in her heart.

But it was Shane, her beautiful Shane, who was the true love of her life.

As if she'd conjured him up, he appeared at the door waving an envelope. 'Sure it is that a letter has come from England!'

Shane now worked at the convent maintaining the buildings and grounds, though he would often say, in English with his Irish accent that she was now fluent in and loved, 'To be sure, the sisters get under me feet!'

Unable to believe that there was at last a letter from Sister Angelica, Marcia grabbed it and ripped it open. What she read shocked her.

'What is it that troubles you? Is Sister Angelica not for being all right?'

As she handed the letter to Shane, Marcia bent double with pain.

'The baby. The baby is coming.'

'To be sure, everything will be all right, me darlin'. You're a whizz at this birth lark now, so you are. Let's be getting you upstairs. I'll go for the midwife.'

Hours later as she lay holding her little girl, who they had named Angelica Madeleine, Marcia said, 'I must write to Mia. I must help her, but most of all, I must save dear Sister Angelica from her distress.'

'From what I have read, you and Mia can be helping each other, me darlin'. Now let me hold me little daughter. Me beautiful Angelica.'

* * *

Standing in the bureau de poste three weeks later, Marcia held on to Shane's hand. He winked his encouragement.

Mia had given a telephone number, and Marcia had booked an overseas call.

The ring tone was clear, as was the voice at the end of the line. 'Hello, Mia Jamieson speaking.'

'Mia! It is Marcia! Oh, Mia, how is beautiful Sis . . . your mama?'

'You're not angry at her?'

'*Pardon?*'

Mia repeated her question in French.

'No, I understood what you said, Mia, but I don't understand why I should be angry?'

This belied the moments she'd had of being cross about everything – emotions she had always quelled.

'Oh, Marcia. I am so short of knowledge of my mama and her history. But as I said in my letter, she is in a turmoil of fear and guilt. I want to help her, but I cannot do that without knowledge. The only key I have to her past is you, Marcia. Can you tell me what happened? What was my mother doing when she met you? And, well, why do you mean so much to her, and how has she let you down?'

'I am Jewish, and she saved me . . .'

Before she could go on the pips sounded to warn that the call would end soon. 'I will write, but tell Sis . . . your mama that I love her, and I am happy. Tell her that Shane is my husband, and we have four children . . .' The line went dead. Marcia didn't know how much Mia had heard of what she'd said, but as she turned to Shane her tears flowed. 'She was like a mama to me, Shane. I've always held her in my heart. I've longed for her to come back but . . . now she's dying . . . So

young. I – I thought that one day I would go and find her
. . . Oh, Shane . . .'

'I wish that I could be taking you to her, me darlin'. But the cost . . . we never have savings, I'm sorry.'

'Don't be. You provide well for us. We have a lovely home, four beautiful children and are happy. That's all Sister Angelica would want for us. I'll write her a letter and tell her all about our life together.'

'You're amazing, Marcia. I've always thought that from the moment you first came to the convent. Sister Angelica used to tell me so much about you whenever our paths crossed. And a couple of times I caught a glimpse of you, me a twenty-two-year-old and you just fourteen, but I knew you would one day be for having a special place in me life.'

Marcia smiled at him, her emotions too fragile for her to respond.

'Let's get you and the little ones home, me darlin'.'

They had to call Joseph and Amos as they'd wandered up the street and joined in a game with other children, but Hans never left Marcia's side since baby Angelica had been born. If not holding her hand, he would be clinging on to her skirt. She understood and made a fuss of him before she tended to her baby's needs.

As all three of her older children crowded around her, she was filled with love for them, and vowed to always protect them.

But then, she wondered how many mothers had made that same vow over the past centuries, and how so often that had been an impossible task for Jewish mothers.

The future would be different, wouldn't it? Nothing like the genocide could ever happen again . . . *Please, God, don't let it.*

* * *

Once home, she sat down and wrote a long letter to Angelica – but then she shelved it as it contained the outpouring of her heart. A dying woman didn't need that.

In the end, she settled on a short letter. After thinking everything through she decided she would begin by addressing it to 'My dearest friend and saviour' as she guessed that Mia would read it out and for her to see 'Dear Sister Angelica' would be a great shock to her.

Trying to put some beauty and light into it, she began by describing where she was.

I am in my garden. It's beautiful here, the sun is shining, and the birds are singing under a lovely blue sky. I am happy and have nothing to forgive you for. You gave me the love that the Holocaust had taken away from me. Be at peace with your soul. You will be forever in my heart. Your loving Marcia.

She hoped this allowed Sister Angelica to let go and take the peace heaven offered and not suffer the pain of this world any longer. She didn't deserve that. She'd brought hope and love to so many children.

Marcia sighed as she thought of how few of them had survived despite Sister Angelica rescuing them. One child stood out in her mind – her sister, Madeleine. She bowed her head and wept.

Chapter Seventeen

Mia

A Love Returned

'Mama, I have some news. I've spoken to Marcia!'

Mama opened her eyes.

Despite how the cancer had ravaged her body in the past three weeks, her eyes still looked bright and lovely. And at this moment, they shone with hope as she lay propped up by a mound of soft pillows.

'Marcia, is she coming?'

'She still lives in France, Mama. And from the little she was able to tell me, I wonder if she can afford to come. I wrote it down as soon as the call ended. Would you like to hear it?'

Mama was the most alert she'd seen her for a long time as she nodded.

'"I will write, but tell Sis . . . your mama that I love her, and I am happy. Tell her that Shane is my husband, and we have four children . . . I love her!"'

Mama's eyes opened even wider. Her mouth went slack.

'Oh, Mama, I know this is a lot for you to take in. I – just wanted to bring you some peace. Marcia isn't angry with you. And now you know that, you can rest easier.'

For the first time in a long time, Mama smiled and then stretched out her hand. Mia took it in her own. Fighting back the tears and not wanting to upset her mama, she had one burning question. 'Why did Marcia twice go to say "sister"?'

An agonized look crossed Mama's face and Mia's remorse was total. 'It doesn't matter, Mama. All that matters is that you've found Marcia and that she isn't cross about anything that happened. She loves you and, as far as I can see, doesn't blame you for anything. And, Mama, she also said that she would write to you.'

Mama smiled again and visibly relaxed but asked, 'Shane? Why Shane? She loved Joseph . . . Did . . . No! Not the lovely Joseph.'

'We can't speculate, Mama. Sometimes, young people fall in love many times before they marry.'

Not sure if this was the time to press her mama for more information, Mia didn't ask who Shane was, or Joseph. Marcia would tell her. But she did say, 'Marcia told me that she is Jewish and that you saved her, Mama. I'm so proud of you.'

'I – I promised to go back for her and her sister . . . Did – did she mention Madeleine?'

'No. There was so little time as it was an international call. You see . . .'

With Mama so alert, Mia explained how she got in contact with Marcia. But that changed when she did.

'Thank you. The convent was my life . . . I'm so tired. Things are coming at me again . . . Don't let them.'

'Hold on to me, Mama. There, rest now. We'll talk another time. Close your eyes, dear Mama.'

When Mama had drifted off to sleep, she looked at peace, making Mia feel better about how far she'd taken all of this.

* * *

As she often did, Mia sat on the bottom step of the steep stairs, giving herself time to recover. And to prepare for Steve's visit, as he'd said he'd call today. She never knew what time as he didn't begin his rounds until after his morning surgery. She looked at her watch, and was shocked to see that it was now twenty past one.

Her tummy rumbled. It'd been such an eventful day and she'd forgotten to eat. And yet, she felt drained of energy. Things had changed rapidly. Her quest to help her mama die in peace was taking its toll.

Lowering her head, Mia was surprised to find that she hadn't come to terms with losing her mama at all. But she had to be unselfish and let her go. Could she, though?

Swallowing hard, she went to rise and had to do so by pulling herself up by the stair rail.

She'd only just stood when there was a familiar tap on the door and it opening hailed Steve's arrival.

She wasn't ready. She plonked back down.

'Hello! Mia?'

'I'm here, Steve.'

'Mia? Are you all right?'

'Yes. Just tired . . . so very tired. And I'm not sure that I'm doing the right thing in trying to help Mama's mind to rest.'

Steve put his bag down and took her hands, helping her to stand. She swayed towards him, finding herself in his arms. He held her to him. 'Oh, Mia, I haven't been able to get you out of my mind.'

He kissed her hair.

Lifting her head, she gazed up at him and saw in his eyes a reflection of her own feelings.

Then her emotions collided, and she burst into tears.

Steve held her close, murmuring soothing words and stroking her hair.

Suddenly he stepped back.

Mia, bereft of him holding her, stared at him.

'I – I'm sorry . . . But I'm forbidden to feel how I do . . . I'm your doctor. I – I could be struck off.'

'But . . . how can we deny how we feel?'

There was a moment of tension between them before Steve took a step towards her and held out his arms. Mia melted into them.

'We can't. I've fallen in love with you, Mia. But you must change doctors before anyone finds out.'

'Can I just stay with Doctor Jones? Is that acceptable?'

'It would be better if you weren't associated with our surgery, except through your mother. You wouldn't be expected to find a new doctor for her at this stage.'

'I'll go to Doctor Price in the morning. Angie will be here to see to Mama. She always takes charge on a Saturday morning, and I get my hair done, or do some shopping.'

'He's a good doctor and a nice man, though hopefully you won't ever need his services . . . Oh, Mia, how did this happen? I've tried so hard to keep you as a friend.'

'It happened for me the moment I set eyes on you, Steve.'

He held her tighter. 'Yes, me too,' he whispered in her ear. The feel of his breath against her skin sent shivers through her.

'I love you, Mia. You seem to have consumed me. I can't stop thinking of you. I see your face in every woman's face I look at. I feel a longing to be with you every minute of the day. I feel like I'm going crazy!'

With this, he let go with one of his hands and sought her hand. Then, to her astonishment, he started to waltz her – a bit clumsily – around the room, while he sang the lyrics of Patsy Cline's 'Crazy'.

Her sadness and frustration turned to happiness, and she found herself giggling as she joined in with the song, ignoring his awkward dance steps.

They ended by hugging one another and laughing out loud.

Mia lifted her head and knew a longing in her heart. To feel his lips on hers would complete her world.

It did more than that. The sensation stirred a longing inside her to be his.

The kiss, gentle at first, then a searing, demanding taking of her heart, lit up her life and gave her hope for the future. She was in love. She'd fallen in love! And the feeling was indescribable. All she knew was that she would never be the same again.

When he released her, she didn't want him to but loved the small pecks he gave her which told her he didn't want to either.

'I love you, Mia.'

Yes, he'd sung it, but to hear those words spoken by him made her his.

'I love you, Steve. With all my heart, I don't know how it happened, but I know I want to live the rest of my life with you.'

His lips met hers again. She clung to him. He was her saviour from all the sadness she endured. A light in her dark tunnel, her everything. She would go to the ends of the earth with him. She was his for ever.

Coming out of the kiss, Steve smiled down at her. 'Saying you want to live the rest of your life with me, was that a proposal?'

Mia felt herself blush. Suddenly she felt she was being very forward. She dropped her head. Steve put his hand under her chin and lifted it. 'I'll remember your words for ever, darling Mia. And one day in the future, we'll make them come true.'

Their eyes locked for a long moment before Steve said, 'I can't believe this. I didn't think it could happen.'

'I've so wanted it to.'

'Oh, Mia. I want to marry you tomorrow and dance with you, in my fashion, every evening. But there's something I have to tell you about me.'

His face was solemn.

'It's nothing serious, is it?'

'Well, yes, it is.'

'Oh, Steve . . . what? I promise it won't make a difference to me . . . to us. But please tell me.'

As if he was telling her he only had weeks to live he said, 'I'm afflicted with flat feet!'

Mia burst out laughing. Steve joined her.

His humour was of the type where he liked to trick her – throw her sideways, as he did with the baked beans incident and just now with his flat feet.

When Steve stopped laughing, he said, 'Well, I've been a lover, a sort-of dancer and a comedian, so I think now I had better be the doctor I came here to be.'

Catching his arm, Mia said, 'And I love every one of those personas as well as when you wear your chef's hat, so I think you'll do for me.'

Steve laughed and took the stairs two at a time.

Mia was still too weary to do anything but walk up at a normal pace, but she was glad when she got there to see Mama resting and not distressed.

Steve turned and looked quizzically at her.

'A lot has happened today that's helped Mama . . . And yet it all went some way to upsetting me.'

'We'll talk downstairs, as it is possible we can be heard. But it does look as though we have the painkillers sorted now.'

After a few checks, none of which disturbed Mama, Steve indicated that they should leave her in peace.

At the door, Mia looked back. There was something different about Mama. She wasn't fighting any more.

Realizing this, Mia's heart sank. She knew it couldn't be long now before she'd have to say goodbye to her darling mama.

Downstairs, Mia told Steve all that had happened.

'But that's wonderful news . . . Are you not happy about it, Mia?'

Mia shook her head. 'It feels like I am assisting her death. My own mama and I want her to die.'

'That's called unselfish love, my darling. The best love there can be. You love your mama, and so you want the best for her and are trying to achieve it for her.'

Mia smiled. 'Thank you, you've really helped me. And yes, that is my motive. I just want Mama out of this pain.'

'So, stop worrying. That's different to caring. Of course you will care and be afraid of what will happen in the future when you're left alone – but you will never be that, Mia. You will always have me.'

'Oh, Steve. I still can't believe it.'

'I know.' He held his arms out to her. When she went into them, he didn't do anything but hold her, and at this moment that was all she wanted and needed.

'After tomorrow, we'll arrange to go out together. You have both Lilly and Angie to call on to step in for you, so no excuses. I want to take my girl to dinner and spoil her, but you must register with Doctor Price first.'

'Lilly's been a godsend. She gives Mama a bed bath twice a week and has shown me how to make sure she doesn't get bedsores. She keeps saying she isn't only doing this for Mama but for me too, and she wants me and Angie to go out for an evening together. So, I know she will come to sit with Mama. Then maybe we could ask Angie and Freddie to come with us?'

'Next time. Our first date should be just for us. I want you all to myself.'

'Is that selfish love then?'

'Ha! Well, it is selfish and unashamedly so.'

Mia laughed. 'I'll work it all out.'

'Make it soon, my darling. I need to be with you when it isn't breaking any of my ethical codes to be so. I don't want to feel guilty and as if I must hide you away.'

'I promise.'

His kiss was a light touch of their lips and then he was gone. To Mia, it was as if part of her life had gone too. She knew she was being silly and that they couldn't be together every minute of the day, but she so wished they could.

Closing the door, she forgot the feeling as she hugged herself and did a twirl. 'He loves me! He truly loves me!'

She wanted to shout it out in the street while doing a joyous dance. But then a cry reached her ears and brought her back to reality as she turned and ran up the stairs.

'I'm here, Mama. You're all right. I'm here.'

Mama lay on her side as if she'd fallen off her pillows. 'What is it? Are you trying to reach something, Mama?'

'Yes . . . the box!'

Mia looked for a box, even though she knew there wasn't one there. 'Someone must have moved it. Is it important?'

'*Mais oui* . . . Please find it.'

This was something new. A box had never been mentioned before. 'What's in the box, Mama?'

'Everything . . . You need to find it . . . It's there, Mia.'

'Okay, I'm sure I'll find it. I'll get Angie to help me. Let's forget it for now as I have exciting news. Steve – Doctor Granger – loves me! We love each other. Oh, Mama, I've fallen in love!'

Mama's smile lit up her weary, drawn, almost yellow-coloured face.

'*C'est merveilleux, ma chérie! Je suis heureuse!*'

'Oh, Mama, to know you think it wonderful and that it makes you happy . . . it's . . . Oh, Mama!'

Though Mia had always tried very hard not to cry in front of her mama over all that was happening, now she found she couldn't control her tears.

'*Ma chère fille, non . . .*'

Always Mama had called her her darling daughter. Climbing onto the bed, Mia lay close to her mama and held her.

'I want . . . I want you at my wedding, Mama. Don't leave me.'

'*C'est la volonté de Dieu.*'

'How can God have a will to take you from me? I need you, Mama.'

Although when tired Mama always spoke in French, she said in English, 'Mia, I – I have atoned. Marcia . . . forgives me . . . You forgive me . . . I loved, like you . . . I knew the happiness . . . I did wrong, and yet, *ma chérie* . . . I never regretted having you . . . just my sin of the flesh . . .'

'Oh, Mama. It wasn't a sin! You were in love with Papa. And that makes me happy. I was born out of love.'

'I – I am almost ready . . . Know that I will always be by your side . . . I'll be with you as you walk up the aisle, *ma chère fille.*'

Mama closed her eyes.

Mia stayed where she was with her arm around her mama. She knew a sense of great peace as though the time to part was close, Mama had said she would never leave her side.

Chapter Eighteen

Angelica

A Shocking Revelation

Angelica let herself drift into her thoughts and allowed her past to come into the present as she and Irene sat on their favourite bench on the mound behind the soup kitchen. Though the van was now closed, there were still people milling around, talking in groups, their topic of conversation being the advances made in the war effort and their fear of Japanese involvement.

She and Irene had been lucky to get the bench and sat huddled against the cold February wind.

However, it wasn't the cold that stopped her enjoying this moment but her worries over Irene. *Why is she dropping things so often, and falling? I must tackle her about it – make her realize that it isn't normal. And I must get her to the doctor.*

Angelica touched her stomach. She was worried too that her little one hadn't moved for hours, when normally it was as if he or she was playing football. But then, she supposed that happened from time to time. For now, she had to concentrate on Irene.

'Irene, when you fell over this morning, why was that? There didn't seem to be anything in your way.'

'I don't know.' Irene's bottom lip quivered as she rocked her pram with one arm. 'It just happened, luv, me leg just went from under me . . . I – I'm scared. It's happened a lot lately, and I'm struggling to do things like buttoning Angie's matinee coat.'

'Why didn't you say? I knew you had some weakness in your wrists, but this is something new.'

'Because you're so near to your time, I didn't want yer worrying.'

'Well, that didn't work, as I've fretted about it over and over. Promise me that we can go to Doctor Preston's surgery tomorrow and tell him all that's going on.'

'I promise. Now, enough about me. I've noticed you looking uncomfortable as we've sat here. You've been rubbing yer back and yer tummy. Are yer sure that you're all right?'

'Well, the baby hasn't moved for a while, and I do have this niggly ache. Maybe we should get home. I'm cold and you must be.'

As Angelica went to get up, the niggly ache developed into a pain that creased her back. 'Ooh!'

'Uh-oh, I know that sound. Come on, we'd better be quick. I've a feeling we'll need Maggie.'

'Oh no. It isn't my time!'

'It's nothing to do with you, luv. If your nipper's ready, then it's coming and that's that.'

As Angelica clutched her stomach when another pain gripped her, Irene turned and shouted, 'Hey, you lot, give me an' hand. Angelica's in labour!'

'What? Blimey! Can yer walk, Angelica?'

Another pain took all the space around her, leaving her unable to identify the speakers. They were all just a sea of faces.

One of them said, 'Aggie, run and tell me Alf to bring his barro'!'

Angelica couldn't think what they needed a barrow for. But she soon found out as Alf arrived and, helped by several of the ladies, lifted her into it.

Her labour then turned into a sort of jolly parade as she was wheeled back home, and the women followed, singing, *'My old man said foller the van and don't dilly dally on the way!'* They showed great glee as they passed a copper and sang the rousing chorus: *'Well, you can't trust a special like the old time coppers, when yer can't find your way 'ome!'*

Angelica felt she would die with the pain and the humiliation, and yet it seemed to mark her as one of them, and for the first time she felt as though she belonged here in Stepney with these kind people. The convent in Limousin seemed a million miles away.

Once home, she was helped upstairs and onto her bed. By now, she couldn't thank anyone, as the pains took her into a world of agony, which seemed to have increased with the arrival of Maggie, who, after assessing her, told her she must begin to push down with every pain in the way she'd seen Irene do.

Straining for the umpteenth time with all the effort she could muster, Angelica thought she would die.

Exhausted, she flopped back. 'I can't . . . I can't do this any more!'

'Oh yes you can! Push . . .'

Angelica had no choice. It felt to her that her whole body was bearing downwards. Suddenly, there was a cry of, 'I can see its head!'

And then, feeling as though she'd split wide open, Angelica sucked in a deep breath.

Before she could release it, a baby's cry filled the room.

'Ah, a lovely little girl! Well done, Mum. Just let me cut the cord . . . There you go! Welcome to the world, little one.'

Angelica smiled through the sweat running down her face and put her arms out to receive her child.

'Let me clean 'er up first, luv . . . Uh-oh, here comes the afterbirth. One more push, only you'll have to do that on your own, Angelica, I have the baby to hold . . . Where is that Irene?'

Raising her voice, Maggie shouted, ''Ave yer that hot water ready for me, Irene? . . . Irene! . . . Where's she got to, eh?'

'Oh, Maggie, give me my baby and go and check. Irene's not well, she's been falling and many other things that aren't right.'

'Well, that's a rum carry-on. Look, hold the baby a moment and let me at least get rid of the afterbirth and put it on the fire.'

Maggie used the newspaper she'd laid under Angelica for the purpose of protecting the bed to wrap the afterbirth in. As she did, she said, 'Listen to how many times it crackles and that will tell yer how many babies you're going to have!'

'What? I don't want any more . . . Besides, I don't have . . . I'm not marrying again.'

'Ha! All widows say that. But it's a lonely life without a man. Anyway, if you're all right, I'll go and see where Irene's got to.'

As Maggie left the room, Angelica looked down at her little bluish baby with streaks of blood all over her and her heart split with love and grief.

Her tears wet the tiny head, her body shook and in French she lamented the loss of Philip and of being denied the love of her sisters back in the convent.

It was then that a scream pierced the air. Followed by, 'Oh, God! Irene . . . Irene, no!'

Holding her baby close to her, Angelica slid out of bed, grabbed a towel and held it between her legs with her free hand as she wearily made her way downstairs. But the towel had to go as she found she had to cling on to anything she could grab hold of to stop herself falling with how weak she felt.

But then, her baby's cries were joined by the much louder and demanding ones of the distressed Angie, and Angelica knew that with no response from Irene, something was terribly wrong.

Her fears clenched her heart as she opened the stairs door to their living room and saw Irene on the floor, her face bloodied, her limp body deeply unconscious.

'Maggie! Maggie! What's happened?'

Maggie halted her swabbing of Irene and turned towards her. 'Oh, God, Angelica, get back to bed, luv. You'll harm yourself. I'll tend to Irene. She must have tripped on something.'

Turning back to the unmoving Irene, Maggie doused her cloth in the bowl of water she had and gently wiped the blood away. Her sigh told of her anguish.

Looking back at Angelica, Maggie said, 'It'll be all right, I promise. I saw young Jimmy in the street, and I've sent him to the corner shop to get them to call an ambulance. So, please, please, go back to bed.'

'Oh, Irene, Irene!'

'Please, Angelica, luv, go back to bed.'

'But there must be something wrong. She's been falling so much lately. And losing strength in her arms! I've been so frightened for her.'

'That don't sound good. But it's no use us speculating, we can only do so much, and I'm doing that. I just need you—'

The sound of clanging bells stopped them both in their tracks. But then Angelica began to shake all over, and her legs gave way. She grabbed the arm of the chair. 'Help me, help me!'

Maggie was by her side in an instant and sat her down. 'Oh, Angelica! You're in shock. Sit quietly for a moment. Hold on to your little one. I'll go and grab a blanket for you.'

Although it was chaos with Angie's screams getting louder and the bells now sounding as though they were in the front room, Maggie kept calm and did what needed to be done. Angelica was glad of this as she felt she was losing control. Every part of her body trembled. 'Oh, Irene, Irene, my dear friend, please get well. Please!'

She didn't call on God for many things, but now she began to pray to Him to help them.

It was Maggie returning at the same time as the ambulance man opened the door that brought the reality of it all back to her.

A portly man with a kind face, whose uniform seemed two sizes too small, entered. 'What have we got here then, eh?'

Maggie explained.

'Right, you've done well, missus. But we're here now. Can you manage the new mum, and we'll get our patient off to hospital?'

'Angelica could do with some medical attention. I think she's in shock.'

'And you are too by the sounds of things. Make a hot cup of tea for you both with plenty of sugar in it – that's if yer have any – and that'll help yer.'

'I think Irene will have some in, but if not, I can scrounge from the neighbours. If they've only got a teaspoonful each, they'll let us have it.'

'Good. Well, there's a crowd out there, so I'll make sure someone fetches your doctor to yer, but we must get going now. We'll take Irene to Mile End General; you can ring them later for news.'

Although she hated tea, Angelica sipped it and began to feel better. The shaking stopped.

'Well, luv, I'm going to have to get Peggy to help me. You and your baby need to be cleaned up and baby needs feeding. I just hope yer milk comes in with the shock you've had. God in heaven, it's been a nightmare!'

Looking down at her now sleeping child, Angelica said, 'But there's Angie to see to. And I'll need to go to be with Irene. It isn't possible for me to stay in bed for the fourteen days as I should do.'

'But yer must, girl! You'll do yourself untold damage. You'll be ill, and yer milk'll dry up! You must make your baby your priority now.'

'No! I cannot! I will be all right. I have read about how in other countries the women have their babies in the fields while they are working. They wrap them up in a sling on their shoulder and continue to work! And I read that they come to no harm. So, I'm going to carry on.'

'I can see you're determined to. Well, it's not up to me, but you'll rue the day, luv.'

* * *

Once Peggy and Maggie had cleaned her up and her baby was fed – a sensation that Angelica had loved – they settled Angie and then left Angelica for a while, promising to take it in turns to pop in to see if she needed anything. Angelica sat back in her chair and let in the nightmare of what was happening.

Loneliness engulfed her. How was she to cope? She felt so weak.

Not letting her fears turn to despair, she made a plan. Firstly, she had to name her baby. Then she had to prepare herself something to eat . . . And then . . .

With what she must do settled in her mind, Angelica felt more in charge. Tomorrow, she would go to Irene. She could do it between feeds. She just had to let her dear friend know that she wasn't alone, and that Angie was all right and well cared for and safe.

With her mind made up, Angelica held her baby to her as she sought to find what best to call her.

Marcia came to mind. But no, she couldn't name the baby after her, as it would be confusing when she went back for her and Madeleine and brought them here. But maybe she could keep to something beginning with 'M' to honour Marcia.

It was then she remembered another child. A child she'd loved dearly.

She'd been brought to the convent one night by her mother, who begged them to save the little girl. Angelica had devoted weeks to caring for little Mia, but despite this, she faded away and died in her arms while her mother slept. No one knew the cause. Only that a weakness had taken the child and rendered her unconscious. The doctor had said that nothing could be done, that she was a child of God and would go back to him.

Well, Mia, you will live again through my little girl.

The next few days were difficult and tiring for Angelica, and she wouldn't have managed without the help of Peggy and Maggie.

She had put Angie to her breast too, and that had soothed the little mite. Angelica loved the moment she sat with both babies feeding, though the arm holding Angie soon ached with her weight.

Life was made easier by Angie being a loving and adorable child who seemed delighted to have tiny Mia by her side, touching her gently and giggling. Despite all she was going through, this warmed Angelica's heart and made her giggle too.

It was in the middle of the night, alone and feeding Mia, that Angelica looked down on the cherub-like face of her baby and swallowed hard. She hadn't let the sadness of Philip not seeing his child affect her, afraid of giving way, but suddenly the thought overwhelmed her and huge sobs wracked her body. *Oh, Philip, my Philip. Why did you leave me?*

Mia became unattached from her breast and seemed to tremble with fear before crying out. Controlling herself and gently soothing Mia, she put her back on her breast and told her, 'You had a wonderful, courageous papa, my darling, but this war took him from us. But to save you anguish, I'll tell you as little as possible about him and nothing of how we met. I am ashamed to let you know who I am really – how I broke my vows, how I sinned with your papa. And I never want you to be rejected by his – your – family. But I know he'll always watch over you.'

A peaceful feeling came into Angelica. To her, it was as if she'd finally laid Philip to rest.

Putting her head back onto the pillow, Angelica wondered how it was that she'd gone from that graceful, ordered life of the convent to the chaos of life in London and not knowing where her next meal was coming from.

Thank goodness, through Philip's cousin having a change of heart, that wasn't so now, and she and Irene were well off. But what of the future? What was wrong with Irene? *Please God it's something that can be put right.*

After a couple of days had passed, Maggie agreed to sit with the babies while Angelica went to the hospital. There'd been no news of how Irene was, and Angelica was desperate to see her.

After a ride in a cab with a chatty taxi driver, she was at last at the hospital entrance.

Going inside, she turned up her nose at the smell of carbolic and made her way along the cream-painted corridor to where she could see a reception desk.

After much questioning as to who she was, the receptionist called the ward.

It seemed Irene had been asking for her, and so Angelica was finally let through and shown to Irene's bedside.

To see her hooked up to oxygen and with a drip in her arm and looking so pale and drawn, with her eyes red from crying, tore at Angelica's heart.

Rushing to her, Angelica leaned over her and held her as best she could, kissing her forehead and stroking her hair.

'I – I'm going to die, Angelica!'

'No . . . no . . . You're just unwell. The doctors will make you better.'

'They can't. I . . . Oh, Angelica. I've something they call MND. Motor something. It'll take all me muscles and make them useless . . . I – I'll die within a year as they've no medication for it . . . I don't want to die, Angelica.'

They cried together, they held hands, and Angelica vowed to care for Irene at home.

There was no objection to this when the doctor was told that Angelica had been a nurse.

By the time Irene came home, Angelica had established a good routine. Mostly, she expressed her milk, as it was easier to feed both babies from a bottle.

Angie didn't need as much now as she was having some rusk biscuits mashed into boiled milk. Though for Mia, her last feed of the day was always at Angelica's breast.

It was a wonderful moment when Irene, brought home by an ambulance, walked in on crutches and saw Angie.

Angie's reaction was immediate. She put out her arms to her mum, giving Irene a joyful welcome.

'She knows me! Oh, Angelica, how? And she's grown so big!'

'I show her your picture every day and talk to her about her mum.'

'Ta, luv. For me baby to know me after all this time!' A tear plopped onto her cheek.

Maggie came out of the kitchen followed by Peggy. 'Now, now, no tears. This is a happy day, luv.'

They both went up to Irene and gave her a hug, then helped her to a seat.

'We've got everything worked out.'

'Yes,' Peggy said, 'and me man's making a contraption to fit onto the wheelchair that the welfare delivered the other day. It means Angelica can take you out for a walk with the babies – well, while they are little still. Though sometimes, we'll look after them while you two go and have a bit of time on your own.'

'We can go to our bench, Angelica!'

'That's the spirit, luv.'

Adjusting took time and life wasn't easy. To Angelica, watching someone she loved gradually losing everything was heartbreaking.

'Somehow . . . we got through.'

'Through what, Mama? You woke me. I'd fallen asleep.'

'Mia?'

'Yes, Mama?'

Putting her hand down, Angelica clutched Mia's arm. In doing so, reality came back to her, and fear clutched her . . . But everything was all right now, wasn't it?'

'I love you, Mama. And I loved lying with you. I'm going to do that every afternoon from now on. It helped you to rest too, and I feel refreshed.'

Fully back in the present, Angelica patted Mia's hand, 'I'd like that, *ma chérie* . . . *Et je t'aime.*'

Angelica knew that Mia would understand that she'd said, 'And I love you.'

Always she'd preferred the French way of saying the words that meant so much to her – Mia, her beloved child, was her world. And to know she was in love, and was loved by Steve, gave her peace.

Chapter Nineteen

Marcia

An Unsettling Encounter

October was a lovely month in Limousin. The heat of the summer had cooled, and the air was fresher. Feeling energized after her two weeks' lying in time following the birth of her Angelica, Marcia decided she would go to the convent. Seeing the Reverend Mother for herself would put her mind at rest as to how she was. And she'd missed being there.

To Marcia, the convent had become her home.

Memories of her real home back in Toulouse were always painful, and yet she longed to go back there one day.

As soon as she could she'd written to Madame Conté, thanking her for her part in saving her life. Once or twice a year since, she would receive a letter from Madame Conté, telling of the neighbours and how often she and her sister spoke of the child they'd saved. She once wrote:

In all the terrible things that happened during the war that we could not change or influence, we were honoured to at least have saved one of God's children. We hope you will have a happy life, Marcia, as that will be all the thanks we need.

Sometimes it seemed that none of it had happened. Everything was so normal now, so how could it have? How could one vile man haven risen up to have such power over others that they did such evil things at his bidding?

But then, she remembered Hans, the good German, and she knew there must have been many like him – doing what they could while seeming to obey orders. Afraid for their own lives and those of their families if they disobeyed.

Dear Hans, we will always remember you.

Getting her children ready for this visit to the convent hadn't been an easy task, but now the eldest three stood in line, their faces shining from her rubbing them with a soapy flannel, and their hair combed, though it was impossible to have it lie flat in the style of the day as all three boys had Irish curly hair. All, too, had their papa's lovely blue twinkling eyes.

'You all look very smart. Now, please try to keep like that for the sisters.'

Marcia smiled as she knew that even if they did, they wouldn't look smart by the time they left. They'd be plied with chocolate biscuits and allowed to play with all the other children in the playground. The rough and tumble of that, added to the chocolate traces around their mouths and on their shirts, would leave them looking like ragamuffins.

Wanting to hug them, but not having much time as the bus would be along soon, she hurried them out of the door. With her baby held close to her she followed them out, just as the bus pulled up outside her gate. 'Don't forget to pick up your flowers, boys!'

Always when they visited, the children took a flower from the garden to lay on the remembrance garden inside the convent. The sisters had made it, and in the centre was a stone with the names of all the children who had died. Dear Madeleine's name was there, as it was on a little vase engraved on a heart within two arms – her arms, as she forever held her little sister in her heart. Though she held her in her nightmares too, as the scene of Madeleine's death haunted her.

'Mama, you always look sad when we arrive at the convent.'

'Yes, Joseph. One day I will tell you why.'

'Is it because of what happened to the Jews in the war?'

This son of hers was growing fast. She nodded, unable to speak her affirmation.

'We have been learning about it at school. I told the teacher that you are a Jew, but that you wanted us to be Catholics like our father. She asked if one day you would come in and speak to the class about your experiences?'

'Maybe, only I don't want you to know, Joseph. Having the memory of it is bad for me, but burdening you with it too would be wrong.'

'I told the teacher that you would say that, Mama, and she said, "It won't be a burden; it will be a sadness." And she said that she hoped that one day you will tell me to help me to understand. You see, Mama, I don't want those things to have happened to you and to our Aunt Madeleine, our grandparents and Aunt Renée.'

For a moment, Marcia felt cross at this teacher. How could she know what was right for her children to hear about the horrors war had inflicted on her and taken from them?

Yes, she had told them of their family, what they were like, how they would have loved them, how her father was the best jeweller in Toulouse and made special pieces – beautiful bracelets, brooches, necklaces and rings for the rich. How happy they were and what a lovely neighbour they had. But nothing else, except that these aunts and their grandparents died in the war. Wasn't that enough for young children to take in?

As children will, Joseph didn't dwell, but changed the subject to his papa's family. 'Will we go to Ireland one day and meet our Irish family then, Mama?'

'Yes, we hope to, but it will cost a lot of money to do so. We barely get by as it is and but for the kindness of the sisters sending produce to us, it would be a lot harder. They cannot afford to pay Papa a good wage, and yet he loves it there. He finds peace, as your papa went through a lot too, you know.'

'Yes. I told my teacher that my papa was a member of the Resistance, and she said all like him should receive a medal.'

Joseph puffed out his chest at this, his pride visible to see.

'Always be proud of all of your family, for whatever they did, or went through. And no matter where they lived, all people suffered.'

As they neared the gates, the sight of the convent walls, as always, brought memories flashing into her mind – happy ones of the noise of the children playing in the enclosed world, feeling safe until the day when the gendarmes or the Germans began to visit as suspicion was raised about the activities of the nuns.

Then it had seemed that she and Joseph and the older children were always alert. But it had worked for a time.

Trying not to let her mind go to the horror of the day it didn't work and the Germans captured them, she ushered her children off the bus and kept her voice light. 'Hurry, children, and be good. You must not let Papa down. He is so proud of you all and loves it when I bring you to his workplace.'

They all grinned up at her. How glad she was that their life was so different to how hers had been.

But her memories, or this playfulness, didn't take what they had been talking about from her mind. Always she knew that Shane could have returned to Ireland. His regiment would have paid his passage, but he chose not to for fear of not getting back to her.

But she knew that it hurt him not to see his family and not to know if he ever would again.

Letters from them were always loving and included her and of course the children. His mother would say how much she longed to see him and her grandchildren.

Remembering this, she felt selfish for longing to see Angelica one more time. If ever they could afford to travel, it would, and must, be to Ireland.

'Can I ring the bell, Mama?'

'You rang it last time, Amos. It is my turn!'

This marked Joseph as the child that he was, as for a moment during their conversation, he had seemed much older than his almost seven years.

Marcia intervened. 'I think it is Hans's turn.'

Hans would never stick up for himself. He had a kind nature, just like the man he was named after. He looked up now and grinned.

'But he can't reach it, Mama.'

'Joseph, if ever a man struggles to do anything, don't shun him, but help him. You can lift your brother; I have seen you do so many times.'

Amos giggled. 'Hans is a man now!'

'No. Boy. Like you!'

With this indignant reply from Hans, Joseph sighed and gave in, lifting his brother. Marcia was glad to see he did it in good spirit and not grumpily. She wanted to instil many values into her children, especially her boys, for she saw it was the male species who caused heartache much more than the female.

Shane, Joseph and Hans were the role models she wanted for them.

Sister Matthew opened the gate.

Like Sister Frederica had all those years ago, Sister Matthew gave a cheerful greeting to callers to make them welcome. Though Marcia remembered that often the lovely Sister Frederica would shirk her duties as she knew Sister Angelica would cover for her. She had a lazy streak, did Sister Frederica!

'Mama, you're smiling again.'

Marcia lost the smile as quickly as it had come. Thinking of Sister Frederica had caused other memories to flood her mind, as the picture of so many faces – those of the children she'd helped to care for and were lost – came to her. Many were Joseph's age or younger. How did they all endure the fear, and the loss of their families?

For the first time, Marcia thought that maybe those who died were the lucky ones. They didn't have the agony of memories. Or the pain of never seeing their families again.

'I like your mama's smile too, Joseph! We don't ever want the sadness of yesteryear to clothe today . . . Hello, my dear Marcia. It is good to see you and the children. We have been busy baking for your visit!'

Marcia laughed. 'Now, don't you be filling the children with too many sweet things, it isn't good for them!'

'Bah humbug, as Ebenezer Scrooge would say!'

The boys giggled.

'You see, they agree! Not all that is bad for the body is bad for the soul! Our true selves love a treat.'

Marcia joined in the laughter. There was no arguing with Sister Matthew's logic. She made it up as she went along, but made it sound as though she was quoting some profound saying of someone from history!

'Well, now that's settled, you boys will find your papa in the orchard, and the school children will be out to play soon.'

'Do they have lessons on a Saturday? But that is Mama's Sabbath!'

Sister Matthew looked uncomfortable for a moment. Marcia rescued her. 'Joseph, it is that the Sabbath is something only we Jewish people keep . . . You are Catholics, but it is the one thing you and your papa make a concession of for me. Not that you are part of it, just that you accommodate it.'

Sister Matthew visibly relaxed. If she thought they were part of Marcia's religion, it wouldn't sit well with her – not that she had anything against the Jews or any other faith, it was just her keeping true to the claim of the Catholic religion that theirs was the one true faith and that brooked no argument from others.

Little did they know that the Jews thought that too. But Marcia knew that there were many people with different beliefs, and each to their own was the way, she thought.

She would have loved her children to follow their Jewish heritage, but agreed with Shane that it might blight their life as even though the Jewish people now had their own land in Israel, they were still vilified in many parts of the world. She hadn't wanted that for her little ones.

The children ran off towards the orchard, a favourite haunt of hers when she'd wanted to be alone or just to be with Joseph, her first love. Still her heart fluttered at remembering him and their devotion to one another.

Sister Matthew brought her out of this reminiscing and Marcia was glad that she did.

'Now we can all coo over the newborn! I didn't want the boys to think they weren't as important with little Angelica's arrival. And, oh, we are all thrilled you chose to honour our dear sister. How we lament her not being here with us any more, and not hearing from her for such a long time.'

'I have news, Sister Matthew. Sister Angelica's daughter has been in touch. The letter I received here was from her.'

'Her daughter! You mean, the letter that came for you . . . She has a daughter! Good gracious!'

Sister Matthew stopped in her tracks and stared wide-eyed at Marcia.

'Yes. You knew that she left here to marry, didn't you?'

'Well . . . yes, but . . .'

How closeted these sisters were. The outside world and how the folk who peopled it carried on was alien to them. It seemed that Sister Matthew at least must have imagined that Sister Angelica would remain a virgin!

A naughty thought made her giggle: *If only they knew how delicious the sins of the flesh were!*

Mary Magdalene knew and yet she gave them up for the love of Jesus. That must have been difficult to do, and though she was a prostitute, she was forgiven. And there lies the hope of all religions – in their forgiveness if they say sorry.

But many German soldiers were religious – would they be forgiven their brutality? Did they smash a Jew's face in with a rifle and then go on their knees at night and say sorry? Were they exonerated from their sin?

'You seem troubled, my dear. I know this place has bad memories for you, but we hope it has good ones too. Let the good ones win today and rejoice in bringing your new child to the sisters who love you and your children.'

She took baby Angelica and her face lit up as she gazed on the little one.

'I'm sorry, Sister, yes, I did let the bad memories win for a moment . . . But, well, this is my adored Angelica.'

'Ah, she is beautiful. Just look at her tiny fingers! God is good to create such perfection.'

Remembering the pain of helping with the birth of one of God's creations, Marcia could have taken Him to task over that part of his design – but then, she would have been told it was Eve's fault!

This exasperated her when the only sin of Eve's was to bite into an apple. She didn't mean to blight all women's lives for ever and a day.

'Come, everyone is waiting.'

When she entered the convent, all the sisters stood in the vast hall. They clapped their hands, then surged forward to surround Sister Matthew and to coo over Angelica.

Marcia was left looking up at the figure of Jesus dying in agony on the cross.

Since the war, she'd thought about his death. Her people had done that. Again, the men were the perpetrators . . . So, there was the capability of brutality in all of us. How could they nail a man to a cross after whipping him and crowning his head with thorns? How could they then mock him as he died in agony? And all because He spoke of different beliefs to them. History really does repeat itself. Why do men need others to believe the same things they do?

Women are rarely the aggressors. Look at these sisters, many of them were here twenty years ago. They didn't discriminate when Sister Angelica brought the Jewish children here. They cared for them and protected them, even allowed them to follow their own beliefs, appointing her and Joseph as their teachers, and they died for them as Sister Frederica had.

'You look deep in thought, dear Marcia.'

'Reverend Mother!' Marcia dashed towards the little woman in a wheelchair whom she loved dearly. 'It is good to see you and looking so well! Shane told me that you were "after looking fine and dandy!"'

They both laughed.

'I am feeling well too. But, Marcia, I want you to know that here, you are allowed your views and beliefs. And always have been.'

Always perceptive, the Reverend Mother must have seen she was struggling with something, but decided not to ask what it was she'd been pondering.

'I know, thank you, Reverend Mother. Did you hear that I had news of Sister Angelica?'

'Yes! How are things? I worry about Angelica. I know she is riddled with guilt.'

'You know?'

'Yes, though it is many years since I wrote to her to send papers she needed—'

'You knew where she was?'

'I did. And I made the decision not to tell you – rightly or wrongly, I believed that Angelica had a right to her privacy.'

'But she promised . . .'

'I know what she promised, dear Marcia. But we cannot always keep those promises.'

'To be in touch with her would have been enough.'

'But that was her right. She knew where I was. She sent a donation and never contacted again – not personally. But we did wonder about the letter that arrived for you from England. So it was from her?'

'It was from her daughter. But why was Sister Angelica asking for forgiveness?'

'Because of the very thing we spoke of. Guilt.'

'What did she have to be guilty of? She saved so many

Jewish children, she fell in love and followed her heart, she has a daughter, and did have a wonderful husband – remember, I nursed Philip too. I knew him as well.'

'It isn't for me to tell you of another's sin.'

'There you have it! She is considered a sinner and considers herself one. She cannot die in peace because she is riddled with your Catholic guilt . . . Oh, Reverend Mother, I am sorry, so sorry, I should not have said that.'

'Yes, you should, my dear, because it is true . . . But you said "die"? My Angelica is not dying, is she? She is but only in her forties!'

The Reverend Mother's distress brought Marcia to her knees next to her wheelchair. 'Yes. Sis . . . Angelica has cancer. Her daughter told me her mother is so full of guilt over me, and other things, but she didn't know why, and that Angelica has never been honest with her about her past. She said she knows nothing of her papa, that she cannot help her mother, who suffers delirium, to die peacefully. I gathered from that that she didn't know that Angelica had once been a nun. That it may be her leaving her vows behind her that was causing her guilt, but I could not break her mama's confidence.'

'Did she keep you a secret too?'

'Yes, though in her delirium, she called my name and asked for my forgiveness.'

'Oh, Angelica. Poor Angelica. In trying to protect others, she has tied a knot around her own soul. And thereby, you have the reason that she never came back for you. Oh, her intention was good, but when it all came down to it, if she'd kept her promise, then her daughter would have known the truth. As would be the case if she answered my letters. She must have felt such pain in leaving her vows – looked on it as a dire sin, that she had to protect her daughter from ever finding out how "bad" her mama was. But the bad was only in her own mind, not in ours, not in God's. She was released from her vows by me.'

'Reverend Mother, we must help her. I should go to her, tell her all you have told me. Tell her that is it okay to be honest with her daughter, that Mia won't think badly of her.'

'Mia?'

'Yes. Mia is her daughter's name.'

'Even in the naming of her child Angelica has given life to another.'

'How?'

'One day, I will tell you, but there is a more pressing task at hand. If the convent paid, could you go to England?'

'Go to Sister Angelica?'

'Yes, you and Shane and the children, go to England. Go to Angelica. Tell her how she should really be thinking. We have the money. Angelica's money. I have never allowed it to be used. Always I kept it in case there was something expensive we needed. We never have. The children's school fees more than cover our needs, as does the sale of produce from our gardens now that we have Shane.'

Marcia could not help blurting out, 'But if you have enough money, why have you always kept my Shane on a low wage? Sometimes, we have difficulty getting through the week.'

'Oh, my dear, I am sorry. I did not know. Sister Agnus does the accounts and Shane never complained to me. I will put that right. No wonder we always have such a good bank balance. But at the expense of you and the children, that is not right. Forgive me for being remiss in not even thinking about it.'

Marcia took the Reverend Mother's gnarled hand. 'No,

forgive me for speaking out. You are a good and kind person and I love you. I'm just so at odds with everything at the moment.'

'Postnatal blues.'

Marcia laughed. 'How do you know about such things? No one believes it is a condition anyway.'

'Well, it is. And you would be surprised just what I know about the world outside these walls. I was the eldest of thirteen children, I saw childbirth in all its raw state and have often berated God about it. And I heard the pleasure of making love and knew the wrath of my mother for a few weeks after she gave birth. I am not as innocent of happenings as you may think.'

Marcia couldn't believe this. Or how knowing it all, this lovely lady still gave up everything to serve God. Perhaps there was something in their beliefs about Jesus after all.

But above everything else she'd been told and that had been a revelation to her, the best part of it all was that she could go to be by Angelica's side.

Chapter Twenty

Mia

Revelations

Mia sat on the sofa, having a moment's quiet. The whirlwind that was Angie getting ready for work had calmed as soon as she'd kissed Mia on the cheek and left.

Mama was washed and comfortable, and Mia needed to gather herself ready for the day.

Since last week when she'd lain with her mama in the afternoon, she'd done so every day and had noticed the benefits it brought. Yes, Mama still had her moments when Mia knew she'd gone into her past life, but none of it seemed to distress her as much as it had done. Mostly it was now centred on Irene and not what had happened in France.

And Mia knew it was helping her too, as she was less tired and coped with the night hours when Mama woke her.

She smiled to herself as the afternoon Steve dropped in came to her mind. Not finding her, he'd run upstairs and found them both asleep.

It had been the brush of his lips on her cheek that had awoken her. When she'd opened her eyes, he'd been so close to her that she'd turned, and with his help had risen off the bed and landed in his arms. He had placed his lips on hers and her body moulded into his.

The moment had been as if it was part of the dream she'd been having about him.

She'd whispered her love and thrilled at hearing his for her. But then Mama had stirred, and he'd become the doctor again.

Sighing to release the feelings the memory had given her, her thoughts went to Marcia and how finding her had helped with Mama so much. *I'm so glad that I kept my promise to Mama that I would, but I wish that today would be the day that Marcia's promised letter arrives.*

No sooner had she thought this than the letter box flapped. Amid the three letters that dropped onto the welcome mat, one was a blue airmail envelope.

Jumping up, Mia ignored all the other post and grabbed this one.

Ripping it open, a flicker of disappointment assailed her as she saw that it was just a short note to her mama. She'd so hoped for explanations – to be told the full story.

But then she put that aside and was glad that she had this. It was beautiful and held all her mama needed to know.

As she went towards the stairs, the telephone ringing stopped her.

The last person she expected to be on the line said in her lovely French accent, 'Mia?'

'Marcia? How lovely. Is everything all right?'

When Marcia told her the reason for the call, Mia's heart soared.

'Oh, Marcia, I am so happy! And you say you will be here in a few days?'

'Yes. Shane has visited the travel agent's and has everything arranged. So, when we are in the hotel, we will contact you . . . Oh, Mia, I cannot wait to meet you and see Sis . . . Angelica. My dear friend.'

'And I cannot wait to hear all about how she became that and how you lost touch . . . Oh, and so much more. But mostly, I can't wait to meet you, Marcia. I feel our lives are entwined in some way.'

'They are. We are joined by your mama and her actions of great bravery. I will tell you all after I speak to her . . . I haven't asked, but we will be in time, won't we?'

'I'll pray that you will be. Mama is stable. The pain relief that Steve has given her is keeping her asleep most of the time.'

'Steve?'

'Oh, that's her doctor . . . Only, he is much more than that . . . He and I . . . Oh, Marcia, you're going to think me mad, but I want to shout it from the rooftops – he and I have fallen in love!'

'Oh, but that is wonderful news! I cannot wait to meet him. But most of all, I cannot wait to meet you, Mia, and to hold my beloved Angelica and in doing so give her peace.'

'Marcia, you keep going to call Mama something else and stopping yourself?'

'I will explain all when I speak to her, Mia, I promise. I'm sorry, but I must speak with her first.'

After they said their goodbyes Mia had mixed feelings. There was something. . . But why was it a secret? And the way that Marcia hesitated in what to call her mama . . . *It sounds as though she is going to say sister, but that cannot be. Mama cannot be Marcia's sister, can she? Or is it another name . . . Cicely? Has Mama had to change her name?* It was all such a mystery, but at last, it seemed she might know more.

* * *

Standing at the bottom of the bed, Mia looked down on her beloved mama. It was good to see her so much more peaceful now.

It was as she turned to leave that her mama said, 'Irene?'

'No, Mama, it's me, Mia.'

Mama opened her eyes.

'I have something for you, Mama. A note, from Marcia. And some exciting news.'

Mama didn't speak, but a look of hope came into her tired eyes and a smile played around her lips.

Mia pulled the bedside chair a little closer and laid the note on the bed where she could see it while she held Mama's hand. As she read the beautiful words, she heard her Mama gasp. Looking up when the short note came to an end, her heart lurched as tears flowed down Mama's face – tears of love and, yes, heartbreak.

'Mama, Marcia is coming to see you!'

'Marcia? She is . . . coming?'

'Yes. Her and her husband, Shane, and their four children.'

'Shane?' Mama's eyes opened wide; her look was one of total surprise.

'Yes, I told you about him when Marcia contacted us last time, and you said you thought she would marry Joseph. Do you know Shane?'

Mama nodded and closed her eyes. 'A brave man, an Irishman . . . He is alive!'

Mia sat quietly, hoping there would be more, but Mama fell asleep. It seemed to her that all the young people of wartime must have been very brave.

The days until Marcia arrived seemed to drag and to be lived in fear as it appeared that Mama was giving up. As if the news of at last seeing Marcia had been enough – a sort of confirmation that she was forgiven for whatever it was she had done. But at last, they were due to arrive today.

Mia looked around the array of foods she'd laid out. Not having a table big enough to sit everyone down for a meal, she'd decided to do what was called a finger buffet. There'd been one at a wedding she'd attended, and she'd really enjoyed it.

Everything looked lovely. Tiny sausage rolls, pork pies cut into slices, a plate of various sandwiches, and some French things that Steve had found in a specialist shop – a soft cheese called Brie, and a bowl of olives.

Father Benedict, who visited regularly, had told her about these and how they were a favourite with crusty bread. Mia hoped the French sticks that Steve had also bought were what they would like.

She'd asked Steve to come along as he wasn't working, but he hadn't thought it wise to be there at the beginning of the afternoon, telling her, 'Too many people will overwhelm Marcia, darling. You and Angie meet her on your own and have your chat. You only need pick the telephone up and I will come when you're all acquainted and, hopefully, know all you need to know.'

But oh, she wished he was here.

'Aunty Angelica is all propped up on a mound of pillows, Mia. I've done her hair and she looks lovely. When are you going to tell her that today is the day?'

'I'd better do it now. But I'm anxious about doing so, Angie. About the effect it will have on her. What if it's too much for her?'

'I understand, love, but she has to know, and will need time to absorb it . . . Come here. I can feel your tension.'

Once Mia was wrapped in Angie's hug, Angie told her, 'It will be all right. Marcia and your mama love one another. Your mama knows that she is forgiven for what seems a promise broken and not a dire sin as we have imagined.'

'You're right.'

'You know, we never did look for that box. We should have done. It could hold some of the answers you seek.'

'Mama hasn't mentioned it since, so I thought it must have been something she dreamed of. I mean, we know every nook and cranny of this house, we'd have seen it before now.'

'But that creaky floorboard – remember? I bet it's there! It's a great hiding place and one we wouldn't have found by chance.'

'Yes. I've often thought about it. I even looked for something to pry it up once. But then . . .'

'Your attention was taken with falling in love. A date with Steve and then waiting for the next one!'

Mia giggled as she came out of Angie's arms. 'You can hardly call them dates! Sitting in here chatting or watching the television.'

'Oh, yes, and what else after I've gone to bed, eh?'

They both giggled now.

'Anyway. I told you that you can go out together, but you haven't. You need to sort that; everyone needs fun together.'

'It's only been three weeks, and besides, Steve has been on call. He gives this number to his secretary to ring if there's a callout, so we have had to stay in.'

'Well, you know now that Lilly can cope, so as soon as Steve has an evening off, let's arrange something. I want to draw Freddie into the family. He's been working away in the Midlands, reporting on a murder case, but that's come to an end. And guess what? He has realized with being away from me how much he loves me! It's been so wonderful.'

'I thought there was something different about you. I'm so pleased, Angie. See if you can get him to come here one day.'

'I'd rather we all went out together. There's a new Chinese restaurant, it's lovely. Things are so much more relaxed over a meal and a bottle of wine. Asking a boy home is like asking him to marry you.'

'Ha, well, you may have to be the one to do that with Freddie, love. He's that slow on the uptake! Right, I'd better go up to see Mama.'

Mia couldn't believe how lovely her mama looked. Angie had gone to so much trouble. Somehow, Mama didn't mind her doing things for her. She supposed it was because Angie was stronger and could help Mama to move more easily.

'Mama? Are you awake?'

Mama's eyes opened.

'You look lovey in that pink bed jacket, Mama.'

A little smile from her mama warmed her heart. 'Angie said . . . special day.'

'Oh, yes, it is.'

Holding her mama's hand in hers, Mia bent over and kissed her. 'You remember I told you Marcia was coming? Well, today is the day, and very soon.'

Mama looked up into Mia's eyes. 'Marcia? My Marcia?'

'Yes.'

'Madeleine?'

Mama had rarely said this name, but when she had it had always been associated with Marcia.

'I don't know, Mama. No Madeleine has been mentioned by Marcia.'

Mama nodded, then closed her eyes. Hearing that Marcia was coming hadn't upset her. She looked calm and had a little smile on her face.

As she went to go out of the room, Mia noticed Mama's breakfast tray was still on the dressing table. Angie must have forgotten it.

When she picked it up, it surprised her to see that the bowl of Complan – a type of food that was meant to be drunk, but they fed to Mama on a spoon – was almost empty. This hadn't happened for a long time as Mama hated it and nearly always clamped her mouth together so they couldn't feed her.

A feeling of hope came into Mia. Maybe, with her mind a lot more settled, they would have her for longer.

An idea came to her then – one that had been impossible with Mama being so weak. Maybe, just maybe, they could get her downstairs sometimes.

Full of hope, Mia told her mama she would be back soon and almost skipped down the stairs.

There was no time to discuss her idea with Angie as the sound of a car pulling up and a knock on the door hailed Marcia arriving.

Mia caught her breath. Then with an attack of nerves she stood staring at the door.

'Mia . . . Mia, open the door. It won't be much of a welcome for them to stand in the street! And if I do it, they will be all confused thinking I am you!'

With this, Mia rushed forward. When she opened the door, she was met with the sight of a beautiful, elegant lady and a gentleman holding a tiny bundle. At their knees were three adorable little boys.

'Marcia!'

'Yes, it is me! Oh, Mia, it is lovely to meet you. This is Shane.'

'Hello, Shane. Please come inside, all of you. It's so good that you're here.'

'Hello to yourself, and it is for being a good day for us too.'

Mia loved Shane's Irish lilt and she grinned up at him, feeling she'd known him all her life.

When introductions were done, Angie asked if she could get them a drink. They had coffee, tea, juice and even a glass of wine to offer.

With this sorted and Marcia perched on the edge of the sofa with Shane by her side, there was a moment of silence.

The child introduced as Joseph asked in French if Mama was glad to be here.

Marcia coloured. 'Hush. Of course we are.'

Angie saved the day. In French, she told Joseph, 'It's overwhelming, as it is a happy and yet sad occasion. Which of you boys likes football?'

The little one, who they knew to be Hans, chirped up that he did, but that the other two were better at it than he was.

'Well, we'll see about that when I'm on your team. Come on, we have a park just down the road and I have a football. I'll take all three of you there and we can have a game. We have two teams, me and Hans against you two. We can decide what we are to be called when we get there.'

Joseph looked at his mama, his face showing an eager expression as he lifted his eyebrows.

'Yes, off you go. And have fun.'

'Sure I'll be putting a bet on the winner.'

'Oh, Papa!'

The one introduced as Amos giggled as he uttered this exasperated comment.

Shane looked all innocent. 'What?'

Everyone laughed and the tension eased.

Once the door closed on the footballers, Shane asked, 'Is Angelica up for seeing us then? Is it well that she is today?'

'Oh, she is! Better than she has been for a long time. I'll take you up.'

'So, it is bedridden she is?'

'Yes. We have a kindly lady who was a nurse come in and she manages to get Mama out onto her chair by her bed, though that hasn't happened for a while as Mama has been too weak.'

'Ah, God love her. She's for being no age. Only a year older than meself.'

Mia nodded. Life was so unfair. Swallowing hard, she said, 'I'll go in first.'

Opening the door, she found Mama with her head to one side and her eyes closed. 'Mama. Mama, Marcia and Shane are here.'

Mama opened her eyes. She saw Marcia and smiled, and then looked towards Shane and just said, 'Shane . . . What . . . ?'

Marcia rushed forward, then gently took Mama in her arms. Both cried with a mixture of joy and sadness. But then sadness won, and Marcia sobbed.

'Now, me little darlin', this is too much for Angelica to be taking. Calm yourself, for her sake.'

Marcia took the handkerchief Shane offered her.

'I'm sorry, so sorry, forgive me . . . I never thought this day would come.'

'No. I didn't either . . . Oh, Marcia . . . I am sorry.'

'*Non*, you must not be! Life happened for us both. All I hoped for you was that you were happy with your Philip.'

'I had him for such a short time.'

To Mia, it was like a miracle. Mama talking was as if she was strong again and fully aware of everything, but then her past had come to her.

It was so lovely to hear Marcia say, 'Many things have happened, Angelica, but love has bound us all these years.'

'It has. I never forgot you . . . but so much . . . so many things I kept inside. I – I was ashamed . . . so ashamed.'

'May I speak in front of Mia? Only she tells me that she knows nothing of your or her own history.'

Mama looked over at Mia then. 'I am sorry, *ma chérie*. Forgive me.'

Going to her side and standing next to Marcia, Mia told her mama, 'Whatever happened to you, I know you are blameless. Whatever decisions you took, they were yours. You are the most wonderful mama, but secrets are gnawing away at you and me. I won't ever feel ashamed of you, not for anything you've ever done. I love you, Mama.'

'She never was for doing anything wrong, Mia. She was a very courageous young lady.'

'May we tell Mia what you did, Angelica?'

'I – I will tell her who . . . I was first . . . Mia, when I met Marcia, I was a nun . . .'

Mia gasped. But then it all began to fit into place.

Between them they told of how Mama had saved fifty Jewish children. Of how Marcia and her sister Madeleine were among them. There was a moment of tears as Marcia told Mama that her sister had died. To Mia, there was more to it than them saying that Madeleine had become ill as she caught a look that passed between Marcia and Shane. But the moment passed as Shane told Mia of her father, how they'd worked with the Resistance together and how courageous he'd been even after he was injured.

Mia had mixed emotions as her parents' remarkable story unfolded, making all the jigsaw pieces of Mama's life and Mia's history fall into place.

Mama put the final piece in for her as she told of how Papa had died soon after he came home from hospital.

'I – I found myself alone . . . expecting a child and abandoned.'

Mia's tears flowed silently, but Marcia gasped. 'Oh, Angelica, my lovely Angelica.'

To Mia, Marcia's sobs were deeper than those of someone lamenting a dear friend's misfortune and she wondered what had really happened to Marcia after Mama left the convent.

Their saying that everyone was all right after the war ended didn't ring true. But if there were things they wanted to keep from Mama, then Mia wasn't going to press them to tell.

She thought about Joseph. From what she knew, he had been Marcia's first love. How sad that he didn't make it through the war years. And how well Mama had taken hearing of his capture as after a tear for him, she'd smiled up at Marcia. 'He would be happy to see us together now, and to see how well Shane is taking care of you, dearest Marcia.'

Looking at her mama, Mia could see that the revelations, and her telling her own truths, had fully released her guilt. She looked happy – truly happy – for the first time in a long time.

Shane lightened the moment. 'And it is that I can tell you, Angelica, Marcia is a handful at times. She has the same headstrong ways you taught her, so she has. And now it is that she has another female in the house with our own wee Angelica. Sure, me and the boys will have a life of it!'

They all laughed, even Mama, a sound Mia hadn't heard in a long time but which warmed her heart. It was so lovely to see how keeping her promise to Mama had been the best thing she'd ever done. Marcia was breathing life back into her.

Chapter Twenty-One

Mia

The Easing of Pain

Kissing Angelica on the cheek once the laughing had died down, Marcia told her, 'Rest now and we will come up to see you in a little while.'

Mia could see that Marcia's heart was breaking. Although she knew Angelica was very ill, it must have been a shock to be faced with the reality of her friend's illness. She must have imagined the Angelica of her youth would be waiting to greet her.

As she stood straight, Marcia looked at Mia, giving her the feeling that she saw and understood the inner turmoil Mia was going through.

I've learned such a lot today and most has been a shock to me.

Once downstairs, Marcia broached the subject. 'Mia, how are you feeling?'

'I'm shocked, saddened, but most of all, glad that I know now.'

'It is good that you feel better for knowing.'

'But, Marcia, it has been torture not knowing, so promise me that when your children grow up, you'll tell them about your life.'

'I am writing everything down. You see, I suffer flashbacks and it helps me to record it all, it gets it out of my head.'

'That's good. I write too, and that helps me, but mine is a novel. I was in journalism, and so this project keeps that part of my brain active.'

'A reporter?'

'Yes – learning to be. Angie is too and is now much higher than I ever got.'

'Then one day you must write about the Holocaust. We must not let the world forget.'

'Marcia, I feel that you didn't tell Mama everything.'

'There are many things that I couldn't, but you have been through enough already today. I will tell you, one day. Now, I just want to hug you. To thank you for finding me and to ask you to keep me in your life as if I am your big sister.'

The hug was a lovely sisterly hug, and Mia felt that a strong bond was forming between them. One that she welcomed as she felt a deep affection for this woman who had shared so much of her mama's life.

As they came out of the hug, the door opened, and Angie was back with the boys. They ran at their mama.

'*Mes enfants*, you smell of lovely fresh air and you have rosy cheeks.'

Mia saw that Amos and Hans had signs of having had a treat around their mouth.

'We had such a good time, Mama.'

This from Joseph was followed by a breathless Hans saying, 'Yes, and we heard bells and then—'

Amos jumped in. 'Then a big van came all painted with bright colours and the driver sold ice cream!'

'And Angie was after buying you one each! The story is on your faces, so it is.'

They all looked mystified at Shane, until Marcia bent down and wet her hankie with her spit and wiped them clean. Then they grinned, though Joseph backed off. 'I can do it myself, Mama!'

'Ah, you are growing up fast, Joseph.'

Mia saw that though Marcia smiled at him, the smile didn't really come from her heart. But then, after all they'd spoken of today, that wasn't surprising.

Baby Angelica suddenly crying out changed things as Shane said, 'Oh dear. It's all this talk of ice creams, it's making little Angelica hungry, so it is.'

They all laughed then as the boys said they were too.

'Well, we've a feast laid out for you. It's in the kitchen. We've only to take the covers off and then we can tuck in.'

'Before that, Angie, can I be taking the boys to the bathroom?'

'Yes, of course, this way.'

Mia turned to Marcia. 'Now, where will you be most comfortable to sit to feed Angelica? Would you like to go to mine and Angie's bedroom to be private?'

'*Non, non, ma chérie*, we French do not have the – how do you say? – embarrassments?'

'Inhibitions.'

'*Oui*, that is the word. I feed my baby wherever I am.'

With this, Marcia opened her blouse, got her breast out and put baby Angelica to it as if it was the most natural thing to do no matter where she was.

And suddenly, it was. When Mia would normally have died rather than do such a thing, she now thought, *Why? It is a natural act and shouldn't be hidden away.*

'I'll go and see to things in the kitchen, and leave you two in peace . . . Only, well, would you mind if I rang Steve to see if he is free to join us? I mean . . . well, if that would be too much for this first visit, it doesn't matter.'

'Oh, I would love to meet him. I can see that he makes you very happy. And that makes me like him already.'

Mia grinned as she went to the telephone and picked the receiver up. Steve answered immediately. 'That was quick!'

'Ha, I was waiting for your call. I've paced the carpet till it's nearly worn out, worrying how it was all going, darling.'

'Ha, you needn't have done. It's wonderful . . . Well, there have been moments, of course, but Marcia and Shane and the children are lovely. It's as if they are my long-lost family.'

'That's so good to hear, my darling. And your mama?'

'It has been a lot for her, so I would like it if you could have your doctor self on first and make sure Mama is all right.'

'Be there in about ten minutes.'

It seemed just a flash in time before he was, as the boys came down and took all the attention. They fussed over baby Angelica, not at all fazed by seeing their mama feeding her. But they then declared they were too hungry to wait any longer for their food, which had kept Mia and Angie busy.

When Steve arrived and introductions were over, she was glad to see how natural he and Marcia and Shane were together. It was as if everyone had known each other for years.

When Mia could get a word in, she said, 'I'll take you up to Mama, Steve, and then we can eat and relax and do all the talking we want.'

She caught hold of his hand as she said this and was glad to have that contact. She'd been too shy to make a big fuss of him when he arrived and apprehensive, too, of how everyone would get on together, but she needn't have worried.

Mama lay with her eyes open, and yet it was as if she wasn't here. She didn't acknowledge them coming in.

'Hello, Angelica. How are you today?'

It was a relief to Mia to see her mama respond immediately to Steve.

'I – I'm . . . well, up and down.'

Steve smiled at Mia. She knew he was pleased to see this change in Mama. To have her answer his question was something he wasn't used to.

'I wanted . . . to say . . . *merci*.'

Steve understood and said, 'You don't have to thank me. It is what I do, try to help sick people.'

'*Non* . . . for Mia . . .'

'Oh . . . I . . . Well, actually, I need to thank you for having such a beautiful daughter, who, I cannot believe, has fallen in love with me! Loving her is easy and I will for the rest of my days, I promise.'

'Will . . . will you marry her soon? I – I want to be here.'

The tears in Steve's eyes matched Mia's as she uttered, 'Oh, Mama . . .'

But then, Steve surprised Mia as he went down on one knee and took her hand.

'Mia, my darling. I have been given permission by your mama to ask your for hand in marriage. Will you marry me?'

'I will . . . Oh, Steve, my darling, I will.'

Mama gave them both a surprise then as she clapped her hands. Mia kissed Steve, and then went to her mama and hugged her. Feeling her mama's arms strong as they enclosed her lifted her heart even more when she hadn't thought it possible.

Then it was Steve's turn to hug Mama.

And Mia thought how much she wished she had a camera to capture this moment, but she would forever lock it in her heart.

As he came out of the cuddle, Steve tapped Mama's back gently and said, 'Well, future mother-in-law, I have to be your doctor for a moment and check that all this excitement hasn't harmed you in any way.'

Mama just gave him one of her beautiful smiles.

When he'd done his checks, Steve said, 'You're as fit as a fiddle!'

Mama giggled, and then once more she surprised them as she asked, 'Can . . . can I come down?' Looking at Mia, she said, '*Ma chérie*, I – I have little time . . .'

Having to swallow the lump in her throat, Mia looked at Steve. 'Could she? Shane and you could carry her . . . It would be so wonderful. I could get the sofa ready for her.'

Steve raised his eyebrows and held his lips between his forefinger and thumb for a moment, and then said, 'Well, why not. We'll go and arrange it, Angelica. Be back soon.'

Once on the landing, Steve pulled Mia to him. His eyes bore into hers. 'I need to say something, my darling. I must make you understand that when a person is very sick, they often rally quite well before . . . well, before the end.'

'But . . .'

'I know. I want you to enjoy having your mama back almost as she was, but I want you to be aware too.'

'Oh, Steve . . .'

'I'm sorry, my love, but now that you know, make the

most of this time. Grab all the memories you can from it, and let's make it the best time that we can for your mama. She wants to see you married. Let's try to do that for her . . . that's if you really want to?'

'I do . . . I do. I want nothing more than that . . . But do we have time? If we post the banns tomorrow, it will be three weeks before we can walk down the aisle.'

'Maybe we can have a mock wedding – I don't know. I'll speak to my solicitor friend tomorrow and find out what the options are . . . Oh, Mia, I love you so much.'

With this, he kissed her gently on the lips. She knew he was holding back as the feelings that were taking them both were difficult to deny.

As soon as they entered the living room and told everyone about Mama wanting to come down, Shane willingly offered his help. 'But how is it that we can do it?'

'There is a method that you may have been taught in the army, Shane, and that is to make a kind of stretcher out of a sheet or blanket.'

'Yes, I know how you mean. It is that we carried your pappy like that, Mia, when we moved him to the truck and then into the convent.'

Mia nodded, but then an overwhelming urge took her. 'Shane, one day will you tell me more about my papa? You must have got to know him well.'

'I can sum him up for you now – handsome, great sense of humour, a leader, but he was for being kind and considerate with it, and likeable. Aye, very likeable. But I will be for telling you specific tales at another time, as it is I have had that look from Marcia not to be taking the stage when it is eager she is to have Angelica down here with her!'

They all laughed, but for Mia, there was a sense of relief, knowing that at last she would learn more about her papa. Shane had memories to tell her. He had spent time with him and got to know him as a person.

Once Mama was down the stairs and snuggled onto Mia's and Angie's eiderdowns that had been laid on the sofa to cushion her, and with a blanket over her and soft pillows to prop her up, she opened her arms and said, '*Bébé?*'

Marcia went to her. 'Angelica, here is your namesake. I will help you to hold her.'

To see Mama gently holding the sleeping baby moved Mia to tears. It was such a beautiful sight, and yet one she knew could never happen with her own child, Mama's grandchild.

Steve's arm came around her and steadied her, and this gave her the courage to cover up her sadness by saying, 'It's just so wonderful to see you downstairs, Mama. It has all overwhelmed me.'

Mama looked up. Her eyes were full of tears too, but she just said, 'I understand . . . I felt it . . . I am thinking . . . the same way . . . but I – I . . .'

Mia rushed to her side and knelt beside her. Slipping her arm around Mama, she said, 'Baby Angelica is beautiful, Mama.'

Mama smiled a tearful smile. 'She is . . . so beautiful.'

The moment passed, Baby Angelica was given to Shane to hold, and tea was served.

By the time this was done, Mama had fallen asleep, and soon after Marcia announced that they would have to go shortly so she suggested that Shane help to get Angelica back to bed.

But Mama looked so cosy and peaceful that Mia said, 'No, leave her. I'll stay down with her tonight. And now I know how it is done, a couple of the neighbours will help me take her upstairs in the morning.'

No one objected. Just looking at Mama snuggled so comfortably and completely resting told them it was the right thing to do.

Saying goodbye was more difficult than Mia had expected. After kissing Mama, Marcia held her close. 'Please come to see me one day. Come to where it all began for your mama, as she was taken to the convent as a very young child.'

'Oh, so after she was orphaned, she was taken to the same convent where she became a nun?'

'Yes. It is as if she drifted into it, when you remember that. But always, she was the sweetest, kindest and the most courageous person.'

'That, I know . . .'

'Me too.' Angie had joined them. 'Aunty Angelica isn't my real aunt – no relation – but she has cared for me all my life.'

For Mia, this brought to the fore the thought she'd had many times – how did Mama cope financially? Where did the money she drew from the bank come from? It was one more mystery for her to solve. But for now, she wanted to hug Marcia again once she'd finished hugging Angie.

As she did, she said, 'I promise to come over to France. I so want to see where Mama grew up and to meet the Reverend Mother, as from all you have told me, Marcia, I know I will love her.'

'You will. She has been through so much pain. She has looked death in the face, and come through it all . . . Oh,

Mia, there is so much to tell you, but I will keep it until you come, as now I know you are a young woman of your word. You promised to find me for your mama, and you did, so I know you will keep your promise to me too.'

After all the goodbyes were said, Marcia went back to gaze down on Mama as she slept. '*Sœur Angélique, va te reposer sachant que je t'aimerai pour toujours.*'

Mia's tears spilled over once more at hearing Marcia calling her mama Sister Angelica and saying: 'Go to your rest knowing I will always love you.' To Marcia, she supposed, Mama would always be 'Sister Angelica', the nun who saved her life.

Chapter Twenty-Two

Angelica

A Peaceful Passing

Already it was May 1945 and Irene had lived months longer than had been forecast.

Angelica sighed. If only there was a cure, as every day of that time Irene had lost more of her abilities. Even her speech was sometimes difficult to understand, and she had lost her mobility, only just managing to use her hands.

Their doctor was amazed at this and said that he wouldn't have expected her to be alive, let alone have any movement. But then, he admitted so little was known about the disease and though he was reading any new paper on it, there still wasn't much progress.

Angelica was just thankful for every second she had her precious friend with her and chatted away to her as she sat in her wheelchair.

Their front room looked so different now, with the sofa gone and replaced by Irene's bed, leaving just enough room for her wheelchair and an armchair for herself.

Under the window stood the playpen, a blessing to Angelica as she could keep the little ones in one place, they could see them both, and they played happily with rag dolls, a few wooden bricks and a train set.

Angie was approaching two and Mia was now fifteen months. Both were bright, sunny natured and adored each other.

A knock on the door interrupted her thoughts . . .

Peggy popped her head around the door. She'd come to look after the children while Angelica took Irene out for some fresh air.

'Morning, luv. So, how far are yer with getting Irene ready then?'

'She's ready. I even managed to get her from her bed to her chair by sliding her and Irene holding on to the arm of it.'

'Well, that's good, luv, but be careful. Yer have to think of not injuring yourself, or where would yer be? . . . Anyway, are yer excited about Churchill's speech later? Me and my Alf cannot wait!'

'Oh, I am, though my best moment was when my beloved France was liberated last August.'

'Yes, it seemed to mark the beginning of the end, but today, luv, we will know that apart from Japan's antics, the war will be no more. They say that crowds are gathering outside Buckingham Palace. But me and Maggie thought we could do something in the street.'

'What are you thinking of?' Angelica was mystified. She hadn't ever heard of anything like this before.

'A party, like they did after the First World War. Don't they do anything like that in France?'

'No, not in the street. I mean, maybe, but I . . .'

Irene tried to join in then, by saying, 'Ah 'ave.'

'Oh, Irene, you never told me about them. So, what do we do, Peggy?'

'Well, while you take Irene for a walk, me and Maggie, with the help of the menfolk, will pinch your furniture – anything that people can sit on or eat off. Maggie's gone into the market – she's heard that there's a stall selling bunting and Union Jack tablecloths. We're a bit late organizing it, but we'll do what we can. But we need everyone in the street to contribute what they can – sandwiches, cakes, tea, milk, sugar, and the local pub's staying open so the men can nip in and get a pint and the women a glass of sherry. Then we'll take it from there . . . Oh, I knew there was something – can we borrow your gramophone, luv? You're the only one in the street with one, and you've some good records, too.'

'Yes, I bought it for Irene. She loves listening to music.'

'Beats us how you two do it. Yer never short of a bob or two and yet we only know about Irene's widow's pension.'

Thinking she owed Peggy and Maggie some explanation, she told Peggy, 'I have an allowance from my husband's estate.' *How easily I keep up this lie of having been married.* 'And initially, I got a lump sum which enabled me to buy this house.'

'Well, you've always been generous to us, luv, and we're grateful to you for that, and glad yer stayed around here with Irene . . . Now, let's get you on your way.'

Manoeuvring the wheelchair, Peggy said, 'I don't know how yer do it, luv. Look at Irene, bless her heart. All clean and shining. Yer a miracle worker.'

Angelica didn't think so, she was just glad for all the nursing techniques she'd learned at the convent. Though none of them were foolproof as her back burned with the ache that had begun in the night.

She'd rolled Irene over to retrieve her wet sheet and the thick layer of newspaper she used to try to protect the mattress when Irene nearly rolled off the other side. Grabbing her and hauling her back to safety had ricked Angelica's muscles.

With Irene safely in the wheelchair, Peggy said, 'I would take her down to Mile End to Regent's Canal. I was down there yesterday, and the embankment is a carpet of buttercups and daisies. It looked lovely.'

'Perhaps I will another day but we're both tired. It's been a bad night with several changes of sheets. I've one lot on the line and was going to do another when we get back, but it sounds like there's more exciting things to do.'

'There is.' They were lifting the wheelchair down the step when she said, 'So, what can you give towards the party, Angelica? I know it's short notice, and yer don't get much time, but anything would do.'

'I have ingredients, but I don't know if I have time to bake.'

'Leave that to me. We've plenty of women who bake and have time to but haven't got the ingredients, or the money. So, can I raid your cupboards while you're gone?'

'Oh, Peggy, you can. Sometimes I just don't know what we would do without you and Maggie.'

'You'll never know that, me darling. Now, off yer go while the toddlers are happily playing.'

Angelica hadn't gone far when she stopped and wiped her brow before peeling off her cardigan. She'd never said, but the pushing of the wheelchair had always been difficult for her, and today with her having this pain, it was more so. Never had she been happier to see their bench than she was now.

'Oh, look, there's loads of buttercups and daisies here too! Don't they look lovely?'

When she sat down Angelica was facing the wheelchair that she'd pushed up to the bench.

Bending down and picking a buttercup, Angelica put it into Irene's hand. What passed for a smile, a kind of grimace but with twinkling eyes, formed on Irene's face. It brought a tear to Angelica's eyes.

'Remember when we first met, Irene? It seems a million years ago and as if we have been friends for ever.'

'Yesh.' Irene tapped her heart.

'And I love you, my darling.'

'A – Ang . . . ?'

'Angie?'

'Yesh. Look af . . .'

Realizing that Irene was asking her to look after Angie tore at Angelica's heart. Was Irene thinking that her time was near?

'Always, Irene. Angie will be with me for as long as I live. I'll bring her and Mia up as sisters.'

Irene managed to nod her head, but as she did so a tear fell from her eye, followed by more. Her body heaved.

Angelica's tears matched hers, as she stood and took Irene into her arms. She had no words. No denial that Irene wouldn't die. No power to stop such a thing happening. And she knew it would be devastating when it did.

Their hug went on for a few moments. Often they did this and it helped them both. Sometimes Angelica would get onto her bed with her and fall asleep with her arm around her.

'I love you, Irene.'

'Ta . . . ta from . . .' Again, Irene placed her hand on her heart and although the word wasn't formed right, it, and the gesture, told Angelica what Irene meant.

Angelica put her head on Irene's for a few minutes before she sat back on the bench.

Irene gave a sound like a giggle.

Angelica couldn't help giggling too, as one emotion took over from the other.

'We're a pair of softies. We've done everything on this bench – planned, laughed and cried. They should name it after us.'

Again, that giggle.

Feeling better, Angelica told her, 'But for now, we still have one another, and a party to go to! Let's go to the market and see what we can buy for it.'

Irene's face brightened. The one place she loved as much as their bench was the market.

When they got there, the stallholders all called out to them and Angelica could see this lifted Irene, as her smile – the special one she had – seemed permanently on her lips.

Everywhere there was a carnival atmosphere, as even stallholders who only sold vegetables had bunting for sale. Angelica thought they must have all been stockpiling for this very day.

By the time they left, Irene's wheelchair had a bag of bunting and one of streamers hanging on the handles and on her knee sat two boxes containing large homemade fruit cakes. Another purchase – two boxes of fizzy drinks – were going to be dropped off by the stallholder later.

When they got back to the street it was a hive of activity. Men were up ladders and hanging out of windows as they fixed bunting and women were spreading tablecloths.

Catching sight of Maggie, Angelica pushed the wheelchair

over to her. 'I have these to contribute, Maggie, and some drinks coming later.'

'Ooh, more bunting. Ta, love. I didn't get much; they were asking such a price for it. Now we'll be able to rival any street round here. Hope you had a good walk. Peggy's with the girls. So, I'm glad you're back as I could do with her here. I've left cakes in the oven and can't get back to them.'

'I'll send her to you. See you later.'

Angelica had only been inside for a few minutes having said her thanks to Peggy, who then rushed out of the door, when her world was splintered by a crescendo of noise. A blast shook her house, taking all reasoning from her and leaving her with a ringing in her ears.

Shocked, she stood still and stared at Irene.

Angie and Mia's terrified screams brought Angelica out of the stupor she'd gone into.

Rushing to the door, the scene that met her resembled the pictures she'd seen of the Blitz.

Maggie's house was no more.

In the confusion of neighbours' shocked voices, two names were yelled over and over.

'Maggie! Peggy!'

Angelica's heart sank as she rushed forward to help those on the ground. 'What happened? Please, please tell me they weren't in there!'

A dazed little boy nodded. 'They went in to get the cakes.' His glazed eyes stared out of his head. Blood ran down his face.

'Run to the shop around the corner. They have a telephone, and ask for police, ambulance and fire engine.'

As he turned and sped away, Angelica looked at the carnage around her. Neighbours she loved lay on the ground, bloodied and crying out with pain.

Some of the women were huddled in a group. 'Fetch hot water, blankets and rags, and if you have any ointment, bring that too. Hurry!'

The sound of distant bells brought some relief to her, but the shock that had kept her strong began to peel away when she knew responsibility for everyone would be taken from her.

Before they arrived, she had covered the injured to keep them warm, and had bowls of hot water at the ready for the treatment of minor wounds.

Looking around her, Angelica saw a scene of devastation framed by brightly coloured bunting, proudly showing the colours of red, white and blue, the patriotic symbol that had kept these brave people going through a terrible war, and was now meant to mark their celebration of its end.

Tears ran freely down her face. She turned and went back inside her own home to find Irene still staring, her body trembling, and the two little ones – resilient as children can be – asleep in their playpen.

'Oh, Irene, *ma chérie*. We've lost our friends, our dear friends.' Sinking to her knees, she lay her head on Irene's lap and sobbed her heart out.

Irene's hand flopped heavily onto her head. Angelica knew that she was trying to give comfort in the best way she could and was seeking it too.

Angelica clung to her. 'It must have been a gas explosion. For weeks now everyone has been saying they could smell gas, but no one did anything about it – not even me! Oh, Peggy and Maggie!'

Irene's fingers drummed on her back. Lifting her head, she could see that Irene looked mystified.

'It was Maggie's house – they were inside. Maggie had cakes in the oven and they went in to get them for . . . Oh, Irene, all they wanted to do was to celebrate the end of the war.'

It had taken weeks for the street to get back to something like normal after the funerals had taken place of the two much-loved women, with throngs of mourners following – a time in which everyone had been kind to Angelica and helped her as much as they could, but one that had seen much deterioration in Irene's condition.

Angelica, worn out and almost at the end of her tether, smiled at her adored Mia and Angie as they happily responded to the antics of Josie, a fifteen-year-old who often baby sat them on a Saturday since they'd lost Peggy and Maggie.

She was a tonic and loved the children.

Brought up in the street, she'd always been a cheerful, outgoing child, and ever willing to help.

Giving Angelica a hand to get the wheelchair down the step, she said, 'Don't worry, enjoy your walk.' Then she kissed Irene. 'I know you'll be going to your favourite bench, Aunty Irene.'

Angelica had always found it strange how children of Britain called older women aunty even if not related, but she liked this tradition and it warmed her heart as this grown-up young girl waved her off and said, 'Take all the time yer need, Aunty Angelica.'

When they reached the bench, Angelica gratefully sank down on it. As she'd taken to doing, she bent and picked a buttercup and put it under Irene's unresponsive hand.

She thought that Irene might not be able to see any longer, or at least not far, so she bent towards her till her face was close. 'I wish I could make you better, *ma chérie* . . . I can't do that, but I can make you a daisy chain necklace.'

Laughing a laugh that didn't touch her sad heart, Angelica gathered daisies and entwined their stalks to make a circle. Irene had taught her how to do this on one of their visits to the bench.

Placing the finished article around Irene's neck, she told her, 'There, you look beautiful, Irene.'

Gently hugging her, she told her, 'Everything will be all right. We'll get through. I know it's harder since we lost Peggy and Maggie, but we're managing. We have each other.'

As she leaned forward Irene looked intently into her eyes, before her head dropped forward.

Angelica gasped as pain sliced her heart. She knew that here, where they most loved to be in all the world, Irene had left her.

Clinging on to Irene's slumped body, Angelica sobbed, and yet she was grateful that her friend had had such a peaceful and, yes, almost beautiful passing, even though it felt that her own life had been cut in half. Now, somehow, she had to find the strength to carry on. To give her little Mia and Angie a good life, and to do as she promised – to bring them up as sisters.

'As the weeks went by, it helped, it really helped me to have my two little girls.'

'Mama, Mama, don't cry.'

Opening her eyes and looking into Mia's kind and concerned ones was disorientating for a moment, but then the pain of the present stabbed at her and she let out a moan.

'Are you in pain, Angelica?'

She knew that voice. It was Steve, the lovely doctor who was going to love and care for Mia. Then Angie, lovely, funny Angie, spoke. 'She's just trying to get out of the washing-up, aren't you, Aunty?'

They all laughed, and Angelica could feel a smile on her own face as the heartbreak of yesteryear left her and she knew the love of today.

Soon, her Mia was to be married. And nothing was going to stop her from being there.

Chapter Twenty-Three

Mia

The Happiest of Days

'Angie, if you've looked out of that window once, you've done it a million times. Freddie will be here when he is!'

'I know, but I can't wait . . . Oh, Mia, he's never been here before. Do you think he'll like it?'

'Of course he will. It'll be heaven to him after a city flat!'

'I know, but his real home is so lovely. Right on the bank of a beautiful lake, in the Lake District. I've seen photos, and it's stunning – huge and, well, expensive-looking.'

'Look, he's used to London and its tenement blocks and rows of terraced houses. And Freddie is Freddie, he's not a snob.'

Angie didn't answer this but just said, 'Lilly's coming. She's just turned into the street. Oh, and so has Steve's car. But where is Freddie?'

'I've never seen you this nervous, Angie. Why don't you busy yourself? Pop up and check on Mama. Make sure she's all right . . . You know, I liked it when she was down here with us. Maybe with Freddie here as well as Steve, we could do that sometimes.'

'I don't know, it's taken ages to get Freddie to come here.

For one thing, he doesn't want to intrude with all that's going on, he sort of feels he'd be in the way.'

'Well, he wouldn't be. Mama's always liked company. Look how she had all the kids in the street in when we were little. And she cried buckets when Josie's family moved away.'

'Yes, there's very few people in the street that she knows now. New ones are buying the houses, flats are being built. It's just not the same place.'

'I know. But also, for Freddie, he wasn't sure of his feelings, so he was afraid to become involved in the family, as if he did find he didn't love me, it would be harder to make the break.'

'Well, that didn't happen . . . Oh, there's Lilly chatting to Steve outside. Go and let them in, love.'

Lilly gave them both a lovely hug. 'How's Angelica today?'

Mia left Angie to tell her as she went into the arms of Steve and received his kiss on her cheek. 'You look lovely, darling. I can't wait for my parents to arrive tomorrow. They're so looking forward to meeting you.'

'And I can't wait to meet them. When I spoke to them on the phone it was just such an easy conversation.'

'Well, they arrive the day before the wedding and I thought I could bring them here, then if your mama is well enough, take them up to introduce them to her.'

'That would be lovely . . . Maybe we could get her downstairs again?'

'I'm not sure we can, darling. We'll see . . .'

'Well, as far as arrangements are going, we only need to pick up Angie's bridesmaid's frock . . . And, of course, I have to ask Freddie to give me away.'

'You've done marvels, darling, and only a few days to go now and you will be Mrs Granger!'

'And I'll have to put up with you moving in and me sleeping on the flipping sofa! Not at all considerate.'

Angie always made them laugh as she said this in a sarcastic, joking way.

Mia did feel guilty about it, but there was no other way, unless she and Steve lived apart, as she couldn't leave Mama.

'Actually . . . well, I haven't said, but I do have news.'

'Well, you can tell me later, Angie. I need to get upstairs to Angelica. I have to read her the next chapter of Catherine Cookson's *Fenwick Houses*, and we want to know if Janey succeeds in turning the house into a guest house!'

'Okay, Lilly. Thanks.'

Mia caught hold of Lilly's free hand. 'We really mean that. Thanks so much for the time you spend with Mama. And for arranging for a wheelchair to take her to the wedding. You've been such a help to us.'

Lilly smiled, though Mia could see she was moved. 'Get on with you. Go and enjoy yourselves.'

With this she hurried up the stairs.

Mia didn't follow her. She'd said her goodbye to Mama, and knew she could safely leave her in Lilly's hands.

There was no time to dwell on this as Freddie appeared then. It had been ages since Mia had seen him – when she'd last been at work. 'Freddie! Lovely to see you.'

Angie playfully shoved her out of the way. 'My turn first, missus!'

Steve put his arm around Mia and grinned down at her. 'It seems we have to wait for me to be introduced and you reacquainted!'

When Angie came out of a blushing Freddie's arms, she said, 'This is Steve, Freddie. I've told you all about him.'

The two men shook hands.

Freddie, a tall, good-looking young man with fair hair, smiled a sardonic smile. 'So, you're the groom-to-be. Nice to meet you as we're going to be future brothers-in-law!'

'What? Angie! You never said!'

'That's my news. Freddie has asked me to marry him! But not only that, we will be moving up to the Lake District . . . Freddie is going to be the northern correspondent . . . I – I didn't want to tell you till we were together, and besides, with the worry over Aunt Angelica, and your wedding, I thought you had enough on your plate.'

Steve reacted first. 'It's wonderful news! Congratulations. I'm very happy for you both.'

He kissed Angie's cheek and once more shook Freddie's hand.

Angie turned to her. 'Mia?'

Recovering from the shock – more from losing Angie than anything – Mia took Angie in her arms. 'Oh, Angie. I'm so happy for you, but I wish you didn't have to move away.'

'Well, we can kip on the floor down here if you like.'

'Ha! No, I don't like. Oh, Angie, you make a joke of everything, but this is massive.'

'Not really, love. We're all grown-up, we need to go our own ways and make our own lives, but nothing will ever break the love between us. Nothing.'

Mia knew she was right, and with Steve's arm squeezing her to give her support, she digested this latest huge shock, and began to see that for them all, it would be a wonderful twist to them going forward to their future . . . It was just how far apart she and Angie would be from each other that was hard to accept.

All this was forgotten as they enjoyed the day together. They had loads more to talk about than Mia's and Steve's impending wedding, though Mia did ask Freddie to give her away, which he accepted, showing his joy. She and Freddie had always got on so well, going on assignments together and just enjoying each other's company.

But mostly, this time helped them to come to terms with all that the future held, though still Mia hated the idea of being separated from Angie for the first time in her life.

Arriving home, Lilly told them that Mama had had a restful day and had loved the couple of chapters she'd been able to listen to.

Freddie surprised them then by asking, 'Is she still awake? I'd like to meet her, and I have something to ask her.'

'Yes, she is, young man, but you won't upset her, will you?'

'No. I've never met her, but I know she isn't well. I promise I'll be very mindful of that.'

With this, Lilly said her goodbyes, and Freddie turned to them. 'I hope you don't mind but I need to ask for Angie's hand.'

'Oh, that's a lovely thing to do. Come on, we'll go up.'

As Mia looked on, it cemented for her what a nice man Freddie was.

Going up to Mama, he said, 'Hello. I'm Freddie. I think Angie has told you about me?'

Mama smiled a weak smile.

'I haven't met you before, as I wasn't sure of everything . . .'

Mama moved her hand towards him, and he gently took hold of it.

'I'm like that, I take my time, but when I'm sure, then that's what I'm sure of for ever . . . I love Angie with all my heart, and I wanted to ask you if I can marry her?'

Mama's smile turned into a glow that lit her face. She nodded her head.

'Oh, Aunt Angelica, thank you. I'm so in love with Freddie, and knew from the start, but I'm the happiest I can be now that he knows he loves me too.'

Angie took hold of Mama's other hand.

Where Mama found the strength, Mia didn't know, but she lifted Angie's hand and put it on top of Freddie's. With this, she closed her eyes.

To Mia, Mama had found further peace with knowing Angie's future was settled.

The next day, Mia woke feeling stiff and tired. She'd spent most of the night with her mama, lying on the bed next to her, or trying to get her comfortable.

Her heart was heavy as she bathed and dressed while Angie looked after Mama. There were only two days left until her wedding, but she couldn't feel the joy she should, couldn't shift the fear for her mama enough to give room for happy thoughts.

But somehow, she must. Steve would be here in a couple of hours with his parents, and she wanted to be at her best for them.

Thank goodness, she thought, that Angie had taken a few days off work to help with preparations, and to prepare for her own wedding day. She and Freddie, after meeting Steve's parents, were going to post their own banns today.

This, too, had stopped Mia from sleeping well. It was difficult to come to terms with Angie's move. If only it wasn't so far away and she could just visit her whenever she wanted to, but that would be impossible as there would be hundreds of miles between them.

Angie calling out that she'd made some toast gave Mia

the push she needed. She quickly finished her make-up and dressed.

She'd chosen to wear a summer dress in navy with white spots. It sported a white sailor's collar and had little white cuffs to its short sleeves. Steve always loved it when she wore it.

Munching her toast and marmalade, Mia listened to Angie's excited chatter about posting her banns, till she suddenly turned and said, 'Hark at me! Going on about my wedding, when you have your future in-laws about to arrive and your head full of yours.'

'No, it's okay, I know how you feel, love, you want to tell the world. But I did want to talk to you about whether you'd had confirmation from the caterers?'

'I have, and I told you not to worry about anything of that nature, that's my job. But as you've asked, they will be here at eleven, after we have left for the church. I'll drop a key in to them the day before. They'll bring some trestle tables and set them out in the yard if the weather's nice, but if not, they will set the buffet out in the kitchen, on the table and on the cabinet. There'll be plenty of room as there'll only be nine of us . . . Oh, Mia, I wish there were more guests for you, but with Aunty Angelica having no one and my mum being an orphan, we have nobody.'

'I know, it won't be like some of the weddings you see coming out of the church . . . Oh dear, we're going to rattle around in that huge building.'

'Ah, but we'll be a happy crowd.'

'We will, except—'

'No exceptions. Your wedding will be a happy day that you will always remember.'

There was no time to chat about this any longer as the

sound of a car engine slowing and then stopping heralded Steve's arrival.

Angie jumped up and took their plates into the kitchen and Mia could hear her frantically washing them under the tap.

Mia went to the door with a huge smile on her face that didn't quiet touch her heart. Angie had said her day would be one to remember, but something told her that it might be, but not for the right reasons.

Steve jumped out of the car, his grin making his face beam as he opened the back door and Mia caught sight of his mother and then immediately his father, who was getting out of the front passenger seat.

She stepped out and went to his mother, who was now standing on the pavement, a small dainty woman with fair hair and blue eyes, which crinkled at the sides as she smiled.

She put out her arms. 'Mia! Oh, it's so lovely to meet you.'

Mia went into a hug full of love and acceptance.

As she came out of it, Steve's father, an older-looking version of Steve, came around the car. 'My turn. We've waited what seems a long time to meet you, my dear.'

His hug was strong, and again, Mia could feel the love they seemed to already have for her.

All she could think to say was, 'Thank you.'

They both laughed. His mum then said, 'No, we have to thank you for bringing the shine back to our son's eyes. You've made him very happy.'

As they shook hands with Angie, Steve's mum said, 'Call us Muriel and Mike. We call ourselves the two Ms.'

This made them all giggle and released any tension that meeting new people often generated.

Their chatter flowed easily after this, and Mia liked them more and more as the time wore on. She loved how they were so ordinary, and how, though retired, they had a zest for life, and talked about the walks they enjoyed and tending to their garden. They were just lovely, ordinary folk, and Mia knew that she would love them.

They took to Angie too, and Angie, as she did with everyone, chatted as if she'd known them for ever.

After about ten minutes, with a welcoming cup of tea made and drunk, and just as Mia was getting anxious and needed to excuse herself to go and check on her mama, Michael said, 'We would love to meet your mum – your mama – Mia. Will it be possible?'

'Yes, she knows you are coming and said she would love for you to come up to see her.'

'I think I should go up first and check her, Dad. Make sure she is up to receiving visitors. Will you come with me, darling?'

Mia nodded and followed Steve up the stairs. At the top, Steve stopped on the landing and turned to her. 'Did she have a good night? Only you look very tired, my darling.'

Mia explained how restless her mama had been.

'I think she was reliving the past again. But though she wasn't distressed in the same way as before, she has been through a lot of trauma, and it must affect her now she is so vulnerable.'

'Yes. Sadly, trauma stays with you more prominently than happy times. But I hope she remembers those too.'

'Yes, she does often giggle.'

'That's good.'

After Steve had kissed Mama on the cheek he said, 'That was from your future son-in-law, who loves you very much, but now I'm going to be your doctor and check how you are, my dear.'

Mama gave one of her giggles in response to this.

Mia felt so cheered by this. And more so when Steve said, 'Well, all seems as well as it can be. And it's good that the pain relief is working. So, how do you feel about meeting my parents? They are here, downstairs.'

'I . . . would like . . . very much.'

Steve beamed down at her, took off his stethoscope and bent over her once more and then surprised Mia by saying, 'You're the nicest future *belle-mère* I could possibly wish for,' before kissing her cheek again.

Then as he straightened, he said, 'I asked Father Benedict to tell me what mother-in-law was in French. I hope I got it right?'

'You did, darling, and it was a lovely thing to do.'

When Muriel and Michael came up and Steve proudly presented them, Muriel immediately went to Mama and held her hands. 'I'm so honoured to meet such a wonderful courageous lady. I just know that we are going to be friends.'

Mama gave one of her lovely smiles as Muriel moved out of the way and Michael took her place. 'And beautiful with it. Now I see where your daughter gets her lovely face from.'

Again, Mama smiled.

Michael seemed overcome as he said, 'We will look after Mia for you.'

For a moment a depressed air descended, until Mama, in the strongest voice she'd used for a long time, said, 'You . . . better had!' then giggled.

This made them all laugh.

* * *

The two days leading up to Mia and Steve's wedding day passed in a whirl of visits by his parents, and last-minute spring cleaning of the house, but the best bit of each day for Mia was when she lay with her mama in the afternoons. One conversation continually revisited Mia. It had happened yesterday, when Mama had said, 'I think it is that you will love France, *ma chérie*. In spring time . . . the trees bloom and . . . the grapevines blossom. Keep your promise to me to go. It . . . means so much.'

'It sounds beautiful, Mama. And I will. I'll go for you, but you will be with me, as France is where you should be.' Mama took hold of her hand. Mia held hers gently as Mama's skin was paper-thin, covering bones with no cushion of flesh.

It was then that Mama had whispered, 'Take a little of me back with you, Mia.'

And Mia had promised, 'I will, Mama, for the convent and for Marcia.'

It was a relief to acknowledge their imminent parting, whereas always she'd tried to hang on to the hope that it wouldn't happen.

Now, as if she'd only blinked, Mia was in her bedroom with Angie getting ready for her wedding.

'Why so pensive, Mia? I knew you would be nervous, but . . .'

'Oh, Angie, Steve is very concerned for Mama. Should we postpone today?'

Mia hated feeling how she was. Angie was trying her best to make everything as it should be.

Already she had her pale lilac bridesmaid's frock on – the colour suited her ivory-coloured skin and didn't clash with her red hair, which she wore piled on top of her head. The skirt of the frock was what was called a 'midi' as it fell to just below her knees. The bodice had a boat-shaped neckline and was fitted to her tiny waist, with three-quarter length sleeves.

'No, of course not. Aunty Angelica is hanging on for this day . . . You do know that, don't you, love?'

Mia nodded.

'You are prepared, aren't you, Mia?'

'How do you prepare yourself for losing someone who is so precious to you?'

'I know, but she hasn't fought to hang on for your wedding to spoil it for you. She's fought to be here on the happiest day of your life. You have to make it so, for her too.'

Taking a deep breath, Mia said, 'You're right. And I will. Let's get my gown on then, we've a wedding to go to.'

Standing a few moments later in front of the full-length mirror that stood in the corner of their bedroom, Mia couldn't believe the reflection was her!

The long white brocade gown she'd chosen, with the same boat-shaped neckline as Angie's frock that made her shoulders look elegant, went into a bodice that fitted into her waist. The skirt belled out and flowed down to just below her ankles.

She felt like a princess as she did a twirl, and more so when Angie fitted her headdress – a simple satin bow attached to an Alice band, from which her short veil flowed.

'Oh, Mia . . .'

'No tears, Angie, or you'll set me off and make my mascara run.'

Angie giggled and dabbed at her eyes.

Mia knew the tears were mixed emotions. Today was a day that marked change in their lives. Mama would leave them very soon, Angie would be married to Freddie in three weeks' time, and she was going to be Steve's wife!

This last thought took away any sadness and filled her with joy.

'Well, I didn't think you could look more beautiful, but you do. That smile shows all the happiness you do, and should, feel today. Today is yours and Steve's day, Mia, love. Come on, let's get you to the church!'

At the church, Mia got the shock of her life when she stepped inside holding Freddie's arm as he pushed her beautiful mama in her wheelchair.

The first ten pews were full of her ex-colleagues! And they all began to clap as she walked forward.

'Thank you, Angie. Oh, I do love you.'

As she looked down at her mama, beaming a lovely smile, Mia thought she looked frail, but so beautiful.

Her outfit – a grey costume, teamed with a new lilac blouse – hung on her stick-thin body.

It was the matching silk pillbox hat, fashioned after those that Jackie Kennedy had made famous, that enhanced Mama's delicate features as it sat on her thick dark hair and gave the impression of who she was – a chic French lady.

Mia wanted to beg God to let her keep her for a few more weeks. But she'd promised that no such thoughts must be allowed today.

Mama glanced at her. 'Be hap – happy, my Mia.'

Mia smiled back as they walked up the aisle to her Steve.

When they came out after the ceremony, her colleagues were waiting for her. They cheered loudly and threw what seemed like tons of confetti, as they shouted how lovely she looked and how they hoped she would be happy.

Lining up for photographs, Mia turned to Angie. 'Thanks, love. That was a wonderful surprise. And I didn't have an empty church echoing every one of my footsteps.'

'They wouldn't have it any different, Mia. They all loved you when you were at work and all ask after you and think you a marvel, which you are . . . I love you, my lovely sister.'

Mia's eyes welled with tears. Angie was a sister to her, no matter that they weren't related. They had adopted one another, and no sisters could be closer or love each other more.

'They're all coming back, you know. Only for the toast, though, they aren't stopping. It's all ready in the yard for you.'

'What? Oh, Angie!'

Once home, Mia was so surprised and pleased to see how Angie had arranged for the caterers to decorate the backyard and to lay out sherry and port for all of the guests. Balloons floated in the breeze and the tables were strewn with confetti.

For the next half an hour, it was so nice to chat to a few of her colleagues, to be hugged by her new mum and dad-in-law, and to see Mama coping as she smiled at everyone from the comfort of her wheelchair and with Lilly in attendance.

Steve gave a wonderful speech, as did Freddie, making everyone laugh as he recalled her bumbling a few things when they were on assignment. Then a shocked Mia was lifted in the air by her colleagues as they all cheered loudly.

They had made the happiest day of her life – a day her mama had been with her too – that bit more special.

But it was Steve who made it into an unforgettable one when they came together later in a fusion of love and exquisite feelings that sealed their love for ever.

Chapter Twenty-Four

Angelica & Mia

Going to Irene

'Mama . . . Mama, you've been asleep all morning. It's afternoon now and I've come to lie with you.'

Angelica opened her eyes. Never had Mia looked so beautiful in a serene way that told her she and Steve were now one.

All she could do was to nod, try to smile and say, '*Je t'aime.*'

'Oh, Mama. I love you too. *Je t'aime.*'

Angelica felt the dip in the mattress as Mia climbed onto it and lay beside her, and felt her arm come around her.

She was safe now. Safe to rest.

The warm breeze brushed her face as she looked over to the green and saw their bench. But then she puzzled at how it could possibly still be there when this was 1963.

The bench had been moved and the green dug up to accommodate building works long ago, and most astonishingly, Irene was now sitting on it and she could talk! She was smiling as she called over, 'Hello, luv, you took yer time getting here.'

Her giggle made Angelica giggle. Then she had the sensation of floating as she went to Irene. They hugged, but it was a strange hug as it seemed they went through each other. But it didn't matter. Nothing mattered as she was back with her beloved friend, and she was all mended and happy and so was Irene. They were holding hands now, but again that felt strange – not like always.

'I had things to put right.'

'Oh, your so-called sins? And did yer?'

'I did. It started with that letter from the Reverend Mother thanking me for sending a donation. You remember, she released me from my vows? But I never felt that those words meant anything and were just said out of kindness.'

'Have yer changed yer mind about that then?'

'Yes. Well, this lovely priest, Father Benedict, came to visit me several times.'

'I was by your side often during your illness, luv, but I couldn't see or hear anyone, I just wanted to be near you.'

'Is that how it happens? As I want to be near to Mia, Angie and Marcia.'

'It does. Yer can only hope they feel your presence. I know Angie has felt mine, and that you have. Yer often said, "Come on, Irene, help me out." And I did what I could.'

Somehow, this seemed enough, when Angelica had been hoping she could be seen. But she didn't mind – nothing seemed as though it could upset her feelings now.

'Anyway, what did this priest do for you?'

Angelica told how he had given her absolution of her only sin – sleeping with a man out of wedlock.

'Not on yer leaving yer vows then?'

'He told me I hadn't done anything wrong in doing that as I hadn't taken my solemn vows.'

'It's all above me. I thought yer had taken your vows?'

'It's the solemn vows that marry me to God. You see, he explained that with the war preventing our bishop from travelling due to the danger he might have been in, and this delaying me from taking my solemn vows, it was only the Reverend Mother's release that I needed and not a dispensation from Rome.'

'And yer got that. But what about Marcia? Did you forgive yourself for not going back? Not that you could go, love.'

Angelica told Irene how that was all forgiven. 'But none of it seems to matter now.'

'No, it won't luv, you've left earth behind. And, oh, Angelica, luv, now you'll rest with me in heaven as somehow we've both landed here despite everything we did that they told us would stop us getting here.'

'Will I see Saint Peter, and . . .' Feeling a little afraid now, she asked, 'And God?'

'I haven't. I just feel this lovely peace. I have no needs, no longings, just happiness.'

This mystified Angelica. It went against all she'd been taught. Maybe she wasn't in heaven? But she'd atoned for everything and received forgiveness. She felt at peace. But what about Mia and Angie, could she really leave them?

'Angelica . . .'

Bringing her attention back to Irene, she took her outstretched hand and was drawn into a hug.

With this, a complete peace came to her. It took all earthly concerns from her and enveloped her in happiness.

Mia

'Mia . . . Mia, darling!'

Steve's voice woke Mia. She took her arm from around her mama and sat up. 'What time is it? Have you got to go back to work?'

'Mia . . . Oh, Mia, my darling!'

Realization came to Mia that Steve had tears running down his face.

Fear clenched her heart as she turned her head towards her mama. 'No, no, no! Mama, don't leave me, Mama!'

She put her head on her mama's still body and rested it on her breast. 'Oh, Mama, Mama, how am I to live without you?'

'Your mama is at peace, my darling.'

Angie's sob brought her attention to her. She had her arms outstretched. 'It's over, Mia. Aunty Angelica is at peace at last. No more pain. Come here and let me hug you . . . I need a hug too.'

Straightening, Mia stood. Angie leaned into her and held her. Together they sobbed until they came to a place of calm encircled in Steve's loving arms.

'You looked so lovely, both of you,' Angie told her. 'I opened the door and smiled. The picture of you holding Aunty Angelica was beautiful. And I thought you were both asleep, but then I saw . . . Oh, Mia, part of me is glad. She died in your arms. She must have felt so loved and safe and that at last she could go.'

They cried again as they looked down at Angelica.

'She looks so peaceful, she's almost smiling.'

As Angie said this, another sob took Mia.

Steve said in a matter-of-fact voice, 'You two go downstairs now, as I have to be Mama's doctor and do some checks and the paperwork. I have my bag as I'd only just come in when Angie heard me and came down to me without waking you, darling.'

Mia allowed Angie to steer her through the door and down the stairs.

Once in the living room she said, 'It was the happiest day of my life yesterday. It was so wonderful, with Mama being there. And at times it was like having her back, she seemed so happy.'

'Oh, Mia, she was, and with having seen Marcia recently too, Aunt Angelica's last few weeks were the best they could be for her.'

When Steve came downstairs Mia got up from where she'd been sitting on the sofa, holding Angie's hand.

'I've done what I have to do as her doctor. We will need to register her death . . . I'm so sorry to have to be making you think of the practical things, darling, when all I want to do is hold you. But do you know where her birth certificate is?'

'I – I only know that there's a box somewhere. Mama told me about it and kept pointing to the floor. If it exists, then it's possible everything is in there. Only there is nothing anywhere else of Mama's. Mine and Angie's are in the drawer of the dresser.'

Angie chipped in then. 'We think the box must be under that creaky floorboard next to the bed, but we've never looked.'

'I'll go and look. And Angie, I think we could all do with a cup of tea, love. It's been a shock to us, even though we knew it would happen.'

Angie jumped up, but Mia did too. 'I'll help. I don't want to sit here on my own.'

In the kitchen, nothing seemed real. It was all as if it didn't belong to now – the now without Mama.

Mia knew Angie felt this too as she came close and put her arm around Mia. 'They say that life goes on, but how can it?'

Once more they were in each other's arms, each trying to feel that everything would be all right, but each still wondering how?

Within a few minutes, they all sat with their hot, steaming, sweet tea, looking at the box Steve had found. A wooden writing box, it seemed to Mia, a strange and frightening object – something that had been hidden from her all her life, and now she had to look at its contents.

Into the silence, and in a gentle voice, Steve said, 'Mia, darling, you should be the one to open it.'

Mia reluctantly slid onto her knees from by his side on the sofa to be level with the box that stood on the occasional table. Steve had placed it there and had moved the table to stand in front of her before sitting down to drink his tea.

The lid opened on hinges, revealing a tray lined with velvet and divided into sections, containing a pen, a pencil and an eraser, a few paperclips, a wooden letter opener and a notepad.

Lifting this out, Mia flicked it open.

'My God! It's about my father!' She read a few lines, then shut it, not able to go on. 'I'll read it later.'

Under the notebook she found two bank books, and a letter addressed to her.

Her hands trembled as she picked up the letter opener.

The sound of sliced paper grated on her heightened senses.

Mia, my dearest daughter,

You brought light into my life when there was only darkness – a darkness held within me that I must atone for.

But for my darling friend, Irene, I would have sunk into this darkness, but she kept me afloat until you arrived and let in the light to help me to live with the sins I had committed.

The letter went on to tell Mia all she now knew – how her mama had been a nun, how she'd met and loved Philip and how he had died from a heart attack after they had crowned that love, leaving her pregnant.

I didn't mean for it to be this way, but I hope that by the time I die, you will know the same deep and consuming love and be understanding of how it happened that you were born out of wedlock.

Your papa was a rich man . . .

Mia read on with astonishment of how they had hopes of doing up her papa's manor house in Surrey and about his cousin turning up and throwing her onto the streets.

'My God, I have relations!'

'Yes, and they have what is yours, but it will be very difficult to prove it. There is only this cousin who knew your mama was pregnant. He could argue that her child belonged to anyone.'

'But wouldn't this letter be a testament to my parentage? And there is the convent. The Reverend Mother and any of the nuns present at the time could testify to my parents' love for each other and how she left the convent to be with my papa.'

'Yes . . . Look, I'm just being devil's advocate here, darling, but you have to remember what your mama has said in the letter, that your papa went straight into hospital and was there for weeks . . .'

'You mean . . . my cousin, or whatever he is to me, could argue that she went with someone else in that time?'

Steve nodded.

Mia knew he was right. This relation of her papa's had shown that he was a ruthless man. Sighing, she went back to what Mama had written to her – words she so wished she'd told her years ago.

It appeared that in her quest to get papers to verify her existence, or to allow her to travel home, she went to visit the cousin.

'He paid her off! So, in a sense, he was admitting I was the rightful heir, and he wanted her out of his hair. So he made her an allowance.'

'Now, that may be more difficult for him to explain.'

Angie spoke for the first time. 'Not really. His cousin had brought this nun over promising her the world, she'd got herself into trouble, he felt guilty for chucking her out and he felt some responsibility towards her – he helped her to buy a house and sort out her papers so she could stay here. He'd have any judge praising him for his kind act and telling him that he went above and beyond. The rotten pig!'

They were quiet for a moment.

Mia raged with many emotions – deep sadness, frustration and anger all assailed her at once.

'My advice, Mia, darling, would be to take it as it is, an explanation, and leave that part behind you. This cousin has all the advantage – the money to see a court case through, the respect of his peers who will judge such a case, and a story that would hold up far better than the truth as your mama tells it to us, and had to live through . . . Thank God she met Irene, who sounds like the loveliest person ever . . . Your mum, Angie – a woman to be proud of.'

Angie's face flooded with tears. 'Thanks, Steve. I – I have always known she was, but I didn't fully appreciate how desperate they both must have been. Rescuing Aunty Angelica probably saved my mum too.'

Mia nodded. It was a can of worms and she wasn't strong enough to open it – nor did she want to or need to. She had all she needed in Steve.

The letter finished with more apologies.

'Poor Mama, she tormented herself over leaving the convent and Marcia and having me out of wedlock . . . Is it a sin to do any of them?'

'I wouldn't say so . . . Well, they do say that nuns are married to God, so there may be some sort of formal procedure – a sort of divorce.'

Angie gave a sardonic laugh as she said the last part of this.

Another silence followed it, but then both Mia and Steve giggled.

However, when they sobered up, Mia said, 'I hope Mama didn't take all this with her and feared that she wouldn't get to heaven because of it.'

'I don't think she did. Look how calm she had become since Father Benedict began visiting her. It's my guess, and what we should believe, that she confessed all to him and he gave her the forgiveness she sought. But . . . well, we will probably never know as what is said in confession is never spoken of by priests.'

'I'd like to know. I'd like to know all the answers. But I don't think that God would look on any of Mama's doings as sins and I hope Father Benedict was able to tell her so.'

Angie agreed with Mia on this. 'Aunty Angelica was a

wonderful woman. She cared for others; she took me in, and look what Marcia told us about saving the Jewish children. What courage it must have taken to hoodwink the Germans as she went backwards and forwards in that rickety old car Marcia told us about.'

Mia smiled then. 'And she couldn't even drive it according to Marcia. She was always being pulled up by the gendarmes for her driving errors and told she must get someone to teach her.'

'Ha, that was funny. But I don't suppose there was anyone to teach her. Although that wouldn't stop Aunty Angelica. She had children to rescue, and she was going to do it, and driving was the only way she could as Shane wasn't available to drive her.'

Steve was thoughtful. 'What must it all have been like? Your mama and Shane were heroes. Unsung heroes.'

They digested this, and all shed a tear at Mama's final words:

My darling, I am sorry to tell you all of this, but remember, I loved you with all my heart. You and Angie – Angelica – were my life. And I will stay by your side in death.

Mia said, 'Mama's last spoken words to me were, "*Je t'aime.*" I love you.'

They huddled together for a moment, all shedding tears at the loss of such a beautiful woman. Mia felt her heart would break, but she took support from her beloved Steve and Angie.

When they came to a calm place they moved on to the second sheet of the letter. This detailed Mama's last wishes.

My darling girls, I have always treated you equally in life and wish to do so in death.

You will have read how I came to own this house, but though the money was provided by Philip's family, it was my beloved Irene's home too and hers before we could buy it. Therefore, I want you both to own it, jointly. Or to sell it and share the proceeds. This will give you security when I am gone.

There is also, in this box, a bank book each. Irene and I opened these in your names, and were trustees until you reached twenty-one, or upon our deaths. We each paid into these accounts for our own child, until Irene died and then I continued for you both.

I want my precious necklace, that I can tell you now marked mine and Philip's engagement, to go to you, my darling Mia.

In a separate envelope you will find a ring. This is from your mum, Angie. She wanted me to give it to you on your wedding day. It comes with all her love. She couldn't write to you as by the time she realized that MND would truly take her life, she was unable to.

Also, there is a treasured brooch of mine that you always loved as a child that I leave to you with all my love and for you to remember me by, my Angie.

At the bottom was her signature, and that of a solicitor with a stamp giving his address.

After a moment, Angie said, 'How lovely to have this brooch, and I have a gift from my mum. How wonderful is that.' She swallowed hard before continuing, 'If only I had known her. Really known her.'

They didn't cry, they were all cried out, but they held hands for a while.

'We were blessed to have had two such strong and wonderful women to bring us into the world, Mia.'

'We were. And we will always honour them, and remember them.'

'Maybe something will occur that we can do to really

honour them – use some of our inheritance to somehow mark their lives. Give it to a charity or something.'

'That's a wonderful idea, Angie. We'll give it some thought, but maybe a homeless charity, and a Jewish one.'

They all agreed on this as they rose to do what they must do for Mama. There were procedures, and Mia wanted to make sure every one of these last things she could do for her mama was done.

It was midnight before Mama had been taken to the chapel of rest at the undertaker's.

Father Benedict had been and blessed her body, telling them that the soul doesn't leave the body for a while.

His prayers helped them all. Even Steve said how he felt better for them as he admitted the whole experience of going through this journey with them had taken a lot out of him. But he said that he was glad that it had led him to Mia and that it had made him more determined to one day be involved in researching cancers and their cause.

Mia was glad, too, that the priest had been able to tell them that Mama had left her vows without sinning and that she was aware of this. 'I'm not breaking her confessional confidence by telling you this as it was not a sin and she didn't need forgiveness, but the only other thing I can tell you is that your mama's soul was ready for God when she left this world and when the time comes she will go to heaven.'

With this, once he'd left and they were all feeling better for everything they had found out, Angie left Mia and Steve to themselves.

The night was still warm after a hot day, and so they went outside and sat on the step together and talked.

Mia related tales of her mama, and Steve of his sister. It was a small part of the healing process but it helped them both.

After this, they felt able to talk of their wedding day, and how wonderful it had been. But it was when Steve asked, 'So, what of the future, Mia?' that she voiced what was her biggest wish.

'I want to go to France to Marcia. I want to give her a hug. She's bound to be very sad when I telephone her with the news and, well, I want to learn more about Mama's past, see the convent and meet the Reverend Mother and any other nuns who knew Mama – visit the world she lived in and has never really shared with me.'

'Is there any room in those plans for us to find a new home?'

Mia held her breath. The thought of moving from the only home she'd known was daunting, and yet, with how Mama had left things, the best option would be to sell and divide the money. She knew Angie would agree.

'Only, I haven't said anything, but . . . Well, I know how it is tearing you apart to face Angie moving away, and so I looked at positions up in the North, nearer to the Lakes, and there is one I would like to apply for. We could buy a home up there. The properties are half the price of here, and—'

'Stop!'

'Oh, Mia, my darling, I'm sorry. I must have sounded so callous, but I wanted to give you something to focus on, something to help you over the next few weeks.'

'I just can't take it all in. It's so wonderful to think I could be near to Angie and Freddie, but I've a whole lifetime to give up, and the biggest change has only just happened.'

'Oh, my darling, let me hold you. I – I was too hasty.'

As he did, Mia let the changes she had to face become real to her. She needed more of a plan than just her visit to France, and Steve was offering her the best possible future she could want.

'Thank you, darling, from the bottom of my heart. Now that it's sunk in, it sounds perfect and I know Mama would want me and Angie to stay together.'

'And how wonderful to be able to bring our family up in the countryside.'

'Ha! You're a fast mover! Here you are having only met me a couple of months ago, you've married me, you're going to whisk me away from all I've ever known, and now you're talking of having kids with me!'

They both laughed. It amazed Mia how she could laugh when the thing she'd been dreading the most had happened. But she felt such a mixture of emotions and, right now, it was a feeling of love and of joy at being with the one she loved.

And they both knew it was a deep love that would last for ever.

Chapter Twenty-Five

Marcia

A Love Laid to Rest

Putting the phone down, Marcia wiped away her tears.

What she had been praying for had happened and her dear Sister Angelica was at peace.

She didn't chastise herself for using the name she'd always thought of Angelica as being called. Mia had said, when she'd slipped up, 'It is how you knew my mama, and how you remember her. It is lovely that you do. She loved you very much. Her passing was made more peaceful because you came to see her and put her mind at rest.'

These were lovely words that helped Marcia.

Going out to the garden, she thought of how Mia had said they would come to France. Marcia knew this would aid her own healing. Being with Mia would be as if Sister Angelica had returned. And it would be good to show Mia and her new husband around the convent. She hoped it would help them to see how life was for the Jewish children during the war. But telling them the truth of the raid by the Germans soon after Sister Angelica left and of the death of her beloved Madeleine, and of Joseph, and so many of those children, wasn't going to be easy.

Why did it happen? How could the world have let it happen?

She sighed as she called out to Hans, 'Time to collect your brothers from school. Come along, hurry, darling, we're late.'

'Mama cry?'

'Yes, darling. Do you remember the lovely lady we went to see in England? The one who was poorly?'

Hans looked unsure.

'Well, she's gone to heaven and we must pray for her soul.'

He nodded, but she could see he didn't understand, she just needed to tell someone.

Hurrying her footsteps, Marcia was suddenly stopped by a voice calling her name – a familiar, yet long-forgotten voice.

Turning in the direction of it, her mouth dropped open, and her eyes opened wide. Composing herself, she heard his name as a desperate whisper on her lips. 'Joseph! Oh, Joseph, where did you come from?'

'Poland . . . Oh, Marcia, I never forgot you, but I hid in a forest after I escaped and didn't know the war was over for years . . . I – I was put into an institution. Confused and . . .'

Putting the brake on the pram, she ran to him and held him . . . 'Oh, Joseph . . . I – I . . . I thought you were dead. Your picture was among those who were . . . I – I can't say it.'

'None of us can. We just say murdered.'

Stepping back, Marcia asked, 'Us? Are you in touch with others?'

'Three of us escaped, but we got separated. Since I came out of the institution, I've seen the others. They saw my story on the news and . . . One of them was Elsie . . . We – we married.'

Marcia's heart lit at knowing he was alive and long-forgotten feelings reignited. She looked into his eyes. Memories hit her in a kaleidoscope of scenes – being in his arms, protected, loved, plans made for the future, his loss . . . 'But that's wonderful. Where is she? How is she?'

'She is in the hotel not far away. She wanted me to find you to tell you.'

Recovered now from being taken through their life together, Marcia made herself say, 'Oh, Joseph, I am so pleased. Have you a family? I too am married. These are my children – two of them, Hans, and Angelica. I have Joseph and Amos in school. I'm on my way to collect them.'

'Joseph? . . . We – we don't have a family, but Joseph? You named your son after me?'

Marcia needed to change the charged atmosphere, needed to be faithful to her beloved Shane, had to stop this fluttering of her heart and stomach. She told herself it was the shock.

With this she made herself laugh. 'Yes, after this boy who was my first love.'

'Oh, Marcia, the war spoiled so much.'

She looked into his eyes. She saw and knew his pain.

'No regrets, Joseph. Nothing can bring the past back – and none of us would want to. We've moved on. I am loved and happy. Are you happy?'

'Yes, but for my demons.'

'Flashbacks?'

'Yes, so many – the cellar, the fear, the horror of Auschwitz. The years in the forest. But good memories, too, of my first love.'

They giggled at this, and it felt good. It put the past where it belonged and their love into perspective.

'Mama, I heard the bell.'

The simple words brought Marcia back to now. 'Yes, Hans, we have to go.'

'Hans? A German name?'

'There were some good Germans, Joseph. Hans was one of them. I'll tell you about him one day. Walk with me, if you have time.'

'I do. So, who did you marry?'

'Shane.'

'What? But that's wonderful . . . He survived!'

Seeing a chance to further lighten the mood, Marcia replied, 'Yes, and he's trying to repopulate the world!'

'Ha! Marcia, you were always so funny, and that's why I fell in love with you.'

'That's why I was your first love. You've fallen "in love" with Elsie.'

'Yes, of course. But ours was such an intense love.'

'Ha, first loves are. But they're too intense to last.'

Joseph was quiet as they walked a few paces. She could feel the tension in him.

'Mine lasted, Marcia.'

Her throat tightened, but she must stop this!

'Don't . . . Whatever you're thinking, don't say it. Be glad that we are alive, and healthy. Be glad that we found love against all the odds. Be glad that we still have some sanity left, even if at times we feel as though we are going mad.'

'I know your insanity, Marcia. I know your pain. We lived it – me longer than you, but I saw what happened. I saw it all, Marcia . . . I stayed on the wall, I lay flat under Sister Angelica's tree . . . I'm sorry, so sorry.'

Marcia couldn't speak as the scene he'd conjured up revisited her for the second time today – Madeleine bloodied and crumpled on the ground.

Shaking the memory from her, she told him, 'My children look like Shane and are of his faith and they all speak English well.' She didn't know why she said this, it just seemed important.

'I'm glad as I cannot see a time when the Jewish people won't be vilified. Better that they are never identified as being Jews.'

'Yes, it seems that way. Giving them to Shane's faith is my way of adding another layer of protection for them and their future.'

They had reached the school gates. There was much needed to clear the air between them. To lay old ghosts to rest. Although it was painful, Marcia knew from old that all emotions needed to go through a process. She couldn't just say goodbye here. She made light of her invitation to him, speaking in English as only in that language could she express Shane. He looked surprised until he heard her out.

'Will you and Elsie come to tea tonight? We would love to have you and Shane won't believe me until he sees you. He has something in Ireland called "the Blarney Stone". I don't know what it is, but it seems to describe everything – good luck, you've kissed the Blarney Stone, or if it's something he doesn't believe, then it's you're giving me a load of blarney!'

They both laughed.

'Have you been to Ireland? As I remember, Shane used to long to go back.'

'No . . . Money's been tight.'

'Then that is what I will do for you. I want to pay Shane back for all he did for me, and you, as your image kept me going, helped me to survive and never faded.'

'Joseph, please.'

'No. I mean it, it did. But then I found Elsie and knew the love I had for her was different. It's just, well, I always kept you in my heart.'

'And I did you, only I thought you were dead. Did you think that of me?'

'Yes. Though I always hoped. I knew the Resistance would try to save you all after you were taken from the convent.'

'How did you find me?'

'Once Elsie said I should find out what happened to you, I engaged a company which was set up to reunite people. You were easy to find as you are still here, but hearing you were alive set up many emotions for me.'

'I'm glad you did . . . It's so good to know you're alive.'

'I'm a rich man, Marcia. Elsie's family were all murdered, but they left a huge legacy for her. It was looked after by the bank – the manager did not agree with Hitler and didn't declare all the fortunes of his Jewish customers. Elsie and I started a jeweller's shop, and now we have a chain of them across many countries.'

'I'm pleased for you, Joseph.'

Her father came to mind – the finest jeweller ever. A familiar pain clutched her heart.

'You and Shane will never want for anything again.'

Not sure how to take this, to go with the excitement in her gut or to refuse anything from him, she was saved from answering as the boys called out, 'Mama! We're here!'

It was Joseph who got to her first. He looked quizzically at Joseph.

'This is the man you were called after, Joseph. He's alive. How wonderful is that!'

Joseph smiled at Joseph. 'We've always thought you . . . well, that Mama and Papa lost you in the war.'

'I had a great adventure. I escaped the Germans and became like a hermit in the forest. And so, here I am, and I'm very pleased to meet you, Joseph.'

Her lovely Joseph beamed as he said, 'I'm named after you.'

'Yes, and I am very honoured.'

'We'll see you later, Joseph. And . . . Oh, but I didn't say!' Turning to her son, she said, 'Joseph, watch your brothers and sister for a moment.'

Marcia walked away from them and motioned for Joseph to follow, and he looked quizzically at her.

'I – I have something to tell you. It is a very long story, but we lost our Sister Angelica today. She died in England.'

'No! I had planned to find her and Philip . . . Is he . . . ? They did stay together, didn't they?'

'He died, not long after they got there.'

Marcia briefly told him what had happened. 'My heart is breaking over it all, but seeing you took it from me.'

'Oh, Marcia, I am sorry. I am glad that you went to see her, though . . . But if, well, if everything hadn't have happened, would you have gone if she had come for you?'

This was something Marcia hadn't thought of, but taking herself back to her love for Joseph, she suddenly knew she wouldn't have left him. That they would have made a life together and looked after Madeleine.

She looked up at him with tears in her eyes and shook her head. 'No, but . . . oh, Joseph . . . I didn't tell Sister Angelica that!'

'You put her mind at rest and that's all that matters.'

She knew he wasn't thinking this. Their eyes held for a long moment, and then she turned and went back to her children, knowing she was taking the past with her.

* * *

The feeling stayed with her as she prepared tea.

It was Shane calling out, 'Isn't it me home and looking for the love of me life,' that brought her out of that world as she felt the familiar lifting of her heart.

Snatching her apron off, she ran through to the living room and into his arms. Her sobs found a release. Her body filled with so many emotions – her love for this man, her loss, her putting to bed the feelings of the past. This was where she belonged.

'Is it Angelica?' Shane asked – always he read her emotions.

She could only nod.

And the nod marked the truth as no feeling of having lost Joseph for a second time entered her. Joseph was an old friend, her first love, and she was glad that he was alive and happy with his Elsie.

Allowing her Shane to steer her to the sofa, they sat down together. There she told him all that had happened today.

He was quiet for a moment, before saying, 'That's for being a shock about Joseph, but a welcome one. And you say he is coming to tea?'

When she said yes, he said, 'Be Jesus, that's a powerful lot to take in . . . Alive!'

Marcia waited. The moment came.

'And is it that old demons have been put to bed?'

She knew what he meant. 'They have been there for ever, my Shane. No one can take me away from you . . . I – I'm sorry . . . You must have known I've always remembered him.'

'Aye, it is so. I've felt his presence many a time . . . So, it is sure you are that . . . ?'

'I love you? Oh, Shane, you're my world, my everything . . . Joseph isn't the reason why I need you so much tonight, it's losing my lovely Sister Angelica for ever.'

His arms tightened around her. She clung to him, knowing her heart was truly at peace. Her Shane was her one true love.

With her new certainty, it was easy to welcome Joseph to her home. And she could see that he'd been through the same emotion, as he doted on lovely Elsie.

Hugging Elsie, Marcia could feel her relief. She showed no tension in her greeting, and hugged Shane in a way that said she understood.

Marcia looked at Joseph. He whispered, 'It is where it should be, in the past.'

Smiling at him, she hugged him. 'A good memory, one of the few good ones that either of us have.'

As he came out of the hug, he beamed at her. It was the smile of someone who loved her as a dear friend. She smiled back at him. 'Come on in. I've cooked coq au vin for dinner. I was taught a long time ago by a wonderful lady by the name of Madame Conté how to make the best.'

'Well, it smells good.'

He looked at Shane. The two men moved towards each other. Both had tears in their eyes. They didn't speak but went into each other's arms and clung on to one another and sobbed.

It was a moment that Marcia would never forget, a moment she had never dreamed would happen – the reunion of two of the bravest men she knew. Two men she loved, but in different ways.

This thought gave her freedom, freedom to love her man with no shackles holding her heart. She knew without doubt that it belonged to Shane completely.

* * *

The evening was partly given over to memories – there was no avoiding them – but Marcia was glad that Joseph made the telling of his escape and time in the forest an adventure for the boys.

Elsie recounted how she was in the cattle car going to Auschwitz when the train suddenly lurched and stopped. Joseph and two others had been working away at releasing a panel of the side of the car, so they took the opportunity and kicked the rotting wood. 'It gave and we all spilled out.'

She hung her head as she said, 'Only three of us got away.'

After a moment, Elsie continued, 'I lost the others, they ran too fast, but I dodged into a farmyard and hid in the cowshed.' Making the boys laugh, she wriggled her nose. 'They never stopped pooing!'

When the laughter died down, she told how the farmer and his wife took her in and cared for her and how she still looked on them as her mother and father today.

The children had lots of questions, but didn't show any sign that they were in any way distressed – there would be time enough to tell them the truth.

After the children were all tucked up in bed, Joseph said, 'I meant it about taking you to Ireland, Shane, but I've been thinking that we should all go to England first to attend the funeral of Sister Angelica. 'We owe her that, Marcia. But how quickly do they bury their dead in England? It is a country I know nothing about – except their bravery in taking on the might of Germany and persuading others to form an alliance that led to our freedom.'

'Oh, Joseph, can you really do that? It would be so wonderful – well, I don't mean . . .'

'I know what you mean, but I need to know how much time I have first.'

This prompted a frantic phone call to Mia, who told Marcia that she would be making the arrangements the next day but that usually funerals took place within four days.

'Is everything all right, Marcia?'

'It is. I have found Joseph, he is married to Elsie . . . There is so much to tell you, but, Mia, God be willing, I will be by your side when you lay your dear mama to rest. It is Joseph who is making this possible.'

'That's wonderful. Oh, Marcia, it will be such a comfort having you there. And though I am mystified over Joseph, I can learn all about it when you come. It will be lovely to meet him and Elsie. Is there anything you want me to do for you?'

'No. Joseph will make all the arrangements. He is sad to never see Sister Angelica again, but he wanted to be there to honour her and all she did for us.'

When she came off the phone, Shane's hug waited for her. As he held her, he asked, 'How is it that you can do this, Joseph?'

'I have my own private plane. It's a simple matter to change the plans I have in place.'

As they lay in bed that night, Shane made her laugh. 'I feel as though I've been hit by a whirlwind and all me dreams are coming true and yet, there isn't a sign of the little people, so there isn't.'

'Oh, Shane, I love you, and your little people and the Blarney Stone, and though I have mixed feelings – sadness over Sister Angelica passing, happiness at having found Joseph and Elsie alive – I'm so very, very happy that you're going to see your mama at last.'

Shane's arm came around her and she snuggled into him to accept his caresses, and his tender kisses, knowing that they would lead to her ultimate happiness as she lost herself in a crescendo of love and beautiful sensations that she knew he would give to her.

The Reverend Mother sat in her wheelchair in the garden next to what was called Sister Angelica's bench and cried tears for the sister she'd lost to the love of a man, and now to God, as she told them her love for Angelica had been a special love.

She hugged Joseph and Elsie, telling them that she'd never stopped praying for them and all the children.

Joseph took her hand. 'Reverend Mother, I want to thank you for all you and the sisters did for us. I remember how we lived in fear with our families, and then when the day came that the Germans were in our street, our parents made us children flee. What would have happened to us without your generous love when you heard of Sister Angelica's plans?'

'It was all down to Sister Angelica, Shane and the Resistance. They were the ones to save you all, I just accommodated you and put into place your care.'

Joseph then told of what he planned to do for Shane, and the Reverend Mother gave her blessing to him being off work for as long as he needed.

Then Joseph said, 'Sister Angelica should be remembered, and I will make sure she is. But there should be something here to remember her by. I would like to donate some money to the convent to open up the cellars and make them into an indoor play area for the children with a plaque on the wall so that every generation taught in this convent knows the story of the Jewish children who were hidden in safety there. And I would like a statue to Sister Angelica, and her bench made so that it will last for years to come, only that should not be touched until after her daughter has been, as Marcia wants her to see it as it was.'

'They are wonderful plans. Thank you, Joseph. And Sister Angelica, as we will always call her, will be in generations of hearts as we will pass her story down the years.'

'She deserves that. And we are all glad that she never knew what happened to her children.'

They said their goodbyes and were waved off by all the sisters. Some of the nuns were more special than others to Marcia as they were here when the convent was a sanctuary to her and Joseph. But she loved them all and in some ways had an easier relationship with those who had arrived after the war as that relationship was free of the shackles of the past.

As they went out of the gate, Joseph looked up at the old oak tree and sighed. 'Will we ever be able to put it behind us?'

Marcia shook her head, 'No. And nor should we – the pain, yes, we should let that heal, but what happened, no. The world needs to know and we – the survivors – should be the ones to tell them.'

Joseph turned to her and took her into a hug. 'If you're brave enough to, then I will be.'

'I am, Joseph. I am.'

Chapter Twenty-Six

Mia

A Heartbreaking Goodbye

Mia stood with Angie on one side and Marcia on the other as she gazed down at her beautiful mama lying in a coffin of white silk.

All that was visible was her face, which, like her name, was angelic, and her hands, which were joined as if in prayer.

Her rosary had been placed around her wrists and then spread over the silk – a symbol of her former life. Mia would so have liked to put something of her papa's in with Mama, to depict her new life and the love Mama had for him, but all she had was the necklace, and she couldn't part with that.

Angie nudged her. 'I brought some things with me . . . Can we lay them with her?'

Mia looked at the photo Angie held. It was one they both loved of Mama and Aunty Irene sitting on a bench.

'And this one as well.'

As she shuffled the photo to the back, Mia gasped. The second one was herself and Angie at age ten and eleven, standing on the doorstep. Mama was behind them, hugging them to her.

'It's okay, I found the negatives too, so we can have copies done.'

As she said this, she handed one of them to Mia and nodded towards the coffin. Mia placed it on Mama's heart. Then Angie did the same with the one of her mum and Mama.

'Now her life is told.'

'Yes, Angie, both halves of her life were precious to her. It's so sad she took such a long time to share the first one with us.'

Angie's arm came around her and together they sobbed out their grief.

Marcia held them, allowing them this moment.

They turned to find comfort in the arms of their menfolk, who led them away.

At the door, Mia looked back at her mama and said, 'I'll go to your convent for you, Mama. Just as I promised.'

Steve held her tighter. 'You will, my darling, you will.'

After the beautiful service they stood around the grave, not wanting to leave.

When they turned to go, Mia took the little pearl box that usually contained the necklace so cherished by her mama out of her purse and said, 'I won't be a moment. Only Mama asked me to take something of her back to the convent, and I thought I would take a little of the earth that will cover her and put it in this little box she loved and bury it by the bench you've told me of, Marcia.'

'That's a lovely idea.'

After she'd gathered the earth, Mia turned to gaze once more at the open grave and then looked up into the sky.

A wisp of blue shaped like a half-moon showed through the cloudy September sky. It was if Mama had smiled her approval.

Once home and when all had been served a hot drink, with Joseph, Elsie and Marcia glad that she offered coffee and not just English tea, the mood seemed to lighten.

It was Joseph who instigated it as he told funny tales of when he was the gardener and Sister Angelica came out to sit on her bench, as it had always been known.

'I took one of my onions over to her as I was proud of how big and white it was. She took one look and said, "Well, I thought if a handsome young man ever brought me anything, it would be a rose, not a smelly onion!"'

They all laughed with him as he said that she soon told him it was the best onion she'd ever seen.

Marcia related next of how she and Sister Angelica were tending to a patient one day when the priest arrived just as they got the patient off the bedpan. 'Father Damion was not a nice man, and we were in a flummox as to what to do with the smelly pan, when Sister Angelica whipped it under the bed, threw a towel over it and then flapped the air with another towel, just as Father Damion came through the door . . . She only whipped him around the face by accident, sending him reeling back out of the room. But if he did smell anything, he didn't say as he was such a baby, moaning and holding his face. Poor Sister Angelica had a fit of giggles and was trying to administer to him while laughing her head off. He was not amused!'

This had them all doubled over, as Marcia had done all the actions imitating Mama and the priest.

'Ah, but I have a tale to tell, so I do. It was when I first went to the convent to ask them to help in the saving of the Jewish children. I rang the bell – a clanger of a thing it was too – when I heard a female voice. And wasn't she cursing like a paddy would if someone nicked his Guinness? Yes, it was for being Sister Angelica!'

Once the laughing died down, Mia, helped by young Joseph and Amos, took plates of English and French finger food around. Lilly helped too by giving the plates out. She and Father Benedict had only popped in for a while but had ended up staying for an hour or more and enjoying all the tales told and the food with a glass of sherry before they left.

But though she loved them all, Mia was glad when Marcia, Shane, the boys and the baby, and Joseph and Elsie, also left around five, saying they were tired, and that they had another journey the next day. As they did, Marcia hugged Mia and begged her not to leave it long before she came.

'Joseph has to leave in two weeks. It would be lovely if you could come before he does.'

'I will try, Marcia, but it depends on when Steve can be released from the surgery for a few days. And we have Angie's wedding in four days too, but we are thinking of it being within the next three weeks that we come. Steve is looking into travel arrangements.'

'I will spend this Sabbath praying you will. But I understand.'

After hugging Angie and wishing her all the luck in the world, Marcia was gone.

To Mia, it was like a huge part of her life had left, but she consoled herself with the thought that it wouldn't be long before they were together again and with all that was going on, she was sure the time would fly.

Already it was evening, and the nights were beginning to draw in.

'Let's listen to music, eh? It will stop us from falling into the doldrums,' Angie said as she was already halfway across the room towards the gramophone.

'Yes, but avoid sentimental ballads or we'll all be in tears, and Mama wouldn't want that.'

As they listened to Elvis singing 'Wooden Heart', the talk turned to their future.

'We have news. Tell them, Freddie.'

Freddie grinned.

'We have a home of our own. Mother and Father have given us one in the grounds of the estate. It needs a bit of doing up, but I've always loved it. It's a cottage and its garden extends to woodland on the edge of Lake Windermere . . . And, well, there's something else . . . Angie told me of your plans, Steve, and I couldn't be more pleased. Have you heard anything yet?'

'No, these things take time. But I've since seen there are other positions going in the area, and I have notified my partner, Doctor Jones, of my impending departure. But there is a lot to sort out before it can happen.'

'Housing needn't be one of them. I spoke to my father. He owns many properties and does have a couple of cottages empty that he lets for holidays in the season. They're fully furnished and equipped. He's willing to let you use whichever one you would like until you sort out buying your own.'

'But that's wonderful news and so kind.' Steve turned to Mia and grinned. 'Well, I can tell by my lovely wife's smile that she is happy about it. Thank you very much, Freddie.'

Mia was battling with her love of this house and how it

would feel to leave it against her great need to be near to Angie. Although it didn't take long for her to decide. She had to embrace the future, and if that meant making changes, then she would adapt.

'That's wonderful. Oh, Mia, I'm so pleased. The only thing marring my happiness was moving so far away from you.'

Angie hugged her, then quickly drew away. Mia was glad as the emotion of them hugging would be too much for either of them. And it was obvious to her that though Angie made light of everything, going away was tugging at her heartstrings too.

As she lay in Steve's arms the next morning, Mia thought of all that had happened to her and Angie in the past year, some of it wonderful but most of it not.

'Well, I have to get up and go to work, darling, I have poorly people awaiting me. Billy Freeman will have another black eye, no doubt. Oh, and Mrs Riley will be in with her piles. And you can bet a pound to a penny that Reggie Flinton will be wanting a sick note for some imaginary illness!'

They both laughed. Mia wondered at her being able to, but it had seemed natural to do so.

Steve looked down at her. 'You look a little better, darling. And I'm glad to see it.'

He bent down to kiss her. When his lips left hers, he said, 'I'll try to get an answer today on when I can be released for a week.'

'I hope you can be, darling. I just feel that the trip to France will be a kind of closure for me before our new life begins.'

Steve looked relieved. 'It will be that, Mia. A new beginning for us all. But before we make the trip up to the Lakes,

I'd like us to stay with my parents for a night. They love you so much and ask me every time they telephone.'

'That would be lovely. And I promise we will.'

Mia thought how hard Steve was working to help her. Arranging things was his way of doing that.

'Well, you and Angie have the best day it's possible to have. I'm so glad she isn't at work.'

Mia smiled at him and gave him a wave as she fought back her tears.

Lying back, she listened for the front door closing, and yet not wanting it to as that would mean he'd left.

She wasn't on her own long, though, as Angie came bounding in with two steaming cups of tea. Putting them down on the bedside table, she got into what used to be her bed but was now shoved up to Mia's to make one bed for her and Steve.

'Mmm, it's still warm, thanks, Steve.'

Mia couldn't help giggling.

'Here. Sit up, let's enjoy a cup of tea in bed and a chinwag, eh?'

'You look as though you want to talk about something specific, love.'

'I do . . . Well, it's this place. We need to make decisions, Mia, love. Things are in place, and I'll be leaving very soon, and you won't be long after me. So, I thought I would pack everything today that I need to take with me.'

'Oh, Angie!'

'No. No tears, no regrets, let's treat it all like a new start. I know Aunty Angelica would want that for us. Didn't she grab with both hands the chance for a new life with the man she loved? Well, she wouldn't want us to do anything different.'

'I know, but . . .'

'You're thinking that it's early days? Mia, my love, that's

the best time to make the changes. If you think about them too long or hang around wondering if it's the right thing for you, you'll get into a rut and it'll be harder. I think today I pack, and you sort out your mama's room. It should be done by you and you alone. You are her daughter and it's the last thing you can do for her.'

'But . . .'

'Please, Mia. We have so little time.'

Mia nodded. 'Okay, I will try.'

'Good.'

They sipped their tea in silence for a moment, then Angie said, 'Now, about the house . . . I know. It breaks my heart too to even talk about it, but we must. We can't leave things. I will be gone in four days, and it will be telephone only contact until you arrive up there with me. I don't want that. I want to help you arrange things. I want us to have a plan.'

Giving in, Mia chatted to Angie about what she wanted to happen, and then listened to Angie's ideas.

Mostly they were the same as her own thoughts had been when she allowed herself to think about it – go to see an agent together and arrange to put the house up for sale in two months' time.

'Do you think Steve will be ready by then?'

'Well, it won't sell straight away so I'm sure we'll be safe with that, but what do you think about the furniture? I would like to keep some.'

'I'm happy about that. And once we know you have a date to come up to be near to me, you can have what you want put into storage and arrange for the second-hand man to come and give you a price for the rest . . . Oh, Mia. I feel so callous talking like this, but . . .'

'No, you're right, Angie, it is what I needed. Thinking of

all the practicalities of changing my life is making it real to me. We have to think how much we want to be together, and how much we want to be with the men we love. All of those things are going to happen, we just need to see to what has to be seen to.'

'Ha, one minute it's me jollying you along and then it's you jollying me along! We're a pair, aren't we?'

'That's how it must be. We both need the support of the other. Now, let's talk weddings. Is everything done? Have you had all the replies to your guest list?'

'We cut that right down and are going to have a party at his parents' later. It'll just be us four, and Lilly, and our colleagues are going to do the same at the church as they did for you. We're still going to the pub and will have their back room for a couple of drinks and then Freddie and I are going off with his parents for our honeymoon in one of the cottages he told you about. His mum is setting it all up for us so we can take care of ourselves and not have to see anyone – though Freddie is taking me to see our new home.'

'Well! That is a change. But I'm glad. I was wondering how I was going to face the society type wedding you originally planned on having.'

'I know. I was so happy when Freddie told me he'd rung his parents and they were fine under the circumstances to throw a party nearer to Christmas for all of their friends and relations, and our colleagues . . . And you and Steve, of course.'

'They sound like nice people, kind and understanding. I'm glad as it really helps if you get along with the family you are marrying into.'

They held hands for a while and then decided they had better tackle their plan.

* * *

Going into Mama's room was something neither wanted to do, not yet. But they knew they must.

Angie crossed the room and opened the window. The breeze swept in, making the air fresher. Mia looked around her. Mama's room had been the same for as long as she could remember, the large wardrobe full of nice clothes and the matching kidney-shaped dressing table with a clutter of bottles of perfume and lipsticks. The polished wooden floorboards were covered with wool rugs in cream and pale blue each side of the bed, and there were pale blue curtains and a matching bed cover. Only now it was empty of the presence that had made it a room of love.

'Will you be all right, Mia?'

'Yes. There's a nice feel in here. Not a gloomy or upsetting one. It's as if Mama has left it ready for me to tackle, and not remained . . . except . . . well, when I look at the bed . . .'

'Well, tackle that first, and get it stripped and the linen in the wash.'

'But that's like I'm getting rid of her . . . Oh, Angie.'

'Don't, Mia. Please, love. We have to do it, so we need to start and to stay strong for one another while we do it.'

Mia swallowed hard. 'You're right. I will start with the bed.'

Two hours later, Mama's room wasn't hers any more. It was just a room – one that didn't hold any good, recent memories and one, Mia convinced herself, that her mama would be glad to be out of as here she'd suffered the pain and mental anguish that had worn her down.

At the door she stood and looked back at the piles of clothes on the bed – one to go to the Salvation Army, and one that would one day make a memory quilt. And next to them the boxes of things to keep and those to throw away.

Closing the door quietly, she went along to what was now hers and Steve's room but had still contained Angie's clothes in one wardrobe and in one drawer of the chest of drawers. Angie was busy packing these.

'Poor you, these last weeks must have been like camping in your own home.'

'It has a bit, but it's been worth it to see you happy, Mia – well, as happy as you could have been the way things were. And I was so glad to help Aunty Angelica to be at your wedding.'

'I've never thanked you, but without you sleeping on the couch we couldn't have been together after our wedding.'

'Well, you were, and I can't wait for it to be like that for me and Freddie . . . Oooh, just three more days!'

It felt as if Angie had just said it, but then it was here, and they were both dressed ready for Angie's big day. She looked lovely in a white satin calf-length frock, and white satin kitten-heel shoes. Instead of a veil, Angie had chosen a satin pillbox hat with a small veil that just covered her eyes.

'You look beautiful, Angie, love. I'm glad you chose to wear your hair like that, swept off your face, but hanging in ringlets down your back. It looks glorious.'

'And you look beautiful too, maid of honour. That peach colour suits you.'

Mia loved her peach satin frock of the same style as Angie's.

'I would like to put my bouquet on my mum's grave, yours on your mama's and then the table centrepiece on the war memorial where my dad is named. Will you help me to do that tomorrow before we leave?'

'I will, love, and it's a lovely idea.'

They hugged then, which seemed to start a whirlwind of

activity as Steve, who'd taken his car for a valet, returned to chauffeur them to the church.

Everything went off well, and Mia was so pleased it had. Freddie's parents were adorable, not a bit snobbish, and made a beeline for them to reassure them that they would love for them to take one of their holiday cottages for as long as they needed it.

No one offered commiserations, which made the day easier, but everyone treated the day as what it was, a happy joining of Angie and Freddie.

The next day, after Angie and Freddie had spent a night in a hotel, they came and picked Mia and Steve up and drove them to the cenotaph. Here, Angie did shed tears as she lay the table centrepiece, a ball of peach roses, on the step. 'I never knew you, Dad, but I've always loved you and always felt your love for me.'

She turned to Freddie for a hug, and a few tears. Always she told Mia that her dad was with her all the time and she felt his presence. It was Freddie who said, 'Today, he's smiling down on you and giving me his blessing to take care of you.'

This made Angie smile.

Next it was to the graveyard, an emotional time for them both as they laid their flowers on Mama's grave and then on Angie's mum's. But as they walked away holding hands, Angie said, 'They are wishing us well, Mia. And we have to make a good life for them.'

'Yes, Angie. It's how we can thank them for the sacrifices they made, to live a life they never had the chance to, with no war hanging over our heads, and no struggling to make ends meet.'

With this, they both stopped and turned to look back.

'We'll make them proud, Mia.'

Allowing her tears to stream down her face, Mia said, 'We will. Once I have fulfilled my promise. Finding Marcia was part of it, now I must complete it.'

Chapter Twenty-Seven

Marcia

Completing Her Family

In Belfast, Ireland, they found a warm welcome, though they were conscious of the Troubles that bubbled under the surface. The town was still buzzing from the visit of John Kennedy in June, and even though this was late September, there was an excitement that the Beatles from Liverpool – the most famous band in the world – would be visiting in November.

But everywhere there were signs of the Troubles. The suppression of the Catholics hit Marcia hard as she could relate to the persecutions they were subject to.

Bridgette, Shane's mammy, was a little woman with wrinkled skin and curly grey hair, and it was clear that Shane had inherited her expressive watery blue eyes.

Marcia loved her the moment she met her and was hugged by her, as Bridgette said, 'My, but you're a fine-looking wee woman, so you are. Will you come in?'

When she greeted Shane, she burst into tears, told him how proud of him she was, but how she wished he hadn't fought the fight of the Englishmen.

'Mammy, it was the fight of the world.'

'Well, we'll leave it there.'

Shane grinned. 'That's for being Mammy's answer when she knows she is wrong.'

Bridgette slapped him playfully, then greeted Joseph and Elsie. 'By, it is that you two and Marcia went through a lot at the hand of that eejit Hitler. I don't know it all, only that Shane was for telling me in his letters, and I'm sorry to the heart of me.'

Joseph and Elsie both hugged her and thanked her.

But it hit her the hardest when Shane said, 'Mammy, these are your grandchildren, Joseph, Amos, Hans and Angelica.'

It was as if she'd been avoiding this moment, as now she looked at the children, sat down and sobbed.

Marcia gently urged them forward.

Joseph put his arms around his granny, and the others followed suit, till they were all cuddling her. Bridgette looked up. Her arms went around them, and she gathered them to her. 'I am loving you so much it is hurting to see you.'

Joseph frowned, but didn't say anything referring to this, he just said, 'And we love you, Granny. Papa shows us your photo that he had in his pocket all through the war, and we kiss you goodnight.'

'Oh, God love you.'

It was Amos, who rarely spoke, but was a deep thinker, who said, 'Granny, why don't you live with us?'

She looked up at Shane. 'Is it that you're never for coming home, Shane?'

Marcia could see that Shane was battling many emotions as he shook his head. 'Me life is with me family in France now, Mammy, but Amos is right, why don't you come, and we can be taking care of you?'

Mammy looked at Marcia, and though she didn't know where she would put Mammy in her little cottage, she knew that she dearly wanted this little lady, who she was already feeling a bond with, to come to live with them.

Going on her haunches beside Bridgette, she told her, 'Mama, I would be honoured to have you with us.'

With tears in her eyes, Mammy said, 'I'm for being good with the wee ones, so I am. I would be a help to you.'

Marcia reached out and took her in her arms. As she did, her little Joseph patted his granny's back.

'Don't cry, Granny, we'll take care of you.'

'It is that Jesus himself sent you to me this day, for I was wondering where me next crust of bread was coming from . . . Oh, it is that I'm sorry for mentioning Jesus.'

Joseph left Elsie's side then and stepped forward. Taking one of Mammy's gnarled hands in his, he told her, 'Never apologize for your beliefs, Bridgette. We should all allow others to follow what they believe is right.'

Bridgette looked up at him and smiled through her tears.

'If you want to come back with us, it can be arranged, Bridgette,' Joseph now told her. 'We're staying for a few days nearby, so we can gather what you want to keep, and have it shipped over to France at a later date, as you'll only be able to take a few of your clothes on the flight back to France with us.'

'Is this really for happening, son?'

Shane had composed himself and now moved Hans nearer and put his arm around his mammy. 'It is, Mammy. I only wish I'd have known that things were as bad as they are.'

'I couldn't be for telling you, son. What is it you could have done? But I haven't even a drop of tea to offer you now you have come all this way.'

'Shane, what do you think to me and Elsie going to the hotel and booking your mammy in with us all?'

'Mammy?'

'I'll do anything, Shane. Now you're here, I'm not for spending a minute without you.'

'Ha, Mammy, you'll not be welcome in me bed, so you won't!'

This caused a giggle that turned into a belly laugh that affected them all.

When they calmed, Bridgette said, 'I could be doing the Irish jig, I'm that happy. But I'll be wanting to say goodbye to my neighbours.'

'Well, we'll throw a party, how would that be?' Joseph told her.

Two days later, Marcia thought that Joseph didn't seem to have any limits to what he could do as she looked around the crowded church hall packed with people. The men all appeared to have a bottle of beer at their lips and the women chatted in what sounded like a different language to Marcia as some of the words she'd never heard.

And Mammy did as she said she would and danced a jig, making everyone giggle, and more so as other ladies of her age joined in. Marcia had to admit that besides being funny to watch, she was in awe of their agility for the ages they were.

Shane was in his element greeting and being hugged by old friends, though some of them expressed their nervousness about such a gathering of Catholics in one place.

Thankfully, it all went off without incident, and as they lay in bed that night, with Shane a little tipsy and as happy as she'd ever known him, he sang her to sleep.

'Welcome home, Paddy, welcome home.
The Scotsman can boast of his thistle,
And England can boast of the rose,

*But Paddy can boast of his emerald isle,
Where the dear little shamrock grows.'*

Marcia smiled to herself. Her own Paddy was truly happy at last, and that completed her world.

When at last the plane took off to take them home, Shane sat with his mammy. 'Will you look at the lovely green that is Ireland, Mammy.'

'No, Shane, I don't want to look back. This is me leaving the shores that brought me happiness and joy but were for being mixed with more sadness and fear than I'm wanting to remember. For haven't I walked me own street to have little boys be throwing stones at me? And stood on me aching legs on the bus and in the queues as the Protestants were served first or took the seats and never were for offering them to me?'

'Joseph and I understand, Mama. We, too, have suffered the same persecution or watched our mamas and grandparents suffer it.'

'Aye, it is that you have, me dear. Best we be putting it behind us, so it is.'

Though she said this, she took Shane's hand, and both had tears in their eyes.

Marcia decided to leave them to their thoughts and concentrated on distracting the children.

It was when they got home in two taxi cabs that they were faced with the reality of where they were to put Bridgette and her clothes.

'You need a bigger house, Shane. Let me see to that for you.'

'No, Joseph, ta, but it is that this is me home.'

'I'll buy you a bed settee then. I haven't seen one, but I hear they are handy. They fold out to make a bed.'

'I was thinking on the plane that I'd be constructing one that came down from the wall for meself and Marcia, and then I could shuffle the two rooms upstairs, so I could.'

'But that will take time, Shane. For now, Mama will have to go in with the boys. The cot could be reassembled for Hans, as he would still fit into it, and then Mama can have his bed.'

'Isn't that me clever Marcia, always comes up with a solution!' Shane grinned at her, and Mama showed her happiness by lifting her skirts and doing a few steps of the jig she did at the party.

This sent the children into fits of giggles and took away everyone's tiredness and frustrations. Marcia smiled. She was going to love having this funny, caring and lovely mammy with her.

It was a few days later and with family life changed, but for the better, that Marcia sat outside with Bridgette as they prepared the vegetables for dinner, and Joseph and Elsie pulled up outside in their rented car.

Still, she hadn't a fixed date for Mia and Steve's arrival, but they had rung and said it might be Friday. That would leave only two days before Joseph had to leave.

Joseph beamed at them.

'Away with you, with your flashing smile and fancy car,' Bridgette said. 'Come sit yourself down and peel a potato or two, for sure it feels as though we're feeding the five thousand.'

Joseph looked mystified.

'It's in the New Testament, Joseph. It seems Jesus was

faced with a massive crowd who he fed with five fishes and five loaves.'

Joseph smiled a sardonic smile, and then nodded. 'He could pull some tricks, that one.'

'To be sure they aren't tricks at all. They're miracles!'

Again, that smile. 'Yes, they are. Very much so. Your Jesus was a good man.'

Before Mammy, as Marcia now called Bridgette, could go off on her preaching of her true religion, which to Marcia was her only fault as it was a sensitive subject, Marcia jumped up.

'I'll get us all some cool lemonade. We seem to be having a hot late summer once again. Grab yourselves a couple of chairs from the kitchen, Joseph, and no more talk about Jesus, Mammy.'

'It's sorry I am. Me tongue runs away with me, so it does. But it's only the banter I am having.'

Joseph grinned but didn't comment, much to Marcia's relief.

When they all sat down sipping their drinks, and just when Marcia had thought that Joseph couldn't come up with anything more, he said, 'It occurred to me that before I go home, there's one more thing I could do for you, Marcia.'

'No, nothing more, Joseph. You have been amazing. I cannot thank you enough, but we are fine now. Please, just enjoy your last days here, and go home knowing you have left a happy family and convent behind you.'

'But you always said you would like to go back to Toulouse and see Madame Conté and her sister, and your old home.'

Marcia's heart skipped a beat.

'Thank you, it's a lovely thought, but I can't get away. Mia will be here soon, and you've already done so much.'

'It will only take a day!'

Marcia so wanted to, and yet did she? Hadn't enough of the past been visited recently? Could she take any more?

Marcia looked around her, at her new mammy, at Hans playing nearby and Angelica sleeping beside her under a sun canopy, and she knew that with her lovely children, and Shane, she was complete. She had her family, and the only other thing she wanted in all the world was to see Mia and to sit on Sister Angelica's bench with her.

The letters that now passed between her and Madame Conté were enough for her, as visiting the past wasn't always a good thing to do.

She shook her head. 'Thank you, Joseph, but I really don't want to go. I am trying to put the past where it belongs.'

Joseph understood. He came to her and held her for a moment, before Elsie did the same, saying, 'I wish Joseph would do that, but maybe after this visit he can.'

'I'll try, my love. It would be good to be free of the shackles of it. And yes, this visit has been a help in that, with me seeing how lives have been put back together and are being lived happily again. And especially finding that you, Marcia and Shane, are alive and happy.'

Elsie took his hand. 'Joseph, I think we should go home now.'

He stood a long moment looking at Marcia, before he said, 'Will you and Shane and the children visit us one day, Marcia?'

'We will, I promise. But won't you stay to see Mia?'

He sighed a deep sigh. 'I think my wise Elsie is right. I think we will go to the convent now, to say our goodbyes, and then fly out tonight. Everything is in place for all I said I wanted to do for the convent. And I hope I've brought a little healing to you, and Shane, my dear Marcia.'

'You have. Will you make sure to see Shane at the convent?'

'I will. And will you promise me that when Mia comes, you will look on it as a joyous thing you are doing for Sister Angelica?'

'Yes, I have this one more thing to do for her – bring her daughter into her old life, so that she can have peace as her mama has.'

'It's been quite a journey, but we're both happy now.' As he said this, he drew Elsie to him.

'We are, Joseph. And we must be thankful for that.'

Marcia opened her arms to him and they hugged. Yesteryear's dreams had been laid to rest. Whether they could ever lay to rest the horrors they experienced and witnessed, Marcia didn't know. But she almost had the last chapter of her book now. She hoped that by the time she wrote 'The End' she would be able to.

Marcia stood with Mammy to wave Joseph off. Mammy's arm came around her and her head rested on her arm.

'We can't be undoing what is done, Marcia, me wee darling, but we can be learning from it.'

'You're right, Mammy . . . Now, let's get these vegetables finished so you can make this Irish stew you're always talking about. And it had better be good enough to beat my coq au vin.'

'Well, if ever a dish sounded rude, that one does. Cock in a van! Ha, there's many a Colleen been caught out with that one, and I'll be for being one of them. For wasn't me Patrick a lively one?'

Marcia burst out laughing. Mammy was sent from heaven and was just the tonic she needed.

Joseph had done so much for them, and one of those things was to complete her family for her by bringing Mammy into her life.

Chapter Twenty-Eight

Mia

A New Life and Finding Peace with the Old One

Two days after Angie's wedding, Mia stepped out of Steve's car and looked around her. Main Street in Quorn, Leicestershire, held such beauty in its old thatched houses and quaint cottages that it seemed a world away from London's East End.

She hadn't dreamed that everything could happen so quickly, but here they were, on an overnight visit to Steve's parents, which would be followed by a two-day visit to stay in the cottage that they'd left to Freddie's mum to pick for them. She'd said at the wedding that she knew the one for them.

'I can't believe we're doing this, darling.'

'I know. It was so good of Doctor Jones to get a locum in and give me this extended time, once I was shortlisted for the interview.'

'I just know you will get it – GP in the Lake District! I never would have dreamed it. It's going to be such a different life.'

'It is, darling, and there will be many changes to come to terms with. So, what do you think to my childhood home?'

They stood outside a thatched cottage. 'It's beautiful.'

Mia had hardly said this when the door opened, and Steve's parents came out to welcome them.

Once inside, Mia truly knew the difference in their upbringing. Hers had been in a terraced house in Stepney, where you had to grow up fast, and with a single parent, and his had been in this beautiful part of the country, in a house that smelled of polish and where thick carpets in reds and golds softened your tread.

A huge fireplace that was made of the wood of an old trunk of a tree took one wall and looked inviting as logs crackled away in its hearth. And big comfy chairs called to you to snuggle into their feather cushions.

'It's lovely.'

Muriel smiled. 'Thank you. And so is . . . Oh, I'm sorry, I forgot. You will be leaving your home behind.'

Giving her a hug, Mia said, 'It's all right. I've come to terms with it all and am looking forward to a new beginning.'

Michael stepped forward. 'My turn for a hug. Hello, Mia. And welcome to our home. It will always be yours too.'

As she went to accept his hug, Mia had to swallow her tears away. 'That's such a lovely thing to say. Thank you.'

He patted her back, and Mia thought her own father would have done that. But before sadness could overwhelm her, Muriel said, 'Come on through, lunch is all ready in the dining room.'

'Ha, lunch! It's a feast fit for a king! She's been baking all morning.'

They all laughed and the tension in Mia broke.

'I think the bathroom first for us and we'll drop our bag in our bedroom. I take it we're in the guest room, Mum?'

'Oh, what am I thinking? Of course, and yes, darling. Though it's no longer the guest suite, but yours and Mia's.

No one but you will stay in there, so we're hoping you will make it your own and leave some clothes and shoes here, then I know you'll always come back.'

'Oh, Mum, the Lake District isn't Timbuktu!'

Michael chipped in, 'You could live around the corner and it wouldn't be near enough for your mother, son. But just humour her and she'll get used to it.'

Steve laughed. 'I'll leave my dirty underwear, like I did when I was a student, how's that?'

Muriel laughed at this and hit out playfully at Steve.

The visit, though only short, was just what Mia needed. She felt at home and loved and as if she'd been granted two new parents. Though no one could replace her own, it gave that feeling of belonging.

They arrived at their holiday cottage in Windermere at two the next day, when Steve's interview was at three. But he didn't panic.

A white-painted building in a row of similar ones, the outside looked charming with its door painted black and sporting a polished brass knocker and pretty net curtains at the windows.

'I'll just pop in with you and freshen up, darling, then I'll have to leave you to it. I've to find the surgery, but it's only a mile away according to the map.'

His leaving her to it was delayed as they walked in and the full charm of the cottage welcomed them. The suite had wooden arms and patterned seats and backs in green with many coloured flowers covering them; the yellow ones were picked out in the colour of the curtains at the two tiny windows. The fireplace was deep-set and laid with huge logs ready to be set alight by the kindling under them. A golden rug covered the front of the hearth and much of the highly polished red stone-flagged floor.

'It's beautiful!'

Steve caught hold of her. 'Just like you, my darling.'

His kiss held a promise and his need of her. She moulded into him. But then she felt bereft as he pulled away and grinned. 'Later, my darling. I'll have to find the bathroom and cool down and make myself presentable. I can hardly turn up like this!'

They went into a fit of giggles as Steve looked down at the bulge in his trousers. 'I'll have to wash in cold water!'

As he went to leave her, he looked back. 'I do love you so very much, Mia. You will be all right, won't you, darling?'

'I will. More than all right, living in a paradise like this with the man I love. Now hurry, or we won't have a chance of this dream coming true.'

She loved his laugh as he went from room to room trying to find the bathroom and then was shocked to find it was upstairs adjoining the one bedroom. 'I didn't expect that! I thought it would be in the yard!'

He hadn't been gone long, and Mia had only had time to explore the house and the lovely back garden laid out with a lawn and flower beds, in which many coloured wallflowers bloomed and nodded a welcome as the breeze caught them, when she heard a car hooter that seemed to be right outside the door.

It was!

'Angie! Oh, Angie!'

Coming out of the lovely hugs Angie and Freddie gave her, Mia said, 'But you're on your honeymoon!'

A glowing Angie replied, 'I know, but what better way to

enhance that than by being with family and friends . . . And we've so much to tell you!'

'Well, wait until Steve comes back or you will have to tell it again. I'll put the kettle on, I've found that at least, and the tea and the fridge. I've not found sugar yet, but I didn't look hard as we don't take it. I know you don't, Angie, but what about you, Freddie?'

Freddie helped with where everything was and they were soon sitting outside at a small round table in the top end of the garden that still had a glimmer of the fading autumn sun.

Their jackets kept them warm, though.

'I have to just ask if you got everything done, Mia?'

'Yes . . . well, no. But there's still seven weeks out of the two months, though we go to France at the end of this week, so that leaves us enough time when we get back. If Steve gets this post, he won't be required to start until the end of November, when the current doctor retires. And Doctor Jones has put out an advert for his replacement and is using a locum until then.'

'Oh, that's a relief. We will come down at weekends as much as we can to help out so it'll all happen. Fingers crossed Steve is successful then everything will fall into place. It's so lovely up here, you will love it. Even the tea tastes nicer.'

'That's the water from fresh reservoirs and we get plenty of rain to top them up too! You London girls will notice the difference in the weather, and it will take some getting used to.'

'Now he tells us the bad bit. Thanks, Freddie!'

They all giggled, but Mia noticed a special look pass between them. A look she knew, as it happened often to her and Steve.

'I can't wait for you to see the lake. Did you pass it?'

'No, we came in off the main road.'

'It's beautiful and we can swim in it and Freddie has a boat too!'

Excitement took away all the sad feelings as Angie carried on extolling the virtues of living in the Lakes. Already, Mia was feeling more positive about this move, even though it was like a different world to her.

When Steve came home, he was full of hope. After greeting Angie and Freddie he told them, 'There were only two of us and the other candidate was quite pompous. He even struggled to greet me when he arrived, so I can't see that he has a bedside manner. Anyway, Doctor Shaw, the retiring doctor, and Doctor Reeves, a much younger man of around my age, told me to expect a call later.'

'That does sound promising, darling.'

'Yes, why don't we book a table tonight at the little cafe on the main road? They do lovely food. Their grilled lamb cutlets with mash and gravy and mint sauce are superb,' Freddie was saying.

'Hmm. Sounds good.'

Mia thought she caught a glimmer of disappointment in Steve's eyes as he said this and looked at her.

Her own feeling matched his. She'd been looking forward to them lighting the fire and having a meal of the bacon and eggs she'd found, with slices of what looked like homemade crusty bread and local butter. And then . . . She didn't let her thoughts go there.

Angie caught on.

'We can do that tomorrow night, Freddie. Mia looks tired. It's been two days of travelling for her.'

'Of course, tomorrow will be excellent. I'll book. Are we

all up for the lamb cutlets? Food has to be pre-ordered or they can't cope.'

To Mia's look of surprise, he laughed. 'Ha, I told you you had a lot to get used to. This ain't London, luv.'

They all laughed at Freddie's funny take on the cockney accent. But to Mia, it was as much the relief of being able to spend the evening alone with Steve that made her so happy.

The call was just what Steve wanted to hear. He was jubilant, grinning at them all and then giving a hearty laugh just before he put the phone down.

Turning to them, his wide smile confirmed what they thought before he told them, 'The position is mine, and they need me ready to take it up on Monday, the fourth of November!'

'We gathered that, but why the laugh?'

'Doctor Reeves jokingly told me, "We need you up and running for the fifth, a night of madness, when they set the world alight around here!"'

They giggled at this as they congratulated him.

The next evening was full of talk of their future, and the lamb cutlets had been as delicious as Freddie had said they would be. But now, Mia dreaded the coming parting from Angie as they donned their coats.

'Well, we'll be off now, Mia. Give me the biggest hug as we face the longest parting we've ever had from each other.'

The hug went on and on as neither Mia nor Angie wanted to let go.

When they did, they both cried, but they allowed themselves to. They'd been through so much.

Angie smiled first. 'We've a lot to look forward to, love.'

Mia cheered up. 'We have, and I'm as excited about it all as you are now.'

'That's good to hear.' Steve's arm came around her and squeezed, then let her go, just long enough for him to say his goodbyes to Angie and Freddie. But once the door was closed on them he took hold of her again.

'Oh, Mia, I've waited all day to get you on my own. I was so whacked yesterday after the journey; I felt I let you down . . .'

'Shh, just kiss me.'

The kiss was different to any he'd given her, more passionate and demanding.

Mia knew an instant response, and yet a different one, a more urgent one than she'd experienced since their wedding. Always, they'd both held a little of themselves back for fear of being overheard by one or another in the house, but now, there was no one and she could be herself.

Her cries at his caresses came from deep within her. Her touching him was uninhibited. And her joy and exquisite pleasure when he gently laid her on the rug and entered her vibrated through her body.

This was a true giving of herself to her man – her husband – her Steve.

When at last her body gave her what she longed for, she hollered with each pulsating gift of love that took her out of herself and made her truly Steve's.

They clung together afterwards, letting their love guide their words as they told of how they had truly felt one.

After a moment Mia thrilled to hear Steve say, 'It will always be like that now, my darling. I love you so much. And now we will have our own home. This cottage to begin with, but I have savings, and you will have your inheritance, so we should be able to put a sizeable deposit down on our forever home.'

'We will. And I know I'll be really happy here until that day comes. It feels like it's mine already – and there are no memories around every corner to trip me up. I can visit which ones I want to when I want to.'

'You, and Angie, must grieve too, my darling. Don't ever hold it in. I will always be here for you, and I know Freddie will be for Angie.'

'I'm the luckiest girl alive to have you, darling Steve.'

'Ha, you don't know me yet. I've been on my best behaviour till now. I can leave a trail of smelly socks and soak the bathroom floor while leaving the soap in the water! Oh, and I rarely put the seat of the lavatory down.'

They giggled at this, but secretly Mia thought, *I hope he does those things, as I don't want a perfect human to live with. I want someone ordinary, with ordinary faults, who I can throw the pillow at if I feel a need to.*

'So, what are your faults then? As it's made me realize with my confession that you may have been on your best behaviour too!'

'Oh, nothing major. I used to drive Angie mad with my make-up all over the dressing table, and not putting my dirty undies in the washing bag . . . Oh, and she's become entangled in my tights strewn on the floor a few times.'

'Ha! I want a divorce right now!'

They were helpless with childish laughter that ended in them kissing and losing themselves and all their bad points in another frenzied giving and taking of the expression of their love.

* * *

A few days later, Mia wasn't sure of her feelings as she stood with Steve and Marcia at the gate of the convent. The bell was exactly as Shane had said it was, clanging so loud it increased her nerves. She looked up at Steve. He touched her arm in a gesture of support.

How often had Mama stood on this very spot waiting to be let into what she must have looked on as her sanctuary?

'*Oh, Mama, were you happy here? I have the impression you were from the tales I've heard. But were you always at odds with yourself?*

The gates creaked as they swung open. And there stood a young woman, not much older than herself.

'Mia! Welcome.'

She stood back, her smile showing her excitement.

As soon as Mia stepped in she was greeted by who she knew was the Reverend Mother, sitting in a wheelchair. Mia hesitated, but then the frail older lady put out her arms.

'Mia . . . So very like my Angelica!'

Mia went to her, bent over and returned her hug. 'It's good to be here, thank you for having me, Reverend Mother.'

As Mia straightened and Marcia introduced Steve, she looked around the yard, made prettier than a school playground with the trees and the borders of flowers. Her eyes fell on the bench. It was exactly as she had pictured it, dappled in sunlight that beamed through the thick foliage of the huge oak tree.

For a moment she saw her mama and went to step forward, but then the image disappeared.

'Go ahead, my dear.'

Walking slowly towards the bench, she could feel that Marcia was with her, and yet everything seemed so surreal, as if she was walking through a mist that clung to her like a spider's web does.

Again, the image. 'Mama?'

'You can see her too?' Marcia asked.

'Yes, like I have never seen her, in a long white gown and veil.'

'Isn't she beautiful?'

'She is the most beautiful I have ever seen her. How long has she been here?'

'I saw her when I came with Joseph, but no one else seemed to.'

Mia wanted to say hello, and run to her mama, but knew it didn't work like that. How she knew, she had no idea. Nothing like this – so beautiful – had ever happened to her before.

As they stood closer, the image faded again. Mia didn't want it to. 'Mama? Mama, don't go.'

'She cannot stay. If she goes and doesn't come back, then she is truly at peace.'

Mia thought it strange how she and Marcia were whispering. It was as if it was just the two of them in the whole world experiencing something that very few ever experienced.

'Shall we sit down, Mia?'

When they sat, Mia saw that Steve was still there, waiting for her. She wanted to beckon him over, but Marcia said, 'I have something to tell you, Mia.'

Listening to the harrowing story of a day not long after Mama left, tears tumbled down Mia's cheeks.

She looked around the yard, imagining the scene and hearing the sob in Marcia's voice.

'I'm so sorry. Poor little Madeleine, but she died a hero. She threw herself onto that soldier to save the Reverend Mother.'

'Yes, I have long thought of her as a hero. But there is nothing to commemorate a Jewish child for such an act.'

'You can do it. I would like to put a plaque on this bench with my mama's name on and a few words to commemorate what she did.'

'Joseph has already said he will build a new one here and commemorate your mama, as well as a statue to her memory.'

'No. I want it to be this one. Surely it can be maintained to keep it for many years? And if it eventually rots away, then yes, the statue will continue to be in Mama's memory, and I will be forever grateful for that.'

'I will tell him, and I am so glad. This bench means so much to all those who knew and remember her.'

'And I want to put the plaque in place myself. I will have it made in brass, and with Madeleine's name on it too.'

'Will you say she was Jewish?'

Mia put her arm around Marcia. 'I will. And we will compose the words ourselves.'

It was a lovely hour that they spent, if a moving one, as they were shown all that Mama had done for the children.

After they said their goodbyes, with an arrangement to come back with the plaque, Shane drove them along the route Mama used to take to collect the children and then into the forest to the sites where she found them.

Mia was in awe of her mother's bravery as Shane described how often she would encounter gendarmes and German soldiers on the way. And then he took her to a blacksmith, who made the plaque for her.

Together, she and Marcia composed the words. Steve told her they were beautiful.

When it came time to part with Marcia they clung together, even though they would be together the next day.

Gently Steve guided her away to take her to the hotel.

Once there she told him the story of the horror of the playground.

He had no words. How could anyone have?

They now realized what an amazing feat it was for Joseph and Elsie to have escaped. Marcia and Shane too, although they had the help of the Resistance. They couldn't think about the fate of those who didn't get away and were taken to Auschwitz.

It seemed no time at all before Mia stood with Marcia once again. The priest, who she'd learned was Father Pierre, blessed the plaque and Shane screwed it to the back of the bench. The words were clear to see:

In memory of Sister Angelica, a courageous saviour of Jewish children 1942–1943. And, resting in her arms, one of those Jewish children, Madeleine Kraus. A child loved and treasured by Sister Angelica, who gave her life to save that of another. May the love they showed on earth be forever felt in this special place that Sister Angelica loved.

Remembered always, with the love of a daughter to a mother, by Mia, Marcia and Angie.

After prayers were said, Mia walked forward with a trowel that Shane had given to her.

She knelt and dug a small hole where she'd seen her mama's feet.

Putting the little box in it, she lifted her eyes. Mama was there again. 'Go now to your rest, dearest Mama.'

Two strong arms lifted her. Arms that loved her. Together, she and Steve walked into the chapel, to pray for Mama and all the Jewish children. And Mia thought, *I have fulfilled my promise*.

Acknowledgements

My thanks to all the wonderful team at Pan Macmillan for all the attention they give to my books. My commissioning editor, Katie Loughnane, whose support and help to get me to the finish line during the difficult time I was going though while writing this book helped me so much. To Rosa Watmough and her team, whose editing brings out the very best of my story to make it shine. And, as always, to Victoria Hughes-Williams, who has played such an important role in my career as my former commissioning editor and now as my structural editor. You always make my story flow.

Thank you to my publicist, Lucy Doncaster, and her team, who seek out many opportunities for me to showcase my work. And to the cover designer (I adore the cover of this book!) and the sales team, who make sure my book stands out on the shelf. My heartfelt thanks go to you all.

And a special thank you to:

My son, James Wood, who reads so many versions of my work to help and advise me, and works alongside me on the edits that come in. I love you so very much.

And finally to my readers, who encourage me on as they await another book, supporting me every step of the way and who warm my heart with praise in their reviews.

Letter to Readers

Dear reader,
Thank you for choosing my book. I hope you enjoyed reading it, and being part of the lives of Sister Angelica, Mia and Angie, and all those who peopled their story.

It was while researching for another book that I came across the story of Sister Denise Bergon, a real-life nun who, during the Second World War, saved the lives of eighty-three Jewish children by collecting them from where they were hiding in the forest and taking them back to her convent. And of Hélène and Ida Bach, two of those children. Their stories inspired me to write fictional events based on what happened to those exceptionally brave people.

Writing a stand-alone book was something I hadn't done for a long time, but I so loved the process, as it freed me up from creating situations that would have to be carried forward in a series. And yet, it left me bereft at the end, as I truly had to leave the characters I loved and move on to my next book.

My next book will be called *Her Hidden Courage*, although its working title was *The Silver Clasp*. Often, the titles an author chooses for her work do not end up on the finished book. They are more of a guideline for us to base the story around.

A Lasting Promise started its life in my imagination as *Mia's Promise* – and yes, having now read it, you can see that was the theme I wrote to. But I so love *A Lasting Promise*, as it encompasses much more of the novel – I thank my editor, Katie, aforementioned in the acknowledgements, and the team involved for their inspiration in coming up with it.

Her Hidden Courage will take us to a different angle of the Second World War, an era that gave us so many courageous people, and which makes me look at myself and ask: how would I have coped? It's an era I love writing about.

In this novel, my protagonists have escaped Poland and the persecution that threatens them and arrive in the East End of London, leaving behind cherished friends and family. Life for them, when they settle on Brick Lane, is cushioned by the grit of the cockney folk; though danger does lurk in the shape of Oswald Mosley's followers, who hold similar views to the Nazis, and rears its ugly and terrifying head when their loved ones eventually arrive in England.

For my protagonists, it is when they finally face their fears and return to Poland to take up different roles in the fight for Polish liberation and the freedom of the Polish Jewish community that their story takes us on an emotional rollercoaster, leaving us hoping and praying that they will return safely and be reunited. But will they?

If you have a question you would like to ask me, or just to chat, I would so welcome hearing from you. I love interacting with my readers. Here is where you can contact me:

My Facebook page, where you can 'like' and 'follow' me: www.facebook.com/MaryWoodAuthor
My Instagram: www.instagram.com/mary.wood.7796420
My TikTok: www.tiktok.com/@marywood616
My X: www.twitter.com/Authormary

And for news and email contact, my website: www.authormarywood.com/contact-subscribe. Here, you can also sign up to receive my newsletter.

Take care of yourselves and others.
Much love,
Mary x

Turn the page for an extract from
Mary Wood's new novel . . .

HER HIDDEN COURAGE

Can she defy the odds to follow her heart?

**Publishing 2026 and available
to pre-order now**

One

Poland, 1937

Tamar clung to Hannah.

Isaac, Hannah's brother, stood looking on.

'We will follow you, Tamar,' Hannah said as she came out of the hug. 'We will, won't we, Isaac?'

Tamar glanced at Isaac. Doing so lifted her world: his tall, slim frame; his dark eyes set in his handsome face; his jet-black hair with a yarmulke – the traditional Jewish cap – covering his crown.

Isaac opened his arms to her.

Tamar's heart, broken by the recent loss of her adored mama and the prospect of having to leave the only world she'd ever known, was soothed a little as a trickle of joy crept into her.

Going into Isaac's arms completed that joy as he held her to him, pulled back her headscarf and kissed her long fair hair.

In answer to his sister, who looked so like him but for her round, wire-rimmed glasses, Isaac said, 'We will, Hannah.' Then his eyes lowered to look down at Tamar again. 'Have faith, Tamar. Papa is looking into arrangements for Hannah and me to join you in England. Mama will not budge, so they are staying here, but she is urging us to go.'

Hannah hung her head. 'I wish Mama would change her mind. I don't want to go without her and Papa. I am afraid for them. But from what we're hearing of the Nazis' treatment of the Jews, and of Hitler's plans for our country . . . our community is afraid. Another family left yesterday – the Goldbergs. So many are gone or are preparing to go.'

Isaac extended his arm to Hannah and held them both close. 'I don't want to leave them either. It will break my heart, but Mama begged me to. She wants to think of us safe in London, but Babacia is not well enough to travel, and Mama wants to care for her, as any good daughter would. She won't leave her. When she passes, Mama and Papa will join us.'

'I don't want Babacia to pass.'

'There are many things in life we don't want, my dear sister, but we must have the courage to face them. Babacia is very weary – she is ready to go to Elohim. She knows He has a place in heaven for her by His side.'

Born and brought up in Mechelinki, Poland, on the coast of the Baltic Sea, Tamar, Hannah and Isaac had always known love, freedom and happiness. Now, trepidation had trickled into the hearts of their fellow countrymen, and in particular their Jewish community. Many were fleeing to America or Britain.

Turning them around to face the sea, Isaac told them, 'Always remember this, our beautiful coast. Remember the times as children when we built things – castles and towers in the sand. And how our bodies tingled with the cold when we swam. Always we laughed. I can hear that sound now . . . Let's do it one more time. Let's swim together.'

'But we don't have our costumes, Isaac,' said Hannah.

'And besides, it will be freezing!' Tamar added.

'Ha! Who needs costumes, Hannah? It is getting dark. No one will come along this way now. And as for the cold, Tamar, my love, we have braved it many times . . . this may be the last chance we have of doing so for a long time.'

With this, Isaac let go of them and stripped off his clothing, leaving only his long underpants on.

Tamar felt her stomach muscles clench as she looked at his strong body. It seemed to spur her on. Dropping her bag, she kicked off her shoes and whipped off her cardigan. Then, without a qualm, she undid the button on her skirt and let it fall before taking her short-sleeved jumper off over her head, exposing her liberty bodice.

'No! Tamar!'

'Come on, Hannah! It feels wonderful!' With this, Tamar loosened her corset and let it drop, taking her stockings halfway down her calves as it did. Bending, she rolled them off fully before stepping out of the crumpled pile of her clothing.

Laughing, she lifted her head. Isaac was staring at her. There was something in his eyes she hadn't seen before. It further enhanced the strange tingling sensations that gripped her.

'I'm leaving you to it. You're mad! Don't be late for tea, Isaac, you know how it upsets Mama.'

As Hannah disappeared out of sight, Isaac stepped nearer to her. 'You're beautiful, Tamar . . . I love you.'

This time, being in his arms was different. The most wonderful feeling she'd ever experienced with him crept over her, and the tingling sensations deepened. Never before had the bare skin of her body touched his.

Isaac stepped back. 'We mustn't. But . . . Oh, Tamar.'

Taking charge, Tamar held his hand and pulled him towards the sea. 'Come, let us swim, my darling. Make memories to look back on and hold dear.'

It wasn't what she wanted to do. She wanted to cling to him, to yield to the desire that gripped her, but she had sinned enough by exposing her flesh to him. Though her liberty bodice and pants covered most of her, they didn't conceal everything her bathing dress would have.

The water stung as if icy cold fingers had clutched her. She splashed Isaac, giggling as he ducked – but then regretted her action as he dived underwater and grabbed her legs, pulling her under. Kicking out at him, she made him release her. Their laughter hung on the air as they surfaced.

For a moment, they held each other's gazes, glimpsing a promise of their future – and yet, would it happen? So many forces were against them. What if Isaac never made it to London? What if the Nazis did the unthinkable sooner than they thought? But then, maybe none of it would ever happen – it would remain a rumour, and they could return and once more know that feeling of freedom.

Wanting that sensation now, Tamar swam along the coastline, allowing the feel of the water, no longer icy, to take away all the bad thoughts and give her peace. Isaac would come to her in London. They would one day marry and return to Poland. And their children would be brought up here and surrounded with love and protection, just as they had been themselves.

As they walked home hand in hand, that dream was shattered. Isaac told her, 'I don't think the Nazis will dare to try to take our country, Tamar. The world wouldn't allow it. We will come back, you'll see . . . Only, it may be sooner for me. Already our armed forces are building in readiness. I – I'm sorry, my darling, but I am thinking of joining the Polish army if nothing changes. I would not be able to stay in London while my fellow countrymen fight.'

Tamar clung tightly to his hand. There was nothing she could say.

Isaac stood still and took her into his arms, and she felt his body heave. Clinging to him, she wept with him. Their world had suddenly collapsed. Why were they hated as a people by the Nazis? What had they ever done to them, or to anyone? They were taught peace and love. Theirs was an ancient religion – the first to recognize one God. They did no harm. They worked hard and contributed to the prosperity of any land they lived in – the only thing they didn't have was a land of their own, since they had been driven out of Israel in biblical times. Always they were persecuted, vilified, and yet she had only known them to give out love.

Isaac lifted his head. He took a deep breath and smiled down at her with tear-soaked eyes. 'Everything will be all right. Our children will know the joys of swimming in the Baltic and playing on the sands. I promise.'

Tamar smiled back and nodded, though in her heart she wondered if it would ever come true.

A few days later, Tamar and Isaac stood at the port of Gdynia, wanting to hold each other, but knowing that it would be frowned upon by Tamar's papa and the other passengers. Hannah had joined them too. They were awaiting the arrival of the ferry that would take Tamar and her papa to Karlskrona, Sweden, the first stop on their long journey.

To Tamar, it felt as though she was leaving her whole world behind – and most of all her mama. It was as if they were abandoning her to the small patch of cold earth that held her body, and yet she told herself: *Mama is happy, she is with Elohim in heaven. He will take care of her, and I will be with her again one day.*

Memories of her mama, fading away day by day, shuddered through Tamar. She looked up at Isaac. Soon his face would fade too, once the ferry drew away from the port, leaving him behind. He would go back to his job as a silversmith until the day he could come and join her. But what of her own life? Papa had told her that he had plans in the world of jewellery. Papa was an expert jewellery-maker, working in gold and silver. He had always dreamed of having his own shop and workshop.

She'd spent many hours with him in his shed when she got home from school, where he taught her the skills of melting silver and fashioning it into delicate, beautiful chains. She had often felt confused about her future, wanting to one day work as a teacher of the languages she loved – mainly English and, though she now hated the people of the country, German. And French, a language she'd only recently studied but loved more than any – it was less harsh, almost poetic in the sounds of its everyday words.

But when she left college two months ago, a week after her nineteenth birthday, Tamar had been lost. Everything she thought might happen – going on to be an apprentice teacher in her local school – had been taken away from her, along with all her dreams.

'Ahh, the ferry is coming. Say your goodbyes, Tamar.' Turning, Papa shook hands with Isaac. 'Maybe by the time you arrive in London, my boy, I will have employment for you. My plans are to look for a shop and workshop of my own. I have contacts there, and I have the money I have saved and the profits from the sale of our house. Keep praying for us.'

'I will, sir, I will.'

Papa hugged Hannah and then turned his back. Tamar knew he was giving her a moment to say her goodbyes.

Her heart broke as she did.

Taking no notice of convention, she clung to Isaac. 'I love you. Come to me as soon as you can.'

'I will, my love. Go now. Don't linger, it is too painful.'

Hugging Hannah to her, Tamar didn't look back at Isaac. She knew he had turned away; had seen the slump of his shoulders and felt the heaving of his body.

'Go, Tamar. We will come soon.' Hannah kissed her cheek, joining their wet faces for a second.

With this final goodbye, Tamar ran to her papa's side and picked up her case. It wasn't heavy. She'd only packed a few clothes and two of her favourite books – *A Christmas Carol* and *Jane Eyre*, both published in German. She could buy English versions when she arrived in London, but these had been given to her by her mama and had been a huge part of her childhood. Tucked inside the cover of *Jane Eyre* was a love note, written by Isaac when he first realized his childhood affection for her had become a true love that would last them a lifetime.

For her, the feeling had come much earlier – she had always known he was her life, her future, not just a playmate.

Loneliness engulfed her as they boarded the boat, and yet it was broken by a trickle of excitement. She had always wanted to see the world, especially the countries whose languages she had learned. Shaking herself mentally, she told herself she would look at this as an adventure. A new phase of her life. Her first steps into adulthood.

Tamar didn't look back from the deck they were seated on. To do so would hurt too much. Isaac would have gone out of sight. And dear Hannah, who had always been like a sister to her, would have walked away with him.

But they would come. They would! She would be reunited with them and held once more by her beloved Isaac. The dreams they had would come true, but in a safe land – a land where they had never heard of Jews being persecuted, only allowed to live in peace to carry out their daily lives.

Their choices had been London or the United States. Both were welcoming refugees fleeing the Nazi regime – or people who were potentially in danger from it. Papa had chosen London because a cousin of his, Ruben, lived there, and had long ago established a firm of silversmiths. This meant that Papa would have employment, and Ruben had communicated that he had found them accommodation. He'd said it was a small flat above a shop owned by a kind and a jolly lady called Elma. Ruben had joked to Papa in his letter that she was the woman he wanted to marry – Ruben was a bachelor, and he said that Elma had never married either. 'But she isn't Jewish and won't hear of converting, so this must remain a desire within me,' he'd written.

Papa had chuckled when he'd read this out to Tamar. His head had shaken from side to side. 'Ruben is incorrigible! A man for the ladies. But then, he was never blessed as I was with a good and beautiful woman like my Miriam.'

Tears had flooded his face, and he'd willingly let her hold him as she'd cried too. But he had soon composed himself, and patted her on the back as he said, 'But it is a new life we must look forward to, Tamar, my dearest. A new life.'

Now Tamar saw the sea stretching out before them, and knew her journey would be a long one – they had to avoid passing through Germany. Tamar thought: *What will this new life have in store for me? How will I cope with it all?*

Sighing, she tucked her arm into her papa's. She would do her best to settle and make life happy for him. He had done so much for her. Even now, it was her safety he was thinking of in uprooting them. As painful as it was for her, it was doubly so for him, as he had to leave his precious Miriam behind.

Papa turned then and looked at her and, as if he was trying to convince himself, patted her arm. 'Everything will be all right. I will make it so.'

Tamar nodded. But in her heart there lay a feeling that not even her beloved papa, who'd always made her world right, could ease the pain. Nothing but being with Isaac again could do that.

If you enjoyed
A Lasting Promise
then you'll love
The Jam Factory Girls

**Whatever life throws at them,
they will face it together**

Life for Elsie is difficult as she struggles to cope with her alcoholic mother. Caring for her siblings and working long hours at Swift's Jam Factory in London's Bermondsey is exhausting. Thankfully her lifelong friendship with Dot helps to smooth over life's rough edges.

When Elsie and Dot meet Millie Hawkesfield, the boss's daughter, they are nervous to be in her presence. Over time, they are surprised to feel so drawn to her, but should two cockney girls be socializing in such circles?

When disaster strikes, it binds the women in ways they could never have imagined. And long-held secrets are revealed that will change all their lives . . .

The Jam Factory Girls series continues with
Secrets of the Jam Factory Girls and *The Jam Factory Girls Fight Back*, all available to read now.

The Forgotten Daughter

**Book One in
The Girls Who Went to War series**

From a tender age, Flora felt unloved and unwanted by her parents, but she finds safety in the arms of caring Nanny Pru. But when Pru is cast out of the family home, under a shadow of secrets and with a baby boy of her own on the way, it shatters little Flora.

Over the years, however, Flora and Pru meet in secret – unbeknown to Flora's parents. Pru becomes the mother she never had, and Flora grows into a fine young woman. When she signs up as a volunteer with St John Ambulance, she begins to shape her life. But the drum of war beats loudly and her world is turned upside down when she receives a letter asking her to join the Red Cross in Belgium.

With the fate of the country in the balance, it is a time for bravery. Flora's determined to be the strong woman she was destined to be. But with horror, loss and heartache on her horizon, there's a lot for young Flora to learn . . .

The Girls Who Went to War series continues with
The Abandoned Daughter, *The Wronged Daughter* and
The Brave Daughters, all available to read now.

The Orphanage Girls

Children deserve a family to call their own

Ruth dares to dream of another life – far away from the horrors within the walls of Bethnal Green's infamous orphanage. Luckily she has her friends, Amy and Ellen, but she can't keep them safe, and the suffering is only getting worse. Surely there must be a way out?

But when Ruth breaks free from the shackles of confinement and sets out into East London, hoping to make a new life for herself, she finds that, for a girl with nowhere to turn, life can be just as tough on the outside.

Bett keeps order in this unruly part of the East End and she takes Ruth under her wing alongside fellow orphanage escapee Robbie. But it is Rebekah, a kindly woman, who offers Ruth and Robbie a home – something neither has ever known. Yet even these two stalwart women cannot protect them when the police learn of an orphan on the run. It is then that Ruth must do everything in her power to hide. Her life – and those of the friends she left behind at the orphanage – depend on it.

The Orphanage Girls series continues with *The Orphanage Girls Reunited* and *The Orphanage Girls Come Home*, all available to read now.